The Iron Mistress

The
Iron Mistress

BY PAUL I. WELLMAN

Doubleday & Company, Inc., GARDEN CITY, N.Y.
1951

With the exception of actual historical personages identified as such, the characters are entirely the product of the author's imagination and have no relation to any person or event in real life.

To Joyce,

WHO KNOWS ALL THE WAYS TO A MAN'S HEART,
AND ESPECIALLY TO THAT OF HER FATHER.

"By Hercules! The man was greater than Caesar or Crom-well—nay, nearly equal to Odin or Thor. The Texans ought to build him an altar!"

—THOMAS CARLYLE, speaking of James Bowie.

Contents

The Iron Mistress

New Orleans, 1817

*N*ew Orleans was, yet was not, a city of the United States in the year *1817*. Since Thomas Jefferson's great land purchase of *1803*, it was recognized as a part of the young American nation by all the world powers. New Orleans, however, had difficulty in so recognizing herself.

In all essentials the city remained a self-contained extension of Europe. Its languages were French and Spanish; manners, arts, cuisines, and customs were Continental; and New Orleans did not forget that it had been what it was for a full century before its vicissitudes threw it to the upstart young Republic of the north.

Americans? The people of New Orleans, and especially the women, regarded Americans as barbarians, who lived, presumably, on a diet of gunpowder and whiskey, and had too much natural violence to be permitted in polite company. Such Americans as came to the city for business reasons quickly discovered it was more convenient and pleasant to live in the new suburb, known as the Faubourg Ste. Germaine, than to encounter continually the superciliousness of the haughty Creole families of the Vieux Carré.

Yet New Orleans was to discover that isolation from the United States, however to be desired, could not long continue. Already in *1817* the process of change was becoming manifest. Its cause was the river: the Mississippi, which was the one great trafficway of the Central Continent.

That year its mile-wide flood carried countless craft of myriad kinds. Steamboats fought upcurrent with threshing side wheels. Ocean-going cargo ships with masts towering incredibly skyward tied up at the wharves. But chiefly the river brought down homemade craft of the frontier, drifting like chips on the current: scows and bateaux, arks, flatboats, broadhorns, barges, keelboats, and even rafts. They were laden with wheat and corn, pigs and poultry, furs, lead, hemp, tobacco—anything to fill the great stone warehouses on the water front, the lusty commerce of a lusty people seeking outlet.

Willy-nilly, fate was overtaking New Orleans in 1817.

Chapter One

1

The cracked bell in the central tower of the Cathedral of St. Louis splintered the air with sound: an immense, accusing voice directed at the last stragglers to Mass. Under the profound arches of the Cabildo young Jim Bowie stepped back to let the people hurry by, and could not help gazing at the marvels of this city with all a back-countryman's unreserved delight.

He was a tall youth—notably tall—with a hunter's tan, a square chin, fair hair, eyes sometimes blue, sometimes gray, and shoulders spreading mightily. He smiled much, and his teeth were magnificent. Most put him down as of a sunny nature, and they were correct. A man might cross him once, or even twice, and get no more than a stare, or perhaps a smile, or even a little apology. But the third time he would be likely to find himself flat on his back from a flailing fist, and if he wanted to carry the matter further, he would be accommodated: though if he preferred to call it quits, Bowie was willing enough to shake hands on it and forget the quarrel. For he was a curious alloy of opposites—a blend of kindliness with savagery.

As if reproaching the tardy, the cathedral bell gave a last expiring jangle and fell silent. In the comparative stillness that followed the subsidence of its mighty voice, Bowie leaned against the stone wall in the shade and listened to the footsteps: quick strides of Creole gentlemen in Hessian boots, soft shuffle of barefoot Negroes, the evocative click of women's small heels. All hastening to worship. This was May, a Sunday morning, the youth under the arches was just twenty-two, and it was his first day in New Orleans.

Across the street raked the iron pickets of the Place d'Armes, a grassy oblong flanked by flower beds and chinaberry trees. The sky was a limpid

3

vault of blue above. A gorgeous day, he considered, although New Orleans folks certainly preferred the shade. One or two did hurry across the open square in the sun, but all others chose the shadow of the Cabildo arches, or those of the Presbytère opposite, even if it meant being tardy to prayer. These Creole women were inordinately careful of their famous magnolia complexions: the men, it seemed, scarcely less so. In the case of the women at least, Bowie conceded that the complexions were worth all the trouble: he had never seen anything prettier, in spite of the way they looked down their noses at an American.

Catholics and foreigners, he thought: yet even with that he knew himself to be the real outlander, and so regarded. A pity, too. Bowie stared at the women passing. They walked and held themselves in a manner proud and graceful and also subtly challenging, so that it was a pleasure to look upon them, as if somehow they made mankind more important and creditable merely because they happened to be a part of it.

He straightened and stood tall, close to the wall, as two Creole girls went by. They were young, in their teens, but women ripened early here and these were most beautifully self-possessed. About their feet their light dresses foamed, the tips of tiny slippers just peeping from beneath now and then, almost furtively, and precious to behold because so infrequently visible. On their heads were white shawls. Of the young man beside their path they seemed unaware, chatting lightly in French. Bowie spoke both French and Spanish, having grown up with them in the bayou country: but this was different from his Cajun patois. Softer and with phrases to which he was not accustomed. Very cultivated French, he assumed, because all Creoles were very high-toned and cultivated and full of airs.

Though they appeared not to see him, he took note that in passing they gave him pointed and unnecessary room. And at the moment when he was staring at their side-faces, he thought he caught a glance from the nearest: a mere gleam, of which he could not be sure, because her lashes were so sweeping that they masked the look, if it were given. Still, he felt she had glanced at him. It was not much, but to a young man it was better than if she had failed to notice him altogether.

His eyes followed her. She was tiny, not even five feet tall, and entirely exquisite. A faint subtlety of fragrance was left on the air by her passing, and her waist was of a stemlike slenderness which his two big hands could have circled without squeezing.

With discontent he glanced down at himself, for she reminded him of his own vastness and clumsiness, matters of which he had not even been conscious before coming to this city where a tapering hand, a small wrist, and a slight and elegant figure were esteemed as much in a man as in a woman, as marks of gentility. On this Sunday morning he was arrayed in

4

his best: coat of dark blue broadcloth, nankeen breeches, white stock, vest of watered silk made by his mother with her own hands, low-crowned black wool hat, and boots gleaming with lampblack and grease. He had felt very fine in Opelousas: but what seemed fine there cried the provincial in every line here in New Orleans.

Everywhere he saw tall bell-crown beaver hats, long-tailed bottle-green coats with shoulders craftily cut and padded instead of merely being stretched to the point of bursting as his shoulders stretched his own garment, cravats instead of stocks, and Hessian boots which fit close to mid-calf and sported tassels as the last breath of sophistication.

Most keenly Bowie felt his bumpkinhood: his hands and feet too large, his height an un-Creole exaggeration of stature, his complexion unfashionably bronzed, his way of walking like that of an elk—long, sure strides and a great swing, good for many miles of forest between dawn and dark, but hardly elegant in a drawing room. But a young man, even when abashed, finds it difficult to keep his eyes from the figure of a pretty woman: so he watched the two slim, disdainful shapes until they disappeared into the cathedral.

For the first time, then, he noticed at the door two men, evidently in some brief argument.

One seemed to be importuning; the other, elegant and elderly, with a gray spike beard, made an angry gesture of refusal, tore himself from the detaining hand, and hastened within. The man who remained outside stood with his head bent in an attitude of profound dejection, gazing at a huge black portfolio which he held under his arm: a quaint figure, slender and of middle height, dressed very shabbily in purplish drab, with fair hair long as a woman's, caught at his nape by a bit of black ribbon, and hanging down behind his shoulders.

Bowie wondered what the argument was about: but it was none of his affair. The cathedral had drained the Rue Charteris of all its people, save the man with the portfolio and himself. Beyond it was the Rue Ste. Ann, running to the river, and at the foot of the Rue Ste. Ann lay the docks of Janos Parisot, the merchant. It occurred to him that he might find that important personage there this morning, so he started along the *banquette* past the cathedral.

Through the open doors he caught a momentary glimpse of vast hollow twilight, pillars receding and altar candles afar. The murmur of the people at prayer came to him like the droning of insects.

"M'sieu——"

A voice of pleading. Bowie halted. The man with the portfolio had stepped aside for him but regarded him with a strange attentiveness.

"Sir," the man said, changing to English, "thee be *Américain?*"

5

The accent was faintly French, yet with a Quakerish style to the words that was puzzling. Bowie surveyed him. He was clean-shaven, tanned, and not unpleasing, though his features were a little fine-drawn as from some weariness. His age would be in the early thirties.

"I am," Bowie said.

"Of the Faubourg Ste. Germaine, belike?"

Bowie shook his head. "Of the Bayou Boeuf, in Rapides Parish."

For some reason the other's face lighted. "A hunter, perhaps?"

"At times."

"I knew it! I knew thee could be none of the trading tribe! By thy eye I knew it. And by the set of thy feet, the one straight before the other as on a forest path! Friend, give me thy opinion on this?"

Surprisingly he went down on his knees before the cathedral doors, laid open his black portfolio, and drew forth a great sheet of paper splashed with color. A painting. He held it up for examination in a way timid, yet somehow appealing and confident, like a young mother holding up her firstborn babe for approval.

"Wild turkey!" exclaimed Bowie.

"The great American cock," the other replied with dignity, in spite of his kneeling posture. *Meleagris gallopavo,* to science. Thee knows the turkey?"

"If I had a shilling for every one I've shot——"

"In such case, will thee point out any imperfection in this representation?" The kneeling man eyed him challengingly, as one who awaits judgment with complete confidence.

"Imperfection?" Bowie stared with genuine amazement. "Why, none, sir, that I can see. It's the very bird—his glittering eye—the wattle and tuft—the way he lays back his wing—I've marked that set many a time. It's like as if he moved before you—every feather in its proper place and true to pattern—why, there's even the sheen of bronze where his gorget catches the sun! Man, is this your work?"

"Aye."

"Then where did you get the trick of it?"

Instead of answering the question, the stranger said, "Thee might care to see more paintings of this order?"

Bowie nodded. In an almost childlike enchantment with the picture he had forgotten his errand and Monsieur Parisot.

The other drew a deep sigh, his woe changing to elation. "Friend, thy praise uplifts me! To find one who sees—and knows!" He grew somber again. "They do not want my birds. Yet how I slave—in the pirogue in the marshes from dawn to dusk—then tramping the streets seeking commissions to paint portraits of spoiled smirking beauties or arrogant rich men who want only that their vanity be flattered—so that I may buy me a little bread."

So bitterly rose his voice that one of the vergers came to the cathedral door and frowned at them for quiet.

"And of them all not one who will so much as glance at my birds—my beautiful birds," moaned the artist, lowering his voice. Amazingly his expression became cheerful again. He replaced the painting in the portfolio, tucked it under his arm, and sprang to his feet. "But at least *thee* will look," he said eagerly. "I hold thee to thy promise! Friend, thee shall gaze at many paintings—glorious paintings of my birds!"

2

Together they walked along the Rue Charteris, and Bowie gaped at the stately Ursuline convent with its many chimneys and its dormered roof. Passing this, they turned up a side street and presently they came to one of the innumerable stairways giving on the street, so characteristic of the Vieux Carré.

"Let us go softly," said the stranger, almost in a whisper. "My landlady is an excellent woman. But she has a—a prejudice against noise. Especially on the Sabbath. I would not disturb her——"

With what seemed unnecessary caution he led the way, tiptoe, to the hall above, where he unlocked a door.

At once an awful odor of death puffed out at them, swirling so overpoweringly from the room that Bowie stepped back from it.

"My heron!" cried the artist.

He seized Bowie by the arm, snatched him within, and shut the door behind him. The stench was such that Bowie was forced to hold his breath, yet he glanced about him with a mighty curiosity as his remarkable host hurried to the window and threw it open to the fullest. Everywhere the walls were covered with paintings, finished and unfinished. Papers with sketches and daubs strewed the floor and were heaped in corners. To one side stood a rumpled bed and a littered washstand, and by the window an easel. Now for the first time Bowie saw the cause of the dreadful odor. Near the easel, dead and putrefying, yet held upright on its long legs in some semblance of life's erectness by an ingenious system of wires, was a swamp heron.

"Alas, *ma belle,*" wailed the artist, "I kept thee too long!"

Almost tenderly he disengaged the disgusting carcass from its wire braces and threw it into the alley. Then seizing a frond of palmetto, he vigorously fanned the air to clear the atmosphere.

"Nay," he cried sharply, "open not the door! The worst will soon be out. And Madame Guchin is—well—strong-minded——"

When he felt he had sufficiently alleviated the unpleasantness, he tossed the palmetto on a heap of the branches and turned to the washstand to lave his fouled hands.

"The paradox of existence," he said. "My heron dies, and rots, and the mongrel dogs of the street presently will devour her, and all that she may live forever. *Voilà.*" His hands dripped above the basin, but with his chin he pointed to the easel.

Bowie stepped to the window where the abominable smell had somewhat cleared. There was the heron, painted as in life, her feathers gleaming, her eye bright, the mirrored waters of her native swamp at her feet, tall palmetto palms in the background.

"Do thee like it?" asked the artist anxiously.

"Like it? It's plain wonderful!"

"Then behold!"

With a flourish the artist opened the black portfolio and began to spread painting after painting on the easel before the window. All were of birds, and Bowie almost forgot the lingering taint on the air in his interest. Many he recognized, as the king woodpecker, which his host called the ivory-billed; the purple martin, courted by the Cajuns with little houses on tall poles because it destroys mosquitoes; the night-long aspiring whippoorwill; the brown pelican with great-pouched bill and surly eyes placed strangely in the top of its head; the stately, dazzling white egret; eagles and owls, hawks and gulls, partridge, quail, plover, geese and ducks, all familiar to his hunter's eye. Most of the smaller birds, to which he had paid little attention in his hunting, he did not know, and his host delighted in naming them for him, seeming to think the least as important as the largest.

"The tufted titmouse," he said, "and a prothonotary warbler"—Bowie blinked at the big word—"and here a ruby-crowned kinglet——"

Expanding, the artist explained his method. He shot birds and used them for models, rather than the stuffed specimens which retained neither natural shape nor color. The wiring which held the dead creatures in attitudes of life was his own invention. He painted very rapidly, he added, because of the perishable nature of his originals—as witness the heron.

Once Bowie uttered an objection. The painting was spirited: four mockingbirds furiously battled a coiled serpent in the crotch of a tree where rested their nest.

"What's wrong with it?" demanded the artist quickly.

8

"Mockers will fight—even a snake—it's their nature. But rattlesnakes don't climb trees—except maybe during a freshet——"

"And why not?" Resentful voice.

"Too fat and sluggish. It ain't their nature. Rather go down in burrows after mice or gophers. Now a blacksnake——"

"Blacksnake? Artistic and dramatic sacrilege! Here thee see a poisonous fanged serpent—death itself—and the brave, brave birds——"

"A blacksnake may not be poison, but he moves like a whiplash. He'd be a sight more dangerous to your birds than any lazy rattler."

"On what authority do thee say this?" cried the artist hotly. "Thee have seen, belike, all rattlesnakes in the world—that thee can say with surety that none climb trees for their prey?" He sneered. "It is I, friend, who am the naturalist. I am the student, observing all works of nature with the greatest scientific care!" His face paled, his teeth seemed to flash, his voice shrilled in surprising and quite unnecessary rage. "It is to be supposed that I—I—know not as much about the habits of snakes as some raw woods ranger——"

Bowie felt his own anger rising, as it does in most men at another's causeless fury. But he wanted no quarrel, so without replying, he turned and walked abruptly out of the room.

Behind, the spate of words ceased. As he went down the stairs he heard the other come out of the door and stand on the landing. Then running steps pursued him, a hand was laid on his shoulder.

"M'sieu——" A soft pleading. "Forgive me. I—I am overwrought and—well—it is just that the truth is so very painful."

Bowie allowed himself to be halted.

"Thee be most perfectly correct—of course—concerning the rattlesnake, wretched reptile!" The artist made a gloomy gesture of despair. "The charlatan's touch—and I know it. Even as I painted it, I knew as well as thee that the sluggish rattlesnake climbs not in trees. 'Twas that made me screech so—my conscience pinched me shrewdly when thee put thy great finger square on my dishonesty."

"It's none of my affair," said Bowie gruffly.

"But wait! I must confess to thee why I fell guilty of such sham. I had hoped through that one painting to gain attention for the others. There's the truth of it! Do thee not think the world might find interest in the death-fight—look thee—between the beautiful birds and the horrid, venom-dripping serpent? And from that, belike, turn to my other pictures of—less melodrama? In God's name, is a man to be damned utterly because he uses a small trick, perchance, for a good end?"

The tone was so imploring, the apology so complete and abject, that Bowie's anger ebbed from him.

9

"At least give me thy name," begged the shabby artist.

Bowie made up his mind. "If you want it, I'll give it. And for the matter of that, I see no harm in the trick, as you call it, for nobody but a woodsman would ever question it. So—my name is James Bowie."

"James? 'Tis my own second name, and we must be friends! I am John James Audubon, painter and naturalist, at thy service. My hand, James Bowie!"

3

Both had forgotten the injunction for quiet. Now they heard a door close in the hall above, followed by the grating of a key in the lock. Next a woman appeared at the head of the stair: a broad, dark woman of middle age, in lace cap and black bombazine dress, who looked down at them with the grimly hostile visage of landladies the world over. In her plump white fingers she held the key which Audubon had left in the door. The artist gazed up at her with a ludicrous combination of consternation, guilt, and anxiety.

"Good—good day, Madame Guchin," he faltered.

In dour silence she stared down at them.

"Is—is that the key—of my room——" he began again.

Her harsh lips opened. "It is no longer your key, monsieur, nor is it your room."

"My—paintings——?"

"Will remain where they are," the woman said obdurately. "I may find them of more substance than your promises, which mean nothing."

She turned her broad back and disappeared down the hall, as uncompromising and unassailable as a frigate which commands an estuary with its guns. Bowie glanced at Audubon. The man seemed caved in, shrinking, as if humiliated almost beyond endurance. His face turned white and he sat suddenly down on the step.

"Are you ailing?" asked Bowie.

"I am ruined. The work of years . . . my whole career——" Audubon's eyes filled with tears, and Bowie, unaccustomed to the emotions of men of this type, was more impressed perhaps than need be by his new friend's despair.

"You're a little behind on your rent?" he said. "Would a loan——"

He drew out his wallet, but the artist rose with frigid dignity.

"Sir," he said, "I own to a faulty memory, but I cannot recall asking thee or anyone for aid——"

Actually, the man was affronted! Bowie found himself apologizing for his own kindly impulse. The despair returned to Audubon's face.

"You've got something worth more than all those paintings," Bowie said.

"What could be worth more than them?"

"The art to make others, as good or even better."

"Rattlesnakes, for example, that remain properly on the ground?"

A wan smile. That smile, under the circumstances, won Bowie. He placed a hand on the artist's shoulder. To his surprise, it trembled. Intuition told him that the fine-drawn look he had attributed to fatigue might be something else. This shabby man, who painted nature with such miraculous fidelity, was famished, actually faint from hunger. He started to say something, remembered Audubon's pride, and thought of a better approach. He grinned amiably.

"I mind a Cajun saying. *A taste of salt makes perfect a soup, a salad, or a new friendship.* If it suits your whim to go along with a little superstition of mine, Mr. Audubon, come have dinner with me, so we can taste salt together and thus seal our friendship."

The artist looked at him sharply. But the grin remained disarming.

"To seal our friendship, eh? That seemeth well thought of——" He regarded Bowie closely again, then with sudden impulsiveness embraced him. "But from this moment call me John! As I shall call thee by thy first name—for I find that I love thee, James!"

Chapter Two

I

Down a street picturesque with the crowds emptied from the cathedral by the conclusion of Mass, Bowie and Audubon walked to the French Market. Once they passed two elegant Creole gentlemen, swinging sword canes, and Bowie got a go-to-hell look from them. Decidedly he was seeing a sufficiency of supercilious bell crowns and sword canes this day. Yet he was never wholly indifferent to a brave show in the sun, and he privately thought that he could name a certain young man whose shoulders might do a great deal more for one of those bottle-green coats than any narrow-backed little Creole ever could do.

When they neared the French Market, close by the levee, a small, lively, wizened little man hurried toward them. He wore a hunting coat and sash, and his cheerfulness was undimmed by the ugliness of a scar that disfigured one side of his face and his nose.

"Jim!" he cried. "I wait for you since long time——"

"I got delayed," said Bowie. "Mr. Audubon, this is my friend who came down with me—Jules Brisson, better known as Nez Coupé."

"*Coupé*—that's right." The little Cajun indicated his disfigured nose with a laugh.

"The best hunter in the bayous," Bowie added.

"Is not so! Jim Bowie is most best hunter in the bayous!"

He fell in beside them. Presently they arrived at a certain Café des Réfugiés, which Audubon had recommended as having a cuisine passable and prices low. Into a paneled room, the walls of which were plastered with handbills and posters advertising bull baitings at the Congo Square, rewards for runaway slaves, stagecoach schedules, and auctions, they were bowed by a rotund *maître d'hôtel* with elaborate shirt ruffles, who gave them a quick appraisal and led them to an inconspicuous corner.

Their table was near and slightly behind one of the two high-backed wooden settles which flanked a wide fireplace. From his seat Bowie saw that the alcove was occupied by a group of young men, of whom only the two at the end of the opposite settle were visible to him. It was evident, however, that all were Creoles, all were well dressed and arrogant. One, with a sallow face, a long lower lip which gave him a petulant look, and a slender black mustache curling foppishly around the corners of his mouth, stared at them, then leaned forward to say something that provoked a laugh.

2

The *maître d'hôtel* began to expatiate with a poet's fervor on the excellences of the menu. Did the messieurs desire a potage? His potages were gastronomic triumphs. He could place before them, if they desired, oysters, terrapin, reedbirds, quail, ortolan, and other delicacies of the first style of culinary perfection. As they hesitated, he observed that the ragout of venison was a dream of gustatory bliss, and the brandies especially imported. Furthermore, there was *la petite goyave*——

"*La petite goyave?*" Bowie repeated.

Was Monsieur not familiar with it? The *maître d'hôtel* became ecstatic. Monsieur was in for a great, a notable experience. *La petite goyave* was the specialty of the house, most famous and most praised by many messieurs of discrimination the world over. He kissed his fingers in rapture. This sublimity, he said, was a drink brewed from the fermented juices of the guava fruit of the West Indies, very bland and delightful, once tasted never forgotten.

"Bring *la petite goyave,* then," said Bowie, "and with it the ragout of venison—at once. My friends are hungry."

Fat face dark with joyful perspiration, the *maître d'hôtel* hurried away and returned surrounded by a cloud of scurrying subordinates, who placed the dinner, smoking and savory, before them. With his own hands he brought a pitcher of amber liquid and glasses: poured, waited with an artist's anticipation as Bowie tasted, and departed happily as the face of the guest showed that the drink was all it was advertised.

"Thee be drinking," observed Audubon, "the favorite tipple of the old buccaneering crew—the Lafittes, Dominique You, René Baluche, and the rest."

"The pirates? I've heard of them. Where are they now?"

"All gone but old Dominique. He's around town, usually drunk."

Audubon began wolfing his food like one starved. Nez Coupé also plunged heartily into the fare. But Bowie continued to sip *la petite goyave,* feeling a pleasurable glow.

In the alcove the young Creoles conversed noisily, with frequent laughter. Bowie became interested in a pair of legs which stretched forth from the end of the nearer settle, differing from the other legs in that they did not sport the prevailing Hessian boots. Instead they were encased in long, fawn-colored pantaloons, very tight at calf and thigh, with straps under the insteps of the small and shapely varnished shoes. He could not see the owner of the legs because of a wing of the settle, but part of an arm and a hand were visible. The latter, slender-boned as a girl's and every bit as white, held a glass of *la petite goyave,* which it raised often to the hidden lips in a manner somewhat erratic, indicating a fairly advanced stage of tipsiness. Bowie decided that he did not care for the fawn-colored legs, or their owner.

3

Audubon, who had taken off the edge of his hunger, relaxed gratefully with his glass, and began to tell of himself—his childhood in France, with some horrendous accounts of the Terror; of the old sea captain who had adopted him, an orphan; of how he came to America as a youth, and was domiciled with a Quaker family, where he got his English speech with its queer thees and thous, his obsession over nature; and a wife, Lucy, a sweet and loyal, and also, Bowie gathered, a long-suffering woman, employed at the present as a governess in a household somewhere upriver, to support herself and her children, so her husband might find his destiny.

All at once he glanced down apologetically at his empty plate. "Forgive my garrulity. I was a-hungered, and drink at such times always makes my tongue overactive." He looked up. "It will do no harm to tell thee that this morning I returned from a field trip of a week's time . . . and my provisions ran out." He paused. "But I sketched in colors a painted bunting—a magical flash of blue-violet, scarlet, and green—beauty to clutch the heart." His face grew rapt, almost mystical, as it always did when he spoke of nature.

" 'Twas in that absence," he went on, "that my poor heron reached the state in which thee saw her. I had forgot her for days. Always in the forest I forget all else." He smiled wryly. "One small matter I forgot was an appointment to paint the portrait of a young lady—a most beautiful young lady, or so she is accounted."

The fawn-colored pantaloons in the settle-alcove had remained in full view, now stretching forth, now crossing their knees, now dawdling negligently. Audubon's back was toward them, but Bowie was gazing at them as the artist uttered the last words. Perhaps he imagined it, but the fawn pantaloons seemed to tense slightly.

"From her father I accepted an advance of ten dollars," Audubon went on, "against a fee of a hundred for the finished portrait. On that prospect I made promises to the good Madame Guchin—promises I could not keep. For since I forgot the initial appointment, the entire agreement is canceled. It was the father with whom thee saw me pleading at the cathedral—old Armand de Bornay, rich as Croesus with sugar plantations and black slaves. To him, ten dollars—or a hundred—is less than a picayune to me. Thee would hardly think him a pinchfist: yet from the furore over the trifling sum involved, thee might suppose it was the price of the Louisiana Territory."

The fawn legs in the alcove drew up rigidly as if their owner suddenly sat erect.

Unconscious of this, Audubon shrugged. "But what would thee? The painted bunting—or the painted beauty? *Peste,* I prefer the bird!"

The owner of the fawn legs was on his feet: all the Creoles in the alcove had risen as if pulled up by invisible strings. The fawn legs stepped around the corner and their owner was revealed as a furiously angry young man in a long, swaggering, scarlet-lined cape. He was slight in figure, with an aquiline face quite handsome, though marred by recklessness and dissipation, and marked by black side whiskers trimmed very close and running to a curved point at the angle of his jaw. For a moment he stood scowling, then strode fiercely over.

"So I find you here!" he said to Audubon.

The artist bore a look of painful embarrassment, with an almost furtive side glance, as if he would have escaped to the outside—anywhere—had it been possible. "Narcisse——" he began weakly.

"You find time, it appears," the other interrupted, "to drink in taverns, if not to carry out your engagements!"

"I beg of thee—my intentions were of the best. But—the day was perfect—I found myself in the pirogue—*pouf!*—a week was gone before I knew it! Ah, my friend——"

"Your *friend?* Have you the insolence to address me in such manner? Perhaps you consider that your patent to make scurrilous reference to Monsieur, my father—to ridicule Mademoiselle, my sister—and in a public place?"

"In God's name, Narcisse!" Audubon was aghast. "I had no thought—an awkward phrasing, perhaps—but that only. My respect for Monsieur de Bornay and my admiration for Mademoiselle Judalon are beyond words. I apologize—most abjectly—for this misunderstanding. If thee wish, I will make my apologies to Mademoiselle—to Monsieur, thy father——"

The Creole's lip curled. "You imagine you will have opportunity for that? The de Bornays open not their doors—for 'apologies'—or any other bootlicking—to liars and dogs—fit only to be whipped like dogs——"

He raised a riding whip which he had in his hand, as if to lash the shrinking artist, but Bowie came to his feet, knocking over the chair behind him.

As one, the Creoles turned toward him, dark and angry, their visages hardening with dislike. Bowie towered over them.

"Messieurs," he said evenly, "you were not invited to this table. I do not know the reason for the dispute, but I do know Monsieur Audubon desires no trouble with you. Be so good as to return to your own place."

The young man with the scarlet-lined cape lowered his whip and looked Bowie up and down arrogantly. "Who may this be?" he inquired.

"My name is James Bowie."

"So his name is James Bowie," repeated the Creole, mimicking most offensively his way of saying it. "An *Américain*—since it is abundantly clear he is no gentleman——"

"As good a gentleman as you!"

"*Vraiment?* In that case you should know that a gentleman does not interfere in what is no affair of his." The Creole's voice was biting.

"What affects my friend *is* my affair——"

"And if not, you make it so? Is that it? Monsieur—what is it—Bowie? Monsieur Bowie! *Mon Dieu,* what a name! I suppose it would be impossible for any *Américain* to comprehend the difference between being a gentleman—and being a clown—a boor—a barbarian——"

On Bowie's clenched fist the knuckles went white. But then he bowed,

15

and the bow was an exaggeration. As he did so, he sought for a name, found it, and when he spoke his sneer matched the Creole's.

"It seems I owe you some sort of an apology—Monsieur Lily Fingers. I had forgot that the conception of a gentleman in this place differs from that of the rest of the world. And that here such a creature should be treated for what he is—as obviously in your own case—a delicate and pap-nerved softling, as pale, as pretty, and almost as masculine as his sister!"

He had devised a brilliantly deadly insult. The Creole's face went white.

"Monsieur!" His hand reached into an inner pocket of his coat.

Audubon and Nez Coupé were up, the latter dragging a short-bladed dirk from his hip.

"No, Nez Coupé——" ordered Bowie.

The Cajun hung poised, snarling like a catamount. In that electric moment Bowie remembered he was unarmed, and balanced on the balls of his feet, waiting for the other to draw.

"Narcisse! I beg of thee!" Audubon's imploring voice.

The Creole gave a chill smile. "I said—I still say—the *Américain* is a born boor. But such as he is, perhaps he should be taught a lesson."

From the inner pocket he brought—not a pistol—but a card case. Deliberately he drew out a small white oblong of cardboard and flung it on the table. Bowie took it up, experiencing a pang of chagrin that he had no card of his own to exchange for it. He read the name.

Narcisse de Bornay

"I am lodging at the Rouge et Noir," he said stiffly. "My name you have."

De Bornay bowed. Bristling, the Creoles tramped out of the tavern.

Chapter Three

I

"He will call thee out, depend on it," groaned Audubon, sinking into a chair.

"That's his privilege," said Bowie.

"Why did thee do it?"

"I wasn't going to listen to him blackguard you——"

"Me? I'll thank thee to let me conduct my own affairs! Narcisse is my friend. He has been drinking, and in his cups his temper is uncertain, that is all. Besides, 'twas no more than I deserved. Most justly he berated me. But thee took it on thyself to intervene, thou great American oaf—and now——" He broke off, wringing his hands.

Bowie was speechless. Under the circumstances, he thought he had conducted himself rather well.

After a moment he said, "If that's the way you think, we'd better part company right here. But just bear this in mind: he insulted me too."

Audubon sat staring at the wine stains on the table, his face woebegone.

"Come, Nez Coupé," Bowie said.

But the artist leaped up. "Wait! Nay, in God's name we be friends!" He seized Bowie's arm. "I'm on thy side, thee must believe me. I go with thee—we must think what to do."

Bowie grunted. As they left the café, Nez Coupé said, "You should have leave me at him. The knife is more quicker than the pistol."

"He had no pistol," Bowie said. "If you'd knifed him, you'd have hung."

Nez Coupé fell into sulky silence. Definitely, this was not according to Cajun notions of how an affair should be conducted.

"Already Narcisse has been principal in three duels," Audubon said dolefully.

This was of interest. "Did he kill his men?" Bowie asked.

"Nay, wounded them, all three. One with the pistol, two with the sword." Sudden hope in the artist's face. "It's by no means sure. Thee may escape with a wound only——"

Bowie laughed a short, ugly laugh. "If he and I fight, I'll make you one promise: *somebody's* going to get killed."

It was like a pronouncement of a sentence of death. The artist shivered slightly, and said no more. Bowie turned toward the river.

2

Though it was Sunday, a brig with a cargo of rum from Havana was being unloaded by a gang of slaves at the Parisot wharf. Bowie watched the Negroes, moving in line like a colony of ants, save that they displayed none of the ants' eager energy in their work. All were strong and muscular, outlandishly dressed in ragged dungarees and shirts of faded linsey, in each face the expressionless vacuity of the slave.

The spectacle was familiar. The dock hands trundled ahead of them two-handled, two-wheeled trucks, shuffling indolently, although a white man in a ship's officer's cap was yelling himself purple at them. Leaning against a stanchion with a coiled whip in his hand was a man in riding boots, with a black beard and a bloodless face: the overseer. He shared none of the mate's excitement, but his eyes ceaselessly watched the slaves as each in turn received an oaken keg on his truck, and slowly trundled it back across the gangplank to the dock, where two of their fellows piled the fat casks high in an open warehouse.

Now and again Audubon glanced at Bowie. "What do we here?" he ventured at last.

"I'm hoping to find Monsieur Janos Parisot."

"The merchant?"

"Yes. I have a letter of introduction from Judge Boden of Opelousas. Do you know him?"

"By sight."

"Buys lumber?"

"Lumber—and many other things."

"My two brothers and I own a lumber mill on the Bayou Boeuf," Bowie said. "John and Rezin are older than I am. Older and steadier, I reckon. Rezin likes to hunt, but he has a practical side. He was the one who discovered the stand of timber on the Bayou Boeuf, but John worked out the details of setting up the saw pit and getting the lumber out."

"And thee?"

Bowie half laughed. "I'm the youngest. And the longest-legged. And maybe the laziest."

"Ha!" said Nez Coupé. "Jim take the pit end of the whipsaw an' wear out both his brothair at the up end in a day's work. Look at those shouldair! Jim get him from the whipsaw!"

"I work hard when I work," Bowie said, "but I can't see a life with nothing but the broadax and the whipsaw. I like to hunt. When I take a notion, I like to get my rifle and be gone for a few days."

"Jim know every cabin an' every pretty Cajun girl for forty mile around," said Nez Coupé. "He nevair miss a cockfight, dance, broom jumpin', or hunt——"

"Sounds bad, don't it?" Bowie grinned. "John and Rezin used to sort of—well, talk with me—once in a while. Until I got big enough so's I could handle 'em both. But we got along all right, until Dr. Carter Carter of Opelousas died. He was buying our lumber."

"So thee seek now a new market?" asked Audubon.

"That's correct. John's about to get married, and Rezin's in politics. So they sent me. That's why I'm here right now—I've been told Parisot visits his dock every day."

An hour passed. Audubon found a shady place, where he sat and talked with Nez Coupé. Bowie remained standing in the sun.

He became aware of a pair of loafers sitting on a coil of rope and watching the unloading with the peculiar enjoyment of loafers the world over at the observation of any kind of labor being done by others. In the manner, likewise, of all loafers, they made free with their comments.

"Wall, now," said one, a tall bearded fellow in brown homespun, "if that ain't the likeliest lot of niggers!"

"Not bad. No—I'd say purty fair," agreed his companion, a fat bald man in a greasy nankeen shirt and leather breeches. It was obvious that they were river boatmen, and equally obvious that neither had ever owned so much as a single slave: yet they discussed the gang on the wharf in a large and expert manner, as elsewhere they might have discussed the fine points of a herd of cattle or horses.

"Nineteen," said the brown beard. "Matched an' in good shape. They'd fotch eight hundred dollars a head at a vendue."

"A thousand's more like it," amended the bald one. "No—I'd say twenty thousand wouldn't be no banter for the lot."

"I dunno." The brown beard had a wiseacre's air. "Them looks like brute niggers, now. Right out of the Congo, I bet. None too well broke. Look at that rascal in the shed—troublemaker if I ever seed one."

He referred to the nearer of the two slaves piling casks. Bowie glanced over. In contrast to the others, this man seized each burden and hoisted it to its place with a kind of savage energy. Yet he was weary: and something more. Through rents in his tattered shirt, Bowie saw ugly weals on the polished ebony body, and the shirt was stained with blood scarcely dry.

The slave had been flogged, no later than this morning, and severely: the kind of flogging that would have prostrated most men. Yet with a lacerated back he worked as none of the others worked, as if driven by some inner frenzy. Alone of them all he wore iron leg shackles, which confined him to short hobbling steps: and toward him, more often than to any of the others, the overseer turned his expressionless grim mask.

Bowie's face showed no change. Slavery was accepted, and this man was another man's property. But, contrary to the opinion of the loafers, the slave in the shed was no brute from the Congo.

Bowie knew him. Quite well. And from a happier time.

The loafers' conversation took a new turn. "I know whar a gang like them kin be bought for no more'n a dollar a pound," said the bald one. "Prime hands, all of 'em."

"Aw, now! Whar?"

"Mebbe I ain't sayin'." These creatures loved to be mysterious.

"Huh! Ain't no sech place. That's why."

The next remark fully caught Bowie's attention.

"Mebbe," craftily said he of the fatness and the baldness, "bein' from Arkansaw, ye ain't never heard of the Lafittes?"

"Hell, everybody knows about them pirates!"

"Some says they're pirates: some says they ain't. Mebbe they done a little piratin'—mebbe they done a little smugglin'. Ain't for me to say." Baldy closed an eye in an indescribable effort to look sly. "But some mighty high-toned gents right hyar in Noo Orl'ns was glad to be sociable with 'em at one time. An' when ole Andy Jackson was fixin' to scrimmage with the British down the perninsular, he warn't too proud to have the Lafittes on his side."

"Andy Jackson didn't need no pirates to lick them Britishers!"

"Think not? Some'd argy that p'int with ye. An' I'm thinkin' Ole Hickory'd be one of 'em. Anyway, the Lafittes is gone now. Some place called Galvez-town, down the Texas coast." The bald head became confidential. "Know who Dominique You is?"

"That ole sot? Shore. Everybody knows him."

"Ole sot mebbe. But Cap'n Dominique was oncet the terror of the Gulf. I reckon he does h'ist enough licker to float him these days. But I ask ye, does he go around in rags? Not him. He eats an' drinks at the very best places, drives a team of blooded bays, an' keeps a fancy quadroon gal."

Brown beard nodded. "That's true. Never thought o' that."

"I bet ole Dominique could tell plenty, if he took a notion——"

"Looky. There's Parisot comin'."

Both loafers rose uneasily from their rope coil. "Reckon we better drift. He don't fancy folks hangin' around his dock."

They slouched away around the corner of the warehouse.

4

The man approaching was past his prime, somewhat portly, with a heavy smooth-shaved face. He wore a long-tailed coat and high hat, walked with a cane, and with his free hand twirled incessantly a key which dangled from a heavy watch chain looped across his waistcoat. Parisot looked suspiciously at Bowie, and then called to the overseer.

"Peters!"

The man went to him, his manner typically respectful and impersonal.

"I've undertaken to clear the ship by morning," said the merchant.

The overseer said, "We're less than half finished, sir."

"You'll work tonight."

"With this gang?"

"It's all I can give you."

The mouth behind the black beard tightened. "Very good, sir." The overseer shook loose his whip, then coiled it again in his hand. Human endurance had limits, even to an overseer's mind. But orders were orders. The braided lash of that whip would be wet with blood before the night's driving was finished . . .

Bowie lifted his hat. "Are you Monsieur Parisot?"

"I am."

"Then I have a letter addressed to you from Judge Sophocles Boden, of Opelousas."

"I have the honor of Judge Boden's acquaintance." Parisot took the letter and scanned it. Bowie found little in him to like. "You are Mr. Bowie?" He extended a limp hand. "From the Bayou Boeuf? I know the country in general. H'mm—Judge Boden mentions that you're in lumber."

"I have a matter of business concerning that——"

"Pardon. I don't transact business on Sunday—except a necessity like this unlading of a ship which has sailing orders."

"I have reason for wishing to discuss matters with you today."

"It will have to be an extraordinarily good reason, sir."

Bowie smiled. "I may be killed tomorrow."

"Did—did I understand you correctly?" Parisot gaped.

"I'm being called out by a gentleman of this city who is, I'm informed, accomplished with his weapons."

"Oh, a duel?" Parisot nodded as one who finds the explanation less startling than he had thought. "What's the nature of your proposal?"

"You purchase lumber?"

"Among other things—yes."

"I am to inquire if you will take the output of a sawmill my brothers and I own together."

"H'mm." A hidden gleam of alertness came into the merchant's eyes. In a casual manner he asked some questions. Bowie named a price.

Parisot fell silent, twirling his watch key. "I must have time to consider your proposition," he said at last. "There are a few points that need examination."

"Haven't I made myself clear?"

"Perhaps. But always there are factors requiring further adjustment. I must consider the risks involved. As it happens, pine lumber is a drug on the market here. Of cypress, on the other hand, I could use all you can send. You suggest mixed shipments in equal quantities. Now if you were to furnish all cypress——"

"At the price I quoted?"

"Naturally."

"Cypress is harder to log—and to saw—as you know, sir. Our price is shaved to the last penny. For cypress only I'd have to ask a higher figure."

Parisot poked with his cane at a knot in one of the wharf planks. "You desire to establish an outlet in New Orleans? You should be prepared to make concessions."

"The price I quoted was fair, sir."

The merchant studied Bowie's face. "Fair? What is fair? You've had small experience with trade, young man. I buy at the lowest price I can bargain and sell at the highest. You wish to settle the business before tomorrow—under the circumstances, these are my only terms."

Bowie looked at the dock owner with a certain longing. But you cannot throttle a man simply because he won't bargain your way. He changed the subject.

"These are your Negroes, Monsieur Parisot?"

"They are."

"Nice lot."

The merchant shrugged. "As good as one can get these days. It's hard to buy prime hands since the government stopped the bringing of slaves into the country."

"That fellow in the shed—where did you get him?"

Parisot turned his gaze in that direction. "That's an example of what I say, Mr. Bowie. He was a house servant. My agent bought him at an auction, because he seemed likely. But he's spoiled and uppity—spent too much time opening doors and polishing silver and pouring wine. Peters! You've had trouble again with that man Sam?"

"Yes, sir," the overseer said. "Had to give him a taste of the snake whip this morning."

The overseer spoke with the icy detachment of his class, handlers of human flesh and blood, whose profession was to accomplish certain things with the units in their charge, using whatever methods were needful to stimulate them to the results desired.

"A bad actor," said Parisot petulantly. "And he can ruin the others. Thinks he's got rights—like resting on Sunday."

"A few weeks in a breaking camp might be good for him," said Peters. Merchant and overseer frowned over at the slave.

22

"He seems to work hard enough," Bowie said.

"When he has to," said Parisot.

"If he's a trained house servant, why put him at common labor?"

"Because I need hands, not house servants!" The merchant turned to the overseer. "Peters, I'm out of patience. That rascal's acted up once too often. Get hold of the factors tomorrow, and turn him over to the breaking camp. I want the fear of God put into him!"

He said it with a peculiar gloating ferocity. Work had ceased momentarily while the hoists brought up more cargo from the hold, and Bowie knew the slave had overheard him.

The implications were sufficiently shocking. Operations of the so-called "breaking camps" down in the Delta were carefully hushed up in Louisiana, but rumors concerning them had circulated for years: whispered stories of strange secret horrors, where the lash sounded day and night, and starvation, the water cure, the thumbscrew, the branding iron—all forms of torment that did not break or maim yet gave exquisite anguish—were employed to destroy any "spirit" in the unfortunates held there, particularly those newly imported from the Guinea coast or the Congo. Bowie had heard of the shocking "wastage" in the breaking process, the deaths and suicides: and how miserable victims who managed somehow to survive came out of the hell-camps little better than idiots, their minds gone, capable all their lives of but one emotion—fear.

The slave called Sam had listened with the terrible fascination of those who are certain of a ghastly doom, yet await final pronouncement of their sentences. Bowie found himself suddenly very unwilling to have this man sent to a breaking camp.

"You got him at the Carter plantation sale?" he asked Parisot.

"I believe so."

"I was acquainted with Dr. Carter Carter prior to his death. A conspicuous gentleman in his day."

"Yes. Most unfortunate that he died without direct heirs. An ornament to the country, Carter Hall, and it had to be broken up——"

"It happens I know this man of yours. He was Dr. Carter's butler. I have a fancy to take him off your hands."

The gleam of alertness flickered again in Parisot's eye, instantly disappearing. He shook his head. "Sorry. He's not for sale."

"Name a price."

"I said he was not for sale."

"You spoke of sending him to a breaking camp."

"I did."

"It might kill him."

"A risk I have to take."

"He'd be little use to you then." Bowie hesitated. "Would you trade him?"

"For another slave?" Parisot was crafty. "Not for a brute nigger fresh out of Africa."

"Would you trade for *two?*"

Parisot grew smooth. "Age and condition?"

"Equal or better."

"When?"

"It would take a little time."

"Days?"

"Six months."

Parisot thought. "If you mean it, there can be but one answer. I agree."

"Good. I'll take the man with me now."

The merchant grinned humoringly. "You're joking. Where's the exchange?"

"My personal note of hand."

"With all apologies, my young friend, I'm afraid a personal note from you wouldn't be very negotiable in these times."

"As security, my one-third of the lumbering concern on the Bayou Boeuf."

Parisot studied him. "You seem to want this slave badly."

"I need a valet."

"Very well. Step to my office. We'll draw up the papers."

"Let me speak to the slave first."

"Certainly." At Parisot's nod the overseer made a motion of his coiled whip and the Negro clanked toward them with his shackles. He was tall and strong, with a slight grizzle at his temples, and a black face which was intelligent, if at the moment bleak and sullen. Bowie could remember that face when it was lit with a smile of welcome at Dr. Carter's hospitable door.

"Sam," he said.

"Marse Bowie, suh." The slave was deferential, yet dignified, in spite of his weariness and pain.

"I'm buying you from Monsieur Parisot."

Sam's eyes flicked to the merchant, to the overseer, then back to Bowie. "Yes, suh," he said. Then, as if the full significance of it had just dawned, "Yes, *suh,* Marse Bowie!"

Bowie looked at Peters. "Have those shackles off of him."

The overseer glanced at Parisot.

"You hear him," the merchant said.

The man with the black beard nodded impassively. He was a slave overseer, and such men were trained to feel no more human emotion in themselves than they recognized in the slaves under them. He began to unlock the irons on Sam's ankles.

Chapter Four

I

Henri Pinchon, owner of the Rouge et Noir tavern, sat in his usual place at his desk which stood behind the bar. On the wall above his head hung a row of large bells, each with a bullet-shaped tongue which, when pulled, continued to vibrate for some minutes after ringing, thus showing to which room above it belonged. Pinchon was short and round, the almost type-perfect host, since he loved his joint and bottle as well as any of his guests, and prided himself on his ability to estimate character at first sight.

For the moment, however, his usual complacency was gone. He had been filled with surprising inner doubts as to his judgment on one customer at least: this Monsieur Bowie. The previous day when he had come to the tavern, Henri ticketed him as a greenhorn who knew not good from bad. The appearance of the scar-faced little Cajun with him confirmed that opinion. The two, therefore, had been assigned the smallest room in the inn, high under the eaves overlooking a dirty courtyard, where they shared a very lumpy bed. Now the good Henri wondered . . .

He rose quickly to his feet. The very pair had entered the public room, accompanied by a man in purplish drab who looked shabby as a beggar, and followed by a Negro in a field hand's ragged linsey. How was a tavernkeeper to conduct himself toward these people?

"Monsieur Bowie——" he said in a low voice. He leaned confidentially over the bar, and Bowie had a whiff of garlic from his breath. "Two gentlemen are here, desiring to see you."

"Who?"

"They are—of the *élite*." Henri rolled his eyes toward the chimney corner and his voice was tinged with respect. The quality of these visitors was sufficiently impressive to give a guest standing merely because such personages saw fit to call upon him.

Bowie turned. Two young men rose and bowed to him together. One he recognized: the long, petulant lip and thin mustache were not easily forgotten. Friends of that fire-eating Creole, Narcisse de Bornay, and their business was not difficult to guess.

25

He walked across the room, and spoke in French. "You wish to see me?"

He of the mustache answered. "There was hardly time for a formal exchange of names at our first meeting, Monsieur Bowie. Allow me, therefore, to introduce my friend and myself. This gentleman is Monsieur Armand Lebain. I am Philippe Cabanal."

"Your servant, messieurs," murmured Bowie, bowing. Lebain appeared to be an ineffectual young man, round-chinned, soft-lipped and proud.

"May we speak in private?" Cabanal asked. "I have taken the liberty of arranging with Pinchon for the small sitting room——"

"If you wish. My friends?"

"*Certainement.*"

Sam, the slave, effaced himself in a corner. With Audubon and Nez Coupé, Bowie followed the visitors to a small room off the main hall, where they turned to him politely.

"We are here on behalf on Monsieur de Bornay," Cabanal said.

Bowie nodded.

"He has empowered us to arrange terms—in the matter of which you know—according to your satisfaction, since you are the challenged party," continued the Creole stiffly.

Another nod from Bowie.

A moment's awkward pause. Then, as if it were distasteful, "Our principal, monsieur, desires us to inquire in what manner you wish his apology to be delivered."

It caught Bowie so by surprise that he wondered if he had heard rightly. "Apology?" he echoed, somewhat stupidly.

"Yes, monsieur."

"I—I believe I do not understand——"

Cabanal drew himself up. "Monsieur de Bornay is a gentleman whose courage has never been questioned. Let that be understood at once. He also has a—let us say an unusual sense of honor—which sometimes induces him to act in an extraordinary manner, or so some of us feel." He paused, as if to convey to Bowie that he, for one, did not approve of what was to follow. "In this instance, he requested us to inform you that realizing he was—ah—somewhat intoxicated this noon, and considering his actions, he feels it your due—and his own also as a gentleman—that he offer his apologies."

This was so utterly contrary to any experience that Bowie could not bring his bewildered mind to frame a reply.

"You are willing to accept the apology?" asked Cabanal, after a moment.

"Why—I suppose so——"

26

"In that case," the Creole said, "we are to ask if you require that it be put in writing, or made to you verbally, in person."

Bowie could have laughed. But the chill formality of the two before him caused him to pick his words carefully. "As to that," he said, "for myself I require no apology at all. If Monsieur de Bornay wishes to retract his words, let him do so to Monsieur Audubon."

"He will do so. Is that all?"

"Yes."

The Creoles stepped to one side and conferred for a moment in low voices. Then they were back, stiff and formal, Cabanal the spokesman as before.

"Permit us to say, monsieur, that we consider this magnanimous of you, especially since it was the purpose of Monsieur de Bornay, who esteems Monsieur Audubon, to make such retraction in his own instance."

He and Lebain bowed. "Now, since so much is agreed between us, shall we proceed to the next part of the business?"

Once more Bowie was baffled. "What other part is there?"

"But surely it is for you now to name to us your seconds, so that the place of meeting and also the weapons can be determined?"

Bowie simply stared. Were these young fools insane?

"Let me understand," he said. "Did I not hear you say that Monsieur de Bornay offers his apologies?"

"*Vraiment.*"

"Then—would that not appear to be an end to the quarrel?"

"Monsieur does our principal less than justice," said Cabanal loftily. "He would never dream of depriving you of the right of upholding your honor against him at the full risk of his own body."

Astonishing, these Creoles, certainly. Bowie was between admiration and exasperation at a man who could think up a dilemma so outrageously contradictory. And the more he considered it, the more reluctant he found himself to fight a duel with an opponent so remarkably inclined, so he said, "Please to inform your principal that my honor is not affronted: and for my part there need be no meeting at all."

Once more they bowed. "We trust this is not merely further magnanimity. He is very ready——"

Bowie exploded at last with laughter. "If he must fight, I'll name you the time and weapons! The time: when next it snows in New Orleans ——"

"But it never snows in New Orleans——"

"I'm aware of that. The weapons: snowballs——"

"Monsieur——"

"Meantime, present my compliments to Monsieur de Bornay, and tell him that I would esteem it a privilege to shake his hand and so close the entire affair—which I'm very ready to say he has conducted in a manner that does him an infinite amount of credit."

The Creoles were unsmiling. In the American's manner was a suspicious levity. His message, moreover, seemed hardly couched in the proper terms. Yet there was something so clifflike in this fair-haired young giant that further arguments did not occur to them.

After a moment they bowed stiffly and withdrew.

2

Bowie found a very respectful Henri Pinchon awaiting him. The gentleman desired another pallet in his room? But certainly. Quarters for the slave? On learning that what apparently was a raw field hand in reality was a skilled house servant, Henri had a proposal. He could employ Sam in the dining room, thus defraying the extra cost of Audubon's lodgings. Bowie accepted.

But when they went up to their third-flight room, Nez Coupé was still snorting. "These peoples—*nom du chien*—too much talk, bah! Lots of time Cajun fight—sometime with gun—sometime with feet—*la savate*—sometime with knife. Like this——" He indicated his scarred visage. "Auguste Cabet—he give me that one. Good frien', Auguste."

"Good friend when he did that to thee?" asked Audubon.

"Oh, Auguste like me plenty." Nez Coupé laughed merrily, as if a disfigured nose was a small matter. "We drunk that time we fight. Me, I fix Auguste so he have stiff arm always. Good fight, that one. An' no talk—like here." Nez Coupé went through a ridiculous little mincing routine of bows and posturings, meantime repeating such words as he could remember of the formal utterances he had heard. "Monsieur. We arrange term. We have priv'lege. He reques' we inform you. Permit us. Magna-magnam—what is this word? Bah!" His scarred face was contemptuous. "Big word get nowheres. Auguste an' me—we get plenty drunk. We fight. No big word. When we get well, we go hunt together like before. We make lots of fun, us."

Bowie sat moodily silent.

"What ails thee, James?" asked Audubon.

"Nothing."

"Assuredly something does."

"I've been a fool."

"In what manner?"

"In every way a man could, I reckon." Bowie gave a short laugh.

"How so? The outcome of the quarrel was most happy——"

"I'm not even thinking about that. This afternoon's what's eating me. It just come over me what a trap Janos Parisot led me into. Played on my sympathies—the old reptile—until I ruined any chance I had for a good deal—obligated myself for everything I own and more—went into debt for fifteen hundred dollars—and all to buy a nigger I've got no more use for than a second set of teeth!"

"Why did thee do it, James?"

Bowie thought back. He had not acted entirely without plan. A sudden secret scheme had suggested itself, endowing him with that surprising calmness in talking to Parisot. But already he was realizing how hare-brained that scheme was. Too ridiculous even to mention.

"I couldn't stand seeing Carter's Sam cut to pieces any longer by that damned overseer!" he said.

Audubon smiled. "Thee be a kindly man, James."

"Hell! I'd have done the same for a horse or dog!"

"And would be kindly still."

For a moment Bowie stared at Audubon. An odd harsh look came into his eyes. "You don't understand me, I reckon. I took one nigger away from Parisot. But I undertook to give him two back. What about the other two?"

The artist's smile faded.

3

Bowie was right: Audubon did not understand him. In some ways he did not understand himself. He was moody the rest of that evening and next morning as they lounged in their room after breakfast. But Audubon amused himself by drawing out Nez Coupé.

"Plenty bird on the Bayou Boeuf," said the Cajun. "Plenty animal—bear—deer—'gator—painter—wolf—*loup-garou*——"

"*Loup-garou?*"

"Oh, *loup-garou*—sure. Bad thing, that one. Look like wolf sometime—sometime change to man—sometime big bat—suck out blood if he find you sleeping—carry off child, suck blood till she die——"

Audubon was curious. He had heard of the superstition of the vampire werewolf—the *loup-garou* of the Cajuns—but this was his first encounter with someone who fully believed it.

"Did thee ever see a *loup-garou?*" he asked.

"Me? No, not see—hard to see, that one. But I been *near* where he come. *Nom de Dieu*—make hair stand up on my neck now when I think about it!"

"How did thee know it was near?"

"How I know? *Le bon Dieu!* Sometime I track wolf—track long time. All at once—wolf track gone. No see him, that wolf track. *Man* track there! No man track before—just there. I stop, me. Thick woods ahead. *Mon Dieu*, John, I hear something in those woods! Something funny. I not know, see? I scare! I think man in there, mebbe, but not like man. How man get in those place, with wolf track? I nevair hear that thing before. *Dieu,* I scare bad! I come back quick from that place." He stopped, and cackled uneasily.

"Thee didn't actually *see* it?"

"No. I not wait—me!"

"It didn't chase you?"

Nez Coupé cackled again. "That *loup-garou*—he have to go pretty fast that time to catch me!"

Bowie had heard this sort of thing before. The Cajun was incurably superstitious, his world peopled by the unseen and inexplicable.

Audubon rose and went to the door as a knock came.

Henri Pinchon, very obsequious, very perspiring, was bowing low before a young man in a tall hat, with side whiskers trimmed to a sharp point at the angles of his jaw.

"This is the room, Monsieur de Bornay. I—I—did not dream these messieurs were friends of yours——"

De Bornay waved him away and entered. For a moment he stood silent, then bowed to Bowie.

"Monsieur, your message was conveyed to me." He spoke a very precise English.

"Yes?"

"Though its proposal was frivolous, I believe I recognized the good will behind it. I therefore have come to express my respects."

The Creole had a smile of peculiar charm: he was very different from the arrogant, drunk and quarrelsome man of the day before.

Bowie returned the smile. "Thank you. And I'll say, Monsieur de Bornay, that I regret my own hasty words——"

"*Chut!* We will not speak of that." Bowie gathered that the hasty words still had power to rankle. They shook hands, and the Creole turned winningly to Audubon.

"John—I was a scoundrel! Can you forgive?"

"Ah, Narcisse!"

"Ah, John!"

In the impetuous French way, they embraced. A pleasant moment.

"Will you be seated?" Bowie said. "On the bed—or John's pallet yonder. I regret we have no better accommodations."

"John's pallet?" De Bornay was surprised, then concerned as the circumstances of Audubon's departure from his former lodgings came out.

"This cannot be permitted!" he said.

"The good Madame Guchin is within her rights," said the artist.

"A pest on such rights! At least we'll get those pictures——"

"I beg thee, Narcisse—no charity." Warning in Audubon's voice.

"Who spoke of charity? A small loan——"

"Would in this case be charity—since I cannot repay it."

"John, John—will you be sensible——?"

"Cannot a man be left some shreds of his pride?" Audubon walked abruptly to the small window and stood with hands locked behind him, gazing stonily out under the eaves.

Bowie found himself wondering at a man who could at one moment accept insults without resentment, yet at another grow angry at an offer of friendly help. But Narcisse seemed to understand.

"How stupid of me," he said. "I had forgot—John, I seem always to do the wrong thing——"

"And I am a fool to take such matters to heart!" said Audubon quickly.

The situation was restored. Presently Narcisse glanced at his watch. "Are you to be long in the city?" he asked Bowie.

"Only a few days."

"In such time as you are here—if you care to see something of New Orleans—will you accept me as your cicerone?"

"Why—many thanks——"

"Then, as a beginning, since it is near noon, will the three of you be my guests at luncheon?"

But Audubon pleaded that he wished to spend the afternoon sketching. And Nez Coupé had a project even more important.

"I have a friend——" he began.

"Bring him along," said Narcisse.

"Him? Who say him? I have enough *him* all time here, *mon Dieu!* This a *her.*" A cavernous grin. "Lots of woman in this place, Jim. Nevair I see so many at one time. Plenty woman like Cajun man here. Down at French Market is one name of Marie. Me, I make woman laugh, that one. Fine woman, her. An' cook! Always she want to cook things——"

Bowie alone accompanied Narcisse de Bornay to luncheon that day.

The fat *maître d'hôtel* at the Café des Réfugiés bent almost double at the door and triumphantly conducted them to a good table near a window, where he personally served them with a light chop, salad, madeira, and frappé. As they were finishing luncheon a group of men, mostly young, entered and crossed to the fireplace alcove, nodding to Narcisse.

"My coterie," he said. "We meet here almost every day to decide upon the evening's diversion."

"I see Cabanal and Lebain."

"Observe the man next to Philippe?"

Bowie saw a short, broad-shouldered man, with a dark, heavy face, eyes cunningly intelligent, and an exceptional muscular structure.

"That is Contrecourt, the *maître d'armes,*" Narcisse said. "One of the best, though his *salle* is less popular than some. He it was who killed Orsini, the Italian fencing master, in the Jewish cemetery last year."

"A duel in a cemetery?"

"One place of many. Usually it is St. Anthony's Square, directly behind the cathedral, which is screened from the street by shrubbery and convenient for impromptu swordplay. If pistols are used, it is customary to ride out to the Oaks of Allard, where a stray bullet is less likely to carry off a citizen wandering unsuspectingly by." Narcisse smiled. "Observe the gentleman to the left of Contrecourt? He with the penciled brows and the gold-embroidered waistcoat?"

"Who is he?"

"The artist Vanderlyn. He's the rage just now in New Orleans, because he understands what our friend Audubon does not—that to succeed as a portraitist, the artist must flatter." He lifted a wineglass delicately between thumb and finger. "Audubon must tell people what he thinks —by word or brush—and the devil take the consequences. He is a genius. Apart from his painting of birds, with which he is so obsessed, he is a landscape and portrait artist of the first quality. Yet he will allow himself no chance for his artistry. He might have more commissions than he could handle, for men like this Vanderlyn are not fit to mix his pigments. But he will not behave himself—show ordinary tact, even."

Bowie nodded. Narcisse sipped, and said, "Perhaps it is the lot of genius to suffer. Originality is seldom welcome in the world. But why go out of the way to suffer?" He paused. "John is too touchy to accept a loan— though it seems not to occur to him that living as your guest is hardly different from borrowing money of you. He must paint portraits to live.

And he persists in treating the finest commissions as without importance."

"Such as—the portrait of Mademoiselle de Bornay?"

Narcisse smiled a trifle wearily. "You don't know the whole story. It was through my efforts that my father compacted with Audubon to paint her. My sweet sister Judalon thereupon invited some friends of her own age and sex to form an audience at the sitting—it's frequently done, giving the portrait thus added importance as a conversation piece."

"Good God!" said Bowie. "And Audubon failed to appear?"

Narcisse shook his head ruefully. "The denouement, of course, was most unhappy. Poor Judalon invited these young ladies to witness her triumph. They beheld instead her ignominy." He considered the wineglass thoughtfully. "A woman is, after all, only human: and I sometimes think a pretty woman is something less than human—toward her own sex at least. These all chanced to be quite charming. It follows that their amusement was quite cruel."

"I can imagine."

"My unhappy sister took to her bed for two days. She is, I suppose, spoiled, and I fear she is well versed in creating a family impasse when she desires. Before she was through with them, my parents were quite beside themselves. Monsieur, my father, is sometimes stormy when angered—but remember, he had some little excuse for it."

Bowie smiled. He was coming to like very much this young man of the gay cynicisms.

"And so," he said, "with the de Bornay interdict upon Audubon, no other New Orleans family will have anything to do with him?"

"Oversimplified, perhaps. But—well, yes."

"And he's lost not only his livelihood, but his life's work?"

Narcisse nodded sadly. "I am attached to him. If there were only some way——"

Bowie thought. "There's one——"

"What is it?"

"If the de Bornays accepted him again, others would also."

Narcisse's laugh was brittle. "You don't know my people. Especially Judalon."

"That is my misfortune."

Narcisse stared at him as if he had been struck by a thought which required considerable digesting.

"Jim," he said, "shall we conspire in behalf of Audubon?"

"In what manner?"

"First, I shall present you to my family."

"You have some sort of a plan?"

"Not exactly. But even a precarious foothold on the wall is a beginning toward carrying the castle——" Narcisse broke off. "You can keep your temper?" he asked anxiously.

"I think so."

"*Bien.* You may have to do so." Narcisse seemed to experience a slight inward amusement at something. "Well, let's join the coterie."

5

They greeted Narcisse with warmth, tingeing off into coolness toward Bowie as introductions were made. At once they ignored the American as they turned to his friend in a volley of French.

"You've heard about the latest challenge?" asked Armand Lebain.

"No."

"Colonel Claridge and Belmonte. Pistols," said Vanderlyn.

"The quarrel?"

"Last night," Contrecourt said. "St. Sylvain's. Cards."

"Claridge will down him," said Narcisse.

"I'm not so certain," said Cabanal. "Belmonte's a big target, but he spends much time at the *salle d'armes.*"

"Five to four Claridge does," Narcisse said.

Cabanal glanced at Contrecourt, who lifted his eyebrows. "Give us a better price, Narcisse," he said. "Look at your advantage. Belmonte's wide as a hogshead. It's like putting up a barn door before a broomstick."

There was a laugh. "Something in what you say," Narcisse agreed.

"What price then?" asked Cabanal.

"Eight to five on Claridge."

"Taken—for a hundred!"

Lebain said, "Another hundred—at the same odds."

A chorus of voices:

"A hundred and fifty here!"

"Louis Chailleau and I will take that between us!"

"A hundred more at Narcisse's price!"

"Done!"

Wallets were out and notations made on a tablet brought by a waiter.

Cabanal smiled at Narcisse. "If I win from you, I'll only be getting back what you've cost me."

"How's that, Philippe?"

"*Mon Dieu,* you're bankrupting us all with those new styles. That spencer coat you brought from London, for instance. I've ordered one— so have all of us. A round hundred it'll cost me. And Cocquelon, my tailor, says he can't possibly get it out for a fortnight, he's so swamped with orders."

Narcisse laughed, looking down at the short, tailless jacket he wore, a precurser of the mess jacket of the future, just then completely new in New Orleans.

"You've heard how this style started?" he asked.

"No. But I do know it's damnably smart."

"Lord Spencer, who's something of an arbiter in London, wagered that he could set a fashion wholly meaningless and unnecessary that would be popular in a fortnight. With that, he called for a pair of shears, whacked off the tails of his coat at the waist, donned his hat, and went for a stroll in Hyde Park. He is, as you know, noted for his taste. Within three days several London dandies were seen wearing the 'spencers.' In two weeks all London had donned the garment."

They laughed, and drank. Bowie sat back, studying the company. Never had he seen young men so gay as these of New Orleans, with minds so occupied with trivialities, so quick to laugh, yet so quick to fury, with faces growing fierce and deadly all in a moment.

A quality of extraordinary vanity here. The *code duello* hung on the air, they moved in an aura of constant danger and seemed actually contemptuous of death, so long as it occurred in the classic manner on the dueling field. A thing pitched to fanaticism. Any affront, however slight and sometimes even unmeant, might send youths out to shed one another's blood: somewhat theatrically, perhaps, but nevertheless with deadly willingness. Yet these men were perhaps no braver than any others when death confronted them in other form than the fashionable and highly stylized duel.

Since the duel bulked so large, it followed that New Orleans was a gathering place for *maîtres d'armes* from all parts of the world: gentry like the man Contrecourt, sitting across from Bowie, twisting his pointed mustaches, hard and dangerous.

Bowie's thoughts were interrupted when Philippe Cabanal leaned over to him. "Narcisse has just told me that you're on your way to the Maison de Bornay."

"So I understand."

"You will meet the divine Judalon. She has New Orleans at her feet, monsieur, myself among others. I even had hopes——" He laughed. "But that's another matter. Mademoiselle Judalon is to my thinking the most beautiful woman in the entire city."

Bowie smiled slightly. "Narcisse insists she has a bad temper."

"Ah?" Cabanal's delicate eyebrows arched. "A lady like this can be forgiven a bad temper—though I do not think Judalon has any more of

35

it than the others. Money—enough money—can compensate for much, even if a woman be clubfooted and hunchbacked. But this woman is beautiful—a perfect divinity. If she wore linsey, she would still be beautiful. It happens, however, that she was born to wear silks, and the silks are fortunate that she wears them!"

Cabanal raised his glass as if toasting the absent lady. Bowie raised his glass also. At that moment he met the eyes of Contrecourt, the swordsman, and with surprise encountered in them a hard glint of dislike.

Chapter Five

I

"Contrecourt—what kind of a man is he?" Bowie asked when he and Narcisse left the café.

"A superb swordsman. A wastrel. A libertine. Why?"

"I wondered."

"You dislike him?"

"I have nothing against him. But he dislikes me."

"Why do you think so?"

"I can always tell it in a man."

Narcisse shrugged. "Perhaps it's not dislike so much as resentment."

"I can think of nothing he could resent in me."

"*He* can." Narcisse gave Bowie a half-smile. "We now perform an experiment. I think I should tell you something of what is on my mind and what confronts you."

"Go ahead."

"I now take you to my father's house, to meet my family."

"Now?" Bowie was alarmed. "I'm—not prepared——"

"Now is the time, for the best of reasons. They will be—to put it bluntly—astonished that I bring you to them. My parents, you must understand, are Creoles of the older stamp. In my case, I recognize the trend of the times, and that whether we like it or not, the *Américains* will soon outnumber us and control everything in New Orleans." He laid a hand on Bowie's shoulder. "Between you and me it would make no difference in any case, for you have won my heart."

"But your family think different—they may not receive us—me, that is."

"We will be received," Narcisse said calmly. "But how my people treat you will depend somewhat on yourself, and somewhat on luck. That's why I asked if you could keep your temper."

36

Bowie nodded uneasily.

"If we do not make the proper impression," Narcisse said, "I warn you that nobody knows the depths of rudeness so well as the very polite."

"Then we're lost. I'm a fool in a drawing room."

"Perhaps not. In any case we must go on. I count on a certain factor with my sister Judalon. Like most of her adorable sex, she is capricious. Perhaps even more so than most, since she is better able to indulge her caprices. That's perhaps a brother's skepticism," he added hastily, seeing the alarm in Bowie's face. "Don't look so very downcast, my friend. You will be something entirely new to her: she may find you interesting because so different." He paused. "It is on this that I'm counting for the success of our little plot in behalf of Audubon. As a stranger who amuses her, you may be able to accomplish for him what nobody else can."

This, with the utmost airy frankness. But Bowie's misgivings grew. Assuredly this young lady seemed most formidable to a man from the back bayous.

"This is at the bottom of what you say is Contrecourt's feeling against you," Narcisse went on. "He is a little jealous."

"In God's name, why?"

"It's a situation. Some of our *maîtres d'armes*—like my own teacher, Malot—are gentlemen. Others, like Contrecourt, live in a sort of whirl of wine, blood and profligacy, dividing their time between their favorite cafés and their *salles d'armes*, flaunting their quadroon mistresses, attired in the last gasp of fashion. They associate, even are courted by, the most prominent men of the city. But—alas for their secret pride—they are never received into female society."

"For what reason?"

"It's perhaps difficult to explain. A fencing master, however skilled and polished, is after all in somewhat the same category as—shall we say— a dancing master—or an instructor in equestrianism. A sort of upper servant. The social ban here is explicit."

"So that's it."

"I suppose it's a source of bitterness to Contrecourt. Perhaps he'd even cause you trouble, if he dared. But he would not dare. You are my friend —and after all, he is a professional swordsman."

Another social ban implied here. The fencing master must not cross blades with an amateur in a serious encounter.

Narcisse said, "Ah, here we are. The Maison de Bornay."

It was a three-story house of brick, standing flush with the *banquette* and heavily shuttered, commodious, but not particularly impressive from the street. When they entered it, however, they stepped into richness, even magnificence. A black butler bowed before them.

"Madame is at home, Pierre?" asked Narcisse.

"*Oui, Monsieur Narcisse.*"

"And Mademoiselle?"

"*Oui, monsieur.*"

"Be so good as to present our compliments, and inform them that I am here with a friend, begging them graciously to receive us."

"*A l'instant, monsieur.*"

The servant vanished, reappeared in a moment to murmur that Madame and Mademoiselle would be charmed to see the visitors in the music room, and led the way down a wide hall. Bowie felt his body tense as if he were about to take a plunge into icy water, as he stepped through the door held open for him.

2

The music room was richly furnished in the Bourbon fashion, with soft curtains of French lace, some paintings of merit on the walls, and beside the window a great carved rosewood pianoforte.

The instrument was magnificent and it was the first of its kind Bowie had ever seen: but that was not what stopped him on the threshold. A girl was seated on the rosewood piano bench, and he had seen her before. Once only. Under the archway of the Cabildo on Sunday morning she had given him one quick side glance, and he had not been able to forget it. That he would encounter her here had not entered his mind.

Dimly he was aware of another, older woman: probably her mother. But the girl had fixed upon herself his entire attention and interest.

Was this the terrifying Mademoiselle de Bornay? She looked the reverse of frightening, sitting beside the great pianoforte which served to emphasize her diminutive perfection. He had an impression of eyes wide and lustrously dark with wonderful curved eyelashes, and high-piled black curls on a small and shapely head. The beauty of a perfect miniature: a miniature painted on ivory.

It required an effort of will to tear his gaze away, and receive his introduction to Narcisse's mother. Madame de Bornay was hardly taller than her daughter, though plump in figure. Her iron-gray hair was carefully dressed, and her fine dark eyes at this moment contained a faint hint of surprise, as if she wondered why her son had brought to them this specimen, with countrified clothes and a frame so huge that it seemed to dwarf almost everything in the room.

Then Narcisse was saying, "Mademoiselle, it is my honor to present my friend, Monsieur James Bowie. Monsieur, my sister, Mademoiselle Judalon Daphne Seraphine de Bornay."

And Bowie found himself dissolving into all bones and knuckles as he made a needlessly awkward bow and blundered out some sort of tongue-tied acknowledgment.

The girl smiled slightly, but the smile instantly disappeared and she gazed at him with that singular expressionless look which women often give a new man: the look that mirrors neither curiosity nor expectation, but a judgment secret and withheld. Her attitude was completely graceful, arms slim and bare, white hands lying loosely together down at one side of her lap. Her gown, of some delicate white silken material, was of the high-waisted, low-cut Empire fashion, and the loveliness of all the world was in the cleft of her bosom, half concealed, half revealed.

The pose was almost too elegant to be natural. A cynical man might have suspected that it was studied, perhaps assumed for the moment: but Bowie was provided with no such insight.

"Monsieur Bowie and I," said Narcisse, to break the silence, "exchanged challenges yesterday."

"Truly?" The girl's face showed a stirring of interest. "But you didn't meet? Why?"

"Happily we discovered that the reason for our quarrel had disappeared."

"A reason, then, is necessary for a duel? I thought gentlemen required only an opportunity—to go bang! with a pistol—or cut-and-thrust with a sword—spill a little blood—and be heroes. Have I been misinformed?"

Her question was addressed not to Narcisse, but directly to Bowie. In her eyes was an equivocal little light; he knew she was debating what treatment she should accord him, and wondered if she was finding amusement in his Opelousas tailoring and homemade waistcoat.

"To tell the truth, mademoiselle," he said, finding his tongue, "we avoided fighting solely because I was certain your brother would cut me to ribbons. And I didn't think ribbons would become me."

"Don't let him deceive you," Narcisse said. "He was ready enough. It was I who wriggled out of it."

"You know your brother sufficiently well to know how much of that to believe," said Bowie.

The equivocal gleam disappeared from the girl's eyes and she smiled: a smile singularly brilliant.

"I know Narcisse well. A friend of his is a friend of this house." Her tone was suddenly cordial.

"Will you sit, monsieur?" Madame de Bornay said formally. But as he turned somewhat awkwardly toward the nearest seat, she added rather hastily, "I think you will be more comfortable on this chair than that one."

He hesitated, looking at her questioningly.

"My mother really means that *she* will be more comfortable if you take the larger chair," the girl said.

She was amused, and he saw the reason for it. The chair toward which he had first moved was one of those excessively frail and spindly things popular in France in the reign of Louis XV—a family heirloom, probably. Bowie's one hundred and ninety pounds of bone and muscle might easily have wrecked it. Hastily he accepted the sturdier armchair, vexed with himself because he was sure the girl enjoyed his confusion.

Thereafter he sipped bitter chicory coffee from a tiny porcelain cup too small for his big mouth, and listened helplessly to conversation in which he had no part: talk quite trivial, quite sophisticated, and quite witty, in so far as he could follow it, encircling the earth, touching the poetry of Chénier and Delavigne, the plays of Diderot and Beaumarchais, and punctuated with anecdotes concerning Madame de Staël, Talleyrand, Mrs. Fitzherbert, Beau Brummell, Fouché, and Napoleon Bonaparte, of which personages, save the last, he had never heard.

Yet though he was lost in the discourse, it enabled him to recover his composure, and even watch Mademoiselle Judalon covertly. A far more captious eye than his would have discovered little to criticize in her beauty. Her features were too small, perhaps, but her mouth was a dainty modeling in coral, her nose delicately patrician. And there were those eyes!

With a sensation of astonishment he suddenly realized that this was the girl Audubon had neglected to paint. He remembered the artist's shrug, and the artist's words: *The painted bunting—or the painted beauty? Peste, I prefer the bird.*

He marveled: what manner of man of flesh and blood was Audubon?

3

Judalon de Bornay was conscious of the glances the visitor was stealing at her, and they did not entirely displease her. She was only seventeen— five years younger than Bowie—but in the wisdom of the affairs of women and men she was a generation ahead of him, with knowledge inborn and then sharpened by experience.

Girls of the Creole race were notably precocious: she had matured early and been in society since her fifteenth year, accustomed to being courted, admired and attended by men, so that their applause had become to her a necessity of life. As for this blond young barbarian, by no means was she yet sure how she would treat him. But his eagerness to please was so evident that she was certain she need merely await her whim to be sure of its accomplishment with him.

Madame de Bornay asked a polite question. "Do you care for music, Monsieur Bowie?"

"Yes, madame," he replied diffidently.

"You are familiar with the pianoforte?"

"No, madame. This is the first I've ever seen."

"Judalon, *chérie,* play something for us, will you?"

"But of course, Mother."

The girl turned to the instrument and played a short selection. Bowie found himself more entranced by the movements of her slender fingers than by the somewhat vapid and trivial music she rendered.

"Do you like it, monsieur?" she asked, as she finished.

"It's choicely pretty," he said, then surprised himself by venturing a compliment. "I admire the graceful way of your hands on the keys, mademoiselle——"

He stopped, but she rewarded him with her brilliant smile. "I didn't know *Américains* cultivated the frivolous art of pretty speeches."

"I meant it sincerely——"

"All the prettier."

"Shall we dispense with the rest of the *bavardage?*" asked Narcisse, who saw his friend being played with, and had a brother's good-natured cynicism toward his sister's little methods.

"Oh, you!" said Judalon, with a tiny pout. Then, "What do you do for music in your own country, Monsieur Bowie?"

"Not much," he confessed. "Of course the Cajuns are great fiddlers, and some play the flute and banjo well enough for dances and broom jumpings——"

"Broom jumpings?"

"A kind of custom. The Cajuns—well—pair off young. It's not often a priest gets into the back bayous, a condition that's mighty tantalizing to couples who've taken fire for each other. So their folks give a big dance and feast. About midnight all the guests make a circle, laughing and joking. A broom is held level, about a foot above the floor, with a man at one end and a woman at the other. Hand in hand, the lovers advance and jump together. It's unlucky to stumble, so they jump high. Commonly, they clear the barrier with plenty to spare, and everyone cheers and laughs. That does it. They're married, as far as the Cajuns are concerned. Of course," Bowie added, at the startled look on Madame de Bornay's face, "the first traveling priest who comes along always gives them the blessing of the Church."

41

Judalon laughed. "You have, perhaps, jumped the broom yourself?"

"No, mademoiselle. My folks wouldn't consider it fitting. They're Scotch Presbyterians——"

"Scotch?"

"Yes, mademoiselle. The Bowies were originally Highland Scotch."

"But you?" Again the amused glimmer.

"I reckon you could call me half Georgian. My mother was raised in Savannah."

"And—all *Américain?*" A hint of a gibe.

He nodded gravely. "All American."

Her glance was fathomless, and turning to the piano she played rapidly another selection. Narcisse gave her a sharp look of annoyance, and turned his eyes quickly toward Bowie. This delighted her, for it was a piece of gay impertinence. The music, which her brother recognized, was from the overture of a new opera, *La Cambiale di Matrimonio,* by a young Italian composer named Rossini, whose music was just becoming popular in Europe, and hence in New Orleans. The feature of this opera, at which the Creoles enjoyed laughing, was an innovation, the first of its kind in any theater: a preposterous stage American, whose name was Mr. Slook, who put his feet on the table, kept his hat on in the house, spat on the floor, and gave away money by handfuls. It was the composer's travesty on what was the common European conception of the gaucherie attributed to all Americans. And this was the peculiarity of Judalon's little dig: it was not directed so much at Bowie, who had never heard of the opera and therefore could not comprehend her intention, but at Narcisse, in revenge for his interruption, and as a piece of raillery at his choice of companions.

"Are you familiar with Rossini?" she asked, when she concluded.

"No, mademoiselle," said Bowie.

"That's from an opera of his." She named it. "When it is presented at the French Opera House here, you must attend. You may find it amusing and edifying."

"And those attending it even more amusing, though less edifying," said Narcisse.

Bowie felt here an undercurrent which he did not understand, but he answered soberly, "If you recommend it, mademoiselle, I will attend it at my first opportunity."

The steadiness of his voice and eyes seemed to create an abrupt change in the girl. On her lips hovered another piece of gay mockery, doubly zestful because its butt was uncomprehending while Narcisse writhed, helpless to stop her, wondering when she would become openly cruel. But suddenly she decided not to utter the badinage after all. This young man was so comely, with shoulders so wonderful, above all so obviously worshipful of her . . . a woman must, after all, concede some dignity to adoration of herself, otherwise she diminishes her own value.

She studied the guest. He *was* huge: and handsome in the way all splendid animals are handsome. She saw how he looked at her, and she sat back with a tiny smile. Judalon knew that light in the eyes of men. Her confidence was enhanced. She contrasted her own small perfection with his greatness. Small women often find a peculiarly intriguing challenge in the stealthy game with big men.

Seeing the change in his sister's eyes, Narcisse relaxed. He too had a game to play, and he believed his first gambit had been successfully offered. This was confirmed when they said their adieus a few minutes later.

Judalon said to Bowie, "Monsieur, we hold a ball at this house next Thursday night. Will you not come as our guest?" At his look of hesitation, she gave him her most dazzling smile and exclaimed, "But of course you will! The card will be at your inn in the morning."

4

Outside, Narcisse said, "My congratulations."

"For what?" Bowie asked.

"Your shoulders. I have always felt that my sister had an eye for fine male shoulders, but I never saw her succumb so readily before."

He laughed at Bowie's flush, gave him a sidewise glance, cocked his hat on the side of his head, and whistled a little tune.

"I see you've no notion how well we progressed," he said presently. "I'll confess to you now that I expected to find the atmosphere at home slightly more frigid than that which I'm informed surrounds the northern pole. Instead—Judalon's most charming smiles, and an invitation to our ball!"

"That was on your account."

"My sister would do nothing on my account."

Narcisse twirled his cane and set his hat straighter on his head. Beside him Bowie walked silently, his mind going back to the girl they had just left, half wondering, half depressed. At the door of the Rouge et Noir, Henri Pinchon met them, bowing as low as his belly would permit.

"Monsieur de Bornay—Monsieur Bowie——" He smiled fawningly. "We were so crowded at the time of Monsieur Bowie's arrival . . . the small room was all we had at the moment. But a suite of two bedrooms and a parlor looking upon the street is now available. I took the liberty of having the luggage removed to it. Your friends await you there."

Bowie said, "The suite—it costs more?"

"Nothing to concern you, monsieur. I dislike annoying my guests about expenses when they are with me. Everything's kept on the tally. Your mere signature is all that's required for anything you desire——"

"But I——"

"A friend of Monsieur de Bornay's is welcome to the best this poor house affords." Again the fawning smile at Narcisse.

Bowie considered uneasily. He had less than one hundred dollars—a large sum to his brothers and himself—but one which seemed to be fading fast here. The smaller accommodations had been satisfactory to him: he was accustomed to worse. But looking at Narcisse, he could think of nothing to say against the new arrangement. Above all, his pride did not wish to admit to this young man either his poverty or his hesitancy about spending what seemed taken for granted.

"Won't you have dinner with me?" he asked.

"I regret—another invitation," Narcisse said. "But I'll drop around for you in the morning. It's my custom each forenoon to take exercise in fencing. A man must keep in practice."

"So it seems," Bowie said dryly.

Nez Coupé and Audubon, he found, had taken possession of the new quarters, which were almost magnificent by comparison with the old. That evening the small Cajun edified them with an account of the glories of New Orleans: glories which appeared to be chiefly feminine. To judge by Nez Coupé's statements, the arrival of a certain personage from the bayou country had created something like a hurricane in the female hearts of the French Market quarter, even though that personage's nose, owing to a previous misadventure with a knife, did not quite meet the more classical standards of beauty.

Chapter Six

I

"I consider Malot, my *maître d'armes,* the leader of his profession," said Narcisse next morning as they left the Rouge et Noir. "His *salle* is much the most popular in New Orleans."

"What about your bet on Colonel Claridge?" Bowie asked.

"I lost it. Who would believe he could miss such a target? I give you my word Belmonte is as broad as he is tall. Claridge should have known money was laid on him and taken no such chances."

"What sort of chances?"

"Oh, he fired on the signal. To the amazement of the witnesses, he missed. Belmonte, who held his fire, heard him muttering. 'Are you praying, Colonel?' he asked. 'Praying nothing,' said Claridge. 'I was making a vow never again to aim at the head.' Poor fellow—he never will aim at the head again. Belmonte shot him through both lungs, and he died this morning. If he'd just aimed at that great midriff, I'd be some hundreds better off this morning."

On the Rue des Expositions, Narcisse pulled a bell at the entrance to a brick building with three stories of shuttered windows. A grave-faced man in a ruffled shirt but with no coat admitted them through the iron grilled door, greeted Narcisse unsmilingly, and led them up a stair.

"That's Olympe, Malot's provost," whispered Narcisse.

The man ushered them into the personal cabinet of the professor of sword. "Have the goodness to wait here," he said, departing.

The room was high-ceilinged, with a mantel on which stood a wood carving, medieval in character, of St. Michael, the patron saint of all swordsmen. French engravings of fencing scenes decorated the walls. In one corner was a shelf of books, chiefly in French or Italian, and some by their appearance very ancient, concerning the sword and its uses. Two or three other books lay on a table in the center, with an inkstand and quill and some scattered papers, across which lay a sword, very fine as even Bowie's inexperienced eye could discern. Most interesting, however, was a full-length portrait of a slender, dark man, with a naked sword in his hand and moody eyes.

"Malot," said Narcisse. "Painted by Vanderlyn."

The door opened. In the man who entered Bowie immediately recognized the original of the portrait. Malot was in his early thirties, soberly dressed, with a lean mustached face, a very high narrow forehead, and a continual flowing grace in every movement. His manner was courteous, almost deferential, as he was introduced.

"Monsieur is interested in *l'escrime?*" he asked.

"I know very little of it," said Bowie.

"Ah?" The *maître's* voice was politely noncommittal. "The sword, it is agreed, is the aristocrat of weapons. But the pistol is correct—quite correct. Although more a thing of chance and less of skill than the blade."

He lifted the thin sliver of tempered steel with its rich basket hilt from the papers on the table. "Regard this. It was given me by the one and only Jean Louis. With this very sword he fought the fifteen fencing masters of the First Imperial Regiment at Madrid in 1813. Monsieur has, of course, heard of that famous assault-at-arms?"

When Bowie shook his head, Malot's expression indicated that he wondered where Monsieur might have spent his life.

"Allow me to relate the circumstances briefly," he said, "for they illustrate my point. Jean Louis, as some do not know, is a mulatto, born in San Domingo and instructed from an early age by Monsieur d'Erapé, who saw in him a precocious child who might have a brilliant career. His color being no handicap in the armies of Napoleon, he was by 1813 a celebrity, victor in many duels, and chief fencing master of the Thirty-first Regiment, then quartered at Madrid.

"A tavern brawl between some men of the Thirty-first and a group of the First Imperial Regiment, which was billeted near, created a regimental quarrel so serious that discipline required exemplary reparation. It was proposed that fifteen representatives of each regiment should engage, taking their turns as long as it was possible to continue the combat. On the day appointed, the two regiments formed a hollow square facing inward, while outside the square the populace gathered as to a bullfight. The first duel was arranged between Jean Louis and Giacomo Ferrari, a celebrated Florentine master."

Malot held the sword at arm's length, and made the blade quiver by the movement of his arm, to show its superbly tempered flexibility.

"Jean Louis, that day, used this sword. He is small and slight of stature, but monsieur, no other man of his side crossed a blade on that occasion. His first opponent, Ferrari, was a giant of a man. With unbelievable precision he parried Ferrari's leaping thrust of the Florentine style and dispatched him with an impeccable riposte. Merely wiping his blade and turning its point to the ground, he awaited the next antagonist. One after another they came: in the sight of ten thousand persons, Jean Louis that day dealt twenty-seven wounds to thirteen opponents, several fatal, without being touched by any of them."

Malot lifted his eyes from the blade in his hand to Bowie's face. "The last two in line were mere provosts. Having seen the best of their side fall in those terrible forty minutes, they commended their souls to God. And God proved merciful. By an accidental flourish, Jean Louis slightly wounded one of his comrades on the leg. A mere scratch, but he almost wept that he should have drawn blood from a comrade. But the colonel of the regiment took advantage of it to declare honor satisfied. Both regiments cheered and fraternized. Now tell me, monsieur, do you suppose Jean Louis could have overcome so many opponents had pistols been used, instead of swords?"

"Perhaps not."

"Almost certainly not! You heard what happened in the encounter of

46

Colonel Claridge and Belmonte? The best shot may succumb to a lucky bullet from a tyro. But in a meeting of swords, the best man wins." Malot laid down the sword. "Shall we repair to the *salle?*"

They passed into a long room, like a gymnasium, with a bare floor and benches along the walls. Narcisse and Malot removed their coats, donned fencing jackets and masks, and took foils from the racks.

"*En garde!*" cried Malot. "Now! The wrist does the work! *Prenez garde!*"

With a slithering whine the thin, bright blades crossed, leaping like living things, so swiftly the eye could hardly follow. The shifting positions of the fencers were movements of grace yet of purposeful utility, the master defending himself merely, while the pupil attacked with the agility of a panther. To Bowie it seemed at first that Narcisse had the better of it. Then he began to perceive the uncanny defense of Malot. The movement of the *maître's* foil was economy itself, he seemed hardly to stir his extended arm, but always the narrow steel interposed itself against the stinging thrusts of the other. All at once he extended in a lightning movement, and returned to a standing position.

"*Touché,*" laughed Narcisse, lowering his foil.

"You crooked your elbow," said Malot. "Keep the kink from your arm and you're difficult enough to reach. Now, again!"

Time after time the bout was renewed, with fury on the part of the pupil, with cold perfection on the part of the master. Each time Malot ended it as he wished, with an incredibly brilliant attack, usually one thrust only, when he saw an instant's opening in Narcisse's guard. At last Narcisse stepped back, laughing and wiping from his forehead the perspiration.

"Ah, Malot, Malot! I can never hope to equal you." He glanced at Bowie. "Will you try him, Jim?"

"I? I've never had one of those things in my hand."

"Then try me."

Bowie took one of the foils. The whip in the thin steel intrigued him and he swished it back and forth, then examined the small rubber button at the tip.

"All right," he said, donning the wire mask which Malot offered, and placing himself in what he conceived to be a posture of defense.

But both Narcisse and the *maître* were at him, scandalized at the position of his feet, his body angle, his grip, a score of other things. When he had adjusted himself as best he could to their directions, he crossed blades with Narcisse. At once he understood how it is possible for a fencer to know instinctively his opponent's movements and inspirations,

47

though he could counter none of Narcisse's. His parries were clumsy, his lunges awkward. In a few passes Narcisse touched him neatly on the breast. They stood back, both laughing.

"My friend," said Narcisse, "do you always have that look when you engage?"

"How do you mean?"

"The fighting face—the killer look. Did you mark it, Malot? Cold ferocity—and while we merely play." He shook his head. "I think I should not like to engage seriously with you, if you become more intimidating as the situation becomes graver."

"You're having fun with me." Bowie's grin was embarrassed. "I wasn't aware of any particular look——"

"No," said Narcisse judgmatically. "In you it would be natural."

"I'm a baby in your hands with these things."

"On the contrary, your reactions astonish me. This is your first attempt with the foils?"

"Yes."

"Few complete novices could hold me off for six *passados*. Eh, Malot?"

The *maître* nodded. "Monsieur possesses an address of body, a muscular brilliance not often seen—especially in one so—so great of stature. I could make of him a swordsman."

Bowie ran his eye along the foil and returned it to Malot. "I reckon I'd do better using this as a whip."

Malot smiled. "We will agree that for the present, in the case of an affair, you should stick to the pistol with which you are familiar——"

"I'm not."

"What are you saying?"

"I can use a rifle, some. But I've never practiced with a pistol. We used to load up Father's old horse pistol and fire her off on the Fourth of July. Otherwise I've never shot one."

Malot stared as Bowie put on his coat. He was still speechless as he led them into a side room. At the door he turned and said, "Perhaps you may see something here which may interest you."

2

Bowie looked about him. Malot, it appeared, was something of an antiquarian, and this room had been fitted up by him as a museum of trenchant arms, which were the central interest of his life. Everywhere on the walls hung dueling weapons of all fashions, some plain, some very rich as to hilt and blade: a bristling array of instruments of death.

Among them also were arms of ancient or exotic kinds: broadswords, poniards, claymores, scimitars, oriental hanjars, cutlasses, even a *gladius* of ancient Roman make, its blade almost rusted away but still displaying the sturdy, deadly design which made the Legions masters of their world.

Bowie's eyes darkened with interest. "What's that?" he asked, pointing to a weapon with a jeweled handle.

"An Italian poniard of the sixteenth century—of the type used by the assassins of the Borgias."

"And this?"

"A French dagger." Malot pointed out an Abyssinian sickle blade, a rare Egyptian knife, a curved weapon with a heavy back which he said was a *kukri* from Nepal. Bowie halted before one of the exhibits, and Malot nodded with the satisfaction of the collector who sees his choicest prizes admired. "I thought you would find that of more than passing interest. A two-handed falchion of the Crusades."

"May I take it down?"

"Assuredly."

Bowie lifted the sword from the wall. It was single-edged, with a two-handed grip and a very wide steel guard. Its most remarkable feature was a round steel weight which slid up and down in a groove along the back of the blade.

"That is a steel apple," said Malot, to Bowie's puzzled look.

"What's it for?"

"Raise the point of the sword upward."

Bowie obeyed. The round weight slipped back against the hilt.

"Now strike—not hard—but to feel the weight of the blade."

Bowie slashed the weapon through the air. With a whir the steel apple slid along its groove toward the point, where it was arrested. Twice he repeated the blows in the air, once easily, once with vigor.

"What a thing!" he exclaimed. "When you strike, the steel apple, running to the point, weights it and adds amazing force to the blow!"

"Medieval armorers were not without their ingenuity," said Malot. "This weapon was to be used against mail."

With a look of deep concentration, Bowie held the sword in his two hands and examined it from point to hilt. He observed the slight curve of the blade, and the fact that it was double-edged toward the point. Presently he replaced the falchion on its pegs and went on down the line examining other weapons.

"This," he said, "is a Scottish dirk."

Malot nodded.

"My uncle had one." Bowie lifted it from the wall and weighed it

49

in his hand. It was something between a short sword and a knife, its steel about two feet long.

"The balance is bad," he said. "You couldn't throw it."

"You throw a knife, monsieur?"

"A little. The Cajuns are great knife throwers."

"Before you is a Spanish *cuchillo*. Try it against the wooden target yonder."

Bowie hung up the dirk and took the *cuchillo,* a straight-bladed knife with a leather-wrapped handle of horn. Turning toward the target, he whipped his arm through the air. The knife sang from his hand, struck point-first in the wood with a sharp rap, and quivered there.

"Bravo, monsieur!" Malot applauded.

Bowie shook his head. "I missed my mark by half a foot. The *cuchillo* is too light." He glanced musingly at the dirk on the wall. "If you could put the principle of the steel apple into that, or something like it, you'd have a pretty deadly weapon."

Malot was watching him closely. "You appear to have an affinity for the knife, monsieur. I have observed frequently such a thing. Some men take naturally to the sword, some to the pistol, as if they were born to it. Often these become great virtuosos with their chosen weapon. With you it may be the knife."

"Somehow it appeals to me," Bowie said. "My Highland blood, maybe." He hesitated. "If I ever fought a duel, I think I'd choose something like this to fight it with."

"A knife—in a *duel?*" The *maître* was shocked.

"Why not? One party at least wouldn't be likely to walk away from a knife fight."

"But—*mon Dieu*—how barbarous——"

"Isn't death itself barbarous?"

"No! A duel should be a thing of art. There is a right way and a wrong way of conducting all things in civilized society—even to the least important. And a duel assuredly is one of the most important. With death as its object, it assumes the noble aspects of high tragedy. Why, therefore, deprive it of beauty?"

Malot's face was very earnest.

"You observe good manners in other acts of your life, I suppose, monsieur? You do not trample upon the little feet of the lady who is your dancing partner? You converse with courtesy and decorum. Even in so crude a performance as eating, you observe etiquette? Why, then, throw all this aside in an affair of honor? Dueling, I repeat, is an art: in my poor opinion the highest of all arts. Honor is precious to a gentleman: when it is gone, he is like a beast. On the field of honor he gives to honor its highest expression. Bravery—artistry—finesse in deportment—honor. These are the four prime essentials of the duel. To these mere expertness in dealing death is only an addendum."

Thus Malot, master of arms, on the one great religion of his life.

Bowie did not reply. He did not feel capable of arguing the point, but his nature was too forthright for this parade. Yet he recognized the fixed immutability of the duel as an institution. Already he himself had received one challenge—from Narcisse. A gentleman, it appeared, must hold himself always ready to face a call. He wished to avoid all quarrels, but if it happened to him . . . he had his reservations about making it a mere flourish of etiquette.

3

"You spoiled Malot's morning," Narcisse said later. "He confided to me that you are a very dangerous man. Since he is a dangerous man himself, that is praise of a sort. But I do not think he approves of your notions."

"I seem to blunder everywhere."

"Not so, Jim. You're different—that's all. Everyone in my coterie is now talking about you, which means that all New Orleans will soon be doing the same. When you come to the ball Thursday night you will meet many people who will know of you and be curious to know more."

"That reminds me—the card of invitation came this morning. I'll send a note of thanks, but I can't attend, Narcisse."

"But, *nom de Dieu,* why not?"

"Many reasons. I ought to get back home. And—well—my wardrobe——" Bowie hesitated. "I've just begun to realize how far behind the mode we are in the bayou country."

Narcisse laughed. "Now that you've opened the subject, I'm willing to admit something of what you say. Fortunately, however, we can remedy that very quickly. We'll stop in at Cocquelon's. It's in the next block. Cocquelon is the best tailor in town: the most expensive, also, but worth it. Always behind with his orders, because he's in such demand. But he cuts the best shoulders in town—your shoulders will exalt him."

"I—I'm afraid I can't afford Cocquelon——" began Bowie dubiously.

"*Pouf, pouf!* If you're short on ready cash, Cocquelon will be delighted to give you credit. I won't hear of your missing the ball. Consider poor Judalon! After all, she invited you personally. And you must think of Audubon. Do you wish to destroy the auspicious beginning we've made—our conspiracy, remember?"

Narcisse took everything for granted in his elegant manner. And Bowie, thinking of the ominous remark about the expensiveness of Cocquelon, and hoping it would not take too much of his small supply of cash, allowed himself to be guided into the tailor shop.

A little yellow man came forward, kneading his hands and bowing. A quadroon, obviously. Quadroon men monopolized most of the tailoring in New Orleans, as their sisters monopolized a certain other profession.

"Cocquelon," said Narcisse, "my friend, Monsieur Bowie, has been— ahem—on a long journey in a remote part of the country. Through a misadventure, the nature of which it is unnecessary to discuss here, he lost his wardrobe. You are to remedy the condition."

Cocquelon surveyed Bowie as if he could easily believe Narcisse's story of misadventure, and gave a little sympathetic clucking sound.

"I suppose you've nothing in stock to fit him?" asked Narcisse.

Cocquelon considered the American's shoulders and shook his head. He had some coats, he said in a high thin voice, but they were designed for the ordinary figure, nothing so magnificent as this.

"Then measure him at once."

With a patter of French the little yellow man darted about, summoning his assistants. They swarmed around Bowie with tapelines, calling off measurements which the master tailor noted on paper.

"How many tail coats, monsieur?" he asked.

"Two at least," said Narcisse.

"One of the new Empire capes?"

"But assuredly."

"A spencer coat?"

"Without question."

"And the long pantaloons?"

"Certainly."

Cocquelon smiled at Bowie, who stood with mouth open, unable to intervene. "Monsieur de Bornay is a boon to us tailors. For you, monsieur, I shall provide the very latest—in cut, adornment, material. You will appear a different person——"

"How soon?" interrupted Narcisse.

"We are overwhelmed with work. A month at least behind orders. But for your friend, Monsieur de Bornay, I make special arrangements— though it will require explanations to my other customers, and sacrifices to myself. So—shall we say a fortnight?"

He smiled, but Narcisse looked as if he did not believe his ears. "Are you speaking seriously?"

Cocquelon recoiled, his smile fading. Monsieur de Bornay was a very important customer.

"By putting everything else aside—at the very earliest—a week, monsieur——"

"Day after tomorrow!" said Narcisse.

Cocquelon was aghast. "Impossible!"

"Day after tomorrow!"

"Mortal man could not accomplish it!"

"Day after tomorrow!"

"Customers all over New Orleans are clamoring for their clothes, abusing me——"

"Day after tomorrow!"

Cocquelon threw up his hands in despair. "Very well, day after tomorrow! I shall have to work my shop day and night—wear out my staff and myself—have fine gentlemen threatening me with personal injuries—but as you say, Monsieur de Bornay—the day after tomorrow!"

They left him pawing at his bolts of goods and whimpering to himself.

"Cocquelon seems eager to please you," Bowie ventured.

Narcisse smiled. "He should. I owe him three thousand dollars."

"Three thous——"

"Cocquelon has many customers who pay him on the nail. He can afford to offend them all—but not the one to whom he is creditor for three thousand dollars. That is well to think about, Jim."

Narcisse laughed and twirled his cane and ogled a pretty girl who came down the street.

Chapter Seven

I

Cocquelon's pantaloons had been difficult to get on because of their tightness, and now they seemed to constrict Bowie's legs. He supposed he would grow used to them. The tall beaver hat also felt top-heavy, and he had not quite mastered the combination of dignity and grace with which a silver-knobbed walking stick should be carried. All in all, however, he was not dissatisfied with himself.

Cocquelon, indeed, had given him a good deal of confidence. The little quadroon wailed over the unreasonable demands of gentlemen, and how they expected the utterly impossible from a poor devil of a tailor, but when he saw his creations so well set off by the American's tall figure, he spread his yellow hands with an artist's joy that was hardly dimmed by his knowledge that he must wait for his money.

So on Thursday evening Bowie walked through the darkness to the Maison de Bornay, half eager to arrive, and at the same time half a mind to turn around and flee back to his tavern. An equipage discharged guests before the house as he approached it, and light streamed out upon them from the open door. He heard French greetings and some laughter. Then he himself was at the entrance.

A black servant in livery took his card of invitation. Another received his hat and cane. A third announced his name. He bowed before Monsieur and Madame de Bornay, receiving from her a formal smile.

"Armand," she said in French, "this is the gentleman who is the friend of Narcisse."

Monsieur, who like many of the older Creoles clung to the old-fashioned formal garb, consisting of pumps with gold buckles, silk stockings, velvet coat and knee breeches, mumbled something vague. Then his narrow, spike-bearded face glanced keenly beyond.

"Ah, Janos, *mon ami!*" he exclaimed. "I've been looking for you!"

Bowie stepped aside. It was his acquaintance, Monsieur Parisot, in a most expensive surtout with a high rolling collar which almost concealed his head. He made quite a parade of saluting Madame de Bornay's hand.

With a degree of confusion, Bowie turned toward the ballroom, and blinked. It was quite dazzling. He had never imagined anything like it. Under the blazing crystal chandeliers the guests laughed and conversed, awaiting the opening of the dance. The women filled the eye to the exclusion of the men. Bare arms, shoulders, and white bosoms gleamed. Eyes and lips were very bright. Light gowns of countless delicate shades made an ever-changing pattern. For these the soberer costumes of the men were only a background.

Narcisse came to him across the polished floor. "I'd almost given you up! I'm *maître de cérémonie* tonight and wanted to see you properly introduced before I began my duties." He looked Bowie up and down. "Cocquelon did well by you, my friend."

"Thanks."

"You dance, of course?"

"Well—country dances."

"Excellent. The opening number is a Sir Roger de Coverley."

"I'm too late to get a partner."

"I think not. I'll arrange——"

"I'd rather watch, for the present."

"Very well. But you're to participate in at least one dance, do you understand? The Virginia reel comes just before intermission. I obtained Judalon's promise to let you take her out."

"Mademoiselle Judalon—I'd be scared——"

"You needn't be. The reel is easy, and she's a very good partner. Furthermore, she's looking forward to it."

"Are you serious?"

Narcisse smiled airily. "Judalon loves novelty. Moreover, she adores drawing attention to herself. I've convinced her that with you she'll be the center of every eye, the subject of every tongue. Very clever of me, I thought."

To Bowie, who saw himself in the light of a sort of public exhibit to provide amusement, the thought was less pleasant.

"Do you see what an opportunity this affords us?" Narcisse said.

"No."

"If only out of perversity, my charming sister is going to be quite kind to you. When the opportunity arises, bring up the subject of Audubon, tactfully. I'm almost sure she will agree to forgive him—if only as a gesture to you."

"Why should she make a gesture to me?"

"My sister is often unpredictable, but she loves to play a game of her own. Perhaps I ought to warn you to be on your guard against her—she has wiles, quite heartless, I fear, and sometimes can make herself a perilous creature for a susceptible man to be around. Are you especially susceptible to female charms, Jim?"

"Why—I—not unusually so, I don't reckon——"

"Well—in this case, you're forewarned. Let her smile at you, and flirt with you, and be very charming to you. Your chance will come——" Narcisse broke off. "I must begin my work."

In one corner of the ballroom a blue-uniformed Negro orchestra was tightening strings on violins and guitars, or running little scales on flutes and clarinets.

"Remember—the reel." Narcisse departed, leaving Bowie by the wall, wondering over the cynicism of a brother concerning his sister.

Gentlemen very high as to coat collar and tight as to breeches conducted ladies who seemed garbed almost in nothing. Sophisticated ballroom dresses were something new to Bowie. He had never seen so much bare female flesh in his life. The gowns were abbreviated both above and below in the French fashion, and clung to supple bodies in a way to make a man look, and swallow, and look again.

On the mantel, the French clock under its bell glass chimed eight silvery strokes, Narcisse lifted his voice to ask couples to take their places, the music struck up, and the rollicking dance began.

Bowie watched only Judalon de Bornay. To his mind nobody compared with her. She came laughing down the middle, and her grace and

55

beauty enchanted him. The top of her head, even with its gleaming dark curls piled high, came hardly to the shoulder of her partner, Philippe Cabanal. Both round captivating shoulders were exposed, and her gown of sheer white crepe was cut audaciously low in front. Her full flounced skirt, fringed at the botton with little artificial rosebuds, reached hardly lower than midway between her knee and ankle, revealing her childlike feet in high French heels, which made her appear tiptoe, as if she might at any moment spread iridescent wings and float away. To the young man watching from the wall, she seemed at once innocent and daring, an intoxicating combination of opposites.

A quadrille followed and was succeeded by a stately *menuet de la coeur*. Still Bowie remained rooted, missing not one movement of the girl, one single expression, as she turned and curtsied and coquetted with her partners, using every pretty trick of eyes and smiles and fan. A deadly little display to watch, even for a young man forewarned and not supposed to be susceptible . . .

2

Narcisse found him by the punch bowl. "The intermission is at ten. The next number's the reel. Come with me."

Bowie hung back bashfully, but he was in for it. Judalon was surrounded by young men, and she moved among them, laughing, protesting, exhilarated. The whole group advanced toward Narcisse and Bowie as if by design, but halted as Janos Parisot, portly and commanding, bowed to the girl.

"Oh, Monsieur Parisot!" she cried in mock despair. "What can a poor girl do? Seven of them! And all desiring to dance at once! If there were only seven of me——"

"Sevenfold, mademoiselle, you could not be more charming." Parisot obviously plumed himself on the compliment.

"Thank you, monsieur." She dropped her eyes.

He cleared his throat complacently. "Perhaps I can relieve you of your dilemma. May I have the honor of this next dance?"

Judalon seemed startled. The man was old enough to be her grandfather. Her eyes encountered Bowie's, and she smiled with relief.

"I regret, Monsieur Parisot, but I have promised this number already."

Bowie felt himself pushed slightly by Narcisse. He bent over the small hand she extended. Then he was walking with her out to the floor.

The Virginia reel was familiar, and for one of his stature Bowie was light and quick of foot. At first he danced by instinct, but within a few moments he was in the spirit of it and enjoying himself. Judalon held out her hands to him and he swung her. Long after he had released her, his fingers retained the memory of her pressure on him. He felt very proud to be dancing with the most beautiful woman in the room, and correspondingly grateful to her for her condescension.

The girl smiled up at him, not displeased. His fine shoulders were set off well by the new coat, and the new pantaloons fit his narrow hips like his skin, revealing the long, powerful muscles of his thighs. His curly hair was newly trimmed, and his sideburns brought out the satisfyingly grim angle of his jaw. Furthermore, his six feet and two inches of height made every other man in the room seem almost insignificant.

Little pots of incense sent tiny wavers of fragrance through the room. About the dance floor, heads leaned together to whisper behind fans. A dream to Bowie: a dream too quickly ended.

The intermission was the time for refreshment, conversation, and flirtation. Ordinarily Judalon would have held court for a dozen men, but tonight she had a different fancy. She tucked her hand into the crook of Bowie's arm.

"Let's go out into the patio. I find it close in here," she said.

Young men bowed as they passed. She flicked one with her fan, nodded gaily to another, spoke a smiling word with one or two, but never halted her progress. Bowie saw disappointment, incredulity, jealousy on their faces. But she appeared to see none of these things. Here and there couples strolled in the courtyard, looking at flowers, conversing in subdued voices.

"Here's a seat by the fountain," Judalon said.

Tongue-tied, Bowie took his place beside her on the stone garden bench. The moon cast their shadows before them.

3

To Judalon de Bornay every man was worthy of appraisal. She was very young, but already she had a well-formed and hard little theory of life: a woman's happiness rested on her power over others, and that meant her power over men, since it was through men that women accomplished all things.

She was quite vain, and only male flattery was worth anything to her. Coquetry was born in her, and she practiced continuously the art of making men do things, taking in it the same elemental joy that a bird might experience in brilliant evolutions of flight. Since first she put on long dresses, she had never been without suitors.

It was no secret to her that men lived in a strange world of their own when they were away from women, being given to dreadful dissipations and violences. Heavy drinking and heavy gambling were taken for granted, and even the keeping of saffron quadroon girls as *placées* in the little colony of establishments on the Rue des Palissades. A woman of good Creole blood ignored the matter. It was safer not to pry too much into the affairs of men even in one's own family, and since the law forbade any thought of marriage with women of colored blood, the position of women with no racial cross was unassailably secure.

And there were the duels. Women usually did not know about them until they were over. Word came next day, usually by roundabout channels. So-and-so was wearing his arm in a sling, or was in bed under a doctor's care. Or most terrible, was dead. One knew a face: perhaps had seen it imploring, or hurt, or happy. And then one did not see the face again, ever. One perhaps attended the Mass: and perhaps even wept a little.

Ladies' names were not brought into these affairs. Nevertheless, Judalon secretly believed she had been the cause—innocent, of course—of at least two. In playing rivals against each other, she had not really dreamed of such eventualities. But six months before young Henri Leconte of Pontchartrain had called out Paul Tourzel, and been pinked on the arm by him with a rapier. Later Antoine Lombardi and Jules Corbaux exchanged shots. Without effect, as it happened, since both seemed to have shut their eyes when they pulled their triggers. Still, it stood as an affair of honor, and increased their good opinions of themselves.

Since they had been rivals for her favor, the result gave her a secret feeling of power. A girl must mean much to a man when he will face death because of her. And it followed that if men were willing to die because of her, they might be made to do other things also—things perhaps more important to her than merely dying.

So now she sat with Bowie and asked him playful little questions. It would have surprised him to know that the questions really were most shrewd and that she was studying him secretly and quite coolly.

He was, she decided, a savage undoubtedly. Very seldom had she encountered a man so unsophisticated. His simple wonder at her, an homage not to be restrained, was too easy, almost laughable. Still, he was different. He would provide amusement, perhaps.

Other couples began going back into the ballroom. They were alone. A new swirl of music came through the French doors.

"An *écossaise*," she said.

"I must not keep you," he replied humbly.

"I care nothing for the dance," she said. "I'm tired—and old Monsieur

Parisot will be in there, waiting to pounce on me. The man's every-where—at every levee, ball, and assembly. An old bachelor, you know. He prefers young girls. If he only could see how they laugh at him behind his back! I'm surprised at the way Monsieur, my father, has taken him up. You'd think they'd been intimates all their lives."

"Mademoiselle——"

"Judalon," she said. "You must call me Judalon. And I shall call you James—no, Jim—because you're Narcisse's friend and therefore mine!"

He was too overwhelmed by this beautiful feminine fiat to reply.

The music came softly, magically. A large brown moth fluttered about them and she clutched his arm, shrinking against him. His body quivered at the touch, and she smiled secretly.

She drew away from her innocent-seeming nearness: it gave him a pang of deprivation. He wanted her nearer, but instead she rose. He stood with her. Their shadows were very close.

"Mademoiselle—Judalon——" His voice shook.

Judalon knew this moment. It was coming now, some blurted avowal, perhaps worth repeating later amid gales of laughter to her friends.

When he spoke, she could hardly believe her ears, and asked him to repeat.

He complied: she had heard him rightly enough. He asked something of her but it had nothing to do with love. She was so kind and understanding . . . wouldn't she forgive Audubon, the painter? . . . he was sure, if she understood the circumstances, she would not hold them against the artist . . . might he not make bold to beg her to reconsider and permit the painting of her portrait after all . . . ?

She was furious. She knew she could never forgive him, and was about to cut him to pieces with mockery and contempt. But another thought came. He deserved a revenge more condign.

She said, "Of course—have Monsieur Audubon come tomorrow. I am sure it can be arranged."

Then she left him so quickly that he could not overtake her before she was indoors. He wondered if he had said something wrong, but in the ballroom she was all beautiful charm again, with a special smile for him, a special tone of voice. He was relieved and happy, and if young men scowled at him, he made nothing of it.

He was watching Judalon with Armand Lebain in the schottische. Beside him the cool voice of Narcisse said, "You're doing well, my friend."

"Am I?"

"Monopolizing Judalon throughout the intermission and keeping her in the patio so that she missed one whole dance."

"You exaggerate."

"I think not. And if I know my sister, she's delighted. This sort of thing enchants her. All her admirers are fuming with rage. She's using you to whip her hounds, and the hounds don't enjoy the lash. Well, you've made enemies: or perhaps my sweet sister has made them for you. But this is without question the time to press your advantage."

"I've done so."

Narcisse was amazed. "How did you succeed?"

"She agreed without hesitation."

Narcisse stared and whistled. "Well, to that extent, it's good."

He turned away.

It sounded like a riddle to Bowie. But when he said good night to Judalon he forgot about it. He hoped she did not give the hand of every young man a squeeze like the one she gave to him.

Chapter Eight

1

Audubon was awake and reading. "How was the ball?" he asked.

"Very fine."

"Monsieur de Bornay?"

"Kind."

"Madame?"

"Gracious."

"And Mademoiselle?"

"Wonderful!"

Audubon filled a long-stemmed clay pipe and began to smoke. "Tell me about it."

"She is charming and generous."

The artist contemplated him and puffed on his pipe.

Bowie said, "I have good news for you."

"Yes?"

"You're to paint her portrait after all."

"I am truly astonished!"

"She regrets the unpleasantness," said Bowie, "and asks that you come to her house this afternoon." He paused. "That should tell you what she's like."

"She asked thee to convey this message?"

"Yes."

"At her own instance?"

"Assuredly. I may have made some small suggestion——"

A long silence. Then Audubon said, "My poor James."

"What ails you?" Bowie felt displeasure.

"I foresee great peril for thee."

"From these Creoles? I fear them not a fly."

"Nay, thee can take care of thyself well enough among men. But——"

"But what?" snapped Bowie impatiently.

"A woman is another story."

"Explain yourself."

"I do believe thee smitten with Mademoiselle de Bornay."

"You talk like an idiot!"

"Even an idiot could see these symptoms," Audubon said.

Bowie reddened. "Well—is there anything wrong with her?" he asked less violently.

"Concerning Mademoiselle I have nothing to say. She is as God made her. But concerning thee I feel most gravely."

"I'm listening."

"This girl is of a different world from thine, James. However desirable a woman may appear, a man who is shaping his career should think strongly before setting his mind on her."

Bowie gave a gruff, short laugh. "If I had any such notions as you suggest—do you reckon she'd think a second time about a bayou man, with no money or prospects, when she can choose from the wealth and family of all New Orleans?"

"May I speak with candor, James?"

"You seem to be doing it already. Keep right on."

"Women sometimes love to play with men. Thee has small experience of the fair sex, my friend. And this one—I think she would require very much experience to cope with—and perhaps even something beyond——"

"As what?"

"Perhaps—*ruthlessness*. A kind of ruthlessness thee do not possess—a kind of ruthlessness I hope thee may never possess—for it means disillusion." Audubon was solemn. "I mark a change in thee, James."

Bowie, unsmiling, waited.

"Thee were a hunter, strong, little caring for foppery or the other superficialities that pass for important in this hive of superficiality. Now I see thee affecting the airs and garments of—well, at least a would-be dandy."

With the peculiar vanity of young men, Bowie found that the "would-be" rankled in his mind.

"I reckon you'd rather have me in linsey or leather?" he grumbled.

"The fop is never respected: the dandy is never a leader of men."

Bowie grunted at that, but Audubon grew more earnest.

"I would not trade thee, James, for ten thousand Philippe Cabanals or even for many Narcisse de Bornays, although Narcisse is much more the man than Philippe. I am an American, yet I was not so born. I am proud that I am now." He took three quick, nervous puffs at the clay pipe. "America is of all nations the youngest, with the greatest destiny. One must know the old, tired countries of Europe fully to understand this. Among nations America is like unto thee, James, among these elegants of New Orleans—unvitiated by the degeneracies of civilization, yet surrounded by a generation of evil, decadence, and dishonor, riddled by diseases of both the body and soul."

Slowly Audubon knocked the ashes out of his pipe, and placed the long-stemmed clay on the table.

"The nearer man approaches the essentials, James, the nearer he comes to the ideal. Is not nature the prime essential, the beginning?"

For the moment at least Bowie could find no argument against that.

"Does it not follow then," said Audubon eagerly, "that the nearer a man lives to nature, the nobler his spirit must become? Observe the savage of the American wild. The closer he approaches the white man's civilization, the more debased he is. Dishonesty, gross appetites, immorality, disease, the whole gamut of degenerative influences work out their will on him. But the red man in his forest, or far out on his plains, is as God intended—splendid, worthy of love and admiration."

Bowie privately considered that the few Indians he had encountered in Louisiana undoubtedly possessed all the disabilities Audubon named, with poverty and dirt added. On the other hand, his father used to tell of sufficiently wild Indians against whom he had fought in Kentucky—and the old man had small respect for them either.

"Return to thy forest, James!" Audubon said. "With rifle in hand and thy eye on the wilds, thee will be closer to perfection than ever in this city, turning out thy toes like a French dancing master and practicing the mincing macaroni ways."

Bowie thought the dig about turning out his toes rather hard, but he only said, "If I did as you say, what would happen to your commission for the portrait of Mademoiselle de Bornay?"

"I should lose it again."

"It means nothing to you."

"It means everything."

"Then rest happy. I'm not taking your advice." Bowie grinned.

They undressed. He blew out the candle and rolled into bed.

After a time he chuckled in the dark.

"What amuseth thee?" came Audubon's sleepy voice.

"You overlooked one big disadvantage in what you call the 'macaroni way.' "

"What is that?"

"Getting used to the clothes. It would be an injustice to Cocquelon to say that my new pantaloons fit me tight as my skin. They fit tighter. When I pulled them off just now, my legs looked like fluted pillars, grooved with the cords of the garment they have worn this day."

2

"How long we stay here, Jim?"

Nez Coupé cocked his scarred head to one side like a terrier.

"You getting tired of New Orleans?"

"Tired? No. Me, I like it plenty here. Fine place, this. But your folks —they want to find out pretty quick, no?"

"I haven't finished my business."

"We been here since week tomorrow——"

"I tell you, I've got to have more time!"

The Cajun's shoulders went up in a shrug. "All right, Jim. Just what you think. Big dance at French Market tonight. I make lots of fun—me." He swaggered out of the room.

Bowie scowled at the floor. Nez Coupé was perfectly right: he was not attending to his responsibilities. So completely was he immersed in matters having nothing to do with the errand on which his brothers had trusted him, that he had not even paid a second business call on Janos Parisot. The thought sickened and oppressed him.

Then he went back to thinking about Judalon de Bornay, going over every episode of the previous evening, and trying to interpret every action, word and look of hers in relation to himself. At times he tried to chill the hope in him by savagely confronting the facts. How could a young lady of her station and training think seriously even once of a man like himself? But then he remembered the dizzying evidences of friendliness she had given him, and how she had favored him over all the others. He remembered also the bitter faces of those confident young Creole bucks . . . Narcisse said he had made enemies.

Judalon . . . you must call me Judalon . . . and I shall call you James . . . no, Jim . . .

Narcisse's warning thrust itself into his mind: *She can make herself a perilous creature for a susceptible man . . .*

He was by no means susceptible. He had known many girls, and never had his head turned by them: he could tell the pretense from the sincere. At twenty-two a man should know his own mind.

With that he rose, nervous as a hunting dog, his young head swirling, wondering when he would see her again. He was face to face with something against which his strength could not avail him. Social barriers. Barriers of money. Barriers of blood. A gulf, invisible but terribly real, and more difficult to cross than any deep and stormy gulf of the ocean.

He was still pacing when Audubon and Narcisse burst into the room.

3

The artist was ablaze. "I've just spoken with Monsieur de Bornay! It is as thee say, James—he renews the commission!"

Bowie raised his head. "Good."

"I begin this very afternoon. Today I am a happy man!"

"Perhaps one of us should go along to keep watch on you, to see that you really appear," Narcisse said slyly.

Audubon's grin was sheepish. "I have learned my lesson, depend on it." *"Bien."*

"With this commission, I can redeem my bird paintings—and also relieve thee, James, of entertaining me—for I return to my own room, which is also my studio——"

"So you walk out on me?" Bowie grinned.

"It is pleasant here—but not conducive. I must work! I go now to make ready." Audubon departed.

Narcisse offered Bowie a cheroot and lit one himself. "You were a sensation last night. Especially with the ladies." He smiled devilishly. "New Orleans doesn't often see a figure like yours. I believe that Judalon was a bit jealous over you, because so many other damsels were chattering——"

"I heard none of this chattering."

"It was out of your hearing, my friend, but well within hers." He reached out his walking stick and gave Bowie a nudge. "Ever see a dog with a bone? The dog is not hungry. He cares nothing for the bone. It may be an old bone, gnawed until all flavor is gone, not even worth the burying. But let another dog come along and cast an eye on that bone. *Voilà!* It becomes a bone of sudden value to our dog, a treasure to be fought for, if necessary to die over!" He laughed. "May I be forgiven the comparison, but that is the way of the ladies also. The tiniest show of interest by other members of their delightful sex enhances a man with them transcendently. Fortunate Jim!"

Bowie managed a lame smile and a lame jest. "Thanks for likening me to a gnawed-over bone."

"I was leading up to this: I think you've played your cards incredibly well. I confess now that when we started our little plot I had only the faintest hope it would succeed. How you managed it, I don't know. But our little Judalon asked me to bring you to the house this afternoon when she begins her sittings for Audubon." Narcisse's cynical smile again. "I suspect that's for the benefit of the other damsels. It may bore you, but it may be good policy. Once the portrait's finished, we can forget the whole tiresome masquerade."

Bowie glanced sidewise at him and thought that brothers as a race were remarkably obtuse. He said, "What if I don't want to forget it?"

Narcisse gave him a stare, then laughed. "You have the driest way about you, Jim." He paused. "In the evening, after the sitting, we'll go to St. Sylvain's, if you like."

Bowie had heard frequent mention of the place called St. Sylvain's. It was, he gathered, New Orleans' premier gambling casino, catering exclusively to the *élite*.

"Almost everyone of importance goes to St. Sylvain's sooner or later," Narcisse said. "It would be a good place for you to meet some of New Orleans' well-known men. And perhaps have a little sport doing it."

Bowie nodded. "Good. That's our evening, then."

4

Bowie heard the buzz of talk before he entered the de Bornay drawing room. When he and Narcisse went in, they saw a half dozen young women, all pretty, and an equal number of young men, among them Cabanal and Lebain, chattering around Judalon, who sat beside a window while Audubon fussed at his easel.

"Odd," Narcisse muttered. "Judalon's never invited gentlemen before——"

Judalon saw them across the room and gave them a vivid smile. "Jim! Come stand by me. I need someone interesting to talk to—while this tiresome business is going on."

He obeyed her. Audubon approached his subject to put her in position, with an anxious eye to the lighting. It took him some moments, and conversation lapsed as they watched him coax Judalon to tilt her head this way slightly, turn her body ever so little in that direction, compose her hands in a certain manner, arrange the draperies of her dress just so.

"Now we have the pose, mademoiselle," he said at last. "Be thee comfortable?"

"How could I be, twisted like this?" she said tartly. But she kept the pose.

Bowie forgot the rest of the room in the picture she made. Hers was a complexion that bore daylight even better than candlelight, seeming to welcome the sharper glare as a means of revealing its perfection.

Rapidly, Audubon began working, sketching the figure, then the face. Behind him there were comments.

"He catches her attitude well."

"The very way she holds her head."

"It is hard to conceive how a man can create such an image on canvas."

"Observe the highlights. Already the portrait is emerging."

Judalon began to devote her entire attention to Bowie. She made him come around, so that she could look at him without turning her head from the way Audubon had tilted it, and chatted gaily.

Had he enjoyed himself at the ball? She must compliment his dancing. It was pleasing to have a partner who was built upon the proportions of a man—with a side gleam at the slight-statured young Creoles, in whom the shot seemed to rankle.

The sitting ended. They crowded about to compliment her on the progress made. She stood up and stretched herself prettily.

"You're weary?" Bowie asked her.

"It's more difficult than one thinks, to sit. The position becomes so cramping. I must move about. Come, Jim——"

All for him. He took her outstretched hand and put it in the bend of his arm. "Where?" he asked.

"The patio. The sun is so bright there."

Not even a look at any of the others.

They walked toward the door which led outside, and Narcisse gazed after them as if puzzled and worried.

5

Judalon said to herself that Narcisse could do nothing about it. Nobody could do anything about what she was doing, and only Narcisse had an inkling of it. Making men do things . . . it always entranced her. She had set certain forces into motion. Now they could work out their own conclusion.

Slowly she walked with Bowie in the sunlit patio, laughingly complaining that her feet had almost gone to sleep from the long sitting.

He was silent.

"Have you an ox on your tongue?" she asked, in the old French phrase.

"No. Just thinking——"

"Thinking what, Jim?" she teased.

"That you're too beautiful—to be true——"

It startled her. But on second glance she was sure he had not intended an ambiguity and accepted the compliment.

"I'm real enough, if that's what you mean," she said. She laughed a little tinkling laugh. "Extraordinary in nothing. Not very wise—and in spite of what you say, not very beautiful after all——"

Narcisse would have said that this was laying it on very thick to wring a compliment. But with a man like Bowie one had to lay it on thick. He rose beautifully to it.

"You are!" he insisted. "The most beautiful girl I've ever known——" This sounded like a repetition, and he boggled down, gulping.

"That's nice of you . . . Jim." Her voice was low and soft.

"Judalon—this may sound like—well, like foolishness to you—I wouldn't blame you. But—but I think about you all the time—I try not to, but I can't help it——"

He stopped, thunderstruck at where this was leading.

She drew a deep breath, and looked down. From it he wrongly took encouragement. "I reckon it's downright presumptuous——" He hesitated, then plunged on, trying to put into words what he had not even thought out clearly. "But—you've made me think you'd at least listen—with kindness. I'm not much. Not now. But I'm *going* to be something. I've got it in me to be the kind of a man a girl like you could look on with pleasure—and respect. Can you believe that . . . and would it make any difference?"

So it was out, Jim Bowie's confession. And exactly as uncouth and awkward as she had expected it to be.

She said, "I think—after that—we'd better go back in."

But he placed his hands upon her arms and stopped her, his face deadly serious.

"Not—until you tell me——"

"Take your hands off me, sir!" She drew herself away and looked at him white-faced. "If you must hear—I never heard anything so preposterous. You believe you've come a long way in a short time, don't you? Well, let me tell you that Narcisse's peculiar fancy for you gives you no right to presume to talk this way to me. If it weren't so—so ridiculous—it would be insulting. But I'll give you an answer—go back and 'jump the broom'—isn't that what you call it?—with one of your Cajun wenches, Mr. Bowie!"

Now she gave a cruel little laugh and left him, pale with anger and humiliation, standing alone in the bright garden.

Chapter Nine

1

Narcisse, alone of the young men, was awaiting their return with the ladies. The others had pointedly excused themselves while Bowie was with Judalon in the garden.

In one glance Narcisse saw from their faces what had occurred. At once he left the house with Bowie.

"I'm sorry," he said after they had walked a few moments in silence.

"Never mind," Bowie said. "I had it coming."

He was still white-faced.

Narcisse said, hesitantly, "I was thinking—this is Friday. Hardly a good night at St. Sylvain's. Some other entertainment—perhaps the theater—would be more enjoyable."

"I'm leaving New Orleans, Narcisse—maybe tomorrow. And we've told several people we were going to St. Sylvain's."

"Does that make any difference?"

"I saw that Cabanal and the rest had left your house too. They've got it in for me. I believe Cabanal's in love with your sister."

"In love?" Narcisse smiled. "I'm not sure Philippe would recognize love if he met it. But he likes our family fortune. Not long ago he offered her his name—and also his debts. He had lost heavily at the casino. His father came from Natchez where they live and was very stern with him, even threatening to cut off his allowance. Philippe was desperate, but Judalon rejected him, and he was quite disconsolate until the following week when his father relented and paid off his debts."

"The fortune hunter!" said Bowie savagely. Then he remembered that his own approach to Judalon might easily be interpreted as the same thing, though he had not so intended it.

"Perhaps," said Narcisse. "But if I resented all the motives that impel gentlemen to pursue my fair sister, I'd be at rapier points with half of New Orleans."

Bowie said, "That brings us back to what we were talking about. If we don't go to St. Sylvain's tonight, won't everybody suspect that I'm afraid to go?"

Narcisse raised his brows, shrugged, and at last nodded. "I follow you. Rapier points and St. Sylvain's. I doubt it would come to that. But you're right—it might be misinterpreted if we didn't go. So—St. Sylvain's it shall be."

2

That evening Audubon accompanied Bowie and Narcisse to St. Sylvain's. After entering the lobby where they were relieved of their hats and canes, they passed into the large dining hall, with wide portals opening to a lounge on either side and an entrance to the gambling casino in the rear. In spite of his unhappy mood, Bowie was impressed by the richness of the place. Paintings, chiefly nudes, decorated the walls, and the wood carver's art was everywhere exemplified in tables, chairs, and sideboards which served the various purposes of the place.

Several gentlemen rather made a point of bowing to Bowie. It was an acknowledgment of a certain standing he had achieved, rather than any indication of friendship. He had been a guest at the de Bornay ball. His friendship with Narcisse was notorious. The qualities that induced one of the great families to accept this *Américain* were not perhaps readily discernible, but it was well to let matters unfold themselves. Meantime, since the de Bornays appeared to be sponsoring Monsieur Bowie—how strange that name!—a formal bow was policy. After all, a bow is noncommittal. One can bow, and still reserve his judgment.

Men were dining at the tables. Bowie saw a graceful figure rise, and acknowledge Narcisse and himself. Malot, the *maître d'armes*. A little beyond him, half a dozen men were seated, among them Cabanal and Lebain, and the duelist Contrecourt. Narcisse's coterie. These did not rise or seem to see them.

"Let's visit the sideboard," Narcisse said. "Everything here is on the house—except the gambling tokens, for which you must pay hard cash. You'll find supper excellent and the wines delightful."

White-capped carvers heaped their plates from a bewildering array: roast turkey, venison, mutton, beef, partridge, quail, fish of every kind, salads, and desserts, all most savory.

The manner in which the coterie had ignored them created a reckless feeling in Bowie. It was he, of course, they had cut. He began almost to hope that somebody—Cabanal especially—would try to make trouble before this evening was over. But all was propriety. Gentlemen about them drank, smoked, and gossiped. Black servants glided about with little silver trays, bearing cigars, liquors and wines, very obliging and deferential.

Audubon said, "There's your friend, Parisot."

The merchant sat alone at a table, gnawing a turkey leg.

"He never gambles," Narcisse said. "Janos Parisot believes only in the sure thing."

"Why is he here, then?" asked Bowie.

"To be seen," Narcisse said. "Observe the burgundy coat at the table beyond? That's Colonel Grymes. The fox-haired fellow with him is Sallou, the moneylender. He's in the same business as Parisot—but without Parisot's tinge of respectability. Parisot lends at usury on commercial enterprises, while Sallou merely lends at usury to those who lose heavily at the gaming table. I see little difference in them—in which I differ from Monsieur, my father, who honors Parisot's card at our house, where Sallou would never dare present himself."

"Who is Colonel Grymes?"

"A gentleman who got his fame defending in court the pirates, Jean and Pierre Lafitte."

That name Lafitte again. Bowie glanced over. The man in the burgundy coat was robust and droll, with a high white forehead and deep lines about his mouth.

"Grymes was public prosecutor," said Narcisse. "Through his undeniably able efforts, Pierre Lafitte, the older brother, was put in the Cabildo, and was on a good way toward the gibbet. But one day Grymes resigned his high office and announced he would defend the freebooter he had previously indicted. Interestingly, Grymes, as public prosecutor, had prepared against Lafitte a case so airtight that Grymes, as defendant's counsel, couldn't free him. So Grymes, as tamperer, took over. One night Pierre disappeared from prison—his jailer had been bribed."

"A jack of many trades, Colonel Grymes," Bowie said.

Narcisse nodded. "He got rich out of the Lafittes, and he's been more or less associated with them or their friends ever since. Usually he's with Dominique You. Wonder where that old buccaneer is tonight?"

As if he divined their discussion, Grymes rose and came in a leisurely, roundabout way, until he stopped at their table. Narcisse and Audubon he greeted. When he was introduced to Bowie, he said, "A buckskin, I'll take oath. Men like you don't grow, sir, on the city streets."

"I've worn more buckskin than broadcloth," Bowie said shortly.

Grymes chuckled and took a chair.

"More buckskin than broadcloth," he repeated. "Begad, sir, the phrase is worthy of the ancients, though nothing ever equaled the Romans for the laconic. Think of Caesar's *'Veni, vidi, vici,'* and Pilate's *'Ecce homo.'* Where will you find utterances like that in this raw country?"

That smooth assumption of superiority again. Bowie was becoming well weary of New Orleans superiority. He said, "I don't know about your Romans, but you can hear sayings as neat as any right in this 'raw country.' I mind last fall, when I saw a country girl fording a creek, carrying a piggin of butter on her head. As she came out of the water, I said, 'Little lady, how deep's the water, and what's the price of butter?' She gave me a merry look, and said, 'To your navel, and ninepence.' Can your Romans beat that, sir?"

It was prompted by resentment, but Grymes gave a great guffaw. "Capital!" he said. "A toast to James Bowie, whose tongue is as agile as his shoulders are broad!"

3

The coterie had gone into the casino, and presently, when Grymes left them, Narcisse said, "Let's enter the haunt of the tiger."

Bowie rose at once, his stubborn recklessness growing. The haunt of the tiger? A good place to confront his enemies.

At least two hundred men were playing at the tables which crowded the floor of the casino. Above the hum of voices rose the rattle of the ivory balls in the roulette wheels and the sharp calls of the croupiers. To one side was a recessed counter, where money was exchanged for gambling tokens: red ivory disks at five dollars, white disks for one. Narcisse bought a hundred dollars' worth, as a shout of laughter and applause came from one of the tables.

"Beaubien's in luck tonight," said the money-changer. "He's making a killing—observe how the others are playing his bets."

"Come on," said Narcisse to Bowie. He was fidgeting, his careless, amused manner gone.

Bowie's mood was attuned to this scene. Men crowded eagerly about tables, servants hurried with glasses on trays, laughter was high-pitched and excited. He experienced a feeling of impending events, fortunes changing rapidly every moment, a sensation almost repellent, yet suddenly enormously fascinating to him.

"Let it alone," Audubon whispered in his ear.

Bowie shook his head. From his pocket he drew some gold coins: fifty dollars. Almost all he had. He was embarking on foolishness, but his bitter spirit impelled him. He took the ten red disks counted out to him.

"I'm for the wheel," said Narcisse.

Bowie said, "I don't understand roulette. But over there's something I've seen before."

"Faro? Good luck." Narcisse departed eagerly and Audubon followed Bowie. For a few turns they watched, while stacks of chips were won or lost on different representations of cards enameled on the cloth. In the middle of the table cover a striped tiger was painted. Bowie remembered Narcisse's expression, "the haunt of the tiger."

He took a vacated seat. He had played faro before, but bets were large here. Might as well risk his whole stake. He placed the fifty dollars on the high card, coppered—to lose. Smoothly the dealer slipped the cards from the box. First a king. Then a seven.

"King-seven." The dealer took in several bets. But the high card, coming first, had lost. Bowie's stack was doubled.

"Place your bets, gentlemen." Another turn. Bowie doubled again.

If gold coins had been stacked on the table, he might have behaved differently. But red ivory chips were not like cash. His feeling for them was only as something to compete with in this game. He was a natural competitor, and this evening an angry one. On the third bet he shoved the entire heap over on the painted ace of spades.

The dealer checked him. "The house limit, sir, is one hundred dollars on any single bet."

Without speaking Bowie divided his stack into three piles. One hundred dollars went on the high card to win, fifty was "heeled" from king to deuce to win, and fifty "heeled" from five to eight to lose.

A murmur around the table. Foolish bet. Almost sure to work against itself by balancing losses against any win. Cards slipped from the box.

"Eight," the dealer announced. Then, "King!"

A chorus of surprise. Bowie had won all three bets. The king had won, the eight had lost, and since king was high, high card had won also. An extraordinary combination of luck. Bowie had four hundred dollars on the table.

At his elbow was a servant with a toddy. He gulped the fiery sweet drink. A burning seemed to flow through his blood. Within him he seemed to have discovered a hidden and unknown inspiration, which fit in perfectly with his bitter recklessness.

He saw Audubon, across the table, staring strangely. Then he forgot everything except the rattle of the chips, the shuffle of the cards, the flat announcements of the banker. He won. And won again. Others began betting on his bets. A fever imbued him. Almost in a trance he was carried along on a resistless stream, which he had no wish to resist.

4

The dealer turned his box on its side.

"The bank is exhausted, gentlemen," he said. "The game is suspended until more tokens are brought from the office."

Stiffly Bowie rose from his chair, taking from the banker a certificate of value. More than two thousand dollars. To Audubon he said, "I want a drink."

Brandy. They stood together by the wall sipping.

The artist said, "Jim . . . you're two thousand dollars ahead. Let's leave —it's after midnight."

"Two thousand," Bowie said. "I started with fifty. Just fifty." His look was almost dazed. "I couldn't lose. Once in a while, but never for long. My hedge bets won, my long chances came off—as if something was guiding me—like a destiny——"

"Come away," said Audubon.

"I can't—not now."

"I beg thee—something has been awakened in thee——"

"What are you talking about?" Bowie said impatiently.

"Listen to me, James. There's an old tale of an English officer in India who brought up as a pet a tiger cub. The animal was fed on milk, as gentle and harmless as a kitten. Once the officer slept in his chair, his hand hanging downward. The tiger, grown now, but still a trusted pet, lay upon the floor and with affection licked his master's hand. Suddenly the officer was awakened by a growl from the striped creature."

Audubon paused, with intense earnestness. "What had happened? He knew! The rough tongue of the brute had abraded the skin of his hand so that a tiny spot of blood had come. Only a drop—but the tiger had tasted it. His loving pet had been transformed by it into a crouching beast of prey, snarling, its great hooked claws extended. Yet for one moment the tiger continued to taste the blood on its master's hand. In that moment the officer lifted a pistol from the table beside him and shot the brute through the head, before it could leap on him, to rend and devour!"

"Well?" said Bowie.

"James—some men have that in them which once having tasted blood never leaves them until it destroys them. I saw the tiger just now—glaring forth from thy eye!"

Bowie stared, half minded for a moment to listen to Audubon's suggestion that they leave. But a voice spoke behind him.

"Well, Jim! The place is buzzing over your *tour de force.*"

Bowie turned. Narcisse was accompanied by Malot. The *maître d'armes* smiled. "It's not often that a player breaks the faro bank here," he said.

"I won only two thousand," said Bowie.

"But many others won also on your play, monsieur."

Narcisse glanced across the room. "Our friends have been less fortunate at the wheel."

Cabanal and the coterie. Some of them were already drunk. Among

73

them was the square figure of Contrecourt. From his eye Bowie received a straight black stare.

A lean and very elegant man in a pearl-gray suit came from the office and glanced about the room.

"That's St. Sylvain himself," Narcisse said.

Malot excused himself. The others watched the owner of the casino as he began moving about from table to table, greeting his guests. Presently he came over to them.

"Ah, Monsieur de Bornay," he said. "I rejoice at seeing you."

"I present my friends, Monsieur Bowie and Monsieur Audubon," Narcisse said.

St. Sylvain gave the impression of icy grayness. Not only was his attire gray, but his hair and slight waxed mustache also. His skin seemed gray, and his veiled eyes were slaty gray.

"Monsieur Audubon, your servant," he said. "Of Monsieur Bowie I have just been informed in my office." He gave a slight smile. "Not everyone is as fortunate as he is. It will take some minutes to rehabilitate the bank. Meantime, you of course wish to continue play, messieurs. What is your pleasure?"

Bowie felt Audubon tug at his sleeve and shook him off.

"What would you suggest, monsieur?" he said.

St. Sylvain bowed slightly. "To suggest is a pleasure. I am about to open a table of baccarat. Will you gentlemen join the party?"

The invitation was an honor in its way, a somewhat dangerous one.

"The play is very simple," said St. Sylvain.

Bowie nodded and glanced down at the certificate of value in his hand. St. Sylvain clapped his hands.

"Bring counters for this certificate to Monsieur Bowie at my table," he said to a servant who came at the summons. With a bow, he led the way.

Audubon hung back. "I'm going, James."

"Good-by, then." Bowie followed St. Sylvain.

5

"Messieurs, I have reserved for you the two chairs nearest the bank at the left," smiled St. Sylvain.

A high favor, since the players nearest the bank were paid first, so that if it was exhausted they stood a chance to receive their money while more distant players went without.

Bowie took the place next to the casino owner, with Narcisse on the other side of him. Across the table was a small man with thin auburn hair turning white at the temples, who was introduced as Monsieur Jarvis. Opposite Narcisse sat a rubicund, portly gentleman named Lombardi. The other three players at the far end Bowie knew: Cabanal, Lebain, and Contrecourt, the professional swordsman.

"The bank is five thousand, messieurs," said St. Sylvain, riffling the deck. "Any part of it, or all, is yours. Bets if you please."

The rules were absurdly simple, somewhat resembling *vingt-et-un*, which Bowie knew as blackjack. Instead of twenty-one, the points were nine or eight, with nine taking precedence. Tens and face cards counted zero. If one had a count of five or less, it was well to ask for a card: if more, to refuse. Only three hands, in each deal, competed: that of the dealer, and of a player on each side of him. After each hand the play moved up the table, so all had a chance to try their luck and pit their skill. But though only two played against the bank each time, all the others could bet, either on their own side to win, or on both sides to win against the dealer. The latter procedure, which required some daring, was called *à cheval*.

Experimentally Bowie pushed forward ten red chips. Two cards slid toward him. He looked: a five and a three. Eight. He turned up his cards. A slight buzz of pleasure rose from his side of the table.

"A card, Monsieur Jarvis?" asked St. Sylvain.

The red-haired man opposite nodded. He took the card and studied his hand. "Six," he said, turning it up.

St. Sylvain glanced at Bowie's eight and turned up his own cards. "Seven," he said.

The gambler had swiftly computed the bets on each side, and since they were slightly heavier on the right than the left, took his loss on the latter to collect on the former.

"The bank is five thousand, two hundred," he said.

Bowie saw the idea of the game. He pushed out three hundred in chips. Narcisse was the player. His count of seven won. Opposite, Lombardi called for a card, got a count of thirteen, and lost. Left seemed to be in luck.

"I'm betting five hundred," Bowie said, *"à cheval."*

"Right's not winning," whispered Narcisse.

"We'll see," Bowie said.

For the first time both sides did win. In three bets Bowie had taken fourteen hundred dollars. Including his faro winnings he had thirty-four hundred.

"The bank," said St. Sylvain, "is two thousand, one hundred."

An impulse seized Bowie. *"Banco.* I take it all."

It was his privilege and took precedence of all other bets.

Imperturbably St. Sylvain dealt to him only. A deuce and a three: a count of five.

"Another card, monsieur?"

"Please."

He looked at the third card and turned up his hand. "Nine."

St. Sylvain pushed over all his chips. "The bank is exhausted. Your pardon a moment while it is replenished." To Bowie he gave his gray smile. "Monsieur's good fortune is exemplary."

Narcisse was silent. Contrecourt and Cabanal frowned over at Bowie, talking together in a low voice. His mouth set stubbornly. If they didn't like it, it was immaterial to him. Before him was more than five thousand dollars in chips.

"The bank is five thousand again——" began St. Sylvain.

"Banco!"

Faces turned on Bowie, growing taut.

"It is you and I then, monsieur?" St. Sylvain dealt. At once Bowie turned up his cards: a trey and a six.

St. Sylvain smiled. "The bank is exhausted again, and for the second time by this gentleman."

Scowls and mutterings about the table. Bowie said, so that all could hear, "I shall propose *banco* each time in the future, if I am able to do so."

Contrecourt rose with a curse.

"Decidedly this *Américain* fool is making a nuisance of himself," he said to Lebain in an undertone which clearly carried. Bowie appeared not to notice. He said, "Would you consider an increase in the bets, Monsieur St. Sylvain?"

"What increase?"

"I have here ten thousand, six hundred. I suggest—ten thousand, six hundred."

An intake of breath from about him. Contrecourt became silent. St. Sylvain glanced about. Eyes, scores of eyes, were fixed on him, waiting to see what he would do. One of those *contre la maison* situations had suddenly risen, which constitute the greatest gambling drama. Every table in the casino was deserted to watch.

"What you propose is contrary to the rules of this house." The gambler's face was icy. "But for this occasion . . . we suspend the rules."

Narcisse sat helpless. The crowd jostled to see. About him Bowie saw faces, Creole faces, hostile faces, in their midst the hard glare of Contrecourt. They all hated him, hoped for his defeat.

Two oblongs of cardboard slithered across the table. He picked up the cards and looked at them. Ace and five. Hard decision. If he drew he

76

risked breaking his hand. If not, the margin for his opponent was wide.

"A card," he said.

It was a trey. St. Sylvain drew almost perfunctorily. Bowie had won again.

"Twenty thousand, I believe?" said the gambler.

Bowie hesitated, and his glance flicked to Narcisse. Perspiration stood on his friend's face. Narcisse was worried . . . Narcisse the brother of Judalon, whose laugh kept repeating in his brain. Twenty thousand and some hundreds more if he stopped now. Twenty thousand was good. But with forty thousand of his own . . . not even the de Bornay girl could laugh at him . . .

He counted. "I have here," he said, "twenty-one thousand, two hundred, to be exact. Will you raise the limit again, monsieur?"

St. Sylvain had a grievous problem. If he lost again to the American he would be more than forty-two thousand dollars down for the night. A very large sum, and if continued this might mean the breaking of his house.

But he nodded.

Colonel Grymes pushed into the circle. Beside him was a man whimsically theatrical in appearance, in a blue military surtout and a tall black stock that almost seemed to cut off his ears. He was slightly larger around the waist than anywhere else, his black hair was plastered with pomatum close to his bullet head, his mustaches were waxed into two upthrusting horns, and across his dark oily face, from the right ear to the corner of the mouth, ran a long white scar.

Philippe Cabanel, unable to stand the suspense, stood up and leaned on the table with both hands, chewing nervously on the end of his mustache. At Bowie's left, Narcisse went white. Complete, tense silence fell.

St. Sylvain shuffled and dealt.

Bowie turned up his hand. Deuce and five of hearts. Seven.

Now St. Sylvain put his two cards face up on the table. All saw that he had a four and a king. An ugly hand. The face card counted as a zero, and since he could draw only one card, it must be either a four or a five to beat Bowie. One five already in the American's hand, and one four in his. In his mind St. Sylvain computed the odds. Eight to one in his opponent's favor.

He must draw. More than forty thousand dollars on the turn of this card. In all the room Bowie and St. Sylvain alone seemed calm.

They all saw the card as St. Sylvain turned it. The five of spades.

"The house wins, monsieur," the gambler said.

A yell of pure relief from the onlookers.

The great young American bull had lost. Victory for the Creoles, victory for their kind, the placation of the secret wish of every heart.

Bowie rose, and the correctness of his attitude was remembered. Not even an eyelash quivered.

He said, "I am finished. Monsieur St. Sylvain, I thank you for your great courtesy."

A servant appeared beside him with a silver tray. He took from it a small glass of cognac.

Chapter Ten

I

Behind him a sudden, sharp question.

Narcisse, pale with anger, had made an inquiry directed at Contrecourt. The swordsman faced him deliberately.

"I remarked, monsieur, that it is a man's privilege to pick his friends, but that all privileges are susceptible of abuse."

In that moment Bowie knew that Contrecourt was dangerously bent on picking a quarrel. Narcisse was aware of it too, but in spite of the duelist's deadly reputation, he did not take his gaze from the other's hard stare.

"Monsieur chooses to speak with ambiguity," he said.

"I will be happy to clarify my meaning," replied Contrecourt.

"Messieurs—let us have no unseemliness in this house," said St. Sylvain.

Narcisse said, "Monsieur St. Sylvain is right. You will step with me into the garden, Contrecourt?"

So simply was the challenge given and accepted, before Bowie could speak, much less try to stop it. He knew he was too late, but he was wildly angry. Narcisse had taken this uneven meeting on himself because of Bowie. He could not match Contrecourt with the sword, any more than he could match Malot, a truth as evident to him as to anyone.

From across the room, Malot hurried. "What is this?" he asked.

"A difference." Narcisse still was pale with anger. "You will accompany us?"

Malot sternly surveyed the duelist. "You must be drunk, Contrecourt. This does not become you. He is an amateur."

"I am ready at any time, to demonstrate to *anyone,* what does and what does not become me," replied the other coldly.

Before Malot could speak, Bowie was confronting Contrecourt. "You mentioned clarifying your remark to Monsieur de Bornay," he said. "Suppose you do so that *all* may understand clearly."

Contrecourt turned on him, his cunningly intelligent eyes lit with some triumph, as if he were about to achieve an end he had planned.

"Gladly." Most offensively, the duelist addressed, not Bowie, but the others about him. "I say that they fight as they game. A large parade—then, *pouf!*"

Bowie's gray glare bored into him. "Who fights so, monsieur?"

Contrecourt could smile his contempt now. "All *Américains.*"

"Any particular *Américain?*"

"If the sleeves fit, suppose Monsieur draws them on!"

"I do so. And I say here, to all, that this Contrecourt is a hired bravo, selling his sword to the highest bidder, no better than any whore who sells her body!"

An *insulte majeure*. Yet Contrecourt was not angry, so much as pleased. "For that," he said, "you shall answer."

"At once!"

Narcisse stepped between them. "Not until this man answers first to me!"

"No, Narcisse!" Bowie said in his ear. "Don't you see—he wants *me*. You happen only to have come between us——"

Narcisse shook Bowie's hand from his arm. "Do me the goodness to let me fight my own quarrels. Malot, will you second me? And you, Jim?"

As quickly, Contrecourt chose his seconds: two men from the Rue des Expositions, whom Bowie did not know. Cabanal and Lebain looked on from the background.

Malot held up his hand. "Someone must be appointed referee." His glance traveled the crowded circle and fell on the dark-faced man with the scar. "Captain Dominique You! Will you act?"

Bowie stared. Was this the famous captain of Lafitte's pirates?

"Gladly," the man said in a full, rich voice.

The crowd opened. Their party of seven passed out. Courtesy kept the others from pushing after them, though many went to the windows. The code was respected by every man in St. Sylvain's.

2

That moon . . . the same moon which had beguiled another garden only the night before . . . now seemed only to give an added ghastliness to this scene.

In their white shirts the antagonists faced each other, Narcisse slender compared to the duelist's powerful breadth. Narcisse was composed and determined; Contrecourt superior and sure.

Swords were brought. Swords always were quickly available anywhere in New Orleans.

"*En garde,*" said Captain Dominique.

The swords sang.

Tragedy. Sheer, senseless tragedy.

Narcisse knew his only hope was in attack. For a few brief, flurrying minutes, he followed thrust with thrust. Then the inevitable.

The professional swordsman saw his opening, and lunged. Back staggered Narcisse. Strange, how the mortal sickness he felt showed in every line of his back as his sword clattered on the gravel walk.

Bowie caught him. Even before he eased his friend to the ground, he knew. A wide descending curtain of blood sheeted the white silk shirt. Narcisse looked up with a question in his eyes . . . question veiling itself in death. He coughed up a mouthful of blood, his slim young legs twisted in one sudden contortion of pain. He was gone.

Bowie laid the lifeless head upon a coat and rose.

The seconds crowded about the stricken man. Contrecourt had not left his place. He stood, the point of his naked sword on the ground, watching the kneeling, stooping group, his face set and still in the moonlight.

"You killed him!" cried Malot.

"I am sorry. I would have preferred to wound him only. But these hotheaded fools must take their medicine."

"By heaven, you'll answer for this to me, Contrecourt!"

Contrecourt smiled coldly. "At your convenience, Malot."

The man had courage. Moreover, this was an opportunity he had long craved. His pupils were few, he was pushed for the money with which to live. If he could defeat Malot, he would at once establish himself as the premier *maître d'armes* in New Orleans. And he believed in himself, absolutely.

"At once then——" began Malot.

"Your pardon." It was Bowie. "Contrecourt meets me first."

"But—Monsieur Bowie——"

Bowie cut the *maître d'armes* short. "I believe the challenge given me takes precedence?" He addressed Contrecourt.

"*Oui, monsieur.*" The duelist was contemptuous: he could dispose of this *Américain* while a man took two breaths, and still be fresh for Malot.

A singing in Bowie's ears. Narcisse was gone . . . Judalon had disdained him . . . every dream in which he had indulged had gone.

He contemplated death, and it was without the instinctive inner shrinking with which nature provides all creatures. A madness was on him, cradled in the black depths of his depression, so that for the first time in his life he felt a desire for the end almost like a suicide before his final act. If he could kill that man, the finish seemed welcome. Yet, in that moment his brain was intensely active.

The duelist was waiting.

He heard himself say, "One of us is going to die tonight, Contrecourt—perhaps both."

"The weapons, monsieur!" said Contrecourt impatiently.

"Sword or knife—take your choice."

A surprise here. Mockingly Contrecourt lifted his blade. "This seems to serve me well enough."

"I'll use a knife, if I can get one."

"A knife against a sword?" Contrecourt shrugged. "It is Monsieur's privilege to choose his way of dying."

Bowie looked at Captain Dominique. "Is there a room hereabouts, empty and bare? It must be completely dark."

"What are you suggesting?" said the duelist. For the first time his composure was penetrated.

"This: it is mine to lay down the terms. You and I will be locked in a dark room. In stocking feet, to move without a sound. He who comes out . . . if either does . . . will be the victor."

Contrecourt's heavy face was a study. This suave swordsman, this killer, did not too greatly value his life: yet in the thought of groping through blackness for an antagonist he discovered something that failed to appeal to him.

He fell back on ridicule. "What outlandish—insane—rules are these? A barbarous backwoods custom, perhaps? An illustration of this man's chawbacon vulgarity? No gentleman would suggest it!"

All at once, a rich, roaring laugh.

"Steel in the dark! This I like!" Captain Dominique You rolled forward with his sailor's gait and looked at Malot. "You agree, monsieur, it is within the right of the man challenged to name his terms?"

"Decidedly."

"Then Contrecourt will either apologize to Monsieur Bowie or abide by these conditions. My friend, do you wish to eat your words?"

Contrecourt angrily shook his head.

"In that case," Dominique said, "we will proceed. As for the knife, Monsieur Bowie, I carry one on me—an old sailor's custom. Will this suffice?"

He reached within the waistband of his ample pantaloons and from a hidden sheath drew a six-inch straight-bladed dirk with an ivory handle inlaid with gold. The knife balanced well in Bowie's grip. He nodded.

They carried the poor limp body of Narcisse inside, and Bowie's mood of doom grew cold, ultimate, conclusive.

Dominique said, "At the rear of this establishment is a storeroom, which is empty and windowless. The very room, it appears, that we need. Messieurs, accompany me!"

3

In the blackness, Contrecourt crouched and felt behind him with his hand for the wall . . . something substantial and reassuring.

They had locked the door. Outside, somewhere, they stood waiting—Dominique, Malot, and the rest.

He took a firmer grip on his sword hilt and wondered where the other was in that room. This *was* darkness. Six inches before his nose he could not discern his hand.

All at once Contrecourt began to regret that he had elected to use the sword in this madman's combat.

With the sword one could keep a knife wielder at a distance and kill—but only if one could see. How to use it when one was blind? In this blackness all his trained lethal skill went for naught.

Contrecourt could face death with bravery: had done so often. But this . . . this was outside of, and beyond, experience. The skin prickled on his back. His shirt was wet with sweat: the sweat of nervousness and fear.

He held his breath, trying to hear the breathing or any soft movement of his enemy there in the inky dark. But though he held it until his lungs seemed bursting, no faint whisper of sound came to his straining ears.

Where was that cursed *Américain?* From what direction would he come? Contrecourt suppressed an instinct to whip his sword wildly about him to keep off the creeping peril: because the sound of the blade slashing the air would betray his position.

Minutes passed, trembling like hours. How long had they been here . . . half an hour? Why, oh, why, did not that fiend move, or do something—anything? Contrecourt wanted to curse—to curse Dominique You, and Malot, and his own seconds who had trapped him into this. But he dared not even whisper.

He became even more tense. It was not a sound . . . so much as the beginning of a mere guess of where a sound was. Frantically, he stabbed in that direction. Only emptiness.

At once he was fearful that the slight rustle of his movement might have told his position.

He listened. Silence was absolute. Only the thumping of the pulse in his own ears seemed unnaturally loud.

Nom de Dieu! To be penned up like this—a polished master of sword—with an *Américain* savage——

He must find a corner. If he could find a corner, with his back in it, the sword would have much greater chance to hold off that silent, inexorable enemy. Perhaps if he moved silently enough the other might grope toward the place he had just quitted and thus reveal himself.

With infinite care, Contrecourt began the stealthy withdrawal. His body was bent, his sword half extended before him. In their silk stockings his feet moved slowly and softly, not sliding but lifted and placed, touched barely on the floor at first and then gradually set down. It seemed the pounding of his heart must be heard more than any sound of movement he made.

To move three feet required an unconscionable time. Still no sound. Still the impenetrable night blackness of the windowless room with its walls of thick stone.

The corner . . . the corner. He reached out a careful, inquiring hand. This must be the corner . . .

With a scream he desperately whipped the blade of his sword around in the dark.

Too late. The other was inside his guard.

There was a sudden dreadful pain in Contrecourt's side and then the blackness of eternity, of death. It was no blacker than the dueling room where he fell with the knife in his heart.

The Maison Rouge, 1818

*B*arataria had been reduced. The last of the buccaneers under Jean Lafitte in the year 1818 roosted on a low sandspit off the coast of Mexican Texas, known as Galvez Island, and the seafaring men of the Gulf prayed that if they were cast ashore it would not be on that coast.

It was not the rocky shore they feared, but the rocky hearts of those who dwelt there. For the people of Galvez-town, which was the name of the pirate settlement, were broken men from all countries: prison breakers, gallows birds, fugitives from justice, thieves, murderers, degenerates, who had made their way to that outland place and held it for the time being against the world.

There, and for the last time, the despicable institutions of piracy and slavery met: the one living off the other. Spanish slave ships were the preferred prey of Lafitte's rovers. In spite of the law forbidding importation of African Negroes, there were always men who, caring little for their good names or the dangers they encountered, were willing to smuggle the cargoes from the captured slavers into the United States, where the expansion of cotton and sugar lands created an insatiable demand for chattel labor.

The year 1818 was the high point of the colony's prosperity. Very soon the American navy would root the settlement out. But meantime every night was a saturnalia, rum and wine were unlimited, blood-lust and cruelty held full sway, women of many races were at any man's whim, slaves were in the barracoon to bring more wealth, and living was high, if foul and vicious, in the merry village of Galvez-town.

Chapter Eleven

1

In the chill breeze that presaged the coming of dawn, the little schooner *Carondelet* heeled over slightly, and Bowie pulled up his collar, thrust his hands in his pockets, and went deep into his buckskin jacket for warmth. A half-moon sailed rakishly through a sea of small opalescent clouds, touching the black waters of the Gulf with highlights, and the stars were just beginning to fade in the faint mounting brightness which grew above the eastward horizon.

It was still night. Bowie listened to the creaking of cordage and timbers, the dull wash of waves, and thought solemn thoughts. Where the bulwarks cast a shadow on the moonlit deck, a long bundle lay. His brother, Rezin, was still sleeping. They had spent the night on deck because the smell and heat of the little cabin were unbearable.

Bowie was glad Rezin could sleep. He had slept little enough on this voyage. Rezin had a habit of rising twice or thrice each night to "look around." Not that there was anything to see except a succession of waves monotonously similar: but Rezin worried.

Rezin was the thinker of the family. A lot more went on in his head than in an ordinary man's, or so Bowie thought. Bowie himself did not worry. At least not a great deal. His mother had a saying, out of the Bible somewhere: *Sufficient unto the day* . . . There was more to it, but he remembered that much. It meant to take things as they came, he reckoned: and that was how he tried to take them. Not that he blamed his brother for concern. It was a concern well justified, and Bowie himself was solely and totally responsible.

Rezin had enough praiseworthy qualities, Bowie considered, almost to make up for those he himself lacked. He was the educated member of the family and could read Ovid and Suetonius in the Latin and quote Shakespeare and Pope rather impressively: especially now that his hair had begun to thin on top, giving him the look of an extra-high and intellectual forehead. Yet he was a good man on a hunt: or in a fight, for that matter. As good as you could want. And there were a lot of downright things about Rezin that Bowie admired: the way he spelled his name, for instance.

Their father, the old Revolutionary trooper, had gone to war so early in life that he had no time to get much schooling, and once he was in the army, he was too busy being a partisan raider under General Marion, the Swamp Fox, to study books. So all his life his notions of spelling were pretty rudimentary. He, for example, had been christened Reason Pleasants Bowie, but he held that the only sensible way to spell a thing was the way it sounded, so he wrote Rezin for his signature.

Since the old man felt that way about it, his son who was named after him saw no occasion to depart from the precedent, although he could spell his way through Noah Webster's *Compendious Dictionary* and back. He signed his name Rezin also, and always would. A streak of loyalty like that was something Bowie could cotton to. A family trait: they always hung together. That was why Rezin was here on the dirty little *Carondelet* on the longest kind of a gamble. Rezin came because of Bowie, and very much against his own better judgment.

2

Bowie remembered the day he returned to the Bayou Boeuf from New Orleans. He and Nez Coupé and the new slave Sam stepped out of the pirogue at the landing, while the early morning mists still blocked out the further forest and lay in streamers at the feet of the nearer trees. The cabin stood back a hundred feet from the bayou, with a stack of firewood on one end of the porch, the skin of a big panther he had killed still tacked on the wall, and a new quarter of beef hung by the door. Everyone was still asleep: not even a wisp of smoke lazied from the mud-and-pole chimney.

His eye took in the logs inside the boom up the bayou, ready to be snaked to the saw pit by the ox teams. There were more of them than when he left: Rezin and John had been working hard, getting ready for the new market he was to arrange. Beyond was the saw pit with its heaps of sawdust.

Another of his mother's biblical quotations recurred to him. *The younger son gathered all together, and took his journey into a far country, and there wasted his substance with riotous living . . .*

The Prodigal Son. Bowie always had despised him, in spite of the scriptural lesson, and secretly sympathized with that older son who had labored to fatten the calf only to see his wastrel younger brother come home and feast on it, doted upon by their father.

Well, John and Rezin would have all reason to look on him in the same light. He was worse than a failure: they could not dream what he had done to them.

His last days in New Orleans had been filled with chill bitterness. There was the death of Narcisse and his own fight with Contrecourt. He remembered the madness, the desire to die with which he had gone into that weird pitch-dark duel, and it was a matter for contemplation. He had never before known such a mood. About it was a smell of sickness that he did not understand or like.

Then Narcisse's funeral. He sat far back in the cathedral, listened to the solemn chanting, and watched the priest fling the holy water. He did not go to the cemetery.

And there was the moment when he stood before the door of the Maison de Bornay, hoping to express his sympathy concerning Narcisse, only to receive an icy message of refusal from Judalon delivered by the lips of the black butler.

With Narcisse gone, he met in every direction coldness such as he had not imagined in New Orleans. Even Malot turned away from him, though Malot knew a just requital had been dealt to the murderer, Contrecourt. To Malot, the purist, Bowie had violated the spirit of the *code duello,* even though he fought within the letter.

Only two in New Orleans were willing to converse with him.

Old Dominique next day sat at the Rouge et Noir with Bowie.

"Knives in the dark!" His great laugh. "A little rich for the blood of these people, hey? But it warms old Dominique's heart, monsieur. I think of the scuffles below decks on the old *Tonnerre,* when a dirk sometimes empty a man's whole basket of guts on the planking . . . Some rum?

"Rum's a man's drink." Dominique smiled. He took a long pull and Bowie sipped, though he did not share the other's admiration for the fiery liquor. Dominique reached forward and laid a hand on Bowie's arm. *"Nom de Dieu!"* he said. "An arm for a cutlass! You'd have made a fortune with us in the old days—with a hundred of hell's prize fiends howling across the bulwarks of a Spanish merchant, and Jean Lafitte cursing from the quarter——"

He smacked his lips.

Bowie said, "You were with Lafitte?"

"With him? I *was* Lafitte! As much a part of him as his right arm, or his black heart. What a man—Jean Lafitte!"

"Why are you no longer with him, Captain?"

"Another rum!" called Dominique, and Bowie saw he did not intend to answer the question.

Presently he said, "Captain, if I told you I had certain business with Lafitte—could you help me find him?"

The old buccaneer did not reply until the rum had been brought. "Would it be expedient to say . . . what kind of business?"

"To Captain Dominique You—yes." Bowie gave a full minute to silence. "I have in mind a speculation—in black goods."

Dominique half closed one eye. "Speculation," he said, "requires capital."

"I can get capital."

"You have lost much money."

"I have other resources."

Dominique drank, his full brown eyes thoughtful, and set down the empty glass. "As for finding Lafitte, that is a hard question. Lafitte is here today—yonder tomorrow——" He broke off with that penetrating glance, the eyelid half closed again. "But . . . I am not often deceived in a man." He seemed to make his mind up. "Show me the color of the money, Monsieur Bowie, and—I may be able to discover information which will be of value to you."

With that half promise, Bowie visited Janos Parisot. Obviously Parisot was surprised to see him: surprised and perhaps a little uneasy. His transaction with Bowie had been unnecessarily sharp, unnecessarily greedy. And with his own eyes he had seen how dangerous a man the American was.

The merchant was gratified when Bowie showed no resentment, but suggested instead a matter of business. From Parisot's standpoint it turned out to be very good business indeed, and he called his clerk. Papers were made out, signed, and notarized, and then he bade Bowie a heartfelt Godspeed.

Finally came the farewell to Audubon. The artist's horror over the events of the night before was apparent, but when he learned that Bowie was returning to his own country, he seemed almost happy.

"I shall miss thee—but at last thee see my viewpoint——"

Bowie shook his head. "I am after money. Money is the one full answer. Men like Monsieur de Bornay respect property. Even a supercilious, pampered female like—like de Bornay's daughter——" He broke off. "John, I am despised here in New Orleans. Because I am *Américain?* No, for Colonel Grymes is *Américain*. It is because I am a poor *Américain*. Well—I shall not always be a poor *Américain*. Remember that I have told you!"

Audubon embraced him and watched him go sadly, as if sure in his mind that his friend had embarked on a course predestined to unhappiness.

3

So Bowie came home to the Bayou Boeuf, ashamed and bitter, to face a difficult explanation to his brothers, touching the business he had transacted on his journey.

He sent a long hail to the cabin. His brothers came out on the porch, then down the path toward him, sleep still in their eyes. But the sleep fled quickly when they had a good look at his long tight pantaloons, his citified coat, his bell crown.

No questions at first. It was seemly to light a pipe, puff deliberately, and speak of commonplaces, as if these remarkable garments were not sufficient to make one drool with curiosity.

John, the eldest, shortest, and darkest of the three brothers, the man of finance in the family, said at last, "Did you make our deal?"

Bowie looked him in the eye. "No."

Another period of pipe puffing. Then Rezin, "What *did* you do?"

"I killed a man."

Nods, and unsurprised puffs of the pipes. "Need killing?"

"Plenty."

More puffs.

"I bought a nigger," Bowie said, "and signed a note for fifteen hundred dollars for him."

"You *what?*"

He repeated it. The brothers forgot their calmness and their pipes.

"Fifteen *hundred*——?" This transcended in importance the killing of any man. An unheard-of price for a slave.

"That him?" asked John.

Sam was called from the landing and examined from all sides. He was eager to please, his eyeballs showing white.

"You'd better be good," growled Rezin.

Sam was dismissed.

A silence. Bowie felt very guilty, but he was in for it. He looked at them with frank directness, an attractive way he had, that sometimes carried a point for him which otherwise might have failed.

"I talked with Parisot," he said.

"Scheming?" asked Rezin.

"Like a wolf. No good to be got out of him. Came back at me with an offer to buy all cypress at the price I'd quoted for mixed lumber——"

"It would ruin us!"

"So I told him. But he's a hard one. Wouldn't give an inch. I waited a few days." Bowie considered it unnecessary to go into the details as to those days. "Went back—thought he might have reconsidered."

"Had he?" John asked.

"Yes. Said he'd offered too much. Quoted a dollar a thousand less."

Rezin and John swore. Then stopped. The Bowies all felt it was little use cursing a man who couldn't hear you.

"I argued," Bowie said. "No good. Finally he came up with an offer to buy us out——"

"*Buy us out?*" They yelled it angrily.

"Offered five thousand, lock, stock, and barrel." Bowie hoped he sounded calm.

"What—did you say?" John asked.

"I laughed at him."

"Good." John was relieved.

"I said we wouldn't take a shilling less than six thousand——"

"Six thous—— But you *did* say we'd take six thousand?" Rezin's voice was almost a whisper.

Bowie nodded. "What's more, I got it. I have the signed option right here in my pocket."

They stared, stunned. Then John's face darkened, and Rezin flared scarlet to the top of his balding forehead. They were good and mad now.

Bowie stepped back, so that the bole of a tree was behind him and he could keep an eye on both of them. A precaution almost instinctive, a hang-over from their younger days when many a time the three of them had fought rough-and-tumble over one thing or another: a source of pleasure and a way of working off steam.

The precaution was needless. They had all passed the boy stage. And even if they had not, they never fought among themselves when there were onlookers. Moreover, Rezin and John had for some time now known there was no profit in jumping this young giant of a brother, even when the two of them teamed against him.

Bowie said, moderately, "This place is too small for us, boys. Even if we had a market—which we haven't—it no more than buys us pone and pork. We've got to get out of this rut."

He paused. They relaxed, no longer clenching their big fists, listening with an air of reserved judgment, like men willing to hear all sides of an argument but convinced against him in advance.

"No matter what we do," he said persuasively, "this little lumber mill's going to pieces. The big outfits will close us out, sooner or later. You know it. I know it."

They waited, their eyes never wavering from his.

"We might as well be flat broke as the way we are. I want to make money—great big money——"

"How?" John asked.

"There's land—a lot of empty land——"

"Speculation?" Rezin spat. "Hell's full of men who went broke speculating on land."

Bowie did not reply directly to that. "We've been here at the end of nothing too damn long, boys. I'm not smart, but I think this country's about to take the biggest running jump in history. And there's no place to go but out. Do you know where *out* is? Right here!"

Their faces changed. He had always been able to carry them with him, to convey his inspiration, whether for a prank, an adventure, or a fight.

"Boys, let's play one game I'm thinking about—to get the money for a still bigger game——"

The door of the cabin opened, and a woman came out.

Her hair was nearer white than brown, but her back was straight and her face calm and kind.

"Ma!" Bowie said. With long strides he went to her, and though he stood on the step below, when he put his arms about her, he had to bend his head to kiss her.

"Why didn't you tell me she was here?" he demanded of his brothers.

"Didn't have a chance," said Rezin.

"I came up Sunday in the pirogue with John," she said. "I must say it was about time. A filthier place I never did see——" Her face crinkled with laughter. "Well, I cleaned it up—with a little help."

John and Rezin grinned. They had been the "help," and her requirements had not been small.

"Well," she said, "what's this about selling the place, just after I got it tidied up?" Again her laughter welled, at their blank faces. "If it's a secret, why do you bellow it all over the woods?"

Rezin said, "All right, Ma. What do you think about it?"

At once she became grave, matriarchal, voicing the law to her clan. "I think only one thing. Whatever you do—do it together. That's the way I want my boys to be."

One by one her eyes sought them out. One by one they nodded.

"Now come into the cabin while I get us some breakfast," she said, "and let's hear what kind of a harum-scarum plan Jim's got in that wild young head of his."

Bowie had not wished to tell his mother, but there was no evading her.

"You won't like it, Ma," he said. "I'm aiming to *run slaves.*"

93

In the long silence that followed, a bluebottle fly made its buzzing at a window clearly heard. He saw the rejection in John's face, the tightening of Rezin's mouth. Gentlemen did not deal in slaves. They were angry and ashamed that he should even mention such a thing before their mother.

But their mother said, "Let's hear Jim's idea."

All three of them stared at her. It was almost as if she had given sanction, and Elva Bowie had been reared a lady. But she had also married a frontiersman, and most of her life had been spent in the wilderness. She had in her the rawhide fiber of it, and now the mother was siding with her boys.

After that came full consideration of Bowie's plan, and Rezin and John saw what she had seen from the first: that there was no other way. Jim was committed to the venture and would have to see it through.

Slaves at a dollar a pound—in a place called Galvez-town. A pirate nest, too. Jean Lafitte—a name familiar enough. He was a famous buccaneer, who would as soon slit your throat as shake your hand. But others had done it. Bowie spoke of Captain Dominique You, who appeared to be a sort of agent of Lafitte's in New Orleans.

They pondered. After all . . . prime cotton hands were worth not less than eight hundred dollars a head anywhere in Louisiana.

Now they looked at Bowie, and perceived that he was not the easy-smiling, lazy brother they had always known. He was determined, reckless, hardened by something.

In the end, when everything had been said, for and against it, the mother spoke her mind:

"I'm not saying Jim acted wise, or acted right. I'm not saying that what he's urging is best. All I'm saying is this: whatever you decide to do, do it together like Bowies."

After that, to show the kind of family they were, John and Rezin voted to sell their property to Parisot, to go along with Jim Bowie and throw everything into his venture—root hog, or die.

Chapter Twelve

I

Bowie thought back on all of this, standing on the slanting deck of the schooner in the chilly pre-dawn. He glanced again at Rezin, sleeping under the bulwark. The *Carondelet* was beginning to pitch in the chop brought by the breeze, and the sky was growing lighter. Ahead, in the bow of the ship, he saw two figures.

For want of something to do, he made his way forward over coils of rope and other obstructions on the dim deck. One of the men was Nez Coupé, boasting as usual.

"So lovely—so young—so much in love with me. It tear my heart when I have to leave from her. Ah, *la petite*—she beg me with big round tears, to take her with me—she cannot live without me——"

"A Cajun wench?" said a strong Irish voice.

"Cajun? No! New Orleanois—the daughter of one of the most grand houses in the city—an' so *charmante!*"

Nez Coupé kissed his fingers. The other laughed.

"I'll bet me life, I know the kind of a house she come from," he said. "One of them places on Girod street, in the swamp district——"

"*Mille sacrés tonnerres!* How you say such a thing, Bourke?" Nez Coupé bristled. "This lady is Creole! Her father is rich like a duke. Sugar. Cotton. Rum. Slave——"

"Faith, a high-toned Creole lady wouldn't spit on you!"

"This show how little you know!" Nez Coupé screeched. "If I mention her name, your ugly Irish eyes bug out like the catfish!" He sniffed scornfully. "But a man of gallantry must nevair mention the names of the so-beautiful creatures who give their hearts to him——"

Bowie came up beside them and leaned on the bulwark.

"Ah, Jim!" said Nez Coupé. "You tell this man that I always speak the truth——"

"You can depend on it, Bourke. I never knew Nez Coupé to tell a stretcher." Bowie eyed the Cajun in the early light. "If he says this poor idiot girl wept over him, you must believe——"

"Idiot!" Nez Coupé cried indignantly. "She is no idiot!"

"Pardon. I should have said insane. Naturally, an insane girl could not leave the asylum——"

"Who say insane?" shrieked Nez Coupé. "What you trying to do, Jim? *De quoi parlez-vous?*"

"She's not an idiot? And not crazy? And yet she'd leave all that cotton and sugar and those slaves belonging to her father, to say nothing of the rum—for *you?* Come now, Nez Coupé!"

"*Sacr-r-ré!*" The Cajun's expression was an indescribable combination of wrath, perplexity, embarrassment, and humor. "*Sacré!*" He burst into a laugh. "Ah, Jim! Lucky I love you. Othairwise, I would cut your throat sometime, you make me so damn mad!"

At that moment Bourke cried out, "A light! Starboard! It must be land!"

As Bowie went aft, the sun was just coming over the horizon, and the master of the *Carondelet* emerged from the cabin house.

"Morning, Captain Hatch," Bowie said.

"Mornin', Mr. Bowie." Hatch was a fat, affable man, with countless small lines crisscrossing his face, which was smooth-shaved except for a tangle of grizzled whiskers under his chin and about his throat.

"The lookout reports a light," Bowie said.

The captain nodded and spoke in the neighing voice of a born Gloucesterman, although he had sailed these Gulf waters for half his lifetime. "If I ain't mistook, we'll see the island soon as we have enough sun. We're under shortened canvas now—need daylight to work in on this cussed coast, navigatin' beacons bein' somethin' the people of Mexico ain't fathomed yet. I might remark, sir, that our landfall seems perfect."

He was complacent. Bowie courteously allowed that it was a surprise to him how anybody could be clean out of sight of land for three days and then stick the bowsprit of his ship square at a given point when he came in sight of the coast again.

"Navigation, sir," purred Hatch. "One of the little things a seafarin' man's got to learn."

The world brightened. Presently Bowie's eyes found the thin sliver of shore ahead, very low-lying, with a white line of surf before it. As the sun broke full over the sea, he even made out what appeared to be a collection of shacks so near the water level that he wondered what kept the big waves from breaking over them when a storm came up. Behind the island stood the tall masts of three ships.

Galvez Island, the stronghold of the old Barataria pirates. He glanced at the fat, cheerful captain—a smuggler, or he would not approach Lafitte's domain so confidently. Bowie wondered how he could look so cherubic when he had been mixed up in the kind of things he must have been.

Rezin woke slowly in the morning sun and climbed to his feet, his face wrinkled with sleep.

"That's her," Bowie told him. "The island."

In the early light Rezin appeared older than his twenty-four years. Although his pleasant face was perhaps not as clear-cut as Bowie's, or as rugged, the family resemblance was strong. Together the two brothers stood staring at the low strip of coast toward which the *Carondelet* slowly forged.

The sun was two hours high before the schooner, hampered by a flawing wind, crossed the bar and sailed around the end of the island. Bowie divided his time between watching the sweating crew work the sails and observing the nearing shore. The rise of land cut off the houses, but the ships' masts, like tall denuded trunks of trees, stood above the shore line and marked their destination.

"They've sighted us," said Hatch. He pointed out two or three small dots on the land: men, watching the incoming vessel. "They know the *Carondelet's* rigging. If they didn't, one of them big fellows behind would be shaking out canvas now to look us over."

In a slow arc the schooner rounded a point, and the inner harbor was revealed: a wide flat bay, a haphazard collection of buildings, some small boats and three ocean vessels at anchor. Nodding to the land swell, the *Carondelet* passed to the lee of the ships.

"*Slaver!*"

A rush of curious sailors across the deck to the side nearest the anchored vessels. They stood stabbing the air with their fingers, their voices an excited babel. The ship was a brig, sharp-built and black-hulled, with a prow like the beak of a bird of prey, and she was anchored between two sloops with open gun ports.

But it was not the look of her that brought that cry from the men at the rail of the *Carondelet*. Something far more insistent, more terrible, stamped her as a thing sullied and profaned by a trade unspeakable. The nostril, not the eye, proclaimed her nature. From her rose a smell abominable and penetrating, sweetish-bitter, sickening, suggesting death and putrefaction, abysmal misery and degradation, filth and pestilence and despair. The horrid stench of the slave ship, once encountered never forgotten, carried across a hundred fathoms of listless yellow water to the staring men on the little schooner's deck.

Hatch squinted. "Lateen spanker gaff," he said. "Spaniard. Didn't I tell ye? Taken recent, an' just in. I'd take bond the blood ain't washed from her decks yet."

Bowie felt a catch at his stomach. "By her stink, she's still got her cargo aboard."

The master shook his head. "Ye'd be hearin' 'em. Niggers on a slave ship keep up a sound continual—moanin', an' cryin', an' squabblin' amongst theirselves—for which ye cain't blame 'em, pore critters, crowded in the way they be—an' mebbe even prayin'—if a heathen nigger can pray. No, the brig's ridin' high an' the cargo's unshipped. But it wasn't no longer ago than yesterday."

Rezin glanced to the shore. "Where's the barracoon?"

"See the red building? That's the Maison Rouge. Lafitte's house. Half fort, half palace. Turkish carpets, carved furniture, gold plate below: cannon on the floor above, like the gun deck of a man-o'-war. Look two p'ints starboard of that an' beyond—see the stockade now?"

Rezin nodded. Then he said, "Looks like a reception committee ashore."

On the beach before the pirate town a crowd was gathering, ominous and turbulent, with now and again a flicker in it as of steel weapons catching the sun.

"If we don't suit 'em," the master said calmly, "we'll likely end up with the buzzards over yonder."

He gestured toward a spit of land some distance from the settlement. Bowie looked with sudden horror. In a rusty black cloud, great obscene birds hung about a row of three gibbets, from each of which dangled a dead man. Some of the vultures soared low, others flapped close to the ground, many roosted villainously on the gallows arms or fought with each other in ghoulish gluttony.

"Officers of the Spanish slaver, I calc'late," Hatch said. He turned to shout orders. The crew leaped to its work, striking sail and dropping hook. The *Carondelet* was at her anchorage.

Already skiffs were putting out from the beach. With a curious significance, Hatch said, "I hope Lafitte's not off on a cruise."

"Why?" asked Rezin.

"It's a hell of a lot safer when he's here. Ain't a man on that island that ain't a devil: an' ain't a devil amongst 'em wouldn't cut your heart out for the gold in your teeth."

Bowie gave a short laugh, but Rezin's face went taut, his light eyes narrowing. He was worrying, not over his own danger, but over the gold they carried. There had been six thousand dollars in the beginning. Dominique You, who arranged to have the *Carondelet* bring them to Galvez Island, had required what he called a "gratuity" for his services. Janos Parisot deducted the "option money" he had paid Bowie—and which, it developed, Bowie had spent on certain tavern and tailoring bills. Finally, Captain Hatch had demanded a cool thousand dollars for his voyage: the rankest kind of extortion, but only he would undertake the voyage. As a result only a little more than four thousand dollars was left to them, and it was carried in money belts, divided equally between the two brothers. The entire resources of the family. Rezin felt a weighty responsibility.

The first of the skiffs, pulled by four filthy oarsmen, neared. In the stern sheets sat a man in a wide black hat, long-skirted blue coat, and leather drawers which left bare his knees above his boots. He leaned his hands on the hilt of a scabbarded cutlass which stood between his feet, silently studying them. The boat scraped alongside, the rowers lay back on the thwarts, and the blue coat climbed aboard.

He was lean and sallow, with black, lusterless eyes, a sparse mustache and a brutal jaw. A sullen, reserved, capricious man. Dangerous, definitely. Was this Lafitte?

"*Buenos días, Capitán Hatch,*" he said unsmilingly.

Hatch nodded. "Captain Diego Porto, these are Señors Rezin Bowie and James Bowie, here on business. You will take us ashore?"

It was a relief at least, to the Bowies, that this was not the pirate chief. In him was every appearance of treachery.

Porto studied them coldly. "*Si, Capitán.*"

4

They stood, four aliens surrounded by hostility, on the sand beach: the Bowies, Hatch and Nez Coupé. Wherever they turned, ugly, threatening faces confronted them, faces of the scourings of the seven seas. A sour odor of unbathed bodies rose with the powdery, trampled dust. Garbs were outlandish—bizarre combinations of pilfered rich garments and filthy rags—leather, linsey, and silk often in the same costume.

The scoundrel look of the pack was heightened in an odd, unnatural way by the presence of women—Negresses, Indians, and Mexicans, as well as fair-skinned women of occidental blood. Among them were two or three girls who looked American and might have been pretty but for their unkempt hair and slattern dress.

Many of the women were big with child. Dirty-faced brats of all racial crosses were in evidence. Buccaneering and breeding went hand in hand on this island. The jet-black Congo Negress and her blond, white-skinned sister moved in full equality here, for all women were at the same level—the lowest.

All at once the snarling animal growl subsided. An avenue was opened in the crowd and through it a dark, heavy figure advanced.

Bowie saw a fattish, olive-skinned face with a sweeping mustache, black hair shot with gray under a wide black hat, an expression morose, a person slightly shabby.

With relief Hatch called out, "Captain Lafitte! I'd begun to fear ye were away! How be ye, sir?"

Bowie was oddly disappointed. He had expected a figure far more elegant and dashing than this. Lafitte said, coldly, "Very well, sir, I thank you. I hope Captain Hatch is well."

"These gentlemen," said the shipmaster, "are the brothers Bowie, and their friend, generally called Nez Coupé. You can vouch for them."

He emphasized the pronoun in a curious way, and it took Bowie two thoughts to realize that *You* in this sentence was not a pronoun at all, but referred to Captain Dominique You of New Orleans.

Lafitte permitted himself a smile, and made a not ungraceful bow. "Your servant, messieurs. I trust we may be of service."

His English was good, though with an accent slightly French. And he had one striking peculiarity: as he spoke, his left eyelid drooped in what seemed a curiously diabolical wink. Later they were to learn it was a habit, amounting almost to a physical failing of the muscles of that eyelid, so that some who had seen him thought him blind in the left eye. Bowie remembered old Dominique's lowered lid, and knew whence he had that trick.

"You must be weary from your voyage," Lafitte said. "Come, we shall make our poor hospitality available to you at once."

The crowd opened again for them to pass, but remained in a sullen mass on the beach for some time after they were gone.

Through the squalid pirate town they walked, and it was even uglier than it had appeared from the sea. Without attempt at order, shacks built of ship timbers, primitive thatched huts, even ragged tents of sailcloth, sprouted like foul fungus growths from the sand. Everywhere filth and refuse strewed the ground. A dirty, prideless settlement, fit habitation for its rascally populace.

5

Upon a slight rise—the average level of the island was not six feet above the sea at high tide—stood the Maison Rouge, a most curious structure, heavy-timbered, two stories high, and painted a blazing red. Through yawning ports on the upper floor glowered the muzzles of cannon, dominating the town and the island.

Lafitte stood politely aside at the door. They entered and gazed about with astonishment. The pirate lived in what he thought was splendor. Tapestries and paintings, looted from many a gutted ship, adorned the walls. Underfoot were costly rugs of Andalusia and Persia. Rich furniture and plate were everywhere in evidence. And all of it, every bit of this wealth and luxury, was arranged with an odd lack of taste: a barbaric, almost ferocious magnificence, but without refinement.

A gray, thin man, very delicate of features, with a high bald forehead and haunting fear in his eyes, received their hats. It was a moment before Bowie realized what made this creature's appearance shocking. He had no ears. Bowie had difficulty keeping his eyes from the vestigial stumps and beastly orifices where the ears had been shorn away. A moment later, with a second shock, he realized the man also was without a tongue.

"Food! *Vivo*—Fernan, you dog!" snapped Lafitte.

The disfigured head ducked in a frightened bow and disappeared.

"My steward," Lafitte said with a curious, cold smile. "You may be interested to know he is a man of noble birth—a Spanish grandee."

"What's he doing here?" Bowie could not help asking.

Lafitte swung his head around at him. "Fernan possesses a distinction he should cherish. He is the only Spaniard of the grandee class who ever stood in my presence and continued to live. It was my whim to have a noble-born Spaniard for a slave. He continues to exist only so long as that whim remains."

Bowie was carefully expressionless. "You appear not to like Spaniards."

The left eyelid drooped lower and the brow blackened. "I can tell you the why of that very quickly—now. But there was a time," Lafitte shot his menacing one-eyed glance at them, "when I could not tell it without cocking both pistols." He drew a shuddering breath. "I owe to Spaniards —to Spanish grandees—much. They ruined me in my youth. I saw my bride die of their brutalities." He breathed softly. "For that I have warred on Spain all my life."

Nobody spoke. After a minute, he said, "I have been called a pirate. But as I hope for salvation, they speak a slander against me when they say I am a pirate. I am a legal privateer, under letters of marque from Venezuela, which is at war with Spain. I attack no vessel of any other nation."

Strange to hear this bloody man justify himself and express a pious hope for the salvation of his soul.

The earless steward appeared with a wide silver tray, from which he placed dishes of dried fish, roast wild turkey, ham, candied fruits, bottles of vintage wine and glasses of lime shrub on a long polished table of mahogany. They sat to this and ate hungrily.

Lafitte partook of a little wine only, half smiling at his guests.

"You were hungry," he said, as if with approval.

"This is a banquet of delicacies," Rezin told him.

"I will give you a secret. This is what keeps my ranks filled with men who will fight for me. Do you know the average seaman's fare?"

"Plain, I reckon."

"Worse than plain. Salt junk, biscuit running with weevil, four-water grog—or plain water that's stood so long in cask that it stinks." He gestured at the food before them. "By contrast, we free traders of Galveztown live on luxuries—real burgundy and madeira, West India preserves, fine hams and potted tongues, dainties in unlimited variety, including the best Havana cigars without stint. Do you blame men for preferring our life to that on a rotten ship?"

It seemed understandable. But Bowie had an instinct for central reasons. "Why do you live on this low-lying island in the mouth of the bay, rather than in some better place within the bay itself?"

"A good question, monsieur. This island is, as you say, low and exposed to storms. But it protects us from a worse danger than any hurricane: the Karankahua Indians of this coast, unspeakable beasts and cannibals."

"They eat human meat? Most Indians abhor——"

"Not these. I'll tell you something that happened in our early days here. When there was a scarcity of women on the island."

"You seem to have plenty of them now," Bowie said.

Lafitte smiled. "Men must have women. Most of ours came perhaps not quite willingly—we took them from captured ships or on coastwise raids. But once here, they seem to accept us—especially after their first pregnancy." He gave a smooth, velvety laugh. "Nothing reconciles a woman to her fate like having a baby. I advise my men to get female newcomers with child as speedily as possible—advice, I may add, which they seem very ready to follow." Again his odious laugh.

Lafitte lit a cigar. "To return to the Karankahuas, generally called Kronks: my men caught a squaw on the mainland and brought her here. We didn't realize the animosity it created among the Kronks. Later four of my people crossed the strait to hunt and did not return. I took a strong party over to search for them. We heard a scream and saw a man running, pursued by the red fiends. When we fired on them, the Kronks dived into the brush, and the fleeing man threw himself gasping at my feet. He was one of our carpenters—Juan Perez, a Mexican. He had seen his comrades eaten before his eyes—*alive.*"

He blew a cloud of smoke through his lips, seeming to derive satisfaction from their horror.

"You find it hard to credit? Perez gave the details on oath. A stake was driven in the ground, fires kindled on either side, and the savages danced for an hour to barbarous music made by tapping with the fingers on their diminutive drums, blowing long cane pipes, and shaking gourd rattles. After that, one by one, each of my men was stripped naked, tied to the stake, tormented with blazing brands, and finally forced to watch while his own suffering body was cut to pieces, bit by bit, with sharp knives, each piece roasted in the flames and devoured before his eyes by the inhuman monsters—until he died."

Lafitte paused grimly. "I'll not weary you with further revolting details. Perez managed to escape. Later we gave the Kronks bloody punishment in a battle. But still none of us would be safe if it were not for the open water between us and the mainland."

Silence fell. Even Nez Coupé's face showed disgust.

A door opened and a woman entered. She was young. And beautiful. They all gazed at her with surprise. Bowie rose instinctively at her entrance, before he noticed that she was a quadroon.

Chapter Thirteen

I

"Pray be seated, monsieur." Lafitte's one-eyed smile. "The lady requires from you no such homage."

The girl's face, fair-skinned with the faintest golden tint, flushed faintly, but she stood gazing with a peculiar doglike intentness at the freebooter.

"Come sit with us, little one," Lafitte said. "Messieurs, this is my housekeeper, Catherine Villars."

Her timid glance at the company said she was eager to please them, and she took a chair opposite Bowie. Without speaking she began to nibble sparingly at the food, her eyes lowered.

Lafitte talked on as if she were not present, but Bowie found it difficult to ignore her. Every movement she made was graceful, her manners pretty, her face delicate and lovely. Yet the majesty of her beauty was veiled by the shadow of her mixed blood. Perhaps the distant strain from the African race had endowed her with that added luxuriance of dark hair, the soft fullness of lips, the tropic warmth of eyes. Such exotic perfections sometimes resulted from the combination of Creole and Negro parentages. The girl was fit for an emperor: and she could never hope to be more than she was—this aging outlaw's mistress.

"You saw the brig in the harbor?" Lafitte was saying to Rezin. "We took her off the Grand Cayman. Unfortunately, she had been becalmed in the Narrow Passage: starvation and an epidemic of flux almost swept her bare of people. Only thirty-six slaves survived of three hundred who started from Fernando Po. Her crew—Spanish, of course—was decimated also. Even before my people boarded her." He paused, with a kind of gloating ferocity. "You saw the vultures at the gibbets? They keep company with the only prisoners brought here alive."

Lafitte's eye ran around the table. Nez Coupé was occupied with his food, Hatch with his wine. Bowie and the girl both had their eyes on their plates. Rezin seemed the only one willing to talk.

"To business, monsieur?" he asked. "How many slaves would you buy?"

"It depends on the prices," Rezin said.

"I have a flat rate, the same to everyone: a dollar a pound."

"How many do you have?"

"We happen to be short. The thirty-six just brought in are all there are on the island at present."

"Their condition?"

"Not good, frankly. But that's really to your advantage, since being a little poor-fleshed, they weigh less. Most of them will soon plump up."

"We have to take them as they come?"

The buccaneer lifted and studied a solid-silver knife which had ducal arms worked into its handle. "I like to give my customers favorable terms. Especially new customers. If you will take as many as thirty, I will let you cull out the six least desirable." He hesitated. "I assume you have the money for them here?"

A glance between the Bowies. He smiled. "I fear you do me less than justice in your thoughts, messieurs. I am a merchant—not a pirate. Good will is important to me. Your money is safer in my strongbox than in your possession. I suggest you place it there at once. You'll get a receipt, a full accounting, and depend on it, more than full value."

Something about the extraordinary rascal compelled belief: besides, they were at his mercy. Rezin said, "We carry the money in belts. And the weight's something onerous. We'll gladly avail ourselves of your offer."

Lafitte nodded. "Now, as to the slaves: you'll be your own judge. And I'm moved to be even more generous. If you take the thirty, I'll throw in the six remaining—for lagniappe, as they say."

"For nothing, Captain?" Rezin's surprise showed in his voice.

"As a premium to new customers. Besides, six slaves are hardly worth the trouble of caring for."

Rezin reserved his reply. The offer indicated to him that the condition of the slaves was worse than Lafitte admitted.

2

At the other end of the table Bowie found himself very conscious of the quadroon girl. An ordinary woman of color would not have won from him a second glance, but this one was far from ordinary.

Everything about Catherine Villars was as if designed for the single purpose of catching and holding male imagination. The curve of her cheek, the sensuous fullness of her parted lips, the sleek lines of her body, all endowed her with a perilous air of provocation. Lafitte, assuredly, was a connoisseur in women.

She was conscious of his attention, for once she glanced uneasily at the buccaneer. But Lafitte was immersed in his talk with Rezin.

Bowie remembered her quick flush when Lafitte told him that she did not "require" from him the "homage" of rising. She must be both sensitive and intelligent, probably well educated also. He found himself regretting her humiliation. It was, after all, no fault of the girl's that somewhere in the past a white man had amused himself with a black woman: or that each in turn of the succeeding line of her female ancestors had experienced the uselessness of negation to white men, bearing daughters nearer and nearer to the pure white strain.

This was a phase of slavery little thought about. Not even the fanatic Abolitionists of the North, trumpeting the evils of the system, ever seemed to consider the silent fate of slave women with regard to their sex. Slave women toiled, but they also were expected to bring forth children, as many as they were able, to increase the slave population. These were not children of love, but of necessity, often conceived under circumstances cruel and bizarre: the sire perhaps a stud Negro, selected for his size and muscularity; or a vicious white overseer with a whip to back up his demand.

A curious new line of reasoning, this was, for a man reared to accept slavery with all its ramifications as a matter of course. So contrary was it to his life's training that Bowie felt almost guilty, as if it were a wrong or unhealthy conjecture. Frowning a little, he addressed himself to his breakfast.

Catherine Villars did not look up. She chewed tiny bites as if she were indifferent to them, and sipped a very little wine, well watered. One must please gentlemen, and gentlemen set great store on daintiness and delicacy in a woman. Furthermore, minuscule portions of food keep slender the figure, and the figure is important, perhaps more so than the face itself, where gentlemen are concerned.

To be a woman was not easy. To be a quadroon woman was hard. To be a beautiful quadroon woman was a lifelong abnegation. In the masculine world only the extreme ascetic who perpetually abstains from all bodily pleasure for the good of his soul equaled the unending self-denial of a woman of Catherine's kind. Her reasons for her sacrifice, however, were exactly opposite from the anchorite's: it was her body, not her soul, for which she lived that ceaseless discipline. Restraint, never-ending restraint, had been preached to her since her earliest childhood. And to what end?

Her body did not and never could belong to her, but to some man—some *white* man—otherwise its beauty and wonder were worthless. Catherine Villars accepted all this without resentment, because she was reconciled to her status as a woman, as a quadroon woman, and as a beautiful quadroon woman.

She heard the fair-haired gentleman across from her speak in a low voice, in French, "You have been on this island long?"

"Oui, monsieur." She did not look up.

"From New Orleans?"

"Oui, monsieur."

"I was recently in New Orleans."

For the first time Bowie found her full glance on him. *"Oui?* And—you found it a charming city—did you not——?"

A sickness in her voice. Homesickness.

He was sorry for her again. "Yes. Most charming——"

All at once she placed her wineglass on the table, rose suddenly, and without a word left the room. Glancing toward Lafitte, Bowie intercepted a stare so concentrated and severe that he could understand the girl's almost frightened departure.

He watched her go. He was facing the door, and just inside the hall, where nobody but he could see her, she stopped and turned. For one instant she regarded him with a strange, expressionless, but ardent curiosity, as if she were attempting to fix him in her mind and answer for herself some secret question. Then she was gone.

3

Except for his one silent stare, Lafitte took no notice when Catherine left the table. When his guests had eaten, he said, "Shall we visit the barra-coon?"

Bowie was glad for the fresh sea air as they walked across the island among low dunes, for it seemed to clear confused thoughts from his mind. The odd, straight look the girl had given him and the suppleness of her figure kept recurring to him.

There was a reason for this. Handsome quadroon girls had a certain reputation, an almost legendary significance, so that a man's mind when thinking of them turned only in one direction. Bowie's brief sojourn in New Orleans had acquainted him with the established system: the quad-roon balls which were the market places for their kind; the dignified mothers in *tignons* who put their daughters through their paces as calcu-latingly as if they were blooded mares, and chaffered for financial terms whereby these daughters, golden-skinned seductresses, bartered their virginity and a lifetime of devotion for a "protector"; and the small ménages on Palisade Street, where they went to live as *placées*.

A planter's son, making his purchase, was reasonably sure he would get his money's worth, for quadroon girls were trained as no girls of comparable virtue possibly ever were trained in the world's long history. Besides countless household skills, they were taught to be realistic without being bitter, to fall in love almost at command, and to be faithful to their paramours when they got them. Above all, the importance of their sex was instilled into them: their one mission in life to entice and hold men by the most primal of seductions—the body. It is likely that the natural warmth of their tropic blood was a mighty asset here: and it is of record that they could concede to their rivals, the white women of the great houses, all the advantage of legal marriage, and still quite easily hold their own with the men.

A girl like Catherine Villars inevitably stimulated heated thinking in a man. Bowie found it difficult to shake off, until they were almost to the barracoon.

The stockade was of rough logs set upright in the sand. At the gate lounged three men, armed and under the orders of Diego Porto, who himself awaited them with a cigar between his lips and a whip in his hand. Bowie, who had disliked Porto at first sight, found he cared even less for him on this second meeting.

Most puzzling to Bowie, in view of Lafitte's expressed hate for Spaniards, were Porto's marked Spanish characteristics: his heavy jaw, sallow skin, eyes and mustache, and particularly his manner of speech.

The man saluted Lafitte. "I have to report a little bad luck, Captain," he said in Spanish. "Two more died this morning."

Lafitte scowled. "The flux?"

"No. Starved themselves. Refused to eat. I tried to persuade them."

"You seem overready to 'persuade' at times, Diego."

Lafitte's manner and voice were impatient. Porto looked sullen.

"They'd have died in a few hours in any case," he muttered.

Lafitte grunted. "Well, I suppose the whip is a necessity when slaves deliberately try to starve themselves to death. Open."

Porto unlocked the gate, and the party filed in.

"Bad, this," Bowie heard Nez Coupé say under his breath.

Within the enclosure several crude shelters covered with dried brush furnished shade, and under these, prostrate or feebly sitting, Bowie counted thirty-four of the most miserable figures he had ever seen. All were fastened by chains to posts, but the chains were needless. Five were women, completely nude and hideous. Drawn black faces turned toward the white men with the dull animal apathy of the savage who has lost all hope.

"There they are," said Lafitte briskly. *"Nègres bruts*—but with the treatment they've had, at least no breaking camp will be necessary for them. Those Spanish swine!" He never overlooked the chance to stress his hatred of Spain, though Spaniards by no means held a monopoly on vicious treatment of slaves.

"They're a sorry sight," Bowie said.

"A little meat on their bones, monsieur! That's all you need. They'll serve you well, out of sheer gratitude." Lafitte was all merchant now, anxious to put the best light on his goods. He glanced around the barracoon. "As to those culls we spoke of, you'll probably not want them after all. I see one or two that look a little past saving."

He gestured. A very tall, impossibly cadaverous slave lay propped weakly on an elbow. His ribs resembled a basket, his joints were swollen, his wrinkled black face was emptied of all expression.

"That fellow?" said Porto. "He's one of the malingerers. Wait—I'll smarten him up a bit——"

He walked over to the prostrate figure. They really did not understand his intention, until with shockingly causeless brutality he began suddenly to lash with his whip. Long, livid weals leaped out on the black skin with every blow: but the slave uttered no sound and hardly stirred, except to throw his head weakly back and forth.

Porto seemed not to hear Bowie's furious shout, until the whip was snatched from his hand, and he was hurled back so violently that he almost stumbled and fell prostrate. When he turned on the American who had thus laid hands on him, his face had a maniacal whiteness of rage.

Bowie paid no attention to him. It was to Lafitte he turned.

"Captain Lafitte! Is this your policy in handling slaves?"

The buccaneer looked from Bowie to the slave, who now was slowly writhing on the ground with his pain.

"No, I assure you!" he said quickly. "You Spanish dog!" he snarled at Porto. "How often must I tell you that whip of yours is too eager? How would you like a taste of it on your own back? Get out of here before the temptation grows too strong in me, and I have you flogged!"

Porto's face went still whiter. Threat of a whipping was a deadly insult. And Lafitte had called him a Spanish dog. A *Spanish* dog. It was well known that Diego Porto was the only Spaniard of full blood on the island, save for the earless steward at the Maison Rouge. A dangerous distinction. Because of it, he had gone to the greatest lengths to prove his hate of his native country and all things connected with it. To have it brought up now and cast in his teeth . . . Porto wanted somebody's blood for this. Bowie felt the hate of black Spanish eyes as Porto walked out of the barracoon.

"I apologize, messieurs," Lafitte said. "Diego is a good man, though something overzealous. He'll hear more from me, I'll promise you. Meantime, please sit at the table yonder. We may as well display at once the slaves."

He was anxious to remove the impression of this unfortunate episode, so that no bad report would go back to New Orleans.

The four visitors took seats at the rough table. At Lafitte's order the men began hustling the Negroes to their feet and prodding them into line.

"Poor brutes," Rezin said. "It's enough to turn a man's stomach."

Bowie's face was stubbornly expressionless.

Past the table the Negroes began staggering, a succession of studies in human misery. Each underwent the same brutal routine of examination, turned about to show all sides, mouth forced open to reveal teeth, flesh pinched and pounded: the women, poor creatures, like the men.

One by one Bowie checked the slaves on a sheet of paper with a stub pencil. Now and again he shook his head.

"Sick," he said once, when a woman was shoved forward and stood with knees shaking, head hung, and naked breasts heaving.

"What's the matter with his leg?" he asked a little later. The slave was examined. The leg had been broken at one time, perhaps in his youth, and had healed crookedly. Bowie waved him aside.

A third displayed bloody toothless gums: his teeth had been smashed out, perhaps here in the barracoon. "He can't eat," Bowie said.

Last in line was the black skeleton Porto had whipped. His head lolled on his shoulders, and two guards supported him to keep him erect. Blood congealed in the whip marks, though it was hard to see how a body with so little flesh could have provided any blood.

"He's not really sick," Lafitte said ingratiatingly. "This fellow will recover fast enough. I've ordered a second big feed for them this evening——"

Bowie shook his head decidedly. "We have no room for him."

Pushed among the other rejects, the slave sank feebly to the ground. Rezin stared at his brother as if this were someone he hardly knew.

Frowning, Bowie studied the thirty he had tentatively selected with the unconscious callousness of the slave dealer, a role already assumed. Even the best of them were in sad condition. Ribs stood out to be counted. On the women, their dried and unfilled breasts hung like flaps of black leather.

"Not very promising," he said dubiously.

"Look at the bargain," Lafitte wheedled. "Those bucks won't average a hundred and twenty pounds to the head, the wenches not a hundred——"

Rezin had done some computing. "At weights like that we have sufficient money for the lot." He added, "What will you do with—the culls?"

Lafitte shrugged. "Oh—dispose of them."

"Knock them in the head and feed them to the sharks in the bay?"

"Something like that. They're not worth keeping."

"I suppose. But it seems pretty beastly——"

Suddenly Bowie stood up. He said, "We'll take the whole lot."

"The culls, too?" asked Lafitte.

"The lot."

"We could hardly get them home, Jim——" began Rezin.

"We're taking them, Rezin. A dollar a pound, Captain Lafitte, and the four odd ones thrown in? Have them put on the scales."

Chapter Fourteen

1

Evening sowed its shadows across the gray Gulf. Formless clouds of a muddy appearance smudged out the sunset without the final blaze of glory. Night's mystery cloaked the island, the lights from pirate shacks accenting rather than diminishing the darkness.

In the dining hall of the Maison Rouge they had finished supper by candle, and Catherine rose from the table and departed. She had not spoken to Bowie during the meal, but there are ways in which a woman can call herself to a man's attention without talk. A fleeting glance, a flutter of sooty eyelashes, these become significant. Once or twice he received from her a full look, and it disturbed him for he was almost sure she was trying to say something.

Rezin leaned over to him. "What made you take the rejects?"

Bowie frowned. "I don't know. Fool thing to do. The *Carondelet's* going to be overcrowded going back."

"It's only three days to the Calcasieu."

"Three days with good weather, but it could change. I didn't like those clouds at sunset."

"Jim."

"What?"

"You took the culls because you were just like I was—couldn't stand thinking about what would happen to them."

"I took 'em because it's a good gamble," Bowie said gruffly. "We might save 'em and make money."

"Just the same, I'm glad you did it." Rezin lowered his voice. "What about that Spaniard—Diego Porto?"

"Well?"

"He's the kind of snake who might try to slip a knife between your back ribs."

Bowie laughed mirthlessly. "Knife one of Lafitte's personal guests? Porto hasn't that kind of gravel in his gizzard."

Lafitte looked over at them. "What's your discussion, messieurs?"

"Planning for tomorrow. We think we'd better load the cargo in the morning," Rezin said.

The freebooter appeared surprised. "I'd hoped to entertain you for at least a day or two."

"We appreciate your hospitality, but time presses."

Lafitte's eyelid drooped. "In such case, we can at least make the present evening memorable. Ah, here is Fernan at last. Move sharp, *cochon,* or I'll trim your nose to match your ears!"

Upon the table the steward began to set many bottles of strange shapes and forms and labels. Quickly he cleared away the dishes of the meal and disappeared. The five men pulled their chairs closer and sampled the contents of these containers of remarkable appearance.

Nez Coupé tasted one after another of the exotic liquors, smacking his lips and making monkey faces. After an hour or two, he began to laugh, and then told a tale without beginning, middle, or end. At last he staggered away, but returned solemnly in a wide curve, swept a bottle off the table and, holding it by the neck, tacked in the manner of a ship against the wind to his room, where he fell across the bed and slept with his bottle clasped to his bosom in drunken affection.

Hatch, who had a sailor's love for rum, discovered that Lafitte's rums were rare and magnificent, and sampled them with head-waggings of approval. At last he began to sing a church hymn of his Gloucester youth in a nasal codfisher's voice, and finally slid majestically beneath the table, where, like a grampus, he snored.

Rezin tried first one, then another of the bottles with pleasure. He exclaimed over the variety and combination of tastes, and when at midnight Lafitte summoned Fernan to lift Hatch from under the table, Rezin rose to his feet with unsteady but stately dignity, and followed the two down the hall, feeling for the wall with one hand to steady himself, and so was gone for the night.

So Lafitte and Bowie remained alone, politely pledging each other, and matching drink for drink. And, becoming intimate in the manner of men growing drunk together, the pirate after a time asked what had brought his guest into slave trading.

"For the making of money," Bowie said.

"True. But there are other ways, perhaps less hazardous——"

"And perhaps more reputable?"

"Better thought of by the conventional mind at least."

"But none with as wide and quick a margin, Captain Lafitte."

"I perceive in you a realism, Monsieur Bowie, unusual in one of your comparative youth."

"I do not see that it is necessary to grow old to understand that money is of all things most important."

"An admirably forthright viewpoint." Lafitte turned this over in his mind. "You will permit nothing to stand in the way of it. Not even love or friendship, perhaps. I admire a man of my own kidney, and it comes to my mind that you and I have a good deal in common."

Bowie nodded slightly. At the time he believed Lafitte meant it as a compliment, but later he wondered if in it was a hint of the satirical. He did not then find it so palatable.

Lafitte sat back and addressed himself assiduously to his bottle, and Bowie with him. The fire in Bowie's brain burned low. It was always so with too much drink. But the fire in his belly burned high, filling him with powers that cried to be used. He wanted to rise and talk, to tell Lafitte of his ambitions and plans; he wanted to wrestle with the pirate and show his strength. But he held himself still and kept from all inclination to babble foolishly.

And so he continued, even after Lafitte began making owlish faces. At last the freebooter gazed about the room as if he had never seen it before, and as the clock struck two, conveyed himself back to his great and magnificent stateroom, locking the door as he always did, before falling in his bed like one poleaxed.

2

Bowie sat alone. He felt wonder that it was he who remained, for he knew he had drunk as much and as often as any. Liquor was working a strange and perilous pattern in his head, a coiled suggestion, dangerous as a serpent in a room.

The woman in the house. Drink brings the thought of women to a man's mind . . .

He thought of Judalon de Bornay. And the thought was bitter, with a return of that chill dreariness of spirit he had known after he knew she had laughed at him.

He thought of Catherine Villars. And this thinking was very different. Somewhere she existed in the mysterious backward chambers of this dwelling, silent, invisible, a continuing provocation. The look in her eyes . . . he was sure he could not have mistaken its deliberate meaning. She seemed to be lurking just beyond the wall, so that he sat in a sort of illogical expectancy, a burning incentive in his flesh, alone in the great hall with the hands of the clock slowly moving toward three.

Thinking was madness. Two women seemed to combat each other in his brain, weaving the pattern of emotions and dreams the world of women creates: aspiration and despair, hope and willingness to pledge life's promise, mystery that baffles yet urges on, resentment burning deep in the core of the heart, promise and disappointment, and over all ceaseless anticipation and preoccupation, whether a man wills it or not.

The room, lighted by a great candelabrum on the table, became hazy, the walls unsteady. This could not long continue. The woman in distant New Orleans receded from his thought, and his mind, twisted by the reeling fumes of alcohol, was filled with the woman who was near. She was choice beyond all expectation, and she had flown those signals to him . . .

He stood up suddenly. She was . . . just beyond that wall, through the door, a few steps down the hall. He would make her confront him face to face and say, yes or no, if she *had* called him, with her eyes . . .

A tiny spark of caution intervened. She was Lafitte's mistress. And Lafitte could be jealous. He had shown it in that one look at the morning table. Headlong foolishness was deadly perilous.

Back and forth he tramped, head lowered, face working with the liquor and the desire, not seeing the tapestry and polished mahogany, not feeling the thick rugs beneath his feet.

The third time he paced feverishly across the room and turned, he halted, almost with a start.

Catherine Villars stood by the table, across the room from him.

3

Whence she came, or how, he did not know. One moment she was not there, the next she was.

He stood dead still, for an instant thinking she was not real, but a product of the brandy heating his imagination. Then he knew that what he was staring at was life, and warm flesh.

She wore a loose green silken robe which clung to every curve of her body. For a moment she hesitated by the table, then she seemed to flow toward him, passing between him and the great lighted candelabrum. One instant her body showed in clear silhouette through the thin silken robe. Apparently it was her only garment: in that moment it was no more than a pale nimbus about the slim, beautiful form.

She passed beyond this direct revealment, and the draped figure was again substituted for the human outline. But Bowie caught his breath. In the backward vault of his brain the picture of her as she had been in that instant remained.

She spoke, a throaty whisper. "The . . . others?"

"Gone," he said. "All gone—to bed."

As if his mind had not ordered it, his hand closed on hers, bringing her to a stop.

"What are you doing here?" His voice was unsteady. "It's nearly three."

He felt her fingers tense slightly in his. "I could not sleep," she breathed. "So warm . . . I did not think anyone was awake."

You are lying, he said to himself. You are lying, and I know you are lying, and you lie knowing that I know it.

"You knew I was here," he said. No accusation, a fact.

"No . . . no . . ."

Her fingers stirred in his hand, made an effort to withdraw, whereupon, mechanically he tightened his grasp. It was a weak effort. She desisted. Drums throbbed in his veins. He drew her toward him.

His hands cupped her shoulders. Soft silk slipped under his fingers. The sculptured wonder of her body . . . She seemed mesmerized into silence, her head back, her wide eyes filled with frightened highlights.

Woman between his hands. Warm, fearful, but not resisting. He thought of another woman. Cold Creole woman, and her chilling laugh. Woman should pay him for what woman had done to him . . .

"No——" Catherine panted. "They—the others . . ."

Alarm. Only alarm, not direct negation.

"Drunk," he said. "All drunk. Dead drunk, Lafitte as dead as the rest——"

He heard her gasp, a startled catch of the breath as his hand ran down her arched back with a sleeking motion, encountered the stunning soft abundance of her hips, and drew her hard against him. Mouth crushed to mouth. Perfumed, soft as velvet, hot as fire, her lips trembled under his kiss.

Now that the die was cast, she seemed no longer afraid.

He sat up and ran his fingers through his hair, still numbed by the drink, and by his emotions. The golden girl looked at him.

All at once he leaped across the room, throwing open the door that led to the back of the house. The full length of the dim empty hall was visible. For a moment he seemed to listen, clenching and unclenching his fists.

"What . . . was it?" She was propped up, half erect, on the divan.

He closed the door slowly. "I thought I heard something. But there was nobody in the passage."

She rose with a startled movement. "Are you sure?"

"There was nobody, I tell you."

For a moment she stood as if poised to flee back to her room. Then she relaxed and pushed up from her face her tumbled hair.

"It is close in here," she said.

"Let me open the door."

"No—not the front door. That side one. It leads to a small garden with a high wall. My garden. I sometimes cool myself at night——" She looked at him. "You said they were all drunk—asleep?"

"Yes."

"I want to . . . may I talk with you?"

Strange, the preliminary. He felt sudden uneasiness, but he could not leave her after what had happened. He followed as she opened the small door and together they stepped out into the velvet night.

Behind them she closed the door. In the darkness they stood near to each other, and Bowie could just make out a dark mass of masonry wall, perhaps eight feet high, shutting off everything but the starless sky.

From the pirate town came a beastly growl accented by louder, sharper sounds: women's shrill, excited laughter; a drunken stave from a far sea chorus; two female voices in high-pitched altercation; men shouting in some tavern, a sudden roar of excitement, perhaps a fight; sobs, somewhere, a girl, alone, crying her heart out.

By night the place seemed to loose forth its whole evil of lust, cruelty, pain and murder. Lafitte's cannon, looking from the upper ports of the Maison Rouge, were no more a defense against a possible invading foe than his threat to the island itself, the visible and necessary sign of his authority.

"Galvez-town's on the move tonight," Bowie said.

She stood very close to him. "Tonight . . . every night."

He disliked this nearness; his uneasiness grew.

After a time she said, "You do not seem pleased with me. Was I not . . . pleasing?"

"Yes," he said. He wanted to let it go at that but she persisted.

"I could continue to be pleasing, monsieur . . ."

He said sharply, "What are you driving at?"

"It is not a small thing I offer."

"Perhaps not. But I'm hardly in a position——"

"You go tomorrow in your ship?"

"I do."

"Monsieur—take me with you."

He experienced a helpless feeling of alarm. When a woman is beside herself, there is no telling what she may do, to what limits of rashness she may be capable of going.

"You are thinking I am crazy, monsieur," she said calmly. "I am not crazy. And I will answer another question in your mind: I am not in love with you. And still a third: although I behaved just now like a harlot, I am not a harlot."

Bowie passed a hand across his forehead. "What are you—trying to say to me?"

"Let me tell you something of myself," she said in the same quiet voice. "I am young. Eighteen. Most women are still girls at eighteen. But I began being a woman early. I was Jean Lafitte's *placée* in my fifteenth year. I loved him and was happy, especially when my baby was born . . . I have a little son."

Somehow the idea that she had a child never had occurred to him.

"When Jean was driven from Barataria, I chose to come here with him. It was a bad choice. I have regretted it every minute of every day." In the darkness she made a gesture with her hands. "Oh, it is true that I am mistress of this house, as much above any other woman in that den of beasts out there as a star in the sky. But also I am a prisoner, as much as if I were in a walled dungeon."

He could see her dim face in the darkness, and her eyes, almost luminous with intensity. "I am forbidden to leave this dwelling, except when escorted. Rum and ruffians being what they are, it is dangerous even for the mistress of this island's ruler to venture forth alone. I know it. But it does not make my confinement less irksome. Especially since Jean has lost his joy in life."

"I had not noticed——"

"You did not know him when I first knew him, monsieur. He is growing fat and forgetting his pride in his appearance. The marks of a man disappointed and bitter. He broods much with the bottle, and though I still study to please him, I believe now he loves me no longer."

116

She gave her head a lift of bitter pride. "I have lost him: but it was to no other woman. I lost him to his advancing years, his troubles, and his failures of ambition and home."

He said, "So you'd run away from him. With me—or perhaps any other man who would take you?"

She considered the question, even his sneer. Then she said, without resentment, "Perhaps so. But not because of myself as you seem to think. It is my baby. This pirate colony is near its end: Jean himself says so. Even here they will hunt us down and he may end hanging from a yard-arm. Then what will happen to us?"

She paused, but as if expecting no answer, went on, "My baby—so little, so sweet, monsieur. Just two years old." A sigh. "Even when I took him to the cathedral in New Orleans to be christened, it was apparent to me that I had brought him into a world cursed for him. I remember the words of the baptismal record: *Pierre Villars, son of Catherine Villars, grifa libra, concubine of Jean Lafitte.*"

She gave a little unhappy laugh. "Concubine. It's a much uglier word, isn't it, than mistress? The interdict of the Church, you see—it would never recognize a connection such as mine, even in a child who was the fruit of it. Yet I am, even in the Church's Latin, *grifa libra*. Free griffe. Not a slave. Called a quadroon, but not a true quadroon. Not an octoroon even. The meaning of griffe is that my colored blood is one sixteenth or less. Hardly distinguishable, do you think?"

He agreed.

"Yet that one sixteenth of my blood is as heavy on my life as a bar of iron," she said drearily. "It will be an iron bar also for my baby son, so innocent, so filled with bubbling laughter, and with a full half of Jean Lafitte's blood in him."

Now Bowie knew full pity for her and her tragedy.

"I would die for him, monsieur, gladly, if it would benefit him. But I must not die. Nobody else would think for him and protect him. I must live and do what I can . . . a woman has so little she can do."

In his heart Bowie wished that he could help her and was moved to do so. But he was not alone involved. To risk his own life—and it would be a savage risk—was one thing. But he could not risk the lives of Rezin and Nez Coupé for any quadroon girl, however beautiful and appealing.

"You think me a wanton," she said.

"No," he said.

"You should. Unless you knew why I behaved like a wanton. You didn't ask me to come." She paused. "You didn't refuse me, either."

She waited, but he said nothing.

"It is held to be prostitution," she continued in her thoughtful low voice, "when a woman does as I have done—in hope of receiving recompense. But sometimes—when it is life or death . . ." Her voice trailed away.

He said, "Let me understand you more clearly, Catherine."

"I will. I thought I was making a payment to you, monsieur . . . before the debt was contracted. A great risk, too, for a woman to take with any man. I was going to tell you that if I pleased you sufficiently to make it worth your while . . . I would be forever what you want me to be to you, with no other obligation than this passage to New Orleans——"

He stood silent, his head bent down. As if she were trying to read his mind, to put into words his condemnation, she said almost eagerly, "You are the first. Believe me, the very first . . . I have never been unfaithful to Jean before."

"I believe you," he said, almost miserably.

A silence. Then, "I lost my gamble, didn't I?"

He said, "I can't take you. There are too many others involved——"

He stopped, looking down at her dim figure standing in an attitude of profound dejection beside him in the darkness.

At that moment a long scream of pain came boring through the night. It was followed by a faint distant snarl of laughter.

"In God's name, what was that?" he exclaimed.

"I don't know——"

Again the faraway scream, edged with agony. Then stillness.

"That was from the direction of the slave stockade!" he said.

"Oh——"

"Could it have been one of the slaves?"

"It is possible. Diego Porto is a brutal man——"

"Porto! Today I snatched his whip from him when he was beating a sick slave. Lafitte threatened him with a flogging——"

She drew a deep breath. "You mean that you left that helpless slave to the mercy of Diego Porto?" It was like an accusation.

"If he touched him——"

"Do you hear the voice any longer?" she said coldly.

No voice now. Bowie knew she was looking at him with something akin to dislike. And contempt, perhaps. Because he had not anticipated what a brute might do to a wretch who had been the innocent cause of his humiliation, and could not escape him or resist.

All at once her fingers clutched his arm.

A sound. Slight. Not far, but close. Very close. Someone was there: just on the other side of the wall . . . Three running strides, and Bowie leaped, caught the top, and with a sidewise twisting swing pulled himself up on the wall.

Running feet. Stumbling through the darkness. A figure, indistinct and dim, hurled itself away in mortal terror. For an instant the head was outlined in light shining from a window of a pirate shack. Bowie caught his breath at the strange familiarity of the shape. Then the figure was gone among the dunes.

Bowie dropped back into the garden. "He was listening. He must have heard . . . everything."

She gave a gasp. "Who?"

"Fernan. I couldn't be mistaken. I saw his head."

"Then—then—we are both as good as dead," she gasped. "He's gone to Diego Porto. They are both Spaniards and he would spy for Diego. Diego must have set him to watch you, and perhaps me."

She clung to him, looking not at him but at the blackness of the wall, as if she would pierce it with her gaze and follow the course of the earless slave, who already was lost in the night.

After a long time, he said, "Could Fernan tell anybody else?"

"I think not . . . but what need?"

"Then it is Diego Porto we must think about."

"It is too late to think now."

She did not weep. Despair was too deep for words. They went in and barred the door. She disappeared, and without bothering to undress he fell across the bed in his room. That night he did no sleeping.

Chapter Fifteen

I

Lafitte had a fancy for gamecocks, and their shrill crowing in his court-yard heralded the dawn. The Maison Rouge stirred, for it kept a sea captain's hours.

Bowie rose, shaved his chin in the bad light, and straightened as well as possible the wrinkles in his buckskin shirt and breeches. It was a silent breakfast. Hatch had bloodshot eyes and a pounding head. Lafitte drank great draughts of scalding black coffee. Not a word came from the usually talkative Nez Coupé. Even Rezin was suffering from the previous night's debauch. Bowie was as silent as the others and more depressed. His mind was weighted by self-condemnation and apprehension.

He watched Fernan move silently about the table, and tried in vain to read that haggard face. Catherine did not come to breakfast. Bowie was sure she was crouching in her own room, after a night sleepless with terror. He was sorry for her: but he hoped never to see her again.

At the recollection of the night before, he experienced the distaste of a man who has been guilty of unmanly weakness. Being drunk did not excuse him. Nothing could excuse him. He felt that he was a traitor to his brother: a traitor of the blackest and most despicable kind. The worst of it was that Rezin and Nez Coupé did not even know the peril in which they stood. Bowie wondered what Diego Porto would do, when the blow would fall. Futility and despair depressed his spirits to their lowest ebb.

He hardly heard the others, discussing in a desultory way the shipping of the slaves. Those muddy-colored clouds of the previous evening had brought intermittent rain in the night, hardly more than a mist, but driven by gusts of wind. Through a window he saw the Gulf, a rough slaty surface capped with white foam. When Rezin speculated that the weather might grow worse, both Lafitte and Hatch shook their heads.

"Little spit of rain and a half gale," said Hatch. "I calc'late it may die down by noon."

It was decided to begin the transfer of the slaves at once.

2

When they stepped out of the Maison Rouge, the air was fresh and almost cold. Across the sky a gray cloud moved unbrokenly, but the rain had stopped.

Except for the insistent shrieks of circling gulls, the soft thud of their boots on the damp sand was the only sound. To their right sprawled the shack town: the place seemed vacant, or dead with sleep. At the barracoon, however, they saw two or three figures.

"Diego's on duty," grunted Lafitte. "Usually he likes to lie abed late of a morning. It does men good to give them the rough edge of the tongue once in a while. Diego is a Spaniard, and a Spaniard is always a treacherous beast, if he thinks you're weak. What happened yesterday will make him obey me more quickly and smartly today. Observe: he comes to meet us."

Bowie felt his belly muscles tighten. The blue coat and the leather drawers with the bare knees advanced toward them on the path through the little dunes, each crowned with its tuft of sea grass and salt-water shrubs. A flight of tiny plover whistled across ahead.

In one moment, unless Porto could be thwarted, Lafitte would know everything. And to Bowie no way of thwarting him occurred.

The Spaniard came to a halt.

"Good morning, Diego," said Lafitte. "Are things ready?"

"Quite ready." Porto grinned viciously.

Lafitte was all business. "Send to the water front to have boats manned. We start shipping at once."

"As you say, Captain. But first, a word with you?"

"Assuredly. Speak."

"Alone, Captain?" On the Spaniard's face a forked look.

"I have hardly time." Annoyance in Lafitte's voice. "It is so private?"

"*Sí*. Most private."

Now it was coming. Diego Porto's revelation . . . the gibbets on the sandspit . . . the clustering black birds of death.

Lafitte nodded, struck by the Spaniard's odd, almost triumphant manner. "Very well, Diego. Excuse us, messieurs——"

He turned aside among the dunes, expecting the other to follow.

But Porto did not follow. He lay flat where he had plowed a furrow in the sand. Above him stood Bowie, rubbing the knuckles of his fist.

The thud of the blow, the grunt of the stricken man, and the sound of his body hitting the ground brought Lafitte about. Amazement turned to black displeasure as he stared at the brief tableau: Hatch, openmouthed and thunderstruck; Nez Coupé, looking from the prostrate figure to the one standing above it, as if he could hardly believe his eyes; Rezin, gaping with consternation; Bowie, apparently gone suddenly mad, scowling down at the man he had felled; Diego Porto, beginning to push himself up from the sand, in a blind, shaking fury.

Rezin found his voice. "Jim—what in the hell——"

Diego was up, dragging at his cutlass. The curved blade hissed from its scabbard. With a choked cry he swung it over his head and rushed wildly at the man who had struck him.

For Bowie it was well that his brother could act with speed and purpose and without waiting to learn what everything was about. The cutlass sang through the air, but its edge bit only sand. Again the Spaniard lay outstretched, tripped this time by Rezin's foot.

Like a great cat Bowie pounced, twisted the cutlass from the hand that held it, and rose.

Diego was up with him, panting with rage, brushing the sand from his garments.

"*Perro!* You die for this," he said thickly.

Bowie said nothing. He was watching the Spaniard as one watches a snake against a sudden lash of its fanged head.

Diego still panted, his heavy jaw hanging, a glazed stare of fury in his eye. "I am going to kill you. I myself will cut your guts out, now!" The violence of his rage seemed to affect him physically, like some stroke of illness.

Guards ran up from the barracoon.

"Seize them!" snapped Lafitte. When the two men were held, he looked upon them with a face suddenly terrible. "Now explain this!"

Diego was frantic. "That son of a female dog without virtue struck me! I claim the right to kill him!"

Bowie relaxed at the words. He had hit the man suddenly and without warning, on the long chance that his crazy Spanish pride would demand personal settlement for the blow before he informed Lafitte of Fernan's report. It had been a very long chance, but it had come off. To Diego Porto the matter had become so intensely personal that only blood, shed by his own hands, would appease him.

Yet, even in his violence, he was sure the American could make no possible explanation for that blow that would not inevitably bring out his guilt. He would permit his enemy to suffer in this dilemma, so for the moment he stood back.

"Captain Lafitte," Rezin said. "I beg you—permit me to talk with my brother. He—he must be distraught——"

"Monsieur James Bowie will speak for himself." Lafitte's drooping eyelid was almost closed. "What he has done cannot be overlooked."

Bowie was ready. "I struck this man—and I will kill him if he insists—for a reason sufficiently good."

"*What* reason, monsieur?" Lafitte was deadly.

"This man—last night—killed a slave, my property! If you do not believe me, look in the barracoon!"

Tense silence followed the accusation. Surprise and something else showed in the Spaniard's face. For this he was not prepared.

"How do you know this?" Lafitte demanded.

"That is beside the point," Bowie said. "Look in the stockade!"

Lafitte turned grimly. "Diego?"

A sick apprehension seized Bowie. He had made a guess, in fact everything was based on a guess, his and Catherine's. Could he have misinterpreted that scream the night before?

On the Spaniard's face was the look of a man who for the first time sees an inescapable pit that has been dug for him. A blow had been given him in public. His notions of honor would not now permit him to make accusations which might appear as an attempt to escape the obligation to wipe it out. Diego Porto was cruel and treacherous: but a Spaniard is not a coward.

"A slave did die last night," he told Lafitte. "The sick one."

"Where is he?"

"I had him taken away."

"Buried?"

"*Seguramente.*"

"I am going to the bottom of this," Lafitte said. "If you have damaged the property of these gentlemen, you will pay for it twice over. Have that body dug up. It will reveal the manner of death——"

The Spaniard raised a hand. "I can spare you the trouble. The man was mutinous. I punished him last night——"

"He died under the lash?" asked Lafitte harshly.

"He died. That is enough. And I will pay for him." Porto looked about him with a white, set pride. "But first this *perro* will answer to me!"

For the first time Bowie drew a full breath. It was settled. He owed very much: to his brother and Nez Coupé, safety; to Catherine Villars, an obligation. Two men on this island knew that which would mean death to himself and all of these. He must stop the tongue of this one. The other—had no tongue.

A dark shadow in his brain. To die, if he could take the other with him, was a thing to be desired. For the second time in his life, he contemplated his end and found it to be without importance. Death could be accepted easily . . . if there were some way to make other matters sure.

On a sudden his eye lit upon the leather breeches his enemy wore. He himself was in buckskin. A thought came and he looked out toward the beach. There in the sand, a great rough log lay, thrown up by some storm in the past.

As if it were another, he heard himself speaking. "Since I am to fight this man, I will show you some sport, Lafitte."

"In what way?"

"A different thing in combats. Do you see that big drift log?"

"Certainly."

"Place us on that log, astride, knee to knee, facing each other. Nail us down to it by our leather breeches. Strongly so neither can get up or elude the other. Strip us to the waist. Then give us dirks—and the signal to begin."

"God, no—Jim——" said Rezin.

Even Lafitte was shocked by what seemed the almost crazed ferocity of these terms, but his eye gleamed with whetted interest. He had made a lifetime profession of death, and here at last was a novelty in it. One of the guards stole away toward the town.

"What do you say, Diego?" asked Lafitte.

"That it is a barbarism worthy of this American scum! If he wants to fight, let him stand up to me with cutlasses like a man!"

"Knives—and nailed to a log. My life against his," said Bowie softly.

"Nailed to a log . . ." The words appeared to have a special charm for Lafitte. His one-eyed smile had gone cruel. "You challenged this man, Diego. It is his to make the conditions. Prepare to fight!"

3

A scurrying of people across the dunes from the town, where word of something vastly to the taste of connoisseurs in death had been brought by a guard. In an ever-growing circle the crowd banked about the log which Lafitte was inspecting, women screaming for a place in the vanguard, their high female voices adding a final horror to the spectacle.

The log had once been a mighty cottonwood, three feet through the trunk, growing on a bank far up the Mississippi. Uprooted by a flood, the tree had been carried down the whole tortuous length of the river and spewed out at last into the Gulf—a thousand-mile journey. Every root and branch had been stripped away, save for a few great stubs which acted as grapples, to fix the log in the sand where it had been tossed. The wood in it was not rotted or soft.

Lafitte almost purred. "Nails will hold here."

From the barracoon a guard brought a handful of square-wrought spikes and a hammer.

"Take your places, messieurs," commanded Lafitte.

Bowie peeled off his shirt. More slowly, Diego stripped to his waist. The Spaniard was shaken with sudden heavy misgivings. Matters had not turned out as he had planned.

He began to wonder if he still should try to tell Lafitte his story, but the opportunity of speaking in private was past. To blare out his chief's dishonor in the hearing of all these people would be an insanity. Bowie would hang, to be sure. Perhaps the other *Americanos* also. Catherine would die, without question. But what of the man whose indiscretion made the entire matter public property, so that all his life Lafitte might be laughed at behind his back? That man might be flayed alive.

Porto decided. This *Americano* must die first.

Torsos bared, they bestrode the log, black glare of hate met by pale stare of deadly purpose. The guard drove deep the nails that fastened them by the slack of their leather breeches to the solid bole.

Three hundred pairs of eyes compared the antagonists. Bowie's body, its muscles standing out like the gnarled roots of an oak, was the more powerful. His face, also, was something to think about, lips tight and almost thrust forward, nose pinched above and flaring at the nostrils, lines deep-bit from eye to cheek, eyes themselves slitted, unwavering. A fighting visage frightful in its separation from any self because of the utter concentration on killing which possessed him.

Yet the Spaniard was strong also, compact, his chest black with hair, and very quick and vicious. Not brawn but lethal skill would decide this combat. Strength against ferocity. The bull against the wolf.

The voices of the pirates rose, haggling over wagers, the odds against the unknown and disliked stranger. They presented an unbroken rank of faces, avid with bottomless cruelty.

Lafitte was examining two straight-bladed sailors' dirks. Only a half-inch difference in their lengths: but many saw that he gave his lieutenant the longer weapon.

The freebooter stepped back. "Now—*fight!*"

The lash of a cobra's head: Diego's whetted blade curved in a gleaming arc at Bowie's armpit. The American threw himself back and aside. Steel just bit his chest. An angry cut, bleeding already, but not deep, severing no muscles.

All the Spaniard's force was in the blow, but missing its full target, it carried past. This was good, for backstroke might be as deadly as stab. And only a heartbeat between them.

In the heartbeat Bowie acted. His fingers clutched for the other's knife wrist: closed on it with a numbing pressure. The bull was exerting himself.

With his free hand, Diego snatched for the prisoned knife.

Too late. Bowie's blade sank deep in his side.

Scarlet blood-gush. A hideous screaming of hate and pain from the Spaniard.

For the second time Bowie struck.

The scream changed to a coughing, a horrid choking of lungs with blood. Porto fell over sidewise, dangling from the log by the nailed leather breeches, black eyes swiftly glazing, knife lost from numbed fingers in the red sticky sand.

From the crowd arose a single, concerted yell of surprise, followed by the babel of many voices.

Bowie sat back slackly while the nails which fastened him were drawn. Freed from the log, he rose. His chest was bleeding. Rage was gone clean from him.

He looked down at his dead enemy, the black Spanish head dangling to the ground, mottled with bloody sand.

No words to say. He turned and stumbled toward the Maison Rouge.

"Where is Fernan?" Lafitte said.

"I do not know," said Catherine. "I brought the basin myself."

On her knees in the Maison Rouge, she was bathing and bandaging Bowie's wound.

Lafitte looked on, approving. To him the conduct of this entire affair, ending so suddenly in a flicker of blades and blood, had appealed greatly. He had seen decision made before action; anticipation that included fore-knowledge of what the antagonist would do, or at least a shrewd accurate guess; movements which did not follow or adapt, but were implicit in a plan. To Bowie he gave the silent sophisticated admiration of the expert player to the champion.

He stirred. "Fernan!"

He rose. "The earless dog! He should have wine here for us now! His back will smart for this!"

He strode back through the hall to find his servant.

They were alone. Bowie said in a low voice, "What will you do?"

"Nothing," Catherine said.

"Fernan?"

"He cannot speak."

"He can write."

"He had only one man in the island in whom he confided. That man is dead. I can only hope——"

He was silent. She swathed bandages over his shoulder and under his armpits. Red spots still showed, so she added more.

She seemed very small, kneeling by the basin with its pink water. She did not look up, did not meet his eye.

He said to himself, she is afraid, deathly afraid.

Quick steps came down the hall. Lafitte stood before them.

He said, in an odd voice, "Fernan."

They turned toward him in dread, the kneeling girl and the man with the white bandages on his naked chest.

After everything else . . . Fernan. What had Fernan revealed to Lafitte?

Bowie felt the girl's hand creeping up the side of his leg, clutching his knee. With a shifting quick glance his eye went about the room for some weapon with which he might strike down the pirate before the extremity.

He heard his own voice, as from a distance.

"What about Fernan?"

"He's dead."

Catherine caught her breath almost with a sob.

"What . . . did you say?" she said faintly.

Lafitte's face darkened with fury. "He took this way to spite me, the Spanish dog! Hanged himself in his quarters. I found him just now in there. Still warm—but dead. *Dead!*"

He seemed to feel it a reflection on his hospitality. To Bowie, he said, "I regret that a thing like this should happen——"

"Don't disturb yourself," Bowie said in a flat, distant voice.

"I'll have the carcass taken away." Lafitte walked to the door.

Again they were alone. Bowie stood up.

"At least you need not fear now."

That was all. Not even a handclasp.

She watched him put on the buckskin shirt.

He walked out of the door, down to the water front where a boat was waiting to take him out to the *Carondelet.*

Chapter Sixteen

I

The canebrake had never felt the sharp pruning knife of civilization. Tall and slender, the canes lifted their feathery tops a good twenty feet above the mucky underfooting, growing so closely that passage through them was won only by hacking a way, or by following an animal trail made by deer and wild cattle going to water.

Down such a trail walked a tall Negro in a blue shirt and faded trousers, with a whip in his hand and a smoothbore musket on his shoulder. He was Sam, Bowie's servant. Behind, in irregular line, came thirty black figures, naked save for cheap linsey breeches. Each carried on his head, in the manner of the African savage, a parcel containing provisions, one cotton blanket, and a set of leg irons with which he himself was confined in camp at night. This was a self-sustained party on the march.

The last man in the procession was Bowie. He wore buckskin and carried a rifle in the crook of his arm and a snake whip coiled in his hand. It was October of 1819. More than a year had passed since he had said good-by to Catherine Villars that morning after he had killed Diego Porto, and Fernan, the steward, had hanged himself—a year and three more journeys to Lafitte's island.

A year had made Bowie older in his look. New lines were etched about his mouth and eyes by the acid of his experiences. Four slave runnings do not add sweetness to the visage. He was hardened. The business of trafficking in human flesh at best was brutal: the whip had to be used because it was the only thing a slave understood. Bowie did not particularly relish seeing his lash bite into the wincing back, but he had flogged many men and accepted it as an inevitable part of his trade, to be done when it had to be done.

This had been a bad trip. He had used the whip, or Sam had used it, with irritating frequency, because the slaves, not knowing of the ceaseless danger of lurking Karankahuas, and having no idea of where they were going, developed a tendency to travel as slowly as they dared, with a backward eye on him: almost deliberately trying his patience as far as it was safe to do so.

Bowie had not realized the strain of it, until now that the danger was over. They had just crossed the Sabine River, the end of the country of the cannibal Kronks. He sighed and squared his shoulders.

Along the narrow runway the slaves walked in single file. Thin stems of the canes drooped to each other above, forming a beautiful and continuous canopy through which the sun did not penetrate, so that they moved in a sort of twilight. Overhead the canes creaked and moaned as they rubbed together, and their leaves whispered.

Ahead was sunlight, the first sign of the canebrake's end. The slaves quickened their pace. It was late, they were weary, and camp would be made here. A few more rods, the canes thinned rapidly, then the growth ceased. Up a rough slope moved the line of black figures, to a grass plain covered by scattered groves of trees. Near one of these mottes water gleamed. The slaves put down their burdens and squatted on the ground in the shade of the live oaks.

Bowie made a quick inspection. The water of the stream which ran into the central swamp of the canebrake was clear at this point. Plenty of dry wood was visible and the foliage above gave shelter. He nodded. At once, under Sam's supervision, the slaves began making little cooking fires and preparing their supper of boiled rice.

Dusk fell. Where Bowie sat on a rough protruding root, Sam brought food: a little bacon and corn pone.

"Everything shipshape, Marse Jim," he reported.

Bowie nodded and ate from his tin plate. He was tired, and Sam was tired. The whole caravan was tired.

"Shall I shackle 'em now, Marse Jim?"

Bowie thought a moment and shook his head. "Let 'em sleep easy. They won't run away now—nowhere to go. Time enough to iron 'em when we reach the border."

Night settled down. Little fires flickered out. In their blankets the slaves rolled to sleep. Bowie also lay down and pulled about him a blanket. He and Sam took turns on watch, Sam the first half of the night, Bowie the last. He saw Sam, the musket across his knees, sitting beside a dying fire.

2

Bowie did not sleep at once. Now that the necessity had passed for continual alertness, thoughts tumbled through his head, crowding for room.

His brothers would be a little surprised when he came in with this gang. Lafitte might be a little surprised too, if he knew about it, though he did not think he would ever see Lafitte again.

This was his first slave venture alone. John and Rezin had told him they had had enough. Thus far, their smuggling had been successful, with legal titles to the slaves obtained from a disreputable customs inspector they had bribed. On three voyages they had cleared a profit of sixty-five thousand dollars. But luck, John and Rezin felt, could not last forever. Both had wives now, and families and money together make some men cautious. Bowie's brothers desired to cease tempting fate.

He did not blame them, nor could he explain to them the reason for this last trip. Partly it was Dr. James Long; partly the old urge to gamble; partly something else.

He remembered the day Dr. Long came to Opelousas, a big, important-looking man, trading on an acquaintance with General Andrew Jackson and a relationship by marriage with General James Wilkinson. He had a courtly manner with women and a certain magnetism to some men, and in the Bowie house he was pleasant and filled with compliments. He had heard, he said, of their position in the community, and also that they had some knowledge of Texas, and he was desirous of enlisting their aid for an expedition he was projecting.

The nature of his expedition? To free from Spanish tyranny the people of Mexico, then seeking to throw off the yoke of foreign oppression. He was quite sonorous as he said this.

When Rezin remarked that the few Mexicans he had encountered seemed lukewarm, to say the least, toward having freedom conferred on them, the visitor said oh, and ah, and there would of course be great honors and rewards for those participating in his venture, if it should be successful, of which he was assured.

The Bowies remained unimpressed.

At the end, the conversation fell off into polite generalities and Dr.

Long, disappointed, prepared to depart. But a name came into the talk at the last moment that interested Bowie. Some of the Natchez men interested in Long's expedition were named. One was Cabanal.

"You mean Philippe Cabanal?" Bowie asked.

"The same. You know him? He has put money into this effort and would have joined us had it not been for his marriage."

"I knew him in New Orleans. I had not heard he had married."

Dr. Long smiled with flashing white teeth. "Philippe married very fortunately, I am told. Into a New Orleans family—the de Bornays. I had the honor of a cotillion with his lady at a ball recently. Can't say I blame a man for hesitating at leaving such a bride. Well. I must get back to my inn. Several await me there. If you change your minds, gentlemen, I'll still be there in the morning."

Bowie had had a good deal to think about that night. So Judalon had married Philippe after all . . .

His own hot flush of anger at this caused him to examine his mind. Was he still infatuated with Judalon? No. He could tell himself with all sincerity, no. How could a man be in love with a woman so shallow, vain, and selfish? She was not even very beautiful.

Wait. Perhaps that was not fair. Yes, one had to concede her beauty. It had, as a matter of fact, held him in a kind of servitude for months. But it was, thank God, over now. If he had any feeling toward her at all, it was hatred: hatred for her self-possession, for her measureless superciliousness, for her beauty and its devilish power to make him uncertain of himself . . .

Next morning, very early, he was at Dr. Long's tavern.

With exasperation and amusement, he thought back on Long's expedition into Texas in which he had participated: the march to Nacogdoches; the bombastic proclamation of a "Republic"; the assumption by Long of the title "General of the Texas Armies," as if he had a hundred thousand men instead of merely two hundred; and finally, the proposal to visit Lafitte's island and interest the pirate in the "cause of freedom."

This was the point at which Bowie's part became important. The expedition to Galvez-town numbered thirty men, including himself, Sam, and "General" Long: enough to discourage spying Karankahuas. While his companions waited ashore, Bowie swam out to the island.

It was a different place, now. Since his last visit it had been smitten by a hurricane which had all but obliterated the settlement. Catherine Villars, still suffering from injuries she had received in the storm, was with her child aboard an anchored ship.

Lafitte sent a boat to the mainland for the ambassadorial party: but "General" Long and his proposals only amused him. He filled his guests with food and wine and compliments, listened to their promises which he assayed as worthless, and dismissed them in a state of confused wondering as to what he intended to do for them, which was exactly nothing. To Bowie he privately imparted that "General" Long was a *chapulin,* that is, a cricket: which is to say someone upon whom it is difficult to keep the thumb.

Bowie did not return to Nacogdoches with Long and the others. He remained with Sam on the island. One visit he paid to Catherine, who was thin and haggard, old it seemed in a few weeks. She told of the terror of the hurricane which had swept waves clear across the island. The weight of the cannon had collapsed the upper floor of the Maison Rouge, killing many women who had gathered in the building for safety, and injuring her own back so she still could hardly walk. She said that Jean Lafitte had been magnificent, rescuing survivors, giving away all his own possessions to alleviate misery after the storm. He would leave Galvez Island very soon now: the American navy had given him warning. She and her child would sail with him.

After that Bowie prepared to return to Louisiana. He had money, and Lafitte had thirty slaves, newly brought in from Angola. He offered to buy them.

"How will you transport them?" Lafitte said. "We have no ships."

Bowie said, "I'll take them overland."

"That's Karankahua country," Lafitte said, then seeing that Bowie was determined, added, "Very well. This is a strong gang of blacks, but you had better be careful. If *les sauvages* discover that your slaves are unarmed, they will catch them and eat them. Perhaps you, also."

He ordered the slaves set ashore with Bowie and Sam, and said goodby. It was the last Bowie ever saw of Lafitte.

Bowie could feel sleep coming to him. He listened to the rustle of the leaves, and the sleeping sounds of his camp. He must get some rest. Sam still sat by the embers with his musket. Bowie willed himself to slumber.

3

Malange . . . Malange . . . Malange.

The slave repeated it to himself: it was his name. They had asked him his name when he came down from the interior of Africa in the slave caravan with an ironwood yoke about his neck. He had told it proudly, for Malange was a chief's name. Since that day he had been called many things, but he always remembered to call himself Malange, the name he had borne when he was free and a Ganguella.

Malange could see the white man's Negro, Sam, nodding heavy-eyed beside the fire. Sam did not think it necessary to be alert; the Indian danger was past, and Bowie himself had said the slaves would not run now. Everyone was sleeping, and Sam was as tired as the rest. His head drooped forward.

Malange lay silently watching him. He was not born a slave. The other slaves, sleeping about him now, knew that he was of chief's blood and respected him accordingly.

He remembered the mountains of Angola: and his village with its high stockade of sharpened poles, the wood smoke and smell of the cooking pots, and the laughter of women; and the drums when the *ochingange* dances were held; and the great hunts when the high grass blazed and the spearmen pinned the antelope and wart hogs that burst from the smoke.

As clearly as if it now sounded in his ears, his mind heard the plaintive song of the women as they pounded meal for the evening. Memory of the song brought back to Malange the happiness of his youth. He thought also of his brother, Samatiete, the brave; and of Kalete, the faithless, his brother's wife; and of Chete, the treacherous friend.

Because of Kalete's faithlessness and Chete's treachery, Malange was a slave in this far country. For Katema, the blind king of the Ganguellas, had sent a caravan to trade at Benguella on the coast, and Samatiete commanded the caravan. On the day Samatiete left, he spoke with Malange, then a weedy youth of eighteen, and explained his trouble. Though wedded less than two months he must leave Kalete, and he enjoined Malange to keep strict watch over her.

Responsibility for Kalete proved not easy. Malange knew her before her marriage: she was his own age, and among the women of the village none was more desired, so that Samatiete had paid over for her to her father seven cattle—more than the conventional price—with trade goods for good measure. But she had in her a secret fire, so that she could not keep her thoughts from men.

First, after Samatiete's caravan was gone, she worked on Malange. And when she saw that he was true to his brother, she became scornful of him, so that he remained out of her sight as much as possible. Then, one day, he found her with Chete in the hut—Chete, the hunter, Samatiete's best friend, and Kalete, Samatiete's wife. They did not see Malange enter the hut. Only when he took from the wall a shovel-headed spear, leaning over the pallet, did Kalete behold him, her eyes suddenly widening with terror.

The spear, however, was not for her. As for Chete, he did not know what was taking place, until the spear entered his back, shrewdly turned

132

so that it slipped between the ribs, and his blood poured over the woman as he died.

The slaying was for Samatiete's honor. Yet, while his hand felt the shaft of the spear still vibrating in Chete's death agony, Malange knew he was doomed. To the Ganguellas, seduction of a woman was not of sufficient importance to warrant the death of a man. Yet he knew he could not have done otherwise: he had heard Samatiete's voice when he spoke of the woman, his brother's heart was wrapped about her.

Ganguella law was condign. A murderer must die as he had put to death the man he slew. If by poison, he drank poison. If by a blow, he died by a blow. It was decreed that Malange should have a shovel-headed spear thrust into his back to let out his life.

But there was an alternative. Sometimes a murderer was sold into slavery, his price going to the family of the murdered man as blood money. Katema, the king, listened to the plea of Samatiete when the brother returned and permitted in the end that Malange be thus sold. So Malange, chained and with the heavy ironwood yoke chafing his neck, marched to the Portuguese slave compound at Loanda. Many, many times he wished he had instead felt the spear in his back.

Malange, who was of the blood of chiefs, looked again at the black man who had been set to guard him, and saw that he was asleep with his musket on his knees. He reached over a hand and nudged the slave next him. The man woke without a sound, his eyes wide. Malange signed to him in the moonlight that freckled the ground under the tree. The slave nudged the man on the other side. None of the Angola natives hesitated in obeying Malange, who was of chief's blood.

4

"I should have let you leg-iron them," Bowie said.

Sam relaxed: his master's voice was moderate, not angry.

"How long have they been gone?" Bowie glanced up at the stars.

"Ah—don' know, Marse Jim."

"It's still hours to daylight. We'll have to wait till dawn to see which way they headed."

At first light they were up for a quick breakfast. When Bowie found that the trail of the fleeing slaves led back into the canebrake, he swore. "The fools! I got them through the Kronk country, and they head right back into it!"

Without hesitation he followed the trail, and Sam followed him. Sam did not like to follow. His eyeballs rolled and his flesh quivered at what he had heard of the Kronks, and the living cannibalism of the wraithlike hobgoblins whom nobody ever saw until it was too late. But he did not dream of disobeying.

As if welded by common apprehension, the fleeing slaves kept together, leaving a well-marked track which Bowie and Sam followed at speed. Before night they found traces of a camp, and Bowie said they were gaining: might overtake the fugitives next day.

But they did not. All that day they pushed into unknown country. Land rose through hills into an almost unbroken plateau, wide seas of plains, scattered mottes, rivers fringed with trees, everywhere the distances extending over horizons wider than any they had ever seen. For hours they would toil to gain the nearest low knob of a hill, to see what would be disclosed from its top. And when they reached that, they would see other hills infinitely remote beyond it. A great, bewildering country. Sam slunk at Bowie's heels like a scared bird dog. To Bowie, however, it was an inspiration: never had he seen a land so big. He could fit into a country like this. He walked with a freer stride, his eyes on the horizons of the great empty landscape.

No sign thus far of Kronks. Once, circling buzzards brought them to the bones of a stray buffalo, hamstrung and devoured by lobo wolves. It had been dead for days, but here the starving slaves had stopped and picked the putrid carcass for a little food.

That afternoon a bluish-gray cloud came out of the north, spreading rapidly across the sky, and a thin cold rain began falling, driven by a bitter wind. They bivouacked in a sheltered arroyo and abided the night. Morning was a dripping grayness, neither dark nor daylight. Rain continued, not hard but steady, and the wind came in raw gusts, so that Bowie pitied the slaves, half naked in this inclemency.

Now the trail was wiped out, but they continued up the valley in which they had been traveling. By night the storm ended, just in time to reveal the setting sun in fiery splendor.

Early in the morning they were afoot again, hoping to find some sign. Water lay in shallow yellow sheets at every depression, and the streams ran bankfull.

Near one of those little temporary lagoons, Bowie came to a stop. In the mud was a human footprint, made since the rain. But the slaves were barefoot. This foot wore a moccasin.

"Kronk," said Bowie. Sam shivered.

Bowie increased his pace, and Sam followed as close as he could. More than any other thing he dreaded being alone. In an hour Bowie halted again. Here half a dozen Kronks had passed. He imagined the ghastly,

scarecrow figures, hardly human, terrible in their abysmal savagery . . .
trotting along in file on some hurried errand.

Very cautiously, they began to follow the trail of the Kronks.

After another hour the trail led to burnt-out fires, embers soaked black
and cold by the rain—a camp of the slaves.

"We're too late," Bowie said. Sam expected him to turn back then, but
he went on.

"There's the trail of the gang," he said. "In a bunch as usual. They
don't know about the Kronks yet. Here the Kronks go. They haven't
sighted the gang, but they know about them."

They kept below the crests of hills, studying each open stretch before
crossing it. Another hour passed.

"Only five Kronks now," Bowie said. "One's gone off, to fetch the rest
of the tribe. God help those poor niggers . . ."

The slave trail was plain and easy to follow.

"Moving slow here," Bowie told Sam. "Maybe they think they're out
of danger of being caught. Or tired. Look yonder! Something's scared
them. Here they stood in a tight knot, talking over something they've
seen. Now they're off at an angle—they're running."

They followed. "I thought so," Bowie said. "The Kronks."

Moccasin tracks. Many moccasin tracks. Some of them right over the
fleeing barefoot tracks.

"Running them toward that arroyo," Bowie said. "That means another
bunch was waiting there. Look at that."

The tracks of Indian and Negro became jumbled. There was no sign
of struggle or bloodshed, but the evidences of surrender were clear.

"They gave up," said Bowie. "I reckon they thought it was going to be
just another kind of slavery."

He halted, and stood staring.

Far ahead, beyond a low ridge, buzzards swooped and soared. No need
to go there. He knew what he would find: scorched stakes, a place of
fires, ground stamped hard by feet of ghoulish dancers in a night-long
orgy, mangled horrors, over which the buzzards now swung and fought.

5

Not yet had Opelousas, the sleepy little town, awakened. For a moment
Bowie stood at the door of his father's white house, his eyes cast down
in the dawn. Sam dropped his bundle on the porch and went silently
around to the back. Slowly Bowie pulled the latchstring. The house was
dark inside, the shutters closed.

He heard someone moving. His mother came from her room in a wrapper, a kerchief about her head.

"Hello, Jim," she said.

"Hello, Ma."

"Travel all night?" Her eyes took in his bundle, his rifle leaning against the wall, his weariness.

"You're ga'nt, Son," she said. "We'll get you something to eat."

When she aroused a servant and gave instructions, she pulled open the shutters. He sat, wearily watching her, and she took her rocking chair, the one she always sat in.

She asked no questions. Instead, she said, "Jim, your pa's gone."

With stupid astonishment, he said, "Pa? When?"

"Four weeks last Thursday. Sudden, the way it came. A fever and a coughing—and it was over."

The strong contours of her face dissolved in aching sorrow.

Bowie did not know what to do. She did not weep. She sat across the room, erect, that one quick change of expression her only evidence of feeling for the man who had been her life for more than thirty years.

So the old soldier of the Revolution was dead. Bowie had been home rarely in recent months, but his father called him "boy" to the end, and was wont to shout orders like a sergeant major, so that everyone in the house jumped to obey him. Still hanging by the fireplace was the ancient cavalry saber, a reminder of Marion's Swamp Raiders. He had been a good deal of a man, the old chief of the Bowie clan. From him this son, sitting with his mourning mother, got his size and strength, for even when the sire began to fail, so that he sometimes drowsed between sentences of a conversation, he still had the shoulders of a buffalo, and no man ever forgot his fierce blue eyes or his roaring voice.

"Ah well," said Bowie's mother. " 'The Lord giveth, and the Lord taketh away. Blessed be the name of the Lord.' "

Scripture came quick to her tongue.

A black servant girl at the door announced breakfast. Pleasant smell. Bowie ate ravenously. When he was filled, his mother said, "What happened, Jim?"

"Bad luck. I lost thirty. Killed. Eaten."

"Eaten?"

Bowie nodded. "The Karankahuas. They're cannibals."

She listened silently to his story. At the end he said, "I'm feeling pretty bad right now, Ma."

"It was bad, Son."

He was laboring with himself, staring at the floor, his big hands twisting together. He did not know of Malange, or that it had required some-

136

one of Malange's blood and nature to prompt the wild flight of the slaves. He had never been able to make himself completely indifferent to slave feelings, as a confirmed slave dealer had to become, and his inward spirit was tortured by a sense of being responsible for what had happened to child-minded people whom he should have watched over more closely.

She let him talk himself out before she said, "You'd better get some sleep, Son."

The mother sat by his bed, hoping he would get the tearing conflict out of his soul. If he would only break . . .

After a time she sighed. He would not break. He could not weep. The demon that was in him would not out. It would drive him on . . . to what ends?

The Vidalia Sand Bar, 1827

*T*he young American nation was gathering itself for its next great outsurge into the wilderness in the summer of 1827. About this there was nothing planned: no weighing and plotting by cabinet ministers or rulers, as might have been true in the older, more cynical, and wearier world of Europe. It was a movement of population as spontaneous, as blindly instinctive, and almost as unthinking as the great herd migrations of animals—the thousand-mile north-and-south yearly trek of the Arctic caribou, for instance, or the rush of the Norwegian lemmings down to the sea. Yet, even though unplanned, the inward urge of a race is forever more irresistible than the schemes of statesmen, however far-sighted, ambitious, or ruthless.

In that summer the frontier knew one of the great historical moments of opportunity. West of the Mississippi River lay uncounted millions of unoccupied acres, and a nation of farmers, thinking of wealth chiefly in terms of land, desired them. Men with courage and luck might get a quick start in life by plunging into the unknown. Passing well, the wagon families knew the dark loneliness, the privations, and the dangers they must face: yet they piled up along the great river all the way from its confluence with the Missouri to its Delta, and gazed across the muddy flood with hungering eyes.

At Natchez, in July of 1827, the river front was covered with cargo boats for miles, moored sometimes three and four deep, their crews fighting and cursing each other, a symptom of the yeasty stirring of a people on the move. And always more flatboats were floating down, the boatmen little better than savages, long-haired and bearded to the eyes, their naked torsos burned by the sun to the color of old mahogany, their wool hats, linsey trousers, and spiked brogans outlandish. Night and day they had drifted, running the peril of sawyers, snags and towheads, and of murderous river pirates; sleeping and eating in sun or storm on the open deck, subsisting on coarse meat and bread devoured out of a common pan or kettle set down among them as if they were so many dogs.

Now at last the boatmen, with an ardent eagerness, saw before them Natchez, the promised end to their long adventure and endless privation. They craved a great carouse, and here it awaited them. What if, in a single night, they flung into the hands of sharks and harlots and tavernkeepers the earnings of weeks of hardship on the river—it was their money, wasn't it? Their right to spend it as they chose? And if they chanced to be knifed in the back and tossed into the night-blackened flood, why that was their business too, and nobody took the trouble to ask what happened to them.

But Natchez—what was it? A city? No, two cities: as separate and distinct as if they were a hundred leagues apart.

Sweeping in a mighty curve, the Mississippi had carved out from its eastern bank a lofty cliff of white and gray rock, at the foot of which, on a narrow strip of mucky ground, stood a huddle of weathered shacks and crumbling brick buildings, stinking with evil. This was the only part of Natchez the boatmen ever saw. Here was the poisonous mecca of sin and debauchery: here crime was habitual, cheating and violence normal, bestial drunkenness universal, death an incident, and harlotry the sole occupation of women. Those women, hard and brazen, equal to any depravity, expecting no kindness from any man, but greedy for the gold of every man, were as good an index as any of the vicious population in that turbulent eddy on the river bottom. This was Natchez-under-the-Bluff.

Through the ruffian settlement, Silver Street raked its narrow course, crisscrossed by dark alleys, each a menacing ambuscade. But Silver Street did not stop there. In a steep slant it climbed the face of the cliff, providing a link with the world above. And there, on top of the bluff, calm and secure, stood the pillared mansions of the rich cotton planters, with their velvet lawns and stately trees, the steepled churches, the courthouse, the ordered shops and cafés.

There gentlemen in rich garb, with stately manners and keen eyes, strolled, or drank fancy drinks, or laid bets, or dealt in slaves and cotton, or paid extravagant compliments to the ladies of their acquaintance whom they met. And here again the women struck the keynote: dainty women, dwelling in unmatched luxury and ease, waited upon by whole retinues of black servants, attended and flattered and spoiled by courtly men, beautiful, idle, sparkling, willful, and very useless. As symbolic of their class as were the harlots of the element below the bluff. And this was known as Natchez-on-the-Hill.

Chapter Seventeen

I

Of the villainous establishments below the Natchez bluffs, none was more villainous than Thomas Grady's tavern. It was particularly so at night, when darkness added to its filthy disreputability, and a few wretched tallow dips built their own winding shrouds of drippings as they threw fantastic shadows. All freshness was excluded from the place, so that its atmosphere was sodden and shamed by smells of stale liquor and bad food, and by the breaths and body odors of the rogues and vagabonds who haunted the place.

Tom Grady himself, a man of limited intelligence, still more limited scruples, and a paunch that could stomach anything, sat in his rawhide chair, caring nothing for fresh air, and listening complacently to the clink of glasses, shrill female laughter, and the overhanging cloud of obscene male discourse which assured him of his inn's popularity.

In the barrel house this July night were five women and four men, excluding himself. Of the women, four were moderately youthful and immoderately hard and brazen: Mother Slappert's girls, who made the inn a soliciting place and plied their trade upstairs. The fifth was the venerable abbess of vice herself, Mother Slappert, fat, cunning, and gray, with enormous breasts sagging under her loose dress.

Four men played idly at old sledge, and the girls looked on familiarly, sitting on chair arms, leaning against shoulders, accepting coarse liberties with giggling complaisance. Grady knew the men: each was a thief and very likely a murderer. Upriver outlaws, three of them. There was Jo Burke, rotund and bald with an evil visage that belied his figure's jovial promise; Buck Sorrels, a great harmless-looking oaf with a foolish grin, who was far from foolish and anything but harmless; and Steve Heacock, gaunt and vulpine, of the three appearing most truly the scoundrel he was.

All of these wore rough river costumes, part leather and part homespun. But the fourth, a burly, swaggering fellow, perhaps forty, was attired in a Bolivar coat and a tall hat, which he wore tilted far over on the side of his head. He had a persuasive, jocular manner, in spite of a trifling oddity of appearance: one tooth in his mouth projected so that it required a constant little effort to cover it with his lip, and somewhat marred his smile.

This fourth man was John Sturdevant: Bloody Jack Sturdevant. Grady knew him to be a murderous fighter at rough-and-tumble or with any weapon. Some said he was the strongest man on the river, a squat Hercules, who had killed six men in single combats. How many other deaths he was responsible for, nobody cared to discuss. Ostensibly a professional gambler—an occupation almost respectable in Natchez-under-the-Bluff— he was given to long absences, and Grady, who heard everything, remembered a whisper concerning a man "with a wolf tooth" who bossed the upriver pirates who lay in wait for unwary flatboats. The barrel-house keeper, however, asked no questions and kept his own thoughts. Bloody Jack Sturdevant was a good customer, spending half his time under the bluff, and at least nine tenths of that in Grady's tavern.

The door opened, admitting for a moment a breath of cool night air, and with it a tall, straight-backed man, who, unlike many tall men, held his head high and proud.

"Howdy, Grady," he said.

The innkeeper hoisted himself to his feet. "Tol'able, Mr. Bowie. An' you, seh?"

Mr. Bowie looked to be in reasonable good health. He was now thirty-two. The years had put no soft flesh on his hard bone and muscle, but they had changed his face. The boyish look was gone. His mouth still could relax genially enough on occasion, but it was set habitually in a stern line, and there was a rugged jut of cheekbones and chin. His eyes, however, told the most about him: they were gray and watchful, and sometimes cold and intimidating.

Bowie was alone here, which argued for a certain self-confidence. It was not considered healthy for gentlemen from the breeze-swept heights above to venture solitary down in this hellhole.

The tavern's familiars regarded him with a variety of speculations. And if the furtive men mentally assessed his possible worth to filching fingers or perhaps a stab in the back, the bold-eyed women gazed at his resolute face and his shoulders—what shoulders!—with a different interest. But the men, after another scrutiny, decided to let alone such obviously dangerous competence: and the women perceived that as far as this gentleman was concerned, they existed not at all.

Grady set a bottle on the bar, but Bowie shook his head.

"What about the horse?" he said.

"He's here, sir." The tavern man put away his bottle. "Yon are the gents that brought him down-river." He called to them.

The "gents" rose, shook off the arms of their girls, and tramped over. With a kind of robust polish that became his style and appearance, Sturdevant bowed, and said, "Sarvant, sir. Honored to meet you, sir." The others only nodded sourly and stood back.

"Drink, gentlemen?" Bowie said. "My pleasure."

They drank his good health in Grady's bad liquor.

"Mr. Sturdevant owns the animal we're discussin'," said the innkeeper.

Sturdevant's lip writhed away from the wolf tooth in a grin.

"Name's Steel Duke, sir. Know of the horse?"

"No." Bowie did not return the grin.

"Out of Bride o' Lammermoor by Forest Duke, who was out of Coquette by Truxton, General Jackson's famous stallion. I presume you're familiar with the line. The Duke's a mighty well-known stake horse around Nashville. Beat some mighty fine horses."

"I'll look at him," Bowie said briefly.

Grady took a lantern and led out into the night. From a hitch rack Bowie untethered a sorrel gelding with white stockings and a blaze on his face. The horse had been ridden recently; dark sweat stains showed about the edges of his saddle blanket.

"What's his name?" Sturdevant asked.

"Ginger."

"Nice-looking bit of blood."

"Yes."

"Steel Duke will make him look like dog meat, sir, meaning no offense, I'm sure."

Bowie took no offense. Grady's lantern winked before them, his fat legs cutting the light like a pair of shears. As they walked along the rough rutted street, a staggering riverman hailed them with groggy exuberance, and would have joined them. Buck Sorrels gave him a push and a kick, and left him sprawled, sobbing in maudlin woe, in one of the black alleys. Over him for a moment Steve Heacock brooded, like a vulture in the dark, then rejoined the party with a curse because the man had no more than a couple of pieces of silver in his pockets.

Beyond the last of the bawdyhouses and saloons, Grady halted and lifted his lantern, while Sturdevant unlocked a padlock and pushed open the door of a shed. The scanty light revealed an interior miserable and filthy, with manure-stained straw and the smell of stables the world over. But in it was a creature that made even these sordid surroundings somehow noble—a magnificent horse, steel gray darkening at all points, clean-limbed, well-ribbed, with every indication of mettle and intelligence in his beautiful head. His eyes seemed to light as he turned his gaze toward them, his delicate ears alert.

"There he is," Sturdevant said. "Judge for yourself."

Bowie's examination was quick and expert. He stood back with a short nod. "He looks choicely good. But I want to see him by daylight."

"He kin beat Major Wright's hoss, Kerry Isle, goin' away," Grady interjected.

"You'll get your money back in no time on stud fees alone," added Sturdevant. "I can furnish a clean pedigree."

Bowie said, "I'm more interested just now in a clean bill of sale."

"Naturally." Sturdevant's grin was gone. He did not like this high-headed man from up above, but business was business. "That I'll guarantee. Recent owner is Squire Levington of Nashville. You're acquainted with him? No? A high-toned gentleman, sir, but if I may say so, a poor judge of cards. That's why the price on this horse is low—five hundred's nothing for an animal like him. But I've no use for a race horse."

Thoroughbred racing in Mississippi still was a gentleman's sport from which the lower element was barred.

Bowie said, "Bring him up to Henderson's stable at nine tomorrow morning. If he's what you say and the papers are regular, the money will be ready for you."

Sturdevant nodded.

"I'll ask you to say nothing of this for the present," said Bowie.

The wolf tooth showed an instant. "I reckon I understand your reasons, Mr Bowie."

Outside, Sturdevant locked the door, and they watched Bowie swing himself on the sorrel and ride up Silver Street toward the bluff.

"Known him long?" Sturdevant asked Grady.

" 'Bout a year. Odd 'un. Big land spec'lator—belongs to General Cuny's syndicate. You heard of them? Nigger valet. Good hosses. Good clothes. A gent. But the damnedest taste for knickknacks. Been in my place plenty of times—every other joint on the street, too."

"He's a rooster?"

Grady shook his head. "Every gal down here's made her play for him, I reckon. No good. It ain't women."

"Then what?"

"Excitement, I reckon. Dotes on gambling."

"That kind of craving ought to be encouraged," Sturdevant said.

"If you're thinkin' soft pickin's, get it out of your skull. That gent's sharp. As sharp with the cards as any man you ever seen. Up to every trick. Paper men—second dealers—holdout men—short-card men—he's onto 'em all. Cheatin's out if you play Bowie."

"Looks like by now he'd of found himself some trouble."

Grady grinned fatly. "He's got a big rep'tation as a fighter. An' I think it's true. They say he's killed a couple of men. A knife fighter, he is, an' thinks up ways of doin' it to curdle your blood. An' he's willin'. Goddamned willin.' That's what chills 'em. Most sharpers, when they find out who he is, don't want no part of him."

Sturdevant grunted. He also had something of a reputation in man killing.

2

As big as a bass drum, the full moon heaved itself over the black forest to the east and drenched the landscape with foggy silver, so swift and blinding that a man had to blink twice to believe it. It made the shadow of the bluff twice as black, so that except for the sound of his horse's hoofs, Bowie's progress up the long incline could hardly be traced.

As he emerged in the moonlight above, he saw two men conversing on the street. By an odd quirk of fate, one of those men was very closely connected with an errand from which he was just returning.

The taller of the pair was Andrew Marschalk, the veteran editor of the Natchez *Herald*: a thin, spare man, with silver hair and a cast of countenance almost sorrowful, save when he chose to be winning. The other was younger, catfooted and nervous, with a narrow dark face, very black hair and mustache, and teeth startlingly white. He was Major Norris Wright, owner of the Irish thoroughbred Kerry Isle, and he was handsome, almost foppish in white leather riding tights and immaculate boots which he tapped continuously with his riding whip.

Bowie would have stopped to speak to Marschalk, whom he respected, but at the sight of the other, he merely nodded and rode on.

"James Bowie—James Bowie," said the major, looking after him. "He rides like an emperor, and gives the imperial nod these days. I knew him, Andrew, when a paper dollar was a fortune to him, and he didn't know good wine from swill."

Marschalk smiled slightly. "Change is life, Major. Some men grow, and the spectacle of their growth is often a little disconcerting."

"Especially when it's a toadstool growth—pushing up overnight, with no substance or value, and with a bad smell to boot."

The editor did not reply directly. "Mr. Bowie appears to have been on some errand of pressing nature," he said.

"A faro game on the landing, probably, if not a rendezvous at some sporting house!"

Marschalk shook his head. "I think you do him injustice. Did you see the sweat marks on that horse? He's come from farther than the landing."

Norris Wright laughed shortly. "Even injustice is more than that man deserves, sir! A bog trotter, sir. A slave-runner. A gambler and a ruffian. Crooked as Aaron's rod, after it turned into a snake, sir!"

The white-haired editor was silent. No man expressed himself, not even to an intimate friend, as Major Wright had done, unless he had notions of backing up the words with some kind of violent action if opportunity arose. And while Marschalk was an acquaintance of considerable time, he was hardly one of the major's intimates. As a matter of fact he was no intimate of anyone's: the austerity of his manner forbade intimacy. What Wright spoke so freely and venomously to him, he would not hesitate to speak elsewhere. This sort of thing led to the shedding of blood.

Wright lifted his hat. "Good night, Andrew. I'm due back at King's."

For a moment Marschalk remained standing where he was. From below the bluff came the brawling noise of the ruffian settlement. The great moon seemed to hang in arm's reach, touching the mile-wide river with a thousand highlights. Far across, the steam ferryboat cast a long path of reflections toward a low dark island near the distant shore.

The editor knew that island. It resembled twenty thousand others in the Mississippi, but it had a significance apart. On the river maps it was called the Vidalia sand bar. But from the upper Ohio, clear down to New Orleans, every steamboat pilot, raftsman, gambler, woodlotter, cotton patcher, flatboater, and catfisher knew it as the Natchez butchering ground: the place of duels, where fiery gentlemen quenched each other's lives, paradoxically whitening honor in the scarlet gush of blood. Marschalk disliked the island and its character. A man gains perspective with age, and more and more each year he deplored every aspect of the so-called "code of honor," with its obligations and excesses. Yet when men set their heads to kill or be killed, there was not much one could do about it.

Major Wright, now. He seemed to like that word, "slave-runner." Not a pleasant word: a fighting word. Remarkable that a man like Bowie could have smuggled contraband blacks into the country to sell them, and still be accepted as a gentleman . . .

The editor smiled slightly to himself. Bowie was, he thought, a compelling sort of man when you came to know him. He had enemies, but he also had friends who seemed quite ready to fight for him. And he made no bones about his record—admitted the slave-running in a sort of frank, disarming way, without condoning it or excusing it. Something about him made one decide not to hold it against him, any more than one held against other friends the indiscretions of youth, committed before they fully understood their grave implications. Too bad, said Andrew Marschalk to himself, that Norris Wright held animosities so deep.

3

Connelly's tavern, with its two white galleries, one above the other, stood on an eminence at the edge of the river bluffs and commanded the finest prospect in Natchez. Bowie turned over his horse to a black stableboy and went directly to the taproom.

As he reached the door, he could hear a voice expounding medical theories with a sort of obstinate insistence. Yellow fever, the voice said, was without question a miasmatic affection, induced by poisonous fogs from the swamps. Consider the yellow fever year of 1825 which decimated New Orleans, the voice adjured someone. A year of inundations, making more extensive marsh areas, and hence the emanation of noxious effluvia from putrescent matter and stagnation . . .

Bowie opened the door and entered. The voice ceased. It belonged to Dr. Samuel Cuny, a potbellied, self-important little man, addicted to long-winded dissertations in medical jargon. His victim, Major George McWherters, Regular Army, retired, leaned against the bar, a long-legged man with very blue eyes and curling side whiskers. His expression changed from boredom to relief at Bowie's appearance.

Four other men in the room also turned to look at Bowie. They had been waiting for him. All were members of the syndicate.

Bowie saw his brother Rezin, growing quite bald now, sitting across the room where he had been playing cribbage with Colonel Samuel Levi Wells, a lean, iron-gray man with black eyes set very close together above the bridge of his long bony nose. The colonel's brother, Jefferson Wells, a little less gray and a little less cadaverous, but with the same narrow-eyed family stamp, was pegging points for them on a brass board.

Seated alone, with a glass on the table beside him and a newspaper in his hands, as if he disdained association with the common herd, was General Richard Cuny, the chairman of the syndicate. The general was imposing, as his brother, the little doctor, was not. He was tall, with a "presence," the euphemism of the day for portliness. His head was very large, with a grizzled frost at the ears, an orator's mouth, and the features of a Roman tribune: the veritable picture of Mars, although the general owed his military title to courtesy and custom, rather than to any warlike achievement. He had served a term as attorney *general* of the state of Louisiana. Not that anybody questioned his personal courage. He had some months before fought a duel with Judge Robert A. Crain, permanently crippling the judge's left arm with a pistol slug.

The general laid down his newspaper and clambered to his feet. "Our Mercury returns!" he exclaimed.

He liked to deal in orotund classical allusions, and when he mentioned the Olympians he never assigned the role of Jupiter to another man, so that by a sort of inference it was reserved for himself.

They all crowded around Bowie.

"Well?" The general bestowed his senatorial smile. "What news?" Bowie shook his head. "No good."

The general's smile faded. "You—you mean the bank refused us the loan?"

"That's it."

"But it was as good as approved last week!" said Colonel Wells, his narrow eyes snapping.

Bowie said slowly, "Major Norris Wright bought into the Alexandria bank this week as a stockholder."

They stared. "It was the syndicate's money!" the general exclaimed. "Wright was nominated by the Crain gang—a figurehead—put there to stop our move——"

Dr. Cuny began to swear in a pointless way, damning Major Wright to seven different kinds of hell.

"Shut up, Samuel!" the general said. As if someone had turned him off, the little doctor became silent. "Gentlemen, this is grave. We need the twenty-five thousand badly. A heavy, a very heavy disappointment. Without that loan I doubt if we can proceed with the Lecompte transaction." General Cuny pursed his lips, considering gloomily. "It's Judge Crain. That man will never get over hating me for putting my mark on him." He brightened a little; it was a subject he never wearied of discussing. "The ball entered his left arm at the wrist, you know, and came out near the elbow——"

The others, who had all heard full many a time the details of how the general had wounded the judge, did not relax their gloomy concern.

"As I came up from the landing," Bowie said, "I saw Norris Wright himself. With Andrew Marschalk." He paused. "And speaking of Wright, I stopped in at Grady's. The horse is here."

They turned to him quickly at that.

"You've seen him?" Rezin asked.

"Yes. Took time for that."

"How does he look?"

"I saw him by lantern, and we'll have another look in the morning. But—I don't think I've ever seen a better horse."

"If he can win the Duncan Cup, I'd give a thousand for a portrait of Crain's face," the general said.

"Or Wright's," said Rezin. "He thinks that Irish chestnut of his can't be touched."

"The horse has been on a flatboat for days," said Bowie. "The race is Saturday, so he's got only three days to find his legs and his speed. But if what they say is true, and we can get him ready—the Alexandria bank loan may not be so important."

They gazed at one another, speculation growing.

"How much?" the general asked.

"Five hundred."

"Share and share. Five hundred into seven portions comes to—well, a little over seventy apiece. Agreed, gentlemen?"

They nodded.

"Since you've made the arrangements, we'll enter him under your name," the general said to Bowie. There were no objections.

"Now, to get a rider," said Jeff Wells.

There, surely, was something to think about.

"My body servant, Orlando, can ride," said Major McWherters, tentatively.

Jeff Wells shook his head. "Orlando's too heavy. Weighs all of a hundred and sixty. That boy of Wright's, Juba, is a real jock if he isn't good for anything else, and he's not above a hundred and ten."

Bowie said, "I've got the jockey. I saw Nez Coupé at Alexandria. He's coming up tomorrow. Nez Coupé can ride and handle any animal that eats hay. And he doesn't weigh a hundred and twenty-five."

"We can see how he does in the workouts," the general said.

Chapter Eighteen

1

Saturday morning Bowie came down late from his room, arrayed in his best ruffled shirt, burgundy cravat, and cinnamon coat. He found Rezin and Nez Coupé in the dining room.

"How do you feel?" Bowie said to Nez Coupé.

The Cajun grinned. "Nevair no better."

He had proved to the satisfaction of all the partners his ability as a race rider in secret workouts down a stretch of back country road in the past two days, and he was dressed in his riding boots and scarlet and white silks which Bowie had provided for him.

"How's the horse?"

"Chipper as one sparrow. Eat his mash an' hay like he no nevair mind nothing."

"Think he can win?" Bowie grinned.

"By God, Jim, I give that horse ride will open your eyes! Steel Duke, he know me like brother—we make lots of fun, us!"

Nez Coupé, whose confidence in himself was magnificent, rose from the table and swaggered off to see about saddling his horse.

Rezin grinned at Bowie. "Dressed to kill, aren't you?"

"Got to look like somebody today." Bowie grinned back. "I'm supposed to be an owner, you know."

Between these brothers was great good will. In ten years their family fortunes had made a remarkable advance. They owned the plantation known as Sedalia, in Rapides Parish, Louisiana; a steam sugar mill at Arcadia, where Rezin lived with his family and his mother; and John, the oldest of the three, had property near Helena, Arkansas, and was being spoken of for the territorial legislature. All of it was due to Bowie, the adventurous, imaginative, and enterprising. Now, however, they were involved in a business crisis, all of them, owing to the refusal of the Bank of Alexandria to make the loan, as Bowie had reported.

"Did old Fraser, the bank president, give any reason for turning us down?" Rezin asked.

"Not the real reason. A lot of bank jargon about collateral and sound principles of finance. He didn't mention that Wright, as a member of the board of directors, had stopped the loan."

"Norris Wright," Rezin mused. "You've got a good enemy there."

"Good? I'd call him bad."

"He doesn't forget that you beat him in the election of '24."

Bowie laughed. "Politics gives a man peculiar notions. Wright got so used to running the Whigs in Rapides Parish, electing legislators, district judges, and the like, that he thought his personal popularity did it. Running for sheriff was just a preliminary for him. The man had his eye on the governorship—he just got too big for his pants."

"You cut him down to his size."

"I reckon he blames me for it. The back bayous came in pretty near a hundred per cent against him. Enough to turn the election."

"Well, he thinks he's got us now, like a coon up a tree."

Bowie nodded soberly. The combination confronting the Cuny syndicate, in which the brothers had heavy stakes, was formidable in resources and influence, and actuated by personal feelings, since most of its members had personal vendettas with men in the Cuny faction. Judge Robert A. Crain was General Cuny's bitter foe. Major Wright hated Bowie. The brothers, Alfred and Carey Blanchard, related to Judge Crain by marriage, had difficulties with the brothers, Colonel Sam and Jefferson Wells. The other member of the Crain group was Dr. Thomas A. Maddox, a sleekly plausible physician, most of whose patients were fashionable women.

The whole financial edifice of the Cuny syndicate was erected like an arch, to which the twenty-five thousand from the bank would have been the keystone. Without the keystone, everything would collapse.

"I'm praying Steel Duke comes through today," said Rezin.

Bowie nodded. "We're betting the pile on him."

To gamble everything on a horse! And on a horse nobody really knew. By this their true desperation was revealed.

The years had wrought some important changes in Bowie. He was a gentleman now, a sought-after guest in the most notable homes. But the tavernkeeper down under the bluff had marked him as a gambler: a gambler with extraordinary luck, who believed in himself to the point of meeting professionals and beating them at their own game. To gamble for himself, however, was one thing: to make decisions, and risk winning or breaking for others, took the pleasure from it and made the gamble a weighty load.

At the moment it seemed to Bowie that fate was always making him the player, the one on whom responsibility was heaviest. Nine years before, he had carried his brothers with him into the wild slave venture. When that reckless scheme paid off in great profits, he persuaded them to go with him into further and greater gambles.

Speculation in land was the great vice of the era. It had lured men like Andrew Jackson, destined soon to be President; Henry Clay, biting his fingernails over his thwarted ambition; Daniel Webster, that pillar of Yankee rhetoric; John C. Calhoun, licking his political wounds, and countless others, celebrated and obscure alike. Some had won, many had lost.

The process appeared so simple: and was filled, really, with so many pitfalls. Land, remote from settlement, could be bought cheaply. With the titles in hand, to reap pyramiding profits one need only hold it until the tide of population moved in his direction and values skyrocketed. But the hidden risks were severe. Competition was keen and ruthless; titles sometimes were not clear or valid, so that a man might lose everything;

finally, there was no predicting when settlement would come, or in what direction.

Yet land speculation appealed to Bowie, and Bowie persuaded his brothers. It was a good combination: John the shrewd, Rezin the adroit, and Jim the powerful and compelling.

Smuggling slaves into the Calcasieu country brought their attention to the Neutral Strip along Louisiana's western border, where land could be bought almost for nothing because conditions were unstable, no man being really sure whether he was in the United States or Mexico. On Bowie's hunch, they put their money in Neutral Strip lands in 1820, and when, the following year, the United States by treaty obtained clear rights to the disputed corridor between the Arroyo Hondo and the Sabine, the brothers made their first big killing. Since then, always led by the restless younger brother, they had kept their resources employed in speculation continually, even to mortgaging the property they had.

To make matters worse, another trouble had arisen. Wholesale lawsuits had been filed in the federal court at Little Rock, Arkansas, seeking to break many titles in Louisiana. Among these were the Neutral Strip titles in which the Bowies had dealt. The land was sold, but the brothers were concerned in protecting their buyers. John Bowie was at Little Rock and had written for help.

"I'm going up Monday morning," Bowie said as they discussed this.

"A long ride," Rezin said.

"Nez Coupé will go along."

Rezin nodded. "You conducted the transactions to buy the land in the first place. You'd be the best one on the stand."

There was more than one reason for hoping the gray horse, Steel Duke, would win the Duncan Cup race this day.

2

At half-past one Bowie and Rezin rode to the track, a half-mile oval, well leveled and scraped, just outside of the town. Starting time was two o'clock, but already a considerable crowd had gathered, and Rezin went off with some friends, leaving Bowie near the judges' stand. Facing the little tower where the judges overlooked the finish was a small grandstand, almost filled by men from the little clearings, in homespun and butternut, and their wives, in calico and linsey.

The lords of the soil, however, who counted their acres by the thousand and their slaves by the score, disdained to rub shoulders with the rabble. Their gleaming carriages paralleled the homestretch in a long line, black grooms at the horses' heads, fashionable loveliness in the up-holstered seats, with gay parasols nodding, calling and waving to each other, very animated and bright.

Most of these ladies had been deserted, temporarily, by their escorts, who circulated in a throng near the judges' tower, looking for interesting wagers. Though the Duncan Cup, an ornate silver trophy, was the ostensible prize of the race, much heavier interests would ride with the jockeys this day. Betting had thus far been slow, however, and all at odds: Major Wright's Irish thoroughbred, Kerry Isle, against the field; or four and five to one against any other horse you named.

The major himself, slim and light-footed, was much in evidence, receiving greetings from his friends, giving laughing assurances to backers, or conversing with a tall, erect man, with iron-gray hair, features well chiseled but cold, and a manner dignified to the point of haughtiness. This was the widely known Judge Crain. Two things about him caught the attention: invariably he dressed in unrelieved black, and his left arm was in a black silk sling. The sling was a reminder of a certain feud still unsettled.

Notably aloof from the judge and the major stood Bowie and General Cuny. The general was resplendent in a plum-colored coat with tails hanging almost to his heels, and a generous breadth of embroidered waistcoat, across which a huge watch chain was swung like the cable of a suspension bridge. An eye-filling sight, the general. But years exert an unhappy disadvantage, and the younger man was a focus of far greater attention, particularly from the ladies.

Presently Bowie excused himself and walked along the front of the grandstand. His free-and-easy way made him a favorite with the butternut contingent, to many of whom he called by name, not sparing his compliments to their gaunt wives.

Up to this time the supporters of Major Wright's entry had been so confident that they posted a standing offer to take all wagers against their favorite. Few bet, for Kerry Isle was acknowledged to be the finest stake horse in Mississippi, and compared with him the other entries appeared almost negligible. The best of these were Montrose, a black stallion with good loins and withers but a rather coarse head, belonging to Colonel Dobson; Baby June, a pretty little filly with a rich red gloss, but a trifle light, owned by Boyce Sparling; and Corporal, a big bay with white stockings, from Four Oaks plantation near Feliciana, reputed fast but with overmassive shoulders which betrayed plebeian blood somewhere in his ancestry.

Just before starting time the ladies in the carriages noticed a stir of excitement near the judges' stand. Men hurried about or gathered in knots for hurried consultations. Presently to the carriages came a report that there was a last-minute entry. By whom? James Bowie. A horse named Steel Duke. The ladies glanced at each other. None of them had ever heard of Steel Duke, so the chattering was resumed.

If the ladies were unperturbed, it was different elsewhere. Steel Duke? Where was he from? Nashville? Good God, what kind of a horse was this, and how did he get into this part of the world?

Judge Crain refused to be ruffled, but Major Wright was anxious. The Crain group had thousands on this race, and Kerry Isle had been a practical certainty. This might make a difference.

The presiding judge, Andrew Marschalk, stalked over to Bowie. "Where's this horse of yours, sir?"

"He's coming now!" someone cried.

A little gnomelike man in scarlet and white jockey's silks, with a scarred visage, rode a gray stallion into the enclosure. Every eye watched as Bowie walked over and laid his hand on the horse's polished neck.

Men who prided themselves on knowing horseflesh studied the newcomer and conversed in excited undertones. The animal, it was agreed, looked fast—very fast. Vein and muscle made a beautiful tracery under his satin gray skin, his barrel was wonderful, his legs delicate but strong, his head showed blood in every line. Speed without question. But what about bottom? Could he match strides for three heats, at a mile each, with a horse like Kerry Isle?

A furious man confronted Bowie.

"You smuggled that critter in!" stormed Norris Wright.

Bowie was calm. "Smuggled isn't the word, Major. I bought him. Here in Natchez. And five thousand dollars says he'll beat your horse."

By a prodigious effort Wright controlled his anger. "I've put up with a lot from you, Bowie!" he said in chilled tones. "But this thing tops all the rest. If your trick beats Kerry Isle—big as you are, and regardless of your reputation—look out for yourself!"

All around them heard the threat. Bowie's face did not change. "What about the five thousand?"

"I'll lay you the five thousand—and another on top of it!"

"Land—six hundred and forty acres in Rapides Parish."

"Done! I'll match you with a section right next to it!"

Black as a stormy sky, Wright turned and tramped away.

The field began filing out on the track, horses milling about, jockeys curbing them or letting them out for brief bursts of speed down past the grandstand. Wright's jockey, Juba, a little hunchbacked Negro with a black face deeply pocked, brought a roar from the crowd as he took Kerry

Isle down at a gallop. The Irish thoroughbred was a big raking chestnut with fine shoulders and a prodigious stride, and his was all the advantage in weights. Uncertainty among his supporters, caused by the spectacular arrival of Bowie's gray, disappeared. The chestnut looked a champion if ever a horse did.

Excited cries arose as betting grew suddenly lively.

"Five to three on Kerry Isle!"

"Seven to thirteen on the gray!"

"The Irisher at seven to five!"

Natchez planters became busy tabulating bets and odds. In the wild excitement money, land, horses, even slaves were wagered. Homespun and linsey in the grandstand bet chiefly in tobacco by the keg and whiskey by the demijohn: and there, because Bowie had been a bayou hunter, the gray stallion ruled as favorite. Even out in the long line of carriages, dainty ladies caught the excitement and made quick little notations with jeweled pencils in small leather-covered notebooks; and such is feminine fancy, that many wagered on the gentlemen who owned the horses, rather than on the horses themselves, so that the chestnut carried small bets because of Major Wright's beautiful manners, and the gray because his master had a head so handsome and shoulders so broad.

3

A brief consultation at the judges' tower broke up, and Bowie, with Dr. Stephen Duncan, crossed the track. The doctor was elderly and good-humored, with a fine forehead, steel-rimmed glasses, flowing gray muttonchops, and the bland confidence of wealth. As donor of the race cup he had something to say about the rules.

Bowie, listening to something the doctor was saying, all at once raised his head.

"Isn't that— Philippe Cabanal?" he asked with surprise.

"Yes. You know him?"

"Slightly."

Cabanal came up. "Hello, Doctor. It's—Bowie, isn't it? How do you do?"

Bowie said, "Very well, thank you. I hadn't heard you were in town."

Not since the night Narcisse de Bornay was killed had he seen Philippe, and he felt in him a curious indefinable change. The man was still well built, well featured, and well dressed, in the world's catalogue a gentleman. But in his face, his nervous vacillating eye, and his loosened mouth beneath the curling mustache, one who was adept at such things could read signs of weakness, or irresponsibility, perhaps even of pride secretly abandoned.

"We're here on a short visit—business," Philippe said.

"We?"

"Yes. My wife is with me." He looked at Bowie. "You perhaps remember her—Judalon de Bornay?"

"I do remember her."

Dr. Duncan said, "In that case, you must come over and pay your respects. Philippe and Judalon are guests at Auburn, and Judalon is here now, in the barouche with Mrs. Duncan."

"Certainly," Bowie said, but he felt a stir of misgiving.

Eagerly Philippe turned to the doctor. "What was the discussion?"

"At the judges' stand? A question concerning the legality of Mr. Bowie's last-minute entry. But nothing in the rules prevents entries at any time before the race. The only question, it seemed to me, was the ownership of the horse, which is not in registry here. A horse entered must belong to the gentleman who enters him, a provision, you understand, to keep out the riffraff. Mr. Bowie avowed his ownership." Dr. Duncan smiled. "Nobody questioned that Mr. Bowie is a gentleman."

Cabanal was worried. "I've got a pretty penny on this race—on Kerry Isle, all of it. What kind of a horse have you got, Bowie?"

"He looks like a prime one," Dr. Duncan said.

"Why did you wait so long to enter him?" insisted Philippe. "Should I hedge, do you think?"

Bowie said, seriously, "I know nothing about him, Philippe. Nothing whatever. He's fast, and he looks good. But I couldn't tell you to bet on him. You see the odds are on Kerry Isle. I'd gladly tell you if I were sure of the horse or had seen him in a race even once."

"I think I'll talk to Norris Wright," Cabanal said, and left them.

"Come over to the barouche," the doctor said.

An increasing reluctance took possession of Bowie. Judalon . . . Ten years since he had seen her, but the mere mention of her name seemed to bring back to him exactly how she looked then, how she talked, how she carried her head and smiled. It made him uneasy, this sharpness of recollection, so that he would have preferred to excuse himself.

"Perhaps you know that both of Mrs. Cabanal's parents are dead?" Dr. Duncan was saying amiably.

"No. I hadn't heard."

"The yellow fever epidemic of '25. In twenty-four hours of each other. Her only brother died previously, very tragically, I understand in a duel of some kind. So except for her husband, the poor girl is alone."

"I regret to learn of it."

"I mentioned it for fear you might inadvertently bring up a painful subject in the conversation, since you knew her before."

"Thank you for telling me."

There was no avoiding the meeting without discourtesy. They walked down the row of equipages, lifting hats and bowing to the ladies in them. He saw Judalon looking at him, her face very still.

She was in a dress of old gold and blue that molded her body down to her waist, then billowed out, and she held a small silken parasol tilted over her shoulder. In the last few steps he thought she had not changed by a single day in all the time since he had seen her.

Beside her, in the barouche, sat Mrs. Duncan, a somewhat fluttery woman of indeterminate age, who greeted him and began an effusive introduction. Judalon stopped her.

"Mr. Bowie and I are old friends," she said.

"You are?" Mrs. Duncan hesitated, a little confused.

"Very old friends. Aren't we, Jim?"

She smiled and held out a gloved hand, tiny as a child's. As he took it, he told himself he had been mistaken: she had changed, but the years had only added to her attraction.

"I've just made a wager," she said. "On your horse—a whole hundred dollars. For old times' sake." Again her smile.

He was astonished at his own pleasure that she should have bet on his horse or remembered old times.

Mrs. Duncan sat back. "The race is about to begin," she said.

"Oh, dear Catherine," Judalon cried quickly, "forgive me for turning my back on you . . . I am so excited meeting—Jim——"

"So it seems," said Mrs. Duncan dryly.

A bugle sounded: followed by the sharp clanging of a bell.

Chapter Nineteen

1

Horses pulled and fretted at the barrier, swerving out and being swung back into place by their jockeys. The starter, a bull-voiced man with a bald head, cracked a long whip and shouted directions at the top of his lungs. Kerry Isle reared, then passaged backward, so that two stewards were required to quiet him and bring him to the barrier again. Steel Duke, however, seemed to be behaving well.

A roar from the crowd: the barrier flew aside. Down the track flashed a riot of silken colors and thundering hoofs.

At the first curve and into the backstretch the horses were bunched, but as they passed the grandstand on the first circuit they began to string out, an azure jacket in the lead. Wright's colors. Dobson's lemon and black were close behind. The scarlet and white Nez Coupé wore seemed lost in the ruck.

From the crowd a howl of shouts and curses and pleas was hurled across the oval.

"Where's that horse of Bowie's?"

"Ain't he never goin' to wake up?"

"He's way back!"

Kerry Isle's backers lifted their voices to a jubilant scream.

Of a sudden, in the backstretch, the gray horse seemed to shake his head and lunge forward. He passed Baby June. Corporal faded. Montrose matched strides briefly, then was left behind. Rounding the last curve, Steel Duke's straining nose was within a length of Kerry Isle's tail.

But the gap did not close. The gray seemed to have spent himself. Or was the scarlet and white jockey holding him back? Bettors, whose hopes had been raised, bellowed their angry disappointment.

"It's the jock!"

"Why don't he give him his head?"

"He's pulling the race!"

"A job! A job!"

Down the homestretch. A two-horse race. And Steel Duke was trailing, beaten by a careless ride.

Then the furious howl of the crowd lifted to a great spontaneous roar, which built and towered as the gray began his drive. Always before, Kerry Isle had taken command in the stretch. But now he found himself unable to shake his rival. Crouched low, his scarlet and white silks whipping in the wind, Nez Coupé lifted the bit, and began using the whip. Juba was flogging his mount.

The chestnut did his gallant best. But the steel-gray head drew forward: now at the flank, now at the girth, now at the shoulder, now head to head. There they seemed to hang.

Twenty yards to the wire.

For a moment they thundered nose by nose, heads outstretched. Nez Coupé, lying along his mount's neck, seemed to convey a call for a last burst of speed. The gray responded.

Under the finish wire he flashed, a clean winner.

The diapason of sound from the crowd seemed to quiver the earth.

His scarred face split clear across with his grin, Nez Coupé circled the gray stallion past the stand and raised his whip to the judges. A handler gave him a shoulder, and he leaped down from the saddle, so that the horse could be led about, preparatory to sponging him down for the next heat.

In the Duncan barouche, a woman was exulting.

"What a beauty! And to think he's yours, Jim!"

Bowie looked up. Judalon was bending toward him, her eyes ablaze, her face beautifully colored with her excitement. She seemed to be espousing his cause. To have a charming woman on one's side is never unpleasant, and he found his old resentment toward her fading fast.

"That first heat was convincing," Dr. Duncan said. "The second may tell the story."

Bowie nodded. He might have gone to the finish wire, but he seemed to be held beside the wheel of the barouche, trying to understand how he could be so acutely conscious of the woman in it, who had laughed at him once . . . and at a time when a race so important to him was being decided.

Again the kaleidoscope of mingled bright silks whirled by in the roar from the crowd. Judalon rose in the barouche, the parasol tilted behind her head, her body a slender curve of feminine excitement. In the din, Bowie found himself straining to hear her voice crying his horse on.

"Scarlet and white! He's ahead—no, the chestnut's right behind him! Steel Duke! Steel Duke! Oh, my beauty! Come on—come on—he's running Kerry Isle into the ground! Oh, he's going to win! He's way ahead —it isn't even close! Two lengths at least! There—he wins—he wins! Oh, what a darling!"

Any man would have called the face adorable with which she looked down at Bowie.

"I'm so glad! I'm so *glad*, Jim!"

He said, "Then it's about perfect for me, Judalon."

Her eyes went beyond him, and her voice cooled. "Here comes Philippe." Putting animation back in her tone, she called out to him, "I won a hundred, dear!"

"I'm glad somebody won." Philippe's voice was bitter. "I lost. A good bit more than a hundred." Fretfully, he turned on Bowie. "I wish you'd given me that tip I asked for."

"I told you I didn't know myself what he could do."

"You bet on him, didn't you?"

"A man naturally bets on his own horse."

Dr. Duncan said, "If you're interested in selling that horse, I'd like to talk with you. Where did you get him?"

"Bought him. Four days ago. From a man named Sturdevant."

"Sturdevant?" asked Philippe. "That gambler under the bluff?"

"Yes."

"I know Sturdevant. Where did he get the horse?"

"He told me he won him in a card game from a Nashville man."

"That's interesting. Very interesting," said Philippe.

Dr. Duncan said, "I'd better return to the judges' stand."

"I'll walk over with you," said Philippe. "Excuse us, ladies—Bowie."

Bowie glanced up and found Judalon watching him with a curious gleam of unsmiling interest in her eyes.

"I hope Philippe wasn't bad hurt," he said.

"I don't know. He's a fool in gambling, and a friend of Major Wright's. You spoke of a man named Sturdevant? He's another of my husband's acquaintances—a very costly one." A hint in her voice of bitterness, or perhaps contempt. "At least *I* backed the right colors," she said, trying to regain her lightness.

Mrs. Duncan said, "There's some kind of excitement at the judges' stand. If I'm not mistaken, they're calling for Mr. Bowie."

He heard his name. "Bowie . . . Mr. James Bowie . . . please . . . judges' stand."

"I wonder what's wrong," he said. "I'd better go."

"Wait," said Judalon. "You must come and see—us—at Auburn——"

"Why—yes——" He hesitated.

"Next week? Say—Wednesday?"

"I'm sorry. I just remembered, I'm leaving Monday for the north."

"Then——" She turned perplexed to her hostess. "Catherine——"

Mrs. Duncan could meet emergencies. "Are you occupied this evening, Mr. Bowie?"

"Why—no—not exactly——"

"Then, perhaps—we're having a few in for dinner. Would you be so kind as to come—your brother, of course, is invited also?"

"It's gracious of you, Mrs. Duncan—most gracious." He hardly knew what to say. "I—I'm sure Rezin will be happy. Yes, most certainly we accept, with profound thanks."

He walked away. Judalon's eyes followed him with an odd blending of expressions: admiration, perhaps; curiosity, probably; speculation, almost certainly.

Troubled faces. Angry faces.

In the center of the crowd of men Andrew Marschalk, white-thatched and imperturbable, stood listening to a cross fire of questions and resentful exclamations.

General Cuny's oratorical visage was dark with wrath. His plump doctor brother puffed and talked in a low voice with Colonel Wells. To one side stood Major Wright, superciliously calm, with Judge Crain and Dr. Maddox, a smooth-faced gentleman with a soft chin and exaggerated white shirt ruffles. Behind these, hardly a member of the group, as if he observed and listened only, was Philippe Cabanal.

"Why at this time?" Jefferson Wells was demanding of Marschalk.

"May I ask the basis?" insisted Major McWherters.

"I have my opinion, sir, of a protest made after a race is run!" boomed the general. As Bowie came up, General Cuny wheeled on him. "The rules have been invoked, sir, and payment of all wagers held up!"

Bowie took a moment to digest that. "What rule?" he asked.

The dry, precise voice of Andrew Marschalk answered him. "The rule that competing horses shall be the bona fide property of gentlemen entering them must be enforced, sir. Otherwise, what is now a sport in which we all take pride and pleasure would degenerate into a shabby knavery."

Very slowly, Bowie said, "Does someone here present question the truth of my statement?"

"No, sir. It is a technical point only——"

"I have here a formal bill of sale. Perhaps that will clear up the questions."

Marschalk thanked Bowie, took the paper and read it keenly. After a moment he shook his head. "I fear this instrument only confirms the stewards and judges in their decision."

Every eye turned on Bowie. He spoke in a dangerously quiet voice. "Then I am to understand, sir, that my status as a gentleman is in question?"

"By no means!" Marschalk said quickly. "The character and quality of Mr. James Bowie are most highly regarded by myself and everyone here present, I am most proud to say, sir. Your mere word, unsupported by any paper or other formal proof, would be sufficient——"

"Then what are we debating?" interrupted General Cuny. "We hear in one breath an objection that appears to be cleared in the next."

His words were pacific, but his voice was not, and he glared angrily at Major Wright.

Andrew Marschalk turned to the general, his manner positive, yet courteous. "Neither Mr. Bowie's word or good faith, nor yours, nor those of anyone here are at issue, I assure you, General. What the stewards feel bound to look into are the word and good faith of the man Sturdevant."

"Sturdevant?" General Cuny for once was startled out of his bombastics.

"He is a known gambler," said Marschalk, "a man of the most shady repute, an habitué of the river front to whom more than one crooked transaction—and worse—has been ascribed."

"I won't attempt to deny that," the general almost mumbled.

"The man Sturdevant," continued Marschalk, "asserts, so I am informed, that he won the horse Steel Duke in a card game. This bill of sale bears not only his endorsement, but a signature attributed to one Joseph Levington, of Nashville, Tennessee. I do not know Mr. Levington. Does anyone here know him? I think not. Taking for granted that such a person exists, might not the animal have been stolen from him? Would you undertake to verify this signature, General?"

General Cuny frowned, puffed out his lips, and shook his head. Andrew Marschalk, who in Natchez was above all petty disagreements, had made his position abundantly clear. Though Bowie had paid over the money in good faith, he might not, after all, be the legal owner of the horse. The signature on the bill of sale might very well be forged.

"The decision is difficult," the editor went on. "But very large sums of money and much property are involved. The delay will be, I am sure, a matter of a few days only. I will dispatch a courier to Nashville at once with this paper, to discover Mr. Levington and verify whether or not it is his signature. If all is in order, notice will be given that wagers shall be paid. If not, the wagers shall be paid on the basis that Steel Duke is disqualified and Kerry Isle declared the winner."

4

Riding back to Connelly's, General Cuny got what comfort he could out of his own conclusions.

"Wright knows as well as we do that the title to the horse is perfectly valid," he told Bowie. "He raises a technicality which will soon be dissipated. I'd as soon say to his face that, in my bringing up, gentlemen don't hide behind technicalities to avoid paying their losses."

Bowie did not reply. Presently the general chuckled.

"The Crain crowd bet their socks on their horse."

Still Bowie was silent.

"Wonder how they learned that we bought Steel Duke from Sturdevant," the general said. "He must have told 'em—there's no faith to be put in that breed of cattle."

Bowie nodded absently, but he had a different theory. Sturdevant had not been seen at the race. Two other men might have given the information: he remembered his casual conversation with Dr. Duncan and Philippe. But Duncan had raised no question concerning the validity of the horse's ownership, and he was not the kind of man to make such a protest to the judges without notifying Bowie of his intention to do so. Bowie was morally certain that Philippe took the information straight to Major Wright.

A sneaking thing to do, and there was no proof, but it was the kind of thing of which Philippe was capable. Bowie had never liked him, not even in the New Orleans days. Always he had suspected that Philippe played a role in the fatal quarrel between Narcisse de Bornay and the professional duelist, Contrecourt: the plot having been, of course, to get rid of Bowie himself, in which Narcisse's fatal intervention had not been foreseen. Yet . . . Judalon, Narcisse's sister, had married Philippe. Surprising how that single fact, which should have no bearing, clouded and complicated matters, and gave indirection to courses of action which otherwise should have been clearly defined.

Chapter Twenty

1

Auburn's great white columns, illuminated by hurricane lamps, gleamed a welcome through the trees. From the moon-brightened turnpike along which they had ridden the mile from town, Rezin and Bowie turned into the avenue to the mansion, which was shadowed by moss-hung oaks.

Rezin was silent and troubled. There was something in Bowie—there always had been something—that aroused in Rezin affection and admiration, not unmixed with pity and even a secret fear for him. Bowie's bluntness and genuineness stemmed from immense inward strength, which was at the same time a source of weakness equally immense.

With a part of the world he was almost irresistible: but he was foreordained, Rezin feared, to be preyed upon always by another part—the subtle, quiet, calculating part of the world, which plays its game with cold and cutting realities. None of the jealousy that sometimes exists even between brothers was in Rezin. He was the elder, but he had long since become the follower of his brother, who was in his mind heroic, like a blond demigod almost: and yet also like a child, to be humored, smiled at, and watched over.

Bowie had broached the matter of the dinner invitation to Auburn as soon as they returned to the inn from the race, and added, "Have you met the Cabanals?"

"Yes," Rezin said. "A day or two before you returned from Alexandria."

"What did you think of them?"

"Of Cabanal, that he is a nobody. Of Mrs. Cabanal, that she's beautiful —remarkably beautiful."

"Anything else?"

"I think remarkably intelligent."

"Nothing more?"

"Perhaps—selfish. Calculating is the better word."

Bowie hitched a shoulder impatiently. "Why does everyone suspect that of a woman merely because she has beauty?"

"Because a beautiful woman is hard to understand, I reckon. Homeliness seems always to clarify a woman's nature, because it appears to have been produced by the weaknesses and virtues of the spirit under it. But beauty gives a woman mystery, because you're damned well sure her spirit's got nothing to do with her looks: she might very likely be the exact opposite of what she seems to be."

After a little silence, Rezin said, "This is the girl in whom you were interested in New Orleans?"

He took Bowie's silence for assent.

"Did your previous experience give you a different impression of her?"

Bowie said slowly, "She's a little older, and there's a change in her that I noticed soon as I talked with her. And then there are some things I don't know—don't understand. How can I judge when I don't know the full story?"

So now Rezin was riding with Bowie to see the woman and to attempt to discover, if possible, what she was.

When they dismounted and entered the great house, they perceived that the company was numerous.

"It's more of an affair than I thought," Bowie said.

Rezin stopped at the entrance to the reception room. "I take it we got a last-minute invitation," he said under his breath. "The whole Crain crowd's here."

It was true. But in spite of that, Bowie looked at the scene with a momentary pleasure. Under these conditions women always were at their best: they reminded him of a cloud of butterflies in the brilliant candle-light.

Individuals began to catch his eye. The tall Blanchard brothers conversed with a pair of pleasant Natchez matrons. Philippe Cabanal stood laughing with Mrs. Duncan. Beyond was Dr. Maddox, talking to the angular daughter of Colonel Dobson, with his studied expression of Byronic sadness, so nicely calculated to impress susceptible women. Major Wright, however, seemed somewhat bored by his partner, a rustic maiden from one of the back plantations, all fluffy curls and flashing teeth, who simpered so adoringly at him that his pain was obvious. On the far side of the room stood Judge Crain, in black as usual, chatting in a courtly manner with Judalon.

"The judge always wears that sling," observed Bowie.

"Not to be ill-natured," Rezin said, "I don't think he needs it. I'm reliably informed that the arm's healed—a little stiff, maybe, but well enough. But the judge isn't one to miss a chance to be conspicuous. That sling, I've no doubt, will be a mark of his personal appearance the rest of his life. The wounded lion, you know."

Mrs. Duncan bore down upon them. So good of them to come. It was almost time to sit down. Did they know everyone here? She was going to ask Mr. Rezin to take in Miss Fulton of Fair Oaks. And would Mr. James be so good as to conduct Mrs. Cabanal?

The gentlemen were enchanted. She fluttered into the room before them in blue brocade and Honiton lace. Pausing in her repartee with Judge Crain, Judalon turned and smiled up into Bowie's eyes. Almost numbingly he felt her old spell beginning to reassert itself over him.

Beside them Major Wright halted with a little bow. "Miss Judalon, your servant. Mr. Bowie."

"Oh, hello, Norris," said Judalon casually.

Bowie stiffened. "Major Wright."

Visibly the two men measured each other. She surveyed them with a little dancing light in her eyes.

"You gentlemen are acquainted, I take it?"

A quick gleam of the major's teeth. "Yes. We hunt in the same country."

"Together?"

"No. Mr. Bowie runs with his own—pack of hounds."

The word "hound" *might* have been a slip. Bowie said, "Our hostess has given me the honor of taking you in to dinner."

"Oh, yes." She smiled and took his arm. To Major Wright she said, "I meant to tell you, Norris. Here comes Mrs. Duncan now. I believe she intends for you to take in your little friend from Feliciana."

167

The dining room was large, the walls covered with hunting prints, pictures of game, and stag heads, and the table, with its snowy cloth hanging nearly to the floor, ran the length of it. Forty sat down that evening to a wonderful banquet of calf's-head soup, saddle of venison, broiled wild ducks, roast turkey, and hickory-smoked ham, with jellies, hot breads, yams, sauces and wines, the dessert followed by nuts of many delicious varieties. But Bowie hardly knew what he was eating, and the jests and laughter and compliments which passed across the table left him out, for he was almost completely occupied by the woman at his side.

At the far end of the table Major Wright sat stiffly with the belle from the remote plantation. It amused Judalon, who called Bowie's attention to it. The Feliciana girl was shaking her curls and flashing her teeth, and the major seemed anything but happy.

"Who is she?" Bowie asked.

"Miss Clarabelle Clevenger. She's set her cap for Norris."

"So it appears."

"He called, I hear, quite regularly at her home. Until recently."

"You mean until you arrived in Natchez?"

"I'm sure that had nothing to do with it. I doubt that there ever was any real attachment—at Feliciana."

"Perhaps not on his side," Bowie suggested.

"He's much too sophisticated for her. She would bore him, as she does now. Look at the little hussy simper, with her saffron face and watery eyes! A diet of veal like that would soon tire his palate."

The description of the Feliciana girl seemed unnecessarily severe.

"The major's a particular friend of yours?" Bowie asked.

"Oh—I've known him two or three years. He comes to New Orleans frequently—he's active in politics, you know—and he and Philippe are great friends." Her smile became impish. "But you and he are *not* great friends, are you?"

"We're hardly intimates."

"Why?"

Now he smiled. "You wouldn't be interested."

She pouted. "In other words, it's none of my affair?"

"Never that. But it's boring and would take so long in telling."

"We must take the time." She gave him a smiling look from the corners of her long-lashed eyes.

Across the table, Rezin was conducting, as well as he could, a conversation with a middle-aged spinster whose chief interest in life was the harp. Rezin had no doubt that the harp was an excellent instrument of music, possibly hardly inferior to the banjo, but "enharmonic compasses," and "transpositions," and "diatonic and arpeggio passages" formed topics in a conversation he discovered most difficult to follow. His attention wandered. He found himself studying Judalon: trying to read her with a scrutiny almost cruel.

No question but that she made an effective picture. Unlike many small women, her movements were not quick or nervous, but rather slow and careless, the movements of a person of infinite leisure and luxury of living. Her face, as she turned it to his brother, appeared in profile extraordinarily delicate and pure, so that he found himself wondering if his thought of her was true after all.

But then she turned her gaze toward him, and he felt a subtle contradiction of the impression she had so eloquently suggested a moment before. Her eyes met his with a single straight look, as if a fencer had extended a rapier blade to measure his opponent. It was veiled instantly, but by so much she made him know that she understood his reservations concerning her. Now she spoke across to him.

"I was just telling Jim what a surprise it was to meet him here."

"Not unpleasant, I hope?" said Bowie, a little fatuously.

"Indeed no. The sight of you is always welcome, Jim—to all your friends. Don't you agree, Mr. Rezin?"

Rezin smiled. "Jim's friends are fond of him. The real ones."

"Perhaps you know his real friends better than he?"

He shook his head. "No, I'd never say that."

"He has so many it's hard to keep track of them, perhaps?" She laughed. "Tell me—are there many *pretty* ones?"

"He doesn't discuss the pretty ones—even with me," Rezin said.

"Truly? Then the days of chivalry aren't entirely gone!"

Rezin sensed a concealed irony in the words: as if she considered his rejoinder rather stupid and laughed at it. A moment later she drew the sting.

"I'm very sure there's one friend on whom Jim can count absolutely— his brother."

In spite of himself Rezin was pleased by her smile. The sledge-hammer boldness of the woman, which in effect secretly derided and defied him, while at the same time openly flattered him—for the impression it made on his brother—stirred in him a kind of reluctant admiration. He knew that here he could hardly be of much help to Bowie.

Dinner ended. Some of the guests were dancing in the ballroom to a piano. Others played at whist in the cardroom. A few engaged in conversation in the drawing room. With one or two other men, Bowie and Rezin smoked in the library, where Dr. Duncan was displaying a newly arrived set of Alexander Pope, handsomely gilt-edged and leather-bound.

Presently, in a low voice, Rezin said, "I saw you talking to the major. What did he have to offer?"

"Nothing worth mentioning."

"You know he's jealous of you, don't you?"

"Why?"

"Mrs. Cabanal."

To Bowie, it was ridiculous, and it angered him. He threw his cigar into the grate and left the library. Judalon was not in the ballroom. She was not in the drawing room. He looked in at the cardroom. She was there, standing beside a whist table at which Wright was playing with Mrs. Duncan as his partner, against Dr. Maddox and Miss Dobson. Her attitude, half leaning on the back of the major's chair to look over his shoulder at his cards, was quite intimate, and he had been laughing with her over something. When she saw Bowie, she straightened at once and came over to him.

Bowie saw Wright's eyes follow her. Perhaps the man *was* jealous.

He said, "You aren't playing?"

"There were five of us," she said. "I was sitting out the hand."

"It will be your turn next."

"No, let them play. You promised me something."

"What was it?"

"To tell me what you've been doing. Let's go in here."

She led him into the solarium.

He attempted to tease her. "Major Wright may not like this."

She gave him a gleaming smile. "Do you care?"

"No." His big shoulders hitched in a shrug. "Where's Philippe?"

"Drinking wine with Mrs. Tichenor of Hawthorne. Aren't you aware that it's practically immoral for a husband to have anything to do with his wife at such a function as this?"

"I'll confess that I wasn't."

"It permits us women who are married to forget it for an evening, and pretend we are belles again."

"You could never be anything else but a belle."

"You're improving, sir!" She laughed and seated herself on a red sofa, beside the great windows which overlooked the yard. "Come here beside me." When he obeyed, she said, "I've heard about you more than once, Jim. Indirectly. One story in particular—about the pirate Lafitte——"

Bowie could be quite frank about that discreditable episode, but he disliked having it brought up by Judalon. She went on.

"Bearding the buccaneer in his den! The audacity of it, the conception, the very ruthlessness! Like a story of old—it might have been told of Raleigh, or Drake, or Cortez. You have a genius for adventure, Jim!"

He was surprised and pleased. "The adventure I don't know about. You might better call it a genius for getting into scrapes."

"And getting out of them—fighting out of them."

He stirred. "I have no hankering for a reputation for fighting," he told her.

"Oh, I didn't mean it in that way! It's—it's just that I've been so interested—*always* so interested, in whatever concerned you."

He stared at her. "That surprises me a little."

"Why?"

"The last time I saw you—in New Orleans—you gave me a—well, a different impression."

Instantly she sobered. "Jim," she said. "Would you hold the thoughtlessness of a giddy girl who did not even know her own mind against someone who truly has many times since wished she could do something—anything—to atone for it?"

She meant the time she had laughed at him. Somehow, he found himself believing her. But there was something else.

"When—Narcisse died——" He paused. A twist like pain went over her face. He went on, "I came . . . next day. To express my sorrow." She was silent. After a moment he added, "I was told at the door that you didn't wish to see me."

Her eyes met his squarely. "You want an explanation of that? I think you deserve one. I did not know—until afterwards. You must believe that. It was poor Father—he could not bear to face anyone who had been connected with Narcisse—or that—horrible affair."

Now he was convinced and felt ashamed. "I should have understood. Forgive me for mentioning it."

"Of course. I could not blame you."

Her voice lingered in a subtly caressing way, almost sadly.

"How different our lives have been, Jim. Mine—those years—they seem to me now like a dream. An idle, uneventful dream, an empty round of

171

social events, trifling gossip, occasional scandals . . ." She ended with a wistful note, her attitude one of resignation to fate almost pathetic, so that his sympathy was strongly aroused.

"Perhaps you think you've missed more than it really amounted to," he said. "My kind of life has meant being hungry often, sometimes dirty, frequently tired to death, and getting into some mighty tough spots— enough to chill your blood when you think back on them. Not very much in it to appeal—to a woman like you."

"How little you know about women! A woman can glory in privations and dangers—if they are with someone she loves." She broke off, and added pensively, "Someone to love. It doesn't seem much to ask of life, does it?"

"You have your husband."

"Philippe?" She seemed almost bitter. "Can I say something to you in complete confidence? I have never loved Philippe. How could I? You know what he is. My marriage was . . . the wish of my father. The two families had been warm friends for a long time. It was never my wish."

The implications were stunning. She said, "Philippe does not love me, either, as I have good reason to know."

He leaned toward her. "Judalon," he said. "Judalon . . ."

She allowed him to kiss her.

Then she jumped to her feet. "What—oh, what have you done?"

Her hands were on each flaming cheek. With a wild and untranslatable look at him, she fled.

For five minutes Bowie sat alone in the solarium. Never in all his life before had he been so shaken. Within him a whole set of resolutions and logical conclusions had been overturned.

When he rose after a time the muscles of his legs were still quivering. Rezin was in the library, deep in bookish talk with Dr. Duncan. Bowie did not summon him. He found Mrs. Duncan and made his farewells.

4

The trees made a dark canopy, shutting out the moonlight, as he rode alone from Auburn. His horse's hoofs thudded softly, insects sang their nocturnal hymns, overhead was a faint stirring of leaves in the night breeze. The rich air was heavy with the perfume of flowers.

He rode in profound abstraction. As lasting as a bee sting, the warm sensation of her lips remained with him. He wondered if she was angry. Convention called for fury from a woman kissed against her will. But

. . . she had returned his kiss. Whether she desired it or not, she had responded to it. At that moment she was not angry, whatever she might have felt later.

Judalon . . . He believed now that he had done her the terrible injustice of misjudging her. They had both been so very young then. She was seventeen, a giddy girl, as she herself put it. Now she was twenty-seven, a magical age in woman, when the luster of girlhood remains, and richness and understanding have been added. And he was thirty-two. Both of them had much greater experience, very much more wisdom, than in those first days they had known each other.

He found her beautiful . . . wonderful. And throughout that evening, as if she defied the opinions of all others, she had shown him how she valued him.

Judalon was married. His mind told him this was an insuperable obstacle, that he must not even allow himself to think of her. Yet all the time, married or no, it was as if she held out to him by voiceless channels a whole infinitude of possibilities, longings and hopes.

Approaching the end of the tree-shadowed avenue, he sensed, rather than saw, his horse's head lift at a sound which seconds later his own ears distinguished. The unmistakable cadence of a galloping horse.

It brought him out of his abstraction. He firmed his reins and pressed his knees on the sorrel's sides. The animal broke into a canter. The trees thinned ahead, and he rode out on the wide turnpike, clear and bright in the moonlight.

He slowed his horse's gait. Now that he was out of that black tunnel of trees, he wanted to know who the oncomer was.

"Bowie!" A hail, peremptory and loud.

He knew the voice: Major Norris Wright.

From the shadows of the trees broke a darker shadow, and a horseman wheeled his mount across Bowie's path on the turnpike, white teeth gleaming in a narrow face.

"Sir! I want a word with you!"

Bowie reined to a stop.

Wright said, "I've watched you this evening, Bowie. Your actions are offensive, sir. You will leave Mrs. Cabanal alone in the future. Do you understand that?"

"On your say-so, Wright, I understand no such thing."

"Philippe Cabanal is my good friend. And I admire Judalon Cabanal. You, sir, owe them both an apology!"

"I don't consider that I need to explain to you, sir, or apologize to anyone!"

"I warn you—let her alone!"

Bowie's mouth set. "You're pretty free with your warnings, Major. Suppose you let Philippe or Judalon tell me."

"That's your answer?"

"Yes."

"Then you'll answer to me—*now!*" Wright's voice was choked.

Bowie saw the pistol in the darkness. The flash lit the ground, the trees, the faces of both men for one quivering instant. The sorrel squatted like a dog, and with the heavy shock of the report in his ears, Bowie felt a jolt at his side, a numbing, but no pain.

The sorrel got back on his legs, and began to plunge, wild with fright. Rage seemed to dim the moonlit scene with a reddish hue as Bowie controlled the horse and circled back.

Staring as if he could not believe, Wright sat motionless in his saddle. "I couldn't have missed him," he said aloud, but to himself.

Bowie's sorrel swung close. "You had no call to fire on me, Wright!"

His own pistol was in his hand. Wright did not stir. His teeth were locked like a wolf's as Bowie thrust the weapon forward. The hammer clicked, but there was no report, no spurt of flame. A misfire.

Bowie hurled the pistol to the ground, and his horse, spurred and reined sidewise, cannoned into the major's mount, almost knocking it off its feet. At the same moment he grappled for Wright.

One powerful hand seized the major by the shoulder, another closed on his elbow. Wright struggled, dashing his bleeding fist again and again into his enemy's face.

Rising in his stirrups, Bowie lifted the other out of his saddle. Together they tumbled headlong to the ground.

A struggle, and a snarling.

"Damn you, Bowie, take your hands off me!"

Terrible fingers reached for Norris Wright's gullet.

A shout, a pounding of hoofs. Other guests leaving Auburn had heard Wright's shot. Men rode out of the avenue's blackness, leaped from horses, dragged Bowie from the major's struggling body.

"Jim—Jim!" Rezin's voice, pleading, expostulating.

"He fired on me. Without warning," Bowie said thickly.

"Come away. Nothing you can do here now."

Bowie's head was clearing, the madness of his rage dying down.

Almost stumbling to his horse, he mounted and rode off with Rezin. Norris Wright stood in a group of his friends, feeling his throat, his pallid hatred clear in the moonlight.

Chapter Twenty-one

1

Bowie, stripped to his waist, stood in Rezin's room at Connelly's. Dr. Cuny stooped over, squinting professionally at his naked side. Just above the waistline a purpling, angry bruise swelled: a bruise fresh and painful, shot with little blood streaks, but after all, only a bruise.

"No doubt of it, the bullet struck here," said Dr. Cuny. "But no penetration—no penetration."

General Cuny began sonorously, "Our James seems to have the invulnerable skin of Achilles——"

"Here's what turned the bullet," Rezin interrupted.

He had examined his brother's waistcoat, and he held out to them a gold watch, smashed and battered. The general and the doctor stared at the disfigured timepiece.

"Let's see it," Bowie said. For a moment he turned the ruined mechanism over in his hand. "It made the ball glance just enough."

"A heavy bullet and a light powder charge," Rezin suggested.

Bowie grunted. "Looks like Norris Wright owes me a new watch."

"What are you going to do about it?" asked the doctor.

"Haven't decided," Bowie said.

The general's Roman features flushed. "This is something that can't be passed over, James. You've got to challenge!"

"I don't know." Bowie seemed to be inwardly debating. "If it's anyone's move, I think it's Wright's."

"Preposterous, sir! Under the code you have every warrant. Unprovoked and treacherous attack, vilification and abuse——"

The general talked as if getting up grounds for a duel was an asset, like money in the bank.

"As to the assault, I reckon Wright's throttle is going to be mighty tender with the finger marks I left on it," said Bowie slowly. "We'll say that things, so far, are about even."

"Do you deny that Major Wright deserves killing?"

"Perhaps he does."

"Then—the cartel, sir. It's a duty!"

"It may be a man's duty to answer a challenge. But I don't consider it's a duty to send one."

General Cuny gaped. "You have scruples against the code, sir?"

"Only against being the initiator."

The general drew himself up somewhat coldly. "I congratulate you, sir, on having suffered no very serious hurt. Now, since it's late and we all need sleep, my brother and I will retire."

Bowie drew on his shirt when the Cunys were gone.

"You think I ought to send a challenge, too?" he asked.

"No," said Rezin.

"Thanks." ·

"But I'm afraid you're going to have to come to conclusions with Norris Wright, sooner or later."

"I reckon."

"There's a treacherous fellow, Jim. An underhanded fellow."

Bowie nodded.

"You mustn't get caught off guard again," Rezin persisted.

He went to his portmanteau at the foot of the bed and opened it. From it he lifted out a knife in a sheath, and brought it to his brother.

"A pistol's all right," he said, "but a knife never misfires. And you can get it into action a lot quicker than reloading a gun."

Bowie examined the weapon. The sheath was rawhide and home-stitched. He drew the blade. An ordinary butcher knife, whetted very keen, but with a cross hilt of hammered brass.

"That brass guard's a good idea," he said.

"I had Manuel, our blacksmith at Sedalia, put it on. Keeps your hand from slipping when you use the knife to bleed or flay game."

Bowie saw an even better use for the hilt. He weighed the knife in his hand. The hilt gave it an awkward balance, the weight up against the handle. No good for throwing. Still, the beginnings of an idea were in him: an idea that had been lying unformed for years. When he was a long-legged youth, he had played at throwing knives with the Cajun boys and achieved a fair skill at it. A knife, to be a good weapon, must be throwable. All at once he remembered, long ago, a room filled with weapons . . . where was it? Oh, yes, the museum of Malot, the New Orleans *maître d'armes*. Some of the things Malot said to him, some of the things he saw and tested there, seemed suddenly to crystallize in his mind.

He said, "Thanks, Rezin," and tossed the knife on the bed. On his face was an absent calm as he put on his waistcoat, with the ragged bullet hole in the pocket, and then his coat. At this moment Rezin felt he knew what was on his brother's mind.

Sure enough, it came out. Bowie asked, "What did you think of her?"

He took it for granted that there was only one "her" worthy of notice at Auburn that night. Rezin did not equivocate.

"She's married, Jim."

Bowie nodded slowly. "I won't see her again. I'm leaving for Little Rock in the morning, instead of waiting for Monday."

At the door, he turned. "Who's the best blacksmith you know?"

Rezin was surprised at the abrupt change in subject. "Why—let's see. There's John Sowell, right here in Natchez. A good man. And Snowden at Opelousas. And what's the matter with Jesse Cliffe at Arcadia?"

"I want somebody who knows all there is to know about steel."

Rezin pondered. "John was telling me about some Arkansas man, last time he was home. Said he knew more about steel than anyone. Let me see—the name is Black. Has a shop at Washington."

"I reckon I'll pay a visit to Washington, Arkansas, on my way north."

"Take you way out of your road."

"I'll make it to Little Rock in time."

"Must be important."

"No. Just a notion."

Rezin was too greatly relieved at finding his brother putting the New Orleans woman out of his mind to argue either for more information or against the long detour.

2

The Territory of Arkansas was divided by a rough line running from its northeast to its southwest corner into two triangles of differing country. The southeast triangle was flat and forested, good, black plantation land, where clearings were being made and cotton planted. The northwest triangle rose into mountains, where most men carried squirrel guns, and turkey-walk cabins stood in small stumped-off patches haggled out of the hillside timber.

Along the dividing line between these regions was a path, skirting hills and swamps, picked out centuries before by the Indians and widened into a wagon trail by settlers, with raccoon bridges across the worst river crossings. Midway on this roadway, sometimes called the Southwest Trail, stood Little Rock, the territorial capital, and at its southwest extremity was the town of Washington.

It was a long journey from Natchez, and Bowie and Nez Coupé had had a sufficiency of salt meat and noisy taverns by the time they reached Washington. They were pleasantly surprised, however, to find that the town was no log-cabin village, that its homes and commercial buildings were well constructed, and that Elijah Stuart's inn possessed clean beds and a decent table.

When they ate supper, which was better than good, Stuart, a big, club-jointed man with a croupy voice and a genial manner, sat at the table with them.

"Know of a smith by the name of Black in these parts?" Bowie asked.

Stuart allowed that, yes, there was a shop owned by James Black, right up Franklin Street, at the edge of town. For good measure, he added that Black had a right smart place and turned out broadaxes, plowshares, and corn knives so damned good that he kept five slaves busy meeting the demand for his product.

Early the following morning Bowie found the shop, a big shed with double doors through which a wagon could be run, a tall brick chimney at the back, and a sign in front which read:

JAMES BLACK
SMITHING AND CUTLERY

He entered the place. Drama is inherent in all blacksmith shops, since smiths deal with fire. Around the walls stood broken wagon wheels, plows, implements, and horseshoes, ready-made and hung in an arrangement according to size. There were three forges, each with its anvil and blower and its water tub to cool white-hot iron. But what caught Bowie's attention was a great blast furnace at the back, like a brick kiln in appearance, something not often seen in blacksmith shops.

A slave, naked to the waist, came up respectfully.

"Mr. Black?" Bowie asked above the clangor at the anvils.

The slave nodded. His black arm indicated the office.

Bowie went in, closing the door behind him to shut out part of the noise. From behind a desk a thin, nervous man, with dark hazel eyes, long black hair brushed back behind his ears, and a forehead greatly wrinkled, gazed keenly at him.

"Mr. Black? My name is Bowie. I've been informed that you make a good cutting edge."

"I make a try at it, sir."

"You have a different tempering method?"

"So they say."

"In what respect?"

Black's face chilled. "By your leave, sir, that's a trade secret."

"I crave your pardon. Certainly, it's your business, sir. I only asked because I have a special job. A kind of knife I want made."

The smith was interested. "I was a cutler before I came West from Philadelphia. Fine knives are a sort of hobby with me, but we don't have much call for them here."

178

Bowie held out a piece of carved wood. "I sort of whittled this out," he explained.

Black nodded. It was customary for men to bring whittled models, since the draftsman's art was almost unknown on the frontier. In long, nervous fingers, he took Bowie's piece of carved white pine and turned it over and over.

"Some novel features in this idea," he said.

"Just a rough beginning of what I mean," said Bowie. From the sheath at his belt he drew Rezin's butcher knife and handed it to Black. "This thing isn't right. Not for a fighting knife. It's too clumsy, lacks balance, and a lot of other things."

In one hand Black held the butcher knife, in the other the wooden model. The superior formation of the latter was evident.

"These are the proportions you want?" he asked.

"Roughly."

Black returned the butcher knife and, taking up a rule, made a series of measurements on the carved pattern.

"Blade, eleven inches long, and an inch and a half wide," he said.

"That can vary a little, according to the balance."

"The heel at the back seems exceptionally thick. I get three eighths of an inch here."

"That's to give it strength. Above all, it must not snap."

The smith nodded. Bowie took the pattern and began to outline some of its features, very carefully. "Observe this: the point is to come at the exact center of the width of the blade. That's to give it accuracy in throwing. Nothing worse than an off-center point when you try to stick a knife in a target. Furthermore, it provides a certain balance which you will appreciate."

Black's eyes gleamed as he nodded again.

"The blade curves to the point convexly from the edge, and concavely from the back," said Bowie. "Both those curves must be as sharp as the edge of the blade itself. They form, in fact, a continuing part of the edge."

"I can see that. An excellent feature. Particularly since you want the blade so thick."

"The cross guard is very important. It should be of heavy brass instead of steel. Also, I want a backing of brass along the heel of the blade, running to where the curve toward the point begins."

"Why brass, Mr. Bowie?"

"Brass is softer than steel. It will catch a cutting edge. In parrying a thrust, the other blade won't slip off so easy."

"Very clear. Very logical."

"The rest of it is naturally up to you, if you want to undertake it."

179

Bowie handed back the model. "The knife must be balanced so it can be thrown. You'll arrive at that when you know the weight of the blade in relation to hilt and handle."

Black nodded. "Of course. A nice problem there."

"There's something else that I'm not wholly sure is possible, but I want to give it to you as a notion——" Bowie hesitated.

"Very well."

"I was once shown a weapon—a kind of sword it was, used by fighting men in the Middle Ages, when they had to cut at steel armor. It had a feature that's always interested me. I've thought it over a good many times since. A weight, called a steel apple, slid in a groove along the back of the blade—toward the point when a blow was struck. It put something extra into the swing, you see—an added power. Naturally a steel apple wouldn't be practical in a knife. But if you gather what I mean—a weighting of the blade, maybe—toward the point—to give a shrewder stroke . . . well, I'll leave that with you for what it's worth."

Black took a long time thinking this over. "It would take study," he said at length. "As for the steel, it will be the best I can make, and that's as good as you can get, if I do say it. You've heard of Damascus steel?"

"Yes, sir."

"The world never saw steel that would take and keep an edge like Damascus, or was as springy, yet strong. It had a peculiar mottling, due to the process of its making. Would it surprise you to know that I make steel with such mottling—perhaps the true Damascus?"

"Indeed, yes," Bowie said.

"I'm not sure it's exactly the same. I discovered the process by an accident. But I'm certain it's the best steel that can be produced by the methods we have today." Black paused, hand at chin, eyes brooding. "And yet, it's possible to make better. Let me show you something."

From a drawer of his desk he took a wooden box, brassbound and locked. With a key taken out of his pocket he unlocked it. Within, on velvet like a jewel, lay an object, dark and irregularly round, half the size of a man's fist. He lifted it out.

"Take it," he said.

In Bowie's hand it was surprisingly heavy. "What is it?"

"Steel. Pure steel. And of a quality never made on this earth."

"Then how . . . ?"

"Let me recite an experience. As a boy, working on a farm in Pennsylvania, I saw a fireball pass across the sky, so bright that it made even the sun seem secondary for a moment, and leaving a trail of incandescent smoke behind it. When it disappeared over the horizon, terrific thunderclaps were heard, and weird sounds which I can only liken to the bellow of oxen, the roar of a fire in a chimney, and the tearing of cloth. This was followed by a detonation like a tremendous explosion. It was the death of a shooting star."

He paused, his keen intellectual face showing the impression made on him by the heavenly visitation. "It terrified the countryside. Many thought it presaged the end of the world. But it started me on a career. I went to the place where fragments of the meteor fell and discovered some pieces, of which this was the largest. Later I learned something remarkable about this piece."

"What was that?"

"Some meteorites are chiefly stone—basaltic rock. Others are chiefly iron, smelted in the heavenly furnace of their own heat as they enter the earth's envelope of atmosphere. But *this* is steel—genuine steel, produced by some process which must have included passage in superheated form through atmospheric ice. Its hardness is such that it is almost impossible to cut it, even with a diamond. These things occur but rarely in meteorites, yet they must have a lesson for us."

With intense seriousness his hazel eyes fixed on his visitor's face. "Mr. Bowie, an examination of the smaller fragments by a noted scientist in the University of Pennsylvania revealed one possible answer to this superior steel. It contains alloys of some kind. Just what these are or how they are combined is impossible to tell. Under our methods it is not possible to combine alloys to make this transcendent steel—at least to my knowledge. But in this small piece is some combining factor. Find its secret for mating alloy and steel, and we will have made a truly great upward step in metallurgy."

He took the dark lump from Bowie and replaced it in its box, which he locked carefully. "That's why it is one of my most prized possessions," he said. "You see I keep it in a jewel box, for it is a true jewel."

Bowie had listened with deep interest. "I believe I've brought my knife to the right man," he said.

"Thank you, sir." Black nodded. "You've given me something different to work on: something which greatly intrigues me. Come back in a month. We'll see what can be accomplished."

3

For a long time after Bowie was gone, James Black sat at his desk turning over in his fingers the whittled wooden pattern. To every part of his nature the problem of the knife appealed. His eyes took in each contour of the blade: the upcurve from the edge, and the downcurve from the spine, both meeting at the point exactly midway of the width of the blade and whetted to equal razor keenness with the edge itself. Clearly a product of thinking, as well as of instinctive judgment of values in a knife as a weapon. New and good: very good. With each minute that he studied the carved model his respect for the man who had brought it to him grew.

To make a knife in this shape was easy: but to give it all the hidden qualities Bowie had suggested would be immeasurably difficult. The matter of balance: Bowie had spoken of the steel apple which threw actual force toward the point as a blow was struck. Such a device was impossible in this knife . . . yet there must be some way to put calculated weight in the blade.

Pursing his lips, he next gave especial attention to the hilt and handle. These must bear relation in balance to the blade itself. A mathematical problem, really, the nicest calculation, and one not readily solved on paper. His experiments must be empirical. Nothing for it but to build a blade and work upon the weights and balances inherent in that.

After a time he rose and went out into the shop. Five trained slaves were at work at the forges, the furnace, or the benches. Two were making wrought-iron nails, a third hammering out horseshoes. He called them to him and gave orders. The furnace was to be permitted to cool entirely. It would be morning before it would be ready for the first part of the experiment, not sooner. Meantime they were to rest.

James Black slept fitfully that night. He was in the tug of an immense inspiration, the pull of an idea. It produced in his mind a constant feverish activity which would not yield to slumber.

Next morning he had his people up at the first dawn and hardly allowed them time for breakfast before he assembled them in the shop. Five black men, muscular and skilled. They looked at him like eager dogs, for they sensed something new. His orders crackled.

"Clean out that furnace. Don't leave a cinder big enough to make your eye water.

"Get a new clay crucible ready.

"Pick out wrought iron. The best we have. I'll look it over myself."

This last proved the importance of the job. Bar iron was good enough for ordinary steel, but so intent was Black on obtaining the nearest possibility to absolute purity that he ordered wrought iron, already refined, and the best of that.

During these preparations he walked about nervously, supervising, personally inspecting every inch of the furnace, even the flue. Not until it was cleaned over and over to his complete satisfaction did he give the order to lay the fire bed.

Taking turns, the slaves began laboring at the bellows. In the bed of glowing charcoal, replaced as fast as it burned away, the wrought-iron

182

bars, cut into short sections, grew red, then white-hot, then white, and at last molten.

Through the day the men sweated in relays. Their master labored more fiercely than any of them, never resting, never taking his eyes from the work, testing and estimating, ordering more fuel, more activity at the bellows. His lean face was a miracle of concentration, as if he fairly willed a perfect process, the carbon from the charcoal to dissolve into the metal and penetrate it, the primary step in changing iron to steel.

All day the furnace glowed: and all the following night. The slaves grew worn and haggard, but they did not diminish their labors, for Black himself, cheeks gaunt, eyes red from smoke, hair disheveled, a smear of soot across his deep-lined forehead, was wearier yet more determined than any of them.

At noon the next day Black ordered the furnace cooled and examined the contents of the crucible. This was steel, but only crude steel, too imperfect for his purpose. The carbon, diffusing into the metal, had encountered particles of slag always present in even the best wrought iron, and formed carbonic gas pockets, which, unable to escape, left molten blisters in the fabric. A further refining, through the crucible process, of this blister steel was needful.

While the furnace cooled Black and his five slaves slept like the dead, but on the morning of the next day, which was the third of this effort, they were all up again at the earliest light.

This was to be the beginning of the most important series of steps. Once again, under Black's own eye, the furnace was cleansed of all impurities. With his own hands he made the crucible of finest clay. The fires were rekindled, the crucible put in place.

4

"Start the bellows!"

The wheezing roar began. Flames leaped up. At the handles a slave grew wet with sweat.

After an hour, at Black's shout, a second man took the bellows. The huge leather lungs, blowing on the fire bed, did not vary their regularity as the slaves changed places, again and again.

More charcoal. Regularly the relays changed. The flaming mass grew white-hot. Hours of this. Then Black gave the signal to stop. The first, or steeling, fire had burned out its course.

Through a smoked glass held to protect his eyes from the vivid glare, he peered into the crucible. Again the furnace was fueled. Again the bellows began their throaty snort.

Flames burned fiercely. Black's men sweated. In the eyeballs of their master was a glare almost furious. This was the second fire. It would be followed by the third, or "killing," fire.

By nightfall Black was satisfied that the contents of the crucible were entirely refined, all impurities burned out. This would have been the normal finish. But he ordered still a fourth fire prepared.

Now he considered very deeply. He went into his office, took out and unlocked the brassbound box, and from it lifted his prized possession of possessions: the jewel of the sky, the piece of a star.

For a moment he weighed it in his hand, gazing lovingly at its black luster and its strange contours. Then he shook his head, drew a deep breath, went out to the furnace and dropped the piece into the molten depths of the crucible.

Bowie's knife was to carry in it the flavor of other worlds, of mysterious space and unknown processes from the infinite itself.

With the continuing roar of the bellows began the period of prayer, for James Black was a prayerful man. The mystical operations by which elements commingled and fused, changing their character into something entirely different, awed him secretly, although he knew more about them than almost any other man. In this was a touch of the hand of God. James Black prayed, if not in words, at least by volition and feeling.

Night. Sparks flew high from the chimney, illumining the roof of the shed and the dark trees about it. Within the shop the red flare of the furnace tinted all the inner timbers with bloody light. Black bodies of the sweating men shone as if oiled, with strange garish highlights.

In that hour James Black was transformed. Like some weird and terrible alchemist of bygone ancient days, he hovered over this scene, as if he were probing into it a mystic formula of transmutation, combined of magic words, strange secret rites, and exorcisms. The shadow, black as ink, from his gaunt pointed shoulders grew gigantically upon the wall and ceiling behind him, batlike and sinister. His face resembled that of a man in profound suffering, eyes bloodshot and staring, mouth compressed and grim, lines deepened, madness, almost, staring out of it. He seemed ready to collapse, for he alone had not rested. But he did not collapse. Biting his lips, his fingers clenched, he drove himself and his men, on and on.

It was toward cockcrow before Black felt that the elements of his steel had sintered into something of sufficient perfection. Even when he ordered the pouring of the molten mass, his heart was in his throat. The final test was at hand. The ultimate proof. All the long process of shaping, tempering, and testing still was to come.

But this was his steel.

As the first gray dawn appeared, the bloom, glowing incandescent, began cooling. The slaves were staggering with fatigue. Last to leave his task was their master; his face like a death's-head.

5

It had been a wearying court session, and Bowie was glad to get away from Little Rock. Sam Doane, the stubborn district attorney, had used every artifice to postpone the trial of the disputed claims, but steadily he had been maneuvered until it was forced to an issue.

Bowie was on the witness stand for days, testifying as to his methods of obtaining land, his methods of disposing of it. Of the one hundred and twenty-six separate cases at issue, one hundred and seventeen had been confirmed by the court, and in this number were included all those in which the Bowie brothers were concerned. It was a great relief, now that they stood clear in the courts.

He was eager to see what had come of the project he had left in Washington with James Black. Once again he sat in the artificer's small office. But this time it was he who turned over in his hands an object: the steel realization of the wooden model he had whittled out of pine.

In his face was a blaze of delight. "I hadn't even hoped it would come off as well as this," he said.

He laid the flat of the blade across his leveled forefinger, an inch or so in front of the cross guard. The balance was perfect.

"It's choicely good." This was the highest praise he knew to give.

"The knife is machined to turn naturally once in the air, in a throw of thirty feet," Black said, deeply pleased.

Bowie's gray eye took in the ivory handle: and the pommel, the cross hilt with balled ends, and the strip welded to the heel of the blade, all of hammered brass.

But it was the blade itself that brought the real gleam to his eye. This was no ordinary knife: no thin polished slip of steel likely to snap like glass or bend at too great a strain. It was as if two or three ordinary knives had been welded together, the backbone powerful. Incurve from spine to point, and outcurve from edge to point, made a harmony deeply satisfying. He tested the edge with a wetted thumb. No razor could be more sinisterly keen.

"That steel will hold an edge as none you ever saw," said Black. "I quenched it seven times. Each time in panther oil."

He took the knife and twanged it with his thumb. From it came a clear, bell-like sound. He returned it to Bowie.

"Try throwing it. That board yonder."

The knife sang through the air, struck, and gave a high vibrant note as it quivered in its target.

Bowie walked over and drew it from the plank. He looked at the cold bluish luster of the blade: it was something like ice. He put it to his tongue: it tasted bitter and raw like the sea. He sniffed at it: it smelt like blood.

"I never thought such a knife could be," he marveled. "What did you do to make it, James Black?"

"Something that can hardly be done again," said Black, his voice almost mystical. "I fused into it a fragment of a star. For better or for worse, this knife of yours has a bit of heaven in it—or a bit of hell."

Chapter Twenty-two

I

Nez Coupé was ecstatic. He spent half an hour lovingly considering the knife's keenness, the firmness of its haft and cross guard, its balance in his fist. He stepped to an oak tree and tried it. A thick branch was sheared through like a melon, and his thumb on the edge found no diminution of the razor keenness. Truly this was a blade beyond all blades.

He gazed at Bowie. "This knife, she is death."

Bowie nodded and took it back, as if he begrudged the time it was in the other's possession. Its mere weight in his hands gave him a sense of power and confidence. Malot, that shrewd appraiser of fighting men, had observed that he had "an affinity for the knife." A true thing. Bowie had killed two men. Each with a knife, a knife utilized for the moment, although he had not particularly versed himself in knife fighting. But each time the knife, though strange and borrowed, had been as an inspired extension of his will.

His new, strange, miraculously keen weapon was as a fulfillment of his nature. His life seemed to focus on it, its hilt in the sheath on his hip gave him a harsh joy. The thing almost went to his head. James Black had spoken of something added: a bit of heaven, or perhaps of hell. Bowie was not far from attributing supernatural properties to his knife.

Painstakingly he cleansed the blade of every tiny vestige of bark or sap left from Nez Coupé's experiment on the oak limb and thrust it back into the sheath.

At Monroe, Louisiana, he and Nez Coupé parted, for the Cajun must take the road west to Arcadia. Bowie continued to Natchez.

He found that Rezin, who had been home in the interim, had returned to Connelly's tavern to await him. After listening to Bowie's report of the land trials at Little Rock, Rezin had news of his own.

"Andrew Marschalk's courier got back from Nashville the week after you went north," he said. "Here's what Marschalk put in the *Herald*."

From his pocket he took a folded newspaper page, and Bowie read:

Be it known to all and sundry, that in the matter brought into question concerning the running horse, Steel Duke, the following has been ascertained: The horse, Steel Duke, was formerly the legal property of Mr. Joseph Levington, a gentleman of Nashville, and passed into the possession of one John Sturdevant, sometimes called Bloody Jack, in the course of a game of bezique played in the City Hotel, Nashville, the 4th, ultimo. Mr. Levington in due form signed the bill of sale to the said Sturdevant, who in turn endorsed it to Mr. James Bowie, when the latter purchased the horse for the sum of $500.00 in cash, the 17th, instant. There exists, therefore, no cloud on Mr. Bowie's title to the horse, Steel Duke, and such being the case, it is ruled by the board of judges and stewards that the race of the 21st, instant, was properly run, Steel Duke being the winner in two straight heats, and gentlemen are notified that they should pay their wagers accordingly.

The Board of Judges and Stewards.
By Andrew Marschalk, presiding judge.

Bowie looked up.

"Most of the bets have been paid," Rezin said.

"What about Wright's?"

"Wright hasn't made a settlement for what he owes you yet, but I'm persuaded that he will."

"I want that five thousand and that cotton farm," said Bowie.

Rezin nodded. "You've been away. Give him time. Whatever Wright is, he's no liar." He grinned. "I hear Judge Crain had to sell property to settle his obligations. It didn't set well with him or with the others. As for us, the bets let us complete the Lecompte land deal. They've done a lot of complaining over at King's tavern."

"Along what lines?"

"For one thing, they're now saying that Joseph Levington of Nashville, while of good family, is prone to lose his judgment when in drink. On the night in question, he was so drunk, so they say, that he didn't know one card from another, and so was bled by Sturdevant. Some of his friends next day urged him to revoke his bet, but Levington signed the bill of sale when it was presented."

"He should. A debt of honor."

"The King's tavern crowd has tried to infer that the incident, to say the best for it, was irregular."

"Gives them some satisfaction, I suppose."

"When you left town so early next morning after the quarrel with Wright, there was a little talk. Your return will put a stop to that, and I think Wright himself never suspected you of running away."

"Huh!"

"Wright's had a month to cool off. He may be ready to drop the matter."

"Don't bet on that," growled Bowie.

To himself Rezin conceded it would be a poor wager. That day in Natchez, sporting bloods were making and taking bets as to whether his brother or Norris Wright would send the challenge, and which of them would die. It was taken for granted that one or the other of the two was living on borrowed time.

"We've had a fracas since you left. Know Montfort Wells of Alexandria?"

Bowie did. Montfort Wells was an older brother of Colonel Sam Wells: an aging man, somewhat palsied and squinting through thick-lensed glasses, since his sight was dimmed by cataracts in both eyes.

"It appears that Dr. Maddox of the Crain party circulated a yarn about old Montfort. Its exact nature I've not been able to learn, since Colonel Wells, naturally, is reluctant to discuss it. But I gather it is of a scandalous nature involving a woman."

Bowie grinned and offered the opinion that the type of scandal alleged might have been taken as a compliment, considering the years and fading manhood of the elder Wells.

Rezin grinned back. "Old Montfort didn't so take it. In spite of his age —he's past seventy—and his palsy, he sent a note to Maddox demanding the source of the story. Maddox refused to state, beyond the fact that it came from a lady patient of his. Yesterday, while in Alexandria on business, he encountered old Montfort, who stepped into his office, fetched out a double-barreled shotgun, and pulled both triggers. His shooting was deplorable—he can hardly make out a moving figure at ten paces, you know. The charge merely truncated the doctor's coat tails and bagged a mule beyond. The animal, which was drawing a cotton cart, overturned the cart and injured the field hand who was driving it. Montfort was deeply mortified because mule, Negro, and cart belonged to a friend of his. Of course he insisted on paying damages. Maddox returned somewhat hastily to Natchez."

Bowie laughed.

"By the way," Rezin went on, "will you dispose of your share in Steel Duke?"

"Dr. Duncan?"

"Yes. Five thousand dollars is the offer. A clean ten-for-one profit. The others all want to sell."

Bowie nodded. "Dr. Duncan spoke to me about it. I wouldn't stand in the way of the others."

"Speaking of Duncan," said Rezin, "reminds me that your friends are still there at Auburn."

"The Cabanals?" Bowie hoped that he appeared casual.

"Yes. A rather lengthy visit, I'd say. For people who aren't kinfolks that is."

"The Duncans are most hospitable. And I think Mrs. Duncan and Judalon are very fond of each other."

"Saw Mrs. Cabanal recently in town. She inquired about you." Rezin paused. "A handsome woman, I'm bound to say, Jim. Mighty small, but handsome. Knows how to look a man up and down as if she were—well —concealing her admiration of him. Hard to get that across, but somehow she does it, and it's flattering in a subtle sort of way."

Rezin ruminated. "Major Wright's been out to Auburn a lot since you left."

"How often?" Bowie said.

"Couldn't say, since I don't keep tabs either on Wright or Auburn. But I'd say over-often. Some of the ladies in the town are beginning to gossip about it, and so it gets to the men, and that's how it came to me. They're saying that Wright's sweet on Cabanal's wife."

"What about Philippe?"

"Don't know. You'd wonder, naturally, why he'd stand for it. He knows about it, surely. Maybe it's all aboveboard—you know how gossip distorts things. In any case, he and Wright are together a good part of the time when he's in town. He's been doing a lot of gambling at King's tavern, and, I'm informed, down under the bluff also."

It was a subject Bowie was willing to drop. The Duncans were respectable. Certainly they knew what was proper and what was not. On the other hand, they were the sort who would never interfere in the affairs of others and would keep their opinions to themselves when guests in their home were involved.

He went to his room, an ugly feeling in him. Judalon . . . She had taken Bowie's kiss, and her marriage had not stood in the way of it. Why not another man's?

In the illogical way of the jealous, he grew angry toward the woman, already condemning her in his mind. No telling what had been going on since he went north. The image of her had remained in his heart and the taste of her on his mouth, a lasting mischief.

Bowie did considerable walking back and forth across the floor, his mind lost in a maze of complications and contradictions. Woman was the inexplicable mystery, her doings not to be computed by any measurement or plan. To deceive, he believed at that moment, was natural in women, even to lie outright was not considered very wrong by them. They practiced the art of dissembling until there was no telling what their true thought was. A man might believe he was foremost with one of them, and find that secretly she was laughing at him, having in reality opened toward another whom he did not even suspect. Cruelty, with such, was an object, a part of their enjoyment of the devious game, because in making a man suffer they saw proof of their power over him.

Yet . . . one had to be fair. Sometimes women were generous to the point of the incredible. Recollection served to remind him that he had received kindnesses for which he might have been more grateful.

Catherine Villars had been the first. There had been others . . . not as many, to be sure, as the opportunities offered. Bowie was likable, free, and good to look upon. He was no skirt chaser: but there were times when it was almost as if he were the pursued. His conscience did not hound him too relentlessly because of what he had accepted from these.

Always he had been mystified by the strange exaltation, naturalness, even innocence of women once they resolved to abandon the familiar cloakings of custom and behavior. A woman might seem remote, cool, inaccessible, living in a different world where a man could reach to her only through the attenuated little tentacles of social contact. Then one night something would steal the sanity from him and her, and he would be left dazed by the suddenness and completeness, the ecstasy and power, the fearlessness and realism, of a surrender which made her seem stronger than she had been before in defense.

Judalon, however, was not to be put in any category, because there was no understanding her. His mind had been troubled ever since that night at Auburn by a succession of illogical hopes, dreams, and self-condemnations, all rising like smoke from the narrow mouth of a jug . . .

What was Norris Wright to her? An ugly rage, an endless dislike of the sleek major burned in him. Wright had tried to kill him. This was something that must be settled between them.

He made up his mind that he would call out Major Norris Wright.

The heat of his jealousy set him to thinking. For a man to be jealous of another man, over a woman who was the wife of still a third man . . . that was not good. About it was something unwholesome, to say the best for it.

Still, he would call out Wright. It was expected of him.

He considered the matter and slid the knife in its sheath on his hip. But this would be no affair of knives. Without any question the major would choose pistols.

3

Next morning a black boy on a long-legged colt brought a note to Connelly's inn. The note was addressed to Bowie, and he recognized the writing, although he had not seen it for ten years. He tore open the small envelope and read:

Mr. James Bowie: The undersigned prays that you come to Auburn, if convenient for you, at 3 P.M. this day, on a matter which she is persuaded is of importance to you. Please answer by messenger.

Faithfully, Judalon de Bornay Cabanal.

Bowie considered the matter for a moment, scribbled a note of acceptance, and gave it to the boy, along with a half dollar.

Here was a mystery. An urgent request to come, at a stated time, on a matter she was "persuaded is of importance." Yet the entire tone of the missive was formal, in the third person. Women sometimes wrote that way, distrusting anything placed on paper. He could feel something beneath this. What, he did not know.

It would take fifteen minutes to ride out to Auburn. That meant he could not start until shortly before three, and it was only ten-thirty in the morning. An eternity, the intervening hours.

He ate lunch with Rezin, saying nothing of Judalon's note, and when his brother, who had business in the cotton exchange, left him, he went to the upper gallery of the inn to sit alone.

Connelly's commanded an unsurpassed view. In a mighty curve the river swept below him, the tree-dotted plain of Louisiana beyond, the distant buildings of Vidalia, and the low-lying island, green and wooded, near the far shore.

The man he least expected to see came out on the gallery and looked at him. Philippe Cabanal.

He hurried over and offered his hand. "Just heard you were back, Bowie. Been gone a long time, haven't you? We've missed you."

Such friendliness was neither timely nor required. Bowie said coldly, "How are you, Philippe?"

"Well enough, I suppose. They told me you were up here. I took the liberty of coming up."

"Certainly." Bowie was wondering now if Philippe knew about the notes exchanged between himself and Judalon.

"Dr. Duncan, who'd been in town, brought word last night that you'd returned from the north. Judalon was as delighted as I." The man smirked. "You know, Bowie, a jealous man might wonder why my wife was so interested. But of course, you two been friends for years, haven't you? I'm not a bit jealous."

Bowie disliked the smirk. He said, "I'm glad to be back. I hope to pay my respects at Auburn soon."

Philippe nodded. A kind of twist came over his mouth, accentuated by the thin curling mustache. "I wanted to talk with you alone. There's—well—a personal thing." He hesitated.

"Go ahead." Bowie wondered where this was leading.

"I find myself in a situation at the moment which is something embarrassing." Philippe gave a little deprecating laugh. "Seems to happen to me most often—my infernal bad luck."

At least it had nothing to do with Judalon. Bowie said, "I'm very sorry."

"I knew I could count on your sympathy," Philippe said eagerly. "That's why I decided to make bold——"

Again he hesitated, as if the matter were hard to bring out. Bowie was struck once more by the change in him. He was dressed foppishly as usual, but his finery did not disguise the distressing air of a man who spends his days seeking favors and getting few.

Philippe began again. "What I want to discuss—how it grinds me to do it!—is the matter of a loan. A sort of loan, that is."

"A *sort* of loan?"

"Well," Philippe said, "that's the awkward part of it." Again the uneasy twist of the weak mouth. "I went a bit over my head in the Duncan Cup. Of course the wrong horse—my luck again. Who'd have dreamed you'd bring in that animal of yours?"

Bowie said, "You can't pay your losses?"

"To put it short, that's exactly it. A bitter draught—I've drunk deep of it more than once."

"Let me understand this. I was under the impression that you had more than enough—with your father's estate—and your wife's——"

Philippe looked down at the floor. "It's unpleasant to discuss personal affairs, but I'll give you an explanation. In confidence, you understand.

My own money is gone. Unfortunate business investments. Could happen to anybody. So we're living on Judalon's income."

"I see."

"Unhappily, her father left it so that she gets it in quarterly installments —not enough, if you'll believe me, to keep us on even a respectable basis."

Philippe gave Bowie a quick glance. "Between us, old de Bornay was far from wise in some of his ventures. Indigo, for one thing. Sank a lot of money in an indigo plantation—a failure, of course. Other bad investments we discovered too late—after the yellow jack carried him off. Old Janos Parisot had him in a nutcracker. That explains why he always kowtowed so, if you remember. After his death the nutcracker squeezed. So Judalon's installment is so small that it's gone as soon as we get it—and before —and we have to wait and scrimp and use our wits until the next comes due. I'd hoped to recoup a little on that horse race. Instead, I'm deeper in than ever."

Bowie was silent, digesting this.

Again Philippe gave him an odd look. "You had a wager with Major Wright."

"I did."

"Perhaps you're wondering why it's not been paid?"

"I supposed because I'd been out of the city."

"You're wrong. He gave me the money and the deed to bring over from King's tavern. I took the liberty of holding it because, as you say, you were away."

"That was quite a liberty, Philippe."

"Don't be angry, I beg of you. You've no idea the straits I'm in."

"You have the payment here?"

"The deed to the land." Philippe drew from a pocket the folded document.

For a moment Bowie glanced it over to see that it was in proper form. Then he looked up. "There was also five thousand in cash."

"Now—this is what I want to bring up. About that money I—I'm going to make a request that I hope you'll find feasible——"

"You don't have it?"

"Please! It happens that I—ah—overextended myself, by just about that amount. Permit me to keep the five thousand—say for ninety days, won't you? It would pull me out of a bad hole." He paused. "It isn't as if it was money you took out of your pocket. After all, you got me in this fix. You really owe me this consideration——"

"What if I don't feel I owe it to you?"

Once more Philippe's sidelong glance. "In that case—perhaps you may feel that you owe it—to Judalon."

Bowie rose so quickly that the other backed away. "What does she have to do with it?"

"Nothing. Perhaps. But you think a lot of her, don't you? Always have." That appraising look. "It would be a terrible humiliation to my wife—if I were denounced. Much worse for her than for me. Don't you think?"

The monumental effrontery of this was its strength.

"Does Judalon know?" Bowie asked.

"Not a thing."

"Let it go as a loan then."

"There speaks the generous friend! You know well that I'd do any favor for you in return!"

Bowie's contempt prevented a reply. Philippe departed, but paused at the door with his smile. "Don't forget. The latchstring's out for you at Auburn. I'm sure Judalon will be eager to see you—any time."

It was as if he were offering his wife's company as a sort of premium for the loan he had just arranged.

4

Worm fence and stone wall set off broad cotton acres, great trees swung bearded streamers of gray moss, and quail whistled across the fields. Bowie trotted his horse down the shaded Auburn drive, left the animal with a stableboy, and went up the steps.

"Mrs. Cabanal?" he said to the servant who opened the door.

"This way, suh." He was conducted to the drawing room.

Judalon was alone. She rose.

"You're prompt. Thank you for coming," she said. "Catherine is taking her nap upstairs, and the doctor's in town. So we can talk for a minute— quite without interruption. Come over here by the window and sit down, won't you?"

He had been looking forward to this, but her manner gave him a profound disappointment, as if cold water had been dashed over his warm expectations. He took the seat she indicated, opposite from her. For a moment she inquired about his journey. Then she said, "You'll want to know why I asked you to come here."

"Yes. I am a little curious," he said.

"The reason was personal. A reason of friendship. I took the earliest opportunity of communicating with you, because of the pressing nature of the matter."

"It must be important."

She regarded him seriously. "Since you got back, have you met Major Wright?"

"No."

"Then, thank God, I'm not too late. Your quarrel with him—I want you to promise me you'll let it go no farther."

This was why she had asked him to Auburn? He was astonished, and at the same time he felt a twinge of resentment.

"I didn't make that quarrel," he said.

"But you can avoid further aggravation of it."

"You really think it's as simple as that?"

"Men are supposed to be rational creatures."

"A man may not seek a quarrel, Judalon, but it sometimes seeks him."

"Why should men be enemies?"

He said, "If I'd lived all my years, and with all my chances made no enemy, I'd feel myself a pretty sorry failure."

She turned that over in her mind. At last she said, "At least promise me that you will not send the challenge. If it comes, let it come from him. Will you promise that, Jim?"

His bitterness was growing. "Why are you worrying over Norris Wright?" he demanded.

"I'm not! Why should I worry over Norris Wright?" An angry flare. "Why do men seek in the most innocent motives of a woman for some hidden interest or meaning?"

"I only asked because——"

"Because of what?" Her eyes challenged him.

"Because I've heard he's been out here a very great deal."

"To see Philippe! And not as often as he would like!" She tossed her dark head. "Major Wright is not as much to my taste as you seem to think. I find him very self-centered, if you want the truth. And much too sure of himself. He seems almost to forget at times that I am a wedded wife. When he knows that you have been here, and that I regard you as a very dear friend, it may dash him, and be good for him!"

It relieved him in a way, yet increased his doubts in another. Evidently she expected him to visit her, often perhaps. Fashionable women had courtiers after they were married. She seemed to think nothing of it. He wondered if, when she and the major were together, the major was the only one who, at times, forgot that Judalon was a wedded wife . . .

The thought chilled him. He said, "Why did you ask this of me, instead of Wright?"

Her mood underwent one of its lightning changes. All at once she was soft and sweet. "Because I know your kindness, Jim, and your common sense. And your friendship. I thought you'd grant me something I earnestly desire. I so abhor bloodshed. It should not be difficult for you to know why."

She meant the death of Narcisse.

"If that's the reason," he said, "I'll promise that if there's a challenge it won't come from me."

Her face brightened. "You make me happy—very happy."

For a moment they sat silently. As if seeking a subject, she said, "I'm sorry Philippe isn't here. I had expected his return before this."

"I saw him. This morning." A casual remark, but instantly Bowie was sorry he had made it. In her eyes was an unsmiling question.

"This morning?" Conviction seemed to dawn in her. "Jim! Did you lend him money?"

It took him back. "Well—not exactly——"

"Did he ask you for a loan, or did he not?" she demanded.

"I gave him no money. Not actual money——" He was floundering.

She leaned forward, her eyes searching his. "Explain that. It's very important to me, and it isn't a mere desire to pry. Jim, tell me!"

"I dislike——"

"Tell me!"

She at least suspected the truth: he decided to tell her part of it.

"It concerns some winnings of mine."

"Winnings from whom?"

"Major Wright."

"He gave Philippe money to pay you?"

She took his silence for an affirmative and for a moment was very still. Presently, with a bitterness he had never known in her, she said, "As prideless as a pot hound—my husband."

She leaned back in her chair, her head against the cushion, closing her eyes. He saw how deeply her pride was hurt, but nothing occurred to him to say.

After a time, she opened her eyes. "It will be no use to ask you the amount. Otherwise I would undertake to repay it as soon as my allowance comes due."

"Don't think of it."

"How can I help it? If Philippe has no pride, I have. Do you know where he is now—what's delayed him? He's with that man Sturdevant; the creature has some hold on him. How much he has taken from Philippe, I don't know, because I have no way of knowing the debts Philippe has piled up here in Natchez since we came. Yours is only one of many. That is why we're still here, cadging on the Duncans. Because, to tell you the brutal truth, we haven't the money to return to New Orleans!"

She rose and walked over to the window. He rose also. Presently she turned to him a face as chill as carved marble. "Jim, this decides me." She closed her lips tightly for a moment. "I am going to divorce Philippe."

She did not speak violently, but he felt violence behind her apparent calm.

"A divorce?" he said stupidly. "It's very hard to get a divorce——"

"I know it's not easy." Still she seemed prompted by a seething inward passion. "It requires an act of the legislature. But I am—not without friends—who have political power. And I have grounds."

Insensibly he had drawn near her. "What kind of grounds?"

"Adultery."

"Judalon!"

"Adultery," she repeated, gazing out of the window. "I have a certain knowledge of a woman he keeps." A flash of distaste on her face. "A wench on Palisade Street in New Orleans. I've known about it for years."

The scene from the window was worth looking at: smooth tree-shaded lawn, a sweep of drive, white paddock fence with the woods beyond. But neither of them really saw it, although both were looking out.

"Don't think me naïve," she went on drearily. "I know men have mistresses. It is winked at; women prefer security to scandal, and therefore suffer. I might even blind myself to it, if Philippe were any excuse of a man. But he is—so despicable. You've seen one side of him—the beggar, cadger. But you know nothing of the other things: his contemptible weakness; his intemperance; his craze for gambling which has impoverished us; his ugly temper and rudeness at times, and his craven crawling for forgiveness at others." She drew a deep, almost shuddering breath. "But this is the finish. As surely as you and I are standing her, I am going to free myself from that man."

She turned to him, all at once very small and frightened of her own resolution. "Oh, Jim, I need your friendship. Divorce is such a dreadful thing—a woman loses so by it. To be an object of pity—of laughter behind my back—of whispered scandal and open sneers. I'm afraid—terribly afraid——"

She seized his hand in both her own and clung to it. Immense emotion surged through him.

"Don't be afraid," he whispered. "When you're free—as soon as you're free—Judalon, will you marry me?"

She looked at him as if she were stunned, her eyes searching his face as if she understood.

"You'd do that . . . for me?" she asked.

"Yes. I mean it, darling."

She carried his hand against her breast, and he could feel her heart beating upon it.

"Dear Jim," she said. "Dear Jim!"

She drew a little breath, almost exultantly. Then she withdrew her hands, took a rose from a vase on the table beside her, and held it delicately to her nose. As if the act cleared her head, she said, "Thank you for that. But I can't answer you now, can I?"

"Why not, Judalon?"

"We must both remember that I'm still a married woman."

The illogic of this baffled him. "But you have decided——"

"When the time comes—perhaps you may ask me—the same question——"

This was not a refusal.

Some things are beyond the power of flesh and blood to withstand. He groped for her. The memory of her lips intoxicated him. He hungered to feel them again.

She put out her arms and held him back.

"No, Jim—don't! You make me leave you!"

There was to be no kiss this time. He dropped his arms, allowed her to escape.

They heard footsteps.

"It's Catherine. Coming down from her nap." In Judalon's voice was sudden relief.

Chapter Twenty-three

I

When Bowie reached the end of the Auburn lane, he saw a horseman galloping down the turnpike toward him from Natchez. It was Philippe. He brought his horse to a jolting stop.

"You've been to Auburn?"

"Yes."

"Made your visit prompt, didn't you?" Philippe's voice was suspicious. Then he said, "Sorry to have missed you."

He lifted his reins, but pulled up his horse again after the animal had begun to move. "Hear what happened?" he asked.

"I don't know what you mean."

"I'm just from King's. Colonel Wells and Dr. Maddox have had an open quarrel. The colonel called the doctor a blackguard to his face—in public! There'll be a challenge without question."

"When did it happen?"

"Not an hour ago. Oh, it's the Vidalia sand bar for certain!"

Pleased by the surprise he had created, Philippe shook his reins and was off.

Bowie put spurs to his sorrel and galloped hard toward the city. As he rode up to Connelly's, Andrew Marschalk's tall, dry figure was descending from a gig driven by a black boy. The veteran editor waited for him in front of the inn and shook hands with gravity.

"A bad business, this," he said.

"Just what occurred?" asked Bowie.

"Dr. Maddox sent a challenge to Montfort Wells as a result of their misunderstanding. Colonel Samuel Levi Wells intercepted the cartel and took it as a personal affront, offering to give satisfaction himself. A most unhappy situation."

They entered the taproom. At the bar, snorting and drinking heavily, was Colonel Wells, surrounded by his friends.

"Andrew!" exclaimed General Cuny. "A pleasure to see you, sir. A great pleasure, I assure you!"

"A pleasure always for me to be in your distinguished company, General. And yours also, gentlemen." Marschalk made a stately bow.

"A glass of bitters, sir?" asked Major McWherters politely.

"Not at this hour, I thank you, sir. I am on an errand, the nature of which you can perhaps guess." Andrew Marschalk invariably spoke very precisely, as if he were dictating a speech, or perhaps an editorial.

A moment's silence. "In behalf of Maddox?" Jeff Wells asked.

The editor shook his head. "No, sir. I hope, gentlemen, that I may act as a representative of yourselves."

He gazed about him with his winning smile. "I see here gentlemen who have the respect of all for their characters, intelligence, and influence. To my regret, I am informed of a quarrel between a member of this group and another gentleman in the city. I have come posthaste, hoping to act as a peacemaker, and counting on your good sense and generosity to help bring about an amicable settlement, for it appears to me that here is an opportunity to assail a barbarous and inhuman practice. Dueling, I am persuaded, does violence to the laws of God, to the best feelings of our own natures, and to the dictates of reason."

Marschalk's musical voice and persuasive personality gave genuine force even to this ponderous speech. He gazed about hopefully.

Colonel Wells said, "Have you made these representations to my opponent, sir?"

"I have, Colonel," said Marschalk gravely.

"His reply?"

"I confess I have not yet obtained his agreement. But I came anyway, hoping I might find here greater forbearance and wisdom."

199

A silence. Colonel Wells said angrily, "You ask me to accept what Maddox has rejected, sir? That man meant to murder my brother! Montfort is an old man, sir, nearly blind. If I held back now, I'd deserve the epithet not only of coward but fool——"

The colonel's liquor was working on him: his close-set eyes were red with fury. General Cuny, the ready diplomat, intervened.

"Your good offices, Andrew, are appreciated. I assure you, sir, that no man in this room but has for your excellent self unbounded respect and admiration."

Marschalk inclined his head slightly in acknowledgment.

"You are determined, sir?" he said to Colonel Wells. "Since I appear unable to bring about a reconciliation, I shall retire." He paused. "But first, may I beseech one member of this party to agree to a provision which may mitigate these unhappy circumstances?" His eye was on Bowie. "It is to you, sir, that I appeal."

"Why to me?" Bowie said in surprise.

"Your disagreement with Major Norris Wright, sir. I fear it might have tragic consequences if either of you were present on this field. May I have your word to remain away from the dueling ground?"

An extraordinary proposal. Bowie considered it.

"You've suggested this, may I ask, to Major Wright?"

"Yes, sir."

"And he——?"

"Agreed, I am happy to say. Provided you agree also."

Bowie would have rejected the proposal a few hours before, but now there were certain considerations . . . a promise given. He nodded.

"If Major Wright agrees, I can hardly do otherwise."

Marschalk thanked him and departed, tall, stately, and composed.

It was almost like awaiting a declaration of war. Scarcely a man in Connelly's taproom but had a personal feud with someone in the King's tavern crowd: old animosities new-heated, by the dispute over the horse race, and the quarrel between Major Wright and Bowie.

In the negotiations between the seconds that evening, Bowie took no part. Judge Crain and Al Blanchard represented Maddox: General Cuny and Major McWherters spoke for Wells. A meeting coldly formal, and terms which could have been foreseen. The place, the Vidalia sand bar. The weapons, pistols at twelve paces. The referee, Andrew Marschalk.

On one point only was there disagreement. Thrice the seconds conferred with their principals before it was settled. Dr. Maddox wished the meeting set off for a week, asserting that he had certain business affairs to settle.

Colonel Wells protested, "Why wait a week for something we can get over in a few hours?"

At the next conference of the seconds, Dr. Maddox once more urged a delay. This time, oddly, he offered a different reason: he wished time to obtain a new set of dueling pistols from New Orleans.

"The fellow's only begging a chance to sharpen his shooting," said the colonel. "If he needs pistols, he can take his choice of mine, and I'll bind myself to use the others!"

At the third conference, about midnight, a compromise was reached. The challenge had been delivered on the fifteenth of September. The meeting was set for the ninteenth, four days later.

2

The word next morning was that Major Wright had left Natchez, gone down-river not to return, at least for some time.

To Rezin this was pure relief. He was anxious over his brother, not so much for fear of any formal encounter, but because there was no telling what might happen if Bowie and Wright met accidentally. A killing might even occur under circumstances that could be interpreted as murder, and the grave penalties of the law invoked. With Wright gone, he felt free to return to Arcadia and urged Bowie to accompany him.

"Not right now," Bowie said.

"Why, Jim?"

Bowie was vague. "A matter or two I've got to settle."

Rezin studied the floor. "I reckon you know you haven't got a better friend than I am."

"That I know."

"In matters—of this kind—a man generally makes a practice of giving in to advice that's bad, and holding out against it when it's good——"

"Speak your mind, Rezin."

"Women are chancy creatures."

This was to be conceded.

"They have a whole different universe of ideas and standards and ways of doing. A man can understand everything there is to know about men, and still not know the first thing about women," Rezin said.

"Wish you'd come to the point."

"I am. One of the constant surprises in life is the way the least kind of a woman can twist the biggest, grandest man around her little finger."

Bowie's face was drained of expression.

"I've seen a tree," Rezin continued. "A hundred foot to the first branch it stood, without a knot or gnurly place on it. You'd think nothing could harm that tree, except maybe a lightning blast from heaven. But it was dead. Why? Because of a little, weak vine. The vine couldn't even stand by itself, but it had twisted its soft arms around the tree, and climbed up the perfect trunk, as if it loved the tree and wanted its protection and company. And all the time it was choking the life out of the tree. Until the great tree was nothing but a dead stub—with the vine still clinging with its arms about it, still blooming and green, still smiling and to all the world still innocent and loving."

"No use pretending I don't understand you," Bowie said. "You're meaning Judalon."

"Yes, I am."

"Then you're stepping where you've got no right to walk, Rezin. Judalon is a married woman. A very respectable married woman. Is that understood?" Bowie's voice was hard.

"It's understood, Jim."

Rezin said no more. He took his saddlebags and left the inn to ride down to the ferry at the foot of Silver Street.

Bowie hated himself for talking like that to Rezin. And for the unangered submission with which his brother took it.

3

It was speedily evident that the delay in the Wells-Maddox duel would have unpleasing results. Natchez found itself possessed of two armed camps, and it was difficult to keep from involvement with one side or the other. A man referred to the quarrel guardedly, if at all, even to his closest friends. The ladies found matters especially bewildering and annoying: one had to display such tiresome adroitness in treading the narrow way between these bothersome hostile parties. Social life was virtually suspended, and the fair element agreed fervently that it would be an enormous relief when the business was over.

For Bowie the days passed heavily and slowly. His thoughts were not clear and manageable; new forces aroused in him and distracted him. Sometimes he lay fully dressed on his bed, staring at the ceiling. Sometimes he played idly and silently at old sledge with some companion in the taproom, drinking more than was good for him. Sometimes he walked alone beside the brink of the bluff, scarcely seeing the magnificence of the river below him, or went equally blindly through the town.

On such a walk as this, the day before the impending duel, he recognized, near the City Market, the barouche and fine bays belonging to the Duncans. At some indefinable call of instinct he quickened his pace.

When he saw Judalon among the market stalls, he was hardly surprised. Her head, on this morning, was bare, and she wore a wide-flowing dress of jade green almost translucent. She did not see him at first, being busy filling a large market basket, which the Duncans' black coachman bore behind her, with purchases from the butchers, greengrocers, and fruiterers.

When he was almost beside her, she cried out as if startled, "Jim! What are you doing here?"

"I was strolling," he said. "I happened to see the barouche——"

"Catherine is indisposed, so I'm marketing for her." She dismissed the butler. "I think that's everything we need, Pomp. Wait for me at the carriage." She turned to Bowie. "Why haven't you been out to see us, sir?"

"This difficulty. I wouldn't like to embarrass you—or the Duncans."

"But you're not involved. You did keep your promise! Jim, I'm more grateful than I can tell you. But I feel like scolding you. You must never allow *anything* to interfere with—well, with anything that concerns our friendship."

All of this with subtle little inflections, and a dimpling, and a play of her eyes, and a graceful way with her head, completely captivating.

He said, "You know it's a torment for me not to see you——"

"Sh-h-h!" She glanced about. "Not so loud——"

"I'm very sorry." He muted his voice.

"You should be. Bellowing in a public place!" But her tone softened as she added, "It seems to me, sir, that I said enough to you—the other afternoon——"

He stood looking at the perfect crescents of her eyelashes lowered against her cheeks, unable to put into words his feelings.

"Pomp will wonder what's keeping me," she said. "You know how servants whisper. I must be very circumspect—particularly now."

"Why now?"

"You'll hear it soon enough, so I'll tell you. Philippe and I had it out." She made a small grimace of distaste. "I hate scenes—and he wept, begged, promised, blew his nose, a distressing spectacle. But I convinced him I meant it—he's gone to stay at an inn."

"When did this happen, Judalon?"

"This morning." She could be so calm about it! "The matter is being placed before the legislature at New Orleans at once. I am persuaded that the passage of the act is only a matter of form and time. Persons politically influential are behind it."

"After that—can I hope, Judalon?" he whispered.

"After that—who knows?" She gave him a dizzying smile.

He watched her shimmering jade-green figure go through the passageways between the market stalls until it disappeared.

4

The first person he saw when he returned to Connelly's was Philippe Cabanal. He was standing alone by the taproom bar, and he was very drunk.

Bowie stopped in the doorway. Never had he beheld such a change in man as had come over Philippe overnight. It was as if a mask had been torn from his face. All pretense at pride and respectability was gone; he had the look of a kicked dog, his face fallen in, his mouth hanging half open under its draggled mustache, his clothes disarranged and soiled with food and liquor. Tomorrow had become, and would remain, a terror in his life.

As if through a mist, he peered at Bowie. "Jim!" he said thickly. "I—been waitin'—see you."

What could he say to the man? Bowie had been angered at Philippe, had despised him. At this minute he came near being contrite toward him.

"Siddown, Jim." Philippe pulled at his sleeve. For a moment Bowie resisted. But as the other almost fell into a chair, calling for brandy, he took a seat across the table. A dusky waiter brought a bottle and glasses.

"What are you doing here at Connelly's?" Bowie asked.

"Livin' here. Gotta room. Wouldn't stay at King's——"

"Why not? Your friends are there."

"Frien's? Wha' frien's? That son-of-a-bitch Wright? He's broken—Jim—he's broken up my home——"

"What do you mean by that, Philippe?"

"Always comin' out to Auburn—ain't he? Huh? Good ol' Philippe—comes to see good ol' Philippe. But he sees more of Philippe's wife than he—does of good—ol'—Philippe."

He poured a glass of brandy and drank it neat.

"Talkin' in corners," he said, his speech thicker each moment. "Private—very private stuff. Didn' wan' good ol' Philippe to hear it. You wanna know why? Well, I'll tell you. Because it was a plot between 'em. Norris Wright an' my wife—bah!"

"What kind of a plot?" A coldness was coming over Bowie.

"Divorce—thass what. Throw me out on my ear—thass what. Throw good ol' Philippe out on his ear——"

Bowie's hand closed on the other's arm. "Wright planned that—with her?"

"Wha' you think? Gone to N'Orleans, ain't he? Wha' for d'you suppose? Why, to put the act through the legish-lature. Thass what."

Bowie sat back. His hand relaxed its grip on Philippe's arm.

Some things were suddenly clear.

That was why Wright departed the very day after the Maddox-Wells quarrel. Why he was so willing to agree not to go to the field of the duel—provided Bowie agreed, which he expected.

It had been the very day after Judalon herself announced to Bowie her decision to divorce Philippe. Why, to be sure. *Persons of political influence.* She might as well have kept it in the singular. Norris Wright. A power in the Whig party. Swinging a lot of weight in the legislative chambers.

And he, Bowie, had let her wheedle him into blundering out once more his love to her . . . making him promise not to call out Norris Wright. Because Norris Wright was the man she meant to marry all the time . . .

Cold fury filled him. At the woman, and at the man.

A good thing that Norris Wright had gone from Natchez.

Chapter Twenty-four

1

The day of the duel dawned clear and somewhat warm. Contrary to the usual custom, the meeting was to take place at high noon. Connelly's was a bustle of warlike preparation, which included not a little alcoholic fortification. Already, by ten o'clock, the bluffs overlooking the river were crowded and onlookers, not a few of them women, filled the galleries at Connelly's. From this vantage the long low island could be seen clearly across the river, and even from the distance of almost a mile many hoped to glimpse something of the proceedings. A telescope or two were in evidence.

At eleven o'clock, Bowie rode down to the landing and saw his friends aboard the steam ferry which would take them to the Vidalia sand bar. There were five in the party: General Cuny and Major McWherters, seconds; Jefferson Wells, witness; Dr. Cuny, surgeon; and Colonel Samuel Levi Wells, principal. The principal was perhaps the coolest of them. He smiled as Bowie squeezed his hand with a fervent wish of good luck.

The Maddox party was crossing in a boat chartered for the purpose. There were five of them also: the seconds, Judge Crain and Al Blanchard; Carey Blanchard, witness; Dr. Denny, surgeon; and Dr. Thomas Maddox, principal. Andrew Marschalk, as referee, had preceded both parties.

When Bowie rode back up to the inn, he observed that the crowd on the bluff was growing greater. A burly figure, with hat tilted on one side of its head, screwed to one eye a long brass telescope such as mariners used: Bloody Jack Sturdevant.

Near him was another figure. Bowie pulled up his horse.

"Philippe," he said.

"Hullo, Jim." Philippe looked the worse for the previous night. His eyes were bloodshot, his face pouched and unshaved.

"Come back up to the inn with me."

Philippe shook his head. "Got a little speculation here. Sturdevant and I. We think we can make out with the telescope what's going to happen. I've got a hundred on Maddox."

"Where did you get the money?"

"Borrowed it——" His eye strayed to Sturdevant.

Bowie said, "You'll lose that bet."

The other laughed wisely. "It may interest you that Maddox has been doing his pistol work regularly the last four days. He can cut the cross, three times out of five, on the word."

Bowie did not hear him. He was looking up the street, on his face an expression of strong attention. At the very verge of the precipice a horseman sat his mount, his attitude one of concentrated thought as he watched the ferryboat churn across the yellow flood. As Bowie watched, he reined back his horse and swung down a side street at a gallop in the direction of King's tavern. It was Norris Wright.

2

As soon as he reached Connelly's, Bowie sent for his servant, Sam.

"I saw Major Wright just now," he said.

"Yessuh."

"He's back in Natchez, after saying he'd be gone until after the duel. I suspect him, Sam. He will not keep his word, and I know it. Pay close attention to me: I want you to take my horse and go down to the landing and watch. If he crosses the river, bring me word at once."

"Yes *suh!*" Sam ran down the steps.

Half an hour later he burst into Bowie's room.

"Marse Jim! Jes' like you say! The major done took a skiff an' bein' rowed over t'other side!"

Bowie struck his hands together. "I knew it! That relieves me of my promise. Sam, get ready to row me across!"

In the side pocket of his coat, Bowie placed a loaded pistol. The tails of the garment covered the sheathed knife at his hip.

3

The sequence of events set off by his bit of gossip concerning Montfort Wells had been upsetting to Dr. Thomas Maddox. Since he had been challenged, the days had been a strain to him, and although he had spent them in assiduous practice with the pistol, he felt none of the confidence in himself that Philippe Cabanal had expressed to Bowie. Too late, however, to do anything but face the consequences. Somewhat pale, but fully determined, he did so.

He had removed his coat and stood watching Judge Crain examine the pistol he was to use. A strange weapon, of course, supplied by the referee, Andrew Marschalk. Maddox wished very much that he might have used the pistol with which he had fired so many rounds at the white target under the tutelage of Judge Crain and Al Blanchard.

They stood in a sandy clearing, screened by trees and brush from the river and the nearer shore. Above the trees, however, the distant white tavern, high on the bluff, seemed to be peering over Maddox's shoulder.

The seconds and others formed two groups, on either side of the line of fire. Already the coin had been tossed and positions selected. There really was little to choose, however, since the sun was directly overhead and the ground perfectly level.

"This way, Tom," said Judge Crain.

A hand was on the doctor's arm. He felt himself guided forward a few steps and placed in position. At twelve paces, a distance which seemed brutally close, he saw the bitter features and close-set eyes of Colonel Wells. Beside Weils stood General Cuny, with his great Roman tribune's head. The general looked at Judge Crain and the judge silently returned the look. Bad blood between the chief seconds.

Maddox felt a heavy weight in his hand. The pistol had been placed there by Crain. Vaguely he glanced down at it. Hammer cocked. Copper cap on nipple. He had only to pull the trigger, and the bullet would be sped.

Blood pounded in his ears as he turned his right side toward his antagonist, to give as narrow a target as possible.

Andrew Marschalk said, "Are you ready, gentlemen?"

Maddox nodded. Wells nodded. Marschalk stepped back.

Now it was coming . . . now was the time . . .

Dry, mechanical voice began a count.

"Make ready—one—two—three——"

Maddox's hand was jolted by the recoil of his weapon. A puff of gray smoke obscured his enemy. Even in the dull solid shock of the almost simultaneous twin reports, he heard the sinister hum close by his head. Very proud he was that he did not duck at the sound of the ball. He hoped his face did not show his agitation.

Smoke drifted aside. Both men still were erect: neither touched.

Maddox experienced great disappointment. If he had only drawn a little blood from Wells, the thing would be over.

Judge Crain, General Cuny, and Andrew Marschalk were in a short, stiff conference. Another shot must be exchanged.

Once more Maddox took his place. Once more he saw the grim visage of Colonel Wells facing him. Once more Marschalk began the measured count. The two shots thudded almost together.

And still neither man had been hit.

In a daze, Maddox saw Marschalk step between them.

"Gentlemen, I compliment you both on carrying yourselves in a manner to excite every admiration." The journalist smiled. "Now, since the most rigid interpretation of the code enjoins no third shot after two have been exchanged, I earnestly pray that this difference be forgotten and a reconciliation take place which will be of profound satisfaction to the multitude of friends you both possess."

With gratitude, Dr. Maddox heard these words. The black hole in the muzzle of Colonel Wells's pistol had looked uncommonly huge and close. He gave a nod. To his intense relief, Wells also indicated a willingness to end the quarrel. The two men came together to shake hands.

In that moment they all saw Major Norris Wright making his way through the bushes toward them, pushing aside the branches with his gold-headed sword cane.

Surprise in Marschalk's face turned to coldness. Intense silence fell.

"Sir," the editor said stiffly, "I must say that I had not expected to see you here."

Wright glanced at the Wells contingent, bristling in a close group, with a spiteful gleam of his teeth.

"The duel is over?" he asked. "I thought I heard the shots. Surely the principals were being reconciled when I appeared? Since the quarrel is ended, can there be any objection to my joining my friends here?"

Marschalk swallowed his strong disapproval. Wright actually had not violated the letter of his agreement, however much he had done violence to its spirit, and the journalist still must play the role of peacemaker.

"There is no objection?" A half question, with a glance at General Cuny. The Roman features did not alter.

Marschalk's face lit up again. "Then I say this is good, very good. A most happy resolution. Let us congratulate our principals as much on their good sense in recognizing the moment when both were vindicated as on the courage with which they upheld their honor." His smile included them all. "We must all be equally happy. I have a little surprise. In the hope that we might reach this very solution, I took the liberty of bringing a hamper over with me. It is here, beside these bushes."

Nobody could exceed Marschalk in charm. He went to the place he had indicated and brought forth a large wicker basket.

"Let us open it," he said cordially. "I think you may find here some wine to suit your palates and a few delicacies for your appetites. The sun is now past the meridian, and what can we do more pleasing than turn what began as a grim occasion into a festive one, lunch in this sylvan spot, and drink each other's healths in good will?"

His manner was irresistible. Stiffness melted. Faces relaxed. Men who had not shaken hands in months did so now.

The kindly old gentleman lifted the hamper's lid. He began distributing to them fried chicken and sandwiches, and produced glasses into which he poured an excellent canary. As they ate, even General Cuny and Judge Crain became almost genial.

4

Andrew Marschalk believed he had brought about permanent peace among the men present. Now he thought he saw a chance to heal still another wound, through the opportune arrival of Norris Wright.

"I consider, Major," he began, "that this is a fitting occasion to bring about friendly relations between yourself and James Bowie—whom you must acknowledge is a gentleman."

For once he had uttered an unfortunate remark. Wright stepped back as if he had been struck, his face paling with anger.

"I acknowledge no such thing!" he exclaimed.

With consternation Marschalk saw his careful planning undone, and made one desperate suggestion. "But—you will shake his hand?"

Wright appeared to be intensely excited. "Never! May I be struck dead, if I ever touch that scoundrel's hand in friendship!"

The words still hung quivering on the air when all present heard the crackle of branches. Bending low to avoid the low-swinging boughs, Bowie stepped into the clearing.

A ghastly silence. Bowie halted, face set, looking at Wright.

But it was neither of these two who set off the explosion.

With a sudden, reckless movement, Judge Crain snatched from his coat pocket a short-barreled pistol.

General Cuny's face grew ashen with fear, then taut with ferocity, as he tugged and tugged to get his weapon, the hammer of which had caught in his garment.

"You and I can settle our differences right now," Crain said fiercely.

Bowie heard the double click of the hammer as it was cocked, saw the judge's pistol come up, and stepped between him and the general, who still was tearing helplessly at his imprisoned weapon.

Already Crain's finger was pulling the trigger. A report. Bowie felt a jolt in his hip. His leg seemed suddenly to lose its strength, no longer able to support him. With a sensation of surprise, he found himself falling and knew he was hit.

Prostrate, he watched General Cuny free his pistol at last, cock it, and fire. The judge winced from a wound in his arm—the same arm the general had wounded once before.

Crain threw down his empty weapon, drew a second pistol, and coldly fired at his old enemy again.

Look of a stricken animal on General Cuny's face. He reeled slowly in a circle and went down. With a cry his brother, the little doctor, ran over to him.

Bowie shook his head to clear it and began levering himself up, pushing with his hands on the ground and dragging his wounded leg. He was erect, holding a sapling with one hand, clutching for his own pistol.

He had it out, cocked, and pulled the trigger at Judge Crain. But his wound unsteadied him. The shot went wild.

Reports of other pistols sounded about him. He hardly knew who fired. Or at whom.

To one side, as if he had no part in the melee, stood Norris Wright, leaning on his gold-headed cane. Time to settle with him later. Bowie wrenched from the sheath on his hip the great knife, and setting his teeth because of his pain, began to hobble across the sand toward Crain.

The judge saw a wild man closing on him. With all his strength he dashed his empty pistol in Bowie's face, and ran, clutching his wounded arm.

He need not have fled. His heavy weapon struck the round knob of its handle on Bowie's forehead. Half stunned, he again fell to the ground.

For a moment he lay there, trying to shake off the blackness that threatened to overwhelm him. He turned on his side, his head singing from the blow, acute anguish shooting in his wounded hip.

Someone cried out a panic warning.

With clearing vision Bowie saw it. Norris Wright had drawn from his cane the long, sharp sword it concealed. Throwing the cane aside, his narrow face murderous, he rushed upon Bowie with the blade.

Everyone watched, struck motionless. Bowie was prostrate, apparently helpless, before the venomous thrust.

With the peculiar fascination of one who sees certain doom approaching, his eyes fixed themselves on the gleaming needle point as it plunged toward his breast.

Sharp, tearing pain. Wright cursed.

The weapon was deep in Bowie's body.

Wright tugged. It was fixed. Again he swore and pulled. Each effort sent a sickening flush of agony through the man on the ground. He clamped his jaws to keep back his cry of pain. But the tough muscles held the blade. Wright could not draw it out.

Furious, the major put a brutal foot on the prostrate body and dragged at the sword once more. The handle came off in his grip, but the steel remained in Bowie's breast.

From Wright another wild curse: but this time for a different cause.

A great hand closed on his wrist. That he had not expected. Instinct sent him into a terrified backward leap. But it was as if an iron shackle had gripped his arm. He felt himself jerked forward, stumbled to his knees, and fell across the bloody body of his enemy.

Momentarily in the sun, Bowie's knife glittered brilliantly.

A cry from Norris Wright, a statement of fact almost irrelevant in its statement of the obvious.

"Damn you—Bowie—you've killed me——"

It ended in a choke of blood. Norris Wright turned over and died.

For a moment Bowie lay still. Then he rolled the corpse aside, pushed himself up from the ground, and staggered to his feet. Blood smeared and spattered him: his own and that of his enemy. The steel blade projected from his body.

For a moment he tried unsteadily to pull it out. Then he gave up and glared about.

Bloody specter of death. Gigantic, dreadful, swaying drunkenly in the clearing where two men already lay dead. Everyone was sure he had his mortal wound: yet everyone knew he was deadly dangerous until the moment he died.

Twenty feet away, tall Alfred Blanchard fired at him. The bullet struck Bowie's left arm, its shock spinning him half around.

He recovered, and dragging his wounded leg, leaped toward the man who had fired on him. Sudden thudding of other reports. Pungent powder smoke prickling the nostrils. Dimly heard, dimly understood.

Bowie's blade, dark with blood now, made an arc. Blanchard staggered backward with a great bloody gash in his arm, ripped by the razor edge.

More shots. Carey Blanchard snapped a pistol at Bowie, who stood with two feet of steel in his body, ready to collapse. Major McWherters fired, his bullet chipping the younger Blanchard's shoulder.

Bowie felt himself falling again, blackness over him.

5

Voices. He heard voices.

Turn him over. Let me examine . . . very singular. The point seems to have struck his breastbone and glanced. No, I believe it did not enter the body cavity. Passed along his ribs around under the muscle sheath. Here's the point . . . extends slightly through the skin at the back. Explains why Wright couldn't get that blade out of him. I shall have difficulty, even with the forceps . . .

Bowie opened his eyes. Blur. Then face. Round fat face. Dr. Cuny bending over him. Others looking down also.

"The general——?" Bowie said faintly.

"My brother is dead."

"I hoped . . . not fatally wounded."

"The carotid artery was severed. Impossible to stop the hemorrhage."

Dry, professional voice. In this moment the little doctor had a strange dignity.

"Sorry . . . so sorry."

"Ease him to his side. Jim, I must hurt you——"

Long, shuddering flame of pain.

Voice, "There it is."

Another voice, "Miracle it didn't kill him."

Bowie's eyes fluttered open again. Andrew Marschalk's austere face, intent with concern. Between pudgy fingers Dr. Cuny held the bloody blade of the sword cane.

"Cold metal," the doctor said. "Bent when it collided with the sternum——"

He stooped again. Bowie's eyes closed. More pain. Probe and scalpel. Two bullets to remove. Medicines and bandages.

As from a great distance, Marschalk's voice. "We must get him across the river."

Voices, many voices about him . . . faint and still more faint . . . strange, cricketlike murmuring . . . night settling thickly.

San Antonio de Bexar, 1829

*A*lready, by the year 1829, the American tide had flowed over into Texas. The filibusters, like Nolan and Long, had not been successful with armed invasion and had paid for failure with their lives. But this was peaceful invasion. Farmers, stock raisers, merchants came at the encouragement of the central government of Mexico, with the twin requirements that they should become Catholics and citizens of the nation.

An adroit policy, Mexican rulers believed. Of the wild and warlike Indians in all Mexico, the most numerous and fiercest roamed the great expanses of Texas. The cannibal Karankahuas, the swooping Comanches, the ever-treacherous Wacos, Tawakonis, and Caddos, the Apaches of endless bloody guile, created a peril so constant that it was impossible to find Mexicans to colonize the area. Even the early Spaniards, who feared nothing, had failed: their missions and presidios, except for those at Nacogdoches and San Antonio de Bexar, were overwhelmed and destroyed, their very locations sometimes forgotten.

In the Americans, self-reliant and formidable, Mexican statesmen believed they had a solution to the Indian problem. Let Americans colonize Texas. Against them the red raiders might dash themselves, and if a few Americans were killed in the process, that was perhaps not too greatly to be regretted. For even in the earliest days of American colonization, some Mexicans disliked the men from the north.

The newcomers accepted the role thrust upon them. In them, the Indians found a foe far more doughty than any they had hitherto encountered. The Karankahuas were all but exterminated in a few bitter campaigns. Others discovered it was well to preserve at least a semblance of peace. Even the Comanches ceased molesting white settlements once they found how deadly American lead could be.

Left alone with no support, military or otherwise, from the Mexican Government, allowed to shift for themselves and live or die, the colonists of eastern Texas kept their modes and traditions and remained in all essentials American. Their towns were American; their systems of local government American, although they used Mexican names—alcalde for mayor, ayuntamiento for town council, and so on. Farming and ranching methods were American, and more successful than those of the natives. The bustling, aggressive atmosphere was American.

Yet through all this, San Antonio de Bexar, the queen city of Texas, remained serenely a city of the Mexican people. Mexican leisure, Mexican laughter, Mexican happiness characterized Bexar. Not for a time yet was it to be violently jarred out of its peaceful existence by the dizzying thrust of progress with all its restless complications.

Chapter Twenty-five

1

Bowie healed very slowly. He had lost overmuch blood, and there was an infection which seemed to devour his system. He hardly remembered when he was taken home to Arcadia. After the fight on the island there were days of sinking when he could hardly breathe, days when he was conscious only of distorted figures and voices not understood, days when pain was fresh and blinding. Then came a confused recollection of an interminable jolting progression, when he fought to keep back the moans that welled up from his deeply lacerated chest.

This was succeeded by welcome ease, his breath no longer choked, and an immense lassitude when he had not the resolution to turn his gaunt head on the pillow. But when mid-December came, bitter cold, though still weak and far under his usual weight, he was recovered enough to go out in all kinds of weather, yet found it pleasant still to sit in the warm chimney corner. At this time from his brother John came a letter, which began:

Dear James: I hve heard how you hve been sick & it must be bad for one of yr usual helth & spirrits. The Natchez fight is all over Ark. & you are famos in these parts, so that I shine by yr reflected glory. When you are strong, why not come to Helena? Wife & I will pleasure in seeing you & there is bear & deer for yr sport . . .

The notoriety of which John wrote was pervasive. Of this the newspapers were palpable proof. Bowie had seen clippings from some: Niles *Register*, the New Orleans *Argus*, the Philadelphia *Times*, the Richmond *Whig*, the Charleston *Courier*, and the Natchez *Herald*. There were many more. Rezin was making a collection of them, and it was he who pointed out that though the versions varied amazingly as to details, they were unanimous in one respect: that Bowie was the central, gory figure in the Vidalia sand bar affair. One paragraph in Andrew Marschalk's article in the *Herald* struck this keynote:

It was Bowie, terrible and bloody, scorning wounds, a steel shard protruding from his chest, yet striding in spite of a crippled leg, with berserk fury into the teeth of pistol fire, animated only by his deadly ferocity, who drove the Crain party into retreat. To the beholder he seemed almost superhuman: a terrifying and invincible Achilles, an avenging demon, the knife he wielded like a modern Excalibur, irresistible against any human defense . . .

Journalism in 1827 was florid, decidedly.

The newspapers voiced an interest that was universal and profound. Every detail of the incident had been discussed in countless cabins, hunters' camps, taprooms, steamboat lounges, and even sophisticated drawing rooms. In the first weeks after Bowie was brought home, people stood for hours outside the house, staring as if trying to see through its walls. A few lank-haired countrymen even pushed to the door and were indignant when denied the sight of him, as if he were an exhibit in some museum, and public property to boot.

Bowie found this curiosity unpalatable.

From Rezin he learned that all the men involved in the duel, save Andrew Marschalk, had left Natchez. The land syndicate had liquidated its holdings, distributed to each partner his share, and the whole future plan of speculative moves was abandoned.

Rezin brought one other piece of news when he returned from Natchez: Philippe Cabanal had gone back to his wife. Bowie could hardly believe it.

"Nothing much she could do but take him back," Rezin said. "Norris Wright was getting the divorce for her through the legislature. If he'd lived, the act for separation of bodies might have passed, and she would have been free. But the divorce died with Norris Wright."

So Bowie had killed that man, only to drive Judalon back into Philippe's arms.

"They've taken a house and are now living permanently in Natchez," Rezin said, "having disposed of their New Orleans residence."

How this affected Bowie his mother understood. One day, when they were alone, she said, "What is she like, Son?"

When he tried to evade her with the futile obtuseness of men, which never fools any woman, she was direct.

"The woman you're eating out your heart over," she said.

"Nobody," he said. "Nobody!"

But then, because he knew his mother did understand all things about him, he told her in briefest sentences.

When he finished, she said, "It's for the best. It seems bitter and hard and endless, but you can get over it. A man like you sets his heart on a thing and holds to it, whether it be a buck, a fortune, a quarrel, or a woman. But you can get over this one. You can get over her, but you never will until you find somebody to take her place. It is not good for man to live alone, as the Good Book says. Son, look for someone to fill your life."

He said nothing. That afternoon he told Rezin he had a notion to accept John's invitation for a visit at Helena.

Rezin approved. "Give you a change," he said. "You're a little weak but you can make the ride. This cold snap is moderating."

"Is Nez Coupé in town?"

"Yes. Helping at the sugar mill."

"Send him to me. I want somebody to ride with." Bowie paused. "I'm going by way of Natchez."

Rezin's face showed his negation.

Bowie said, "It's not what you think. I'm through with her. But you tell me Dr. Duncan has bought Steel Duke. He hasn't paid for him because I have yet to sign the bill of sale."

"That's correct." Rezin was relieved.

"I'm going to see Duncan and finish up that business. After all, five thousand dollars isn't anything to throw away."

2

He did not wait for the weather to moderate. Skim ice was on the ponds and small streams, trees were bare of leaves, and the ruts in the roads were frosted when he and Nez Coupé rode out of Arcadia. The Cajun, in a long blanket capote, sang and whistled, and called to any woman he chanced to see.

"*Mon Dieu,* Jim," he said once, "is lots pretty woman here. See that one, how she smile? Like Nez Coupé plenty, her."

"She was only laughing at that capote you're wearing."

"How you talk!" Nez Coupé was indignant. "You can't tell difference between woman smiling at man she admire an' woman laughing at something funny? I feel sorry for you, Jim. They all like fine man. I bet I make lots of fun with that one."

Having by this thought restored his own good humor, he frolicked and sang all the way to Natchez.

As they rode up Silver Street from the landing, a cadaverous individual in a battered bell crown stared at them gap-mouthed. At the top of the bluff, a couple craned their necks and said something in a low excited voice Bowie could not understand. On the gallery of Connelly's, a group of men separated as they went up the steps.

"That's him," one of the men said in a loud whisper.

Another said, "Look at his eye!"

The winter weather which had lapped in Arcadia had not extended to Natchez. Here the atmosphere was almost warm, and when he was conducted to his room in the tavern, Bowie found it stuffy. He opened a window slightly to freshen the air. A snatch of talk came in filled with exaggerated misunderstanding.

". . . new principle in steel, I hear. Cuts through bar iron and is weighted so a man can throw it same as a dart."

He closed the window. The knife was with him always now, but also it seemed much in the minds of the world.

He was eager to finish his business with Dr. Duncan and be away. Next afternoon he rode out to Auburn. The doctor took him to the big barn to see Steel Duke and told of his plans to enter the gray stallion in the four-state racing circuit before retiring him to stud. Money was to be paid over in drafts, equal sums to each of the two Bowies, the two Wellses, and Major McWherters, a double sum to Dr. Cuny because of the dead general's share.

Bowie signed the bill of sale, and Dr. Duncan asked about his health.

"I'm well, I think," he told the physician. "A slight stiffness in the chest, and I tire more easily than I used to."

The other nodded. "I observe that your face is thin, and you must be fifteen pounds underweight. A long rest and plenty of food for you, my friend, before you become again the man you were."

When Bowie rode back to the inn, Nez Coupé was waiting for him.

"Note come for you," he said.

"Let me see it," Bowie said, and took it to the window to read:

Jim: I have just learned you are in Natchez, and cannot express my joy that you are about again. I must see you. Can you possibly arrange to ride alone along Linden Road at Sunset this evening? J.

He read it through twice, then tore the note to pieces. If Judalon was waiting on the Linden road, she could wait until midnight for all of him. He would not be guilty of the foolishness of obeying this summons. It was too late, anyhow. The sun was almost setting.

Five minutes later he was galloping the sorrel gelding toward the Linden road which led out through the forest.

Behind him leafless branches made a dry point against the red western sky, every bare trunk black as India ink, and a stone wall gray in the fading light.

He came around a curve where the thickness of the woods cut off the sunset glow. A woman on a brown mare came bobbing toward him from the darkening east.

Bowie brought the gelding to a stop. The horse blew his nostrils. He wanted to go, tossing his head against the bit and dancing on his trim hoofs.

Judalon cantered up. She was wearing a riding habit of green trimmed with gold braid and a small green hat with a close-lying plume of yellow. Where it embraced the horn of the sidesaddle, her knee rounded under the dress, and the skirt rippled like a brave banner in the breeze.

He said, "Your note came."

"I thought you had not gotten it. I've been riding poor Winnie back and forth." She patted the brown neck with her gloved hand.

"Why did you want to see me?" he asked.

She held her face high, with an unsmiling dignity, but the air had brought color to her cheeks. "Now that you're here, I don't know what to say."

Their eyes clung together.

"Perhaps," he said, "we can talk better if we dismount."

She opened her mouth to protest, but without waiting for her answer he swung to the ground. Wordlessly she watched as he took her bridle, holding both horses. Then she rested a hand on his shoulder and slipped to the ground. Beside the horses, she seemed smaller even than he remembered her.

He took time tethering the animals, and she studied him. When he returned to her, she said, "You have been very sick. When I first saw you, I could hardly believe—so gaunt——"

"I'm coming back fast."

"I'm very glad."

The road was growing dark.

He said, "I suppose you'll never forgive me."

"For what?"

"The thing that happened—on that island."

She seemed weary. "It happened. Nobody can blame you . . . can they?"

"You asked me to let the quarrel go no farther."

A tired smile. "A ridiculous request, wasn't it?"

"You were in love with Norris Wright."

"You've no right to say such a thing!"

"But it's true, isn't it?"

"He was a friend. Devoted to me."

"More than a friend!"

"No!"

"More than a friend!"

"No, no, no!"

"I say yes!"

He turned her roughly so that she faced him. Suddenly she put both hands before her eyes and broke into a storm of weeping.

He looked at her, his anger fading. "I'm sorry," he said gruffly.

"I thought—you were my friend, too," she sobbed. "But—but—you only torture me——"

Her tears affected him powerfully. "It wasn't to torture you. It is only that I also was in love with you—then——"

She ceased sobbing. "Loved me . . . then?" she asked. "Is it all over, Jim?"

She looked up at him, small and appealing, the tears still sparkling on her cheeks.

"No. No, Judalon," he said unsteadily. "Not over—never all over——" Almost blindly he reached out and took her hands.

Weakly she tried to draw back. "Jim—no—someone may come——"

He crushed her body to him, and kissed her, almost brutally, again and again.

She did not resist or try to pull away: yet there was no yielding to him, no response. He released her.

"Are you through?" she said coldly.

He looked down, ashamed. "Forgive me. I lost my head."

She seemed to consider that excuse carefully. "A man is, I suppose—what he is. And the invitation I sent you to this secret meeting—it does not surprise me that you drew from it the wrong conclusions."

"I haven't even learned why you sent for me," he said humbly.

"Once you said there was—nothing you would not do for me."

"I say it again."

"But do you mean it?"

"Try me."

"If you mean it, you can help me. It's about Philippe—and that man Sturdevant. I don't know how Philippe is involved with him—but I fear greatly that in some manner Sturdevant is using him—some disgraceful way—it would crush me if it came to light——"

"You are so concerned for Philippe?"

"Not that. I'm weary of protecting him—of watching over his weaknesses. But what involves him involves me without any escape——"

"You don't love Philippe!" he burst out. "You must leave him—go with me—go west to Texas. I'd lay down my life for you, Judalon—nothing I won't get for you—it's a great new country—we could start everything afresh——"

She said, "Do you realize what you're suggesting?"

"I'm offering a lifetime of devotion——"

"I have a husband. To divorce him now—even if I desired it—would be impossible. Thanks, primarily, to what you did—on that island. Now you do me the great compliment of proposing that I go with you—as your kept woman—your mistress——"

"No!" he said hoarsely. "I never meant such a thing!"

"What else could you mean, sir? Help me mount."

He gave his hands for a step-up for her boot. When she had arranged herself in the saddle, with the reins in her hand, she looked down at him. He did not trust himself to speak.

"Good-by," she said.

"Judalon——" He took an almost despairing step toward her.

"Good-by, Jim." She cut the mare with her whip and galloped toward the city, her small figure black against the afterglow.

She did not look back at him.

4

Lemon-yellow light from the windows illumined the dark streets of Natchez-under-the-Bluff, and the hurdy-gurdy sound of barroom music already had begun.

Bowie pushed open the door of Grady's tavern. For a moment he stood looking about the dirty dimness of the place and observed that for once Mother Slappert's girls were not in evidence. A Portuguese freighter had just tied up at the landing, and the crew was at liberty: every member of that dedicated sisterhood of lechery was busy in the little nunnery of vice above the tavern room.

At a round table sat Jack Sturdevant with his mock-jovial look, his Bolivar coat, and his tilted hat, and three others whom Bowie knew: red, bald Jo Burke, Buck Sorrels of the deceptive good humor, and vulturine Steve Heacock. As he expected, Philippe Cabanal also was at the gaming table, and with him a youth, dressed well but with the recklessness of inexperience written all over him. Bowie knew the youth: John Lattimore, son of Dr. William Lattimore, a respected planter down the river.

Tom Grady pushed his leather-aproned belly against the bar.

"Whiskey," Bowie told him. "And none of the white, either."

"Right, sir. The best Monongahela." Grady set over the dram.

Bowie took his time drinking it, his mind filled with strange dark thinking. A man has something that fills his life, such as passion for a woman, and it is taken away. Afterward he suffers a thirst of the spirit, like one parched on salt cod without water.

But furthermore, once a man has loved a woman, even when she treats him badly, he remains curiously in bondage to her for a time, even after he has come to hate her. A paradox, difficult to understand, but most surely true. Judalon had met Bowie on a country road, and once more it was only to use him. He knew it, but he had an instinct for writing conclusions, making certain no obligations hung over him. One who knew him well might have marked on this night in his look a black sense of futility. To him it mattered nothing what happened: he was in the mood of great danger, capable of throwing himself away without a thought.

Presently he finished his glass and walked over to the gaming table. They were playing bluff—a short card game, the jacks and nines wild. Young Lattimore was sweating. Though the evening was young, he had already lost five hundred dollars, and he dreaded what he would have to report to his father next day.

Cabanal had lost little or nothing. It was clear to Bowie that Sturdevant was bleeding Lattimore: the others were fill-ins, and Philippe the decoy who had brought the boy to this den. This was what Judalon had hinted. How many others had Philippe led down here? With how much gold from the top of the bluff had Sturdevant lined his pockets?

"Good evening, Cabanal," Bowie said.

Philippe nodded uneasily and glanced at young Lattimore. Sturdevant looked up, his face growing less jovial. The three men from upriver sized Bowie up. He paid no attention to them.

A showdown. Sturdevant won a small pot: Lattimore's money again.

Bowie said, "You seem to be running in bad luck, John."

"Awful." Lattimore pushed the damp hair back from his forehead.

"Sometimes it changes your luck to leave your chair a few minutes."

Lattimore clutched at any hope. "I—yeah, that's so—I've heard that. Would—would you sit in for me a few minutes, Mr. Bowie? See if it's this seat—or—just me?"

Bowie looked Sturdevant in the eye. "Agreeable with you?"

"No objection."

Bowie slid into the vacant chair. Everyone in the room, except perhaps young Lattimore, knew a silent challenge had been delivered in a manner indescribably personal between Bowie and Sturdevant.

Conversation ceased and faces tensed. Cards slid over to Bowie.

"Open the pot, Cabanal?" he said.

Sturdevant studied him with narrowing eyes. They played a few hands. Bowie took his next calculated move.

"Another deck, Grady!" he called loudly, and dashed his cards on the table.

Silence for a moment. Then, "May I ask why?" Sturdevant said dangerously.

He knew what Bowie would answer. If he dared.

Bowie dared. "This deck is strip-carded."

It was in the open.

"You accuse me of running a brace game?" Unconditional threat.

For answer Bowie slid the cards through his fingers, tossing certain ones, face down, on the table. "Turn those cards up," he said coldly. "They're the wild ones—jacks and nines—or I'm a liar."

Sturdevant sat still, his hands on the table, his lip sliding back from his wolfish fang. He did not turn the cards up.

Bowie laughed, hard and mean. "Trimmed top and bottom for a sucker deal—why, they're not even trimmed smooth!"

Sturdevant rose slowly, and Bowie with him. To the gambler this was something very serious. He had a reputation to maintain. Six duels and six dead men. Cock of the walk on the river. He could not let himself be faced down now.

Everyone knew about Bowie's fights, but Sturdevant made a series of quick calculations. He was almost as tall, and far broader than the other. He had strength to throw a man over his head. Most important, he marked in Bowie's face the telltale signs of long sickness, in his way of holding himself an unwonted weakness of body. No time could be better than this: the advantages were with the gambler.

Sturdevant's grim lip covered the jutting fang. "You'd better explain that, Bowie!"

"Any way, and any time you want."

"Here?"

"The light's not good, but it might do——"

"As good a place as any," Sturdevant growled. "They tell me you call yourself a knife fighter. Knives—in a circle?"

Bowie nodded. "And left wrists strapped together?"

Bloody Sturdevant did not believe anyone could beat him in a knife fight. Six men had tried. They were dead, all of them. But this final pro-

223

posal caught at his breath. He had courage, however, his one rare virtue.

"Get ready!" he said.

Voices, suddenly raised, had attracted the curious. From outside the barrel house, men pushed in. A rumor scurried above, and Mother Slappert's girls left their secret chambers to come down the stairs with their greasy Portuguese consorts. The venerable mother abbess herself preempted a seat on the bar from which she could watch unimpeded.

Sick with fear, young Lattimore wiped his cold, perspiring palms on his trousers. His father's cotton money was gone. Now he feared for his life.

Philippe Cabanal had gone pale, but not entirely with dread. An excited inner speculation drained the color from his face. Somebody was to be killed. Whoever it was, Philippe stood to win.

He was so deep in Sturdevant's power through debt that he had become no more than a shill, forced to lure victims to the inn to be fleeced. If this role ever were discovered, his disgrace would be complete and he feared Judalon already suspected it. He hated Sturdevant and feared him. Should the gambler die, Philippe would be free.

Comparing the antagonists, however, he believed that Bowie, gaunt from his wounds and illness, would be the one to die. He knew nothing of the interview an hour before on Linden Road, but he was sure Bowie was in love with Judalon. Already she had almost thrown Philippe aside for Norris Wright. So long as there was a strong, powerful man—such as Bowie—on whom she could work her enticements, there was always a likelihood that she might rid herself of her husband. Philippe hated Bowie because he, himself, was too cowardly to resent his meaning for Judalon.

To Bowie, the situation had become intensely simple. Sturdevant dared not lose face before the desperadoes, river toughs, and harlots who comprised his world. He must face Bowie, man to man, and let the others stand back. At this minute, therefore, there was no danger of a stab in the back or other treachery.

Thomas Grady shuffled forward, paunch swinging, lips flapping. At Sturdevant's glare, his protest died.

"A piece of chalk!" the gambler ordered.

Grady hurried to bring it from the tally board.

"Draw me a circle on the floor."

"How big, Sturdevant?"

The gambler's tusk gleamed. "Ten feet across, Bowie?"

Bowie nodded. Puffing in the manner of fat men when forced to stoop, Grady drew a crude circle.

Coats were off, and sleeves were rolled up, revealing the gambler's forearm thick and hairy, Bowie's pale along the inner arm, the flesh not yet fully firmed.

Gasping like a fish, his cheeks alternately purple and gray, Tom Grady bound their wrists together with turn on turn of leather thong. The tavern man did not desire to referee this fight. His eyes rolled at them pleadingly, but the faces were inflexible.

They stepped into the chalked circle. It seemed very small. Avid faces walled it about in solid mass, dirty bodies crowding so close that the front line braced back to keep from being projected into the ring itself. A smell of onions and raw whiskey and many bad breaths.

Bowie's free hand fell on his knife hilt. Steve Heacock handed to Sturdevant a foot-long splinter of steel—a hideous thing, double-edged, needle-sharp, a frontier dagger known as an Arkansas toothpick, made for murder and for that alone.

Not on this weapon, however, but on the knife Bowie drew from his sheath, every eye concentrated. A low murmur. Expert appraisal of the blade, the incurve and outcurve at the point, the brazen backstrip and cross guard, above all the deadly fashioning to cut with the keenness of the razor and the momentum weight of the hatchet. This was the new, revolutionary weapon of which there had been such talk, its value to be demonstrated here before them—against human flesh, blood, and bone.

Grady said almost apologetically, "You ready, gents?"

Sturdevant gave a curt nod. Bowie's head moved almost imperceptibly in assent. Glances of the two men held as if interlaced.

At the full reach of their arms pinioned together, they faced.

Sturdevant crouched in the manner of a wrestler, his weight on the balls of his wide-set feet, his dagger blade held a little before and to one side of his body.

Bowie was more erect, his left foot advanced slightly, his head well back. The knife was held with the thumb alongside the blade, about waist-high. Head and throat of the opponent do not enter into the calculation of a born knife fighter. The torso is the target—the belly by preference. His attitude, tigerishly alert, stated the terms of the whole man.

For perhaps ten heartbeats Grady waited. Homely natural sounds from without came in unnaturally loud as men and women held their breath: a horse's hoofs in musical staccato, a hearty voice in greeting, a banjo distantly clinking.

Grady said, "Go to it!"

The chalked ring became a sudden flurry of desperate action. Sturdevant swung his dagger. The blow came low—savage thrust cutting inward for Bowie's bowels—a calculated first stroke to decide everything in a single gasping second.

A voice cried, "Sturdevant!" as if designating already the victor.

But Bowie's response was unforeseen. Instead of thrusting, his body heaved backward, with a great jerk of his pinioned arm. It caught the gambler off balance, threw his thick body half around and deflected the viper thrust almost invisibly swift from his hip.

The knife flickered, intervening against the dagger. Parry almost magical.

Now onlookers saw the first of the knife's great qualities. The brass spine was a perfect counterguard: it caught the dagger's edge and held it, then as the men glared into each other's eyes, blade against blade, let it slide slowly to the hilt, where it was stopped.

An instant thus: less than a heartbeat.

With a movement smooth, shifting, and deadly, Bowie slipped under the other's guard and gave his counterstroke.

Not the belly. His blade bit into the knife arm instead. All saw it: steel sinking deep into flesh, clear to the bone. Flesh turned white, then blue. Then a spattering spurt of blood as Bowie drew back his weapon.

Something clattered to the floor. Sturdevant's dagger.

The gambler looked down stupidly at his bleeding arm. Leaders and muscles were severed: fingers had lost all power to grasp and hold.

Sturdevant raised his eyes. He was helpless. But he waited his end, standing on his feet, unafraid.

Deliberately, Bowie cut the thongs that held their wrists together with the point of his knife. Sturdevant heard him say, "I'm not going to kill you. But understand this: my friends aren't your meat."

Bowie wiped the blade of his knife, returned it to its sheath, and tossed the handkerchief he had used on a table, from which it was seized and became, bloodstains and all, a souvenir prized and exhibited until it was worn to shreds.

With Lattimore and Philippe, he passed out of Grady's tavern.

Chapter Twenty-six

1

Sturdevant lay on one of Mother Slappert's beds, and two of her girls took turns laying wet cloths on his bandaged wound. A down-at-heels doctor, who received his pay in rum but had known better days, had sewed up the gash, bound it, and told him the truth about it.

Sturdevant was deeply hurt. In his pride, for one thing. But more serious was the assured fact, which now he at last admitted even to himself, that his hand and arm would be crippled all his life. No longer could he wield a knife with that right hand. Worse, the fingers, deadened by the cutting of nerves and ligaments, never again might hope to recapture the delicate skill essential in card handling. If ever he played again, Sturdevant must play honestly.

He dismissed the girls and called to him Jo Burke, Buck Sorrels, and Steve Heacock.

"Get Bowie," he said to them.

They nodded, eyes fixed on his face.

"No mistakes. I want him dead."

Again they nodded.

"Put a watch on the tavern where he stays. Find out where he's going. Then finish him! I don't care how you do it, but make sure. I'm leaving tonight. Upriver."

They signified their comprehension.

Agony drew his lips back from the fang. He recovered. "Follow me when you've done this job. Don't come back to me until you've finished it. Take no chances. A country road at night, if you can. *But make it sure!*"

They departed to carry out the orders he had given.

2

At the top of the bluff Bowie said good night to his two companions and rode on to Connelly's. Young Lattimore certainly had an abundance of lesson. Rake's progress had lost its charm for him.

Philippe hardly spoke. He had been freed of an incubus. Bloody Jack would gamble no more. As a Judas goat, Philippe was of no use to him now. He could almost feel grateful to Bowie.

At the tavern, Bowie said to Nez Coupé, "We'll eat a bite and ride tonight."

Nez Coupé was doleful. "Where we spend night?"

"Sleep out if we have to. I don't want another night in this town."

As they ate, Bowie discovered that already his fight under the bluff was filling the town. Through the shutters of the dining room, a voice came.

"Bloody Sturdevant, ye say? An' Bowie done it?"

"Aye. My cousin seen it. Not an hour ago. In Tom Grady's barrel house it was. Funny place for gentry to be brawling."

"Gentry? I dunno Jim Bowie's such gentry."

"Mebbe not. But he's a ring-tailed fighter. Bloody Sturdevant—mighty few could come off best with him."

"Bowie's a devil—sure."

"Tell me he flashed a knife to turn a man sick at the sight."

"Aye. Everybody's talkin' of that knife."

Bowie finished his meal in silence. Tom Grady's barrel house, public opinion seemed to hold, was no place for a gentleman to be brawling. In fact, there seemed to be some question as to whether Jim Bowie belonged to the gentry at all.

This, he now believed, was what had destroyed him with Judalon. It was destroying him everywhere. His reputation for turbulence, for bloodshed. A belligerent . . . more scum than gentleman. He was very weary of this sort of distinction which he had never sought.

An hour later he and Nez Coupé rode out of Natchez past King's tavern, with its high brick foundation and clapboard walls. Always Bowie had avoided the place, because it was the headquarters of Wright and Crain, and he gave it now a back glance only. Strangely, he had the impression of a figure, indistinct on the darkened gallery, which seemed to be watching him. The figure disappeared, and he rode on.

This way led to the Natchez Trace. It was the best of the several bad roads, and they planned to follow it until it verged too far eastward, then strike toward Helena along one of the northward trails, thus avoiding the rough river route, which followed the cliffs and swamps and spurs of the Mississippi.

An old, notorious way, traveled by countless wayfarers in the past, yet always lonely. Murderers had lurked in it, and men had been killed for what little they carried, their bodies tossed into some ravine or otherwise indifferently disposed of, so that skeletons always were being found, their ribs trellising the vines of some thicket.

Nez Coupé was unhappy. He was afraid of nothing that lived and could be understood, but he believed firmly in spectral visitation, and this dark road through the forest made his skin creep. To him the Natchez Trace was peopled after dark by the ghosts of murdered men, and particularly by the ghosts of the men who had committed the murders and had been executed for their crimes.

Most earnestly Nez Coupé hoped he would meet no specters on this eerie night journey.

Moss-draped branches overlapped their heads, intensifying the night blackness, so that the horses walked gingerly, feeling their way and snorting softly now and then at the underfooting. The choked bellow of a bull alligator announced the proximity of a swamp: and distantly, Nez Coupé heard the long howl of a running wolf.

But was it a wolf? Might it not be the dread *loup-garou,* with fire eyes and man-wolf shape, hurrying to intercept and waylay travelers in this uncanny place?

Silence closed in. Nez Coupé's ears strained. Even the sound of the horses' hoofs seemed muffled. The road began to descend, perhaps to the marsh ahead. Loneliness twisted the Cajun's bowels with foreboding. For once he was wordless, the nearness of panic in his soul. His pony's nose was at the sorrel's haunch, following as close as possible, in its master's desire for close companionship with Bowie.

They passed a cabin in a small clearing. Through its windows of paper, coated with hog's lard, light showed cheery and yellow.

"Jim—we get bait an' bed here, mebbe?" Nez Coupé ventured.

Bowie did not seem to hear.

"Horse—he need some rest—you think?" Nez Coupé was plaintive.

"They've been resting all day," Bowie said shortly.

Nez Coupé sighed and urged his pony closer. Trees blotted out the cabin lights. All at once there were stars overhead. Their horses' hoofs sucked in muck. Whispering stalks lifted their tips far overhead, seeming to make a solid black wall on either side: a canebrake.

This was a prime place for concealment. Nez Coupé knew wild beasts preferred canebrakes, also that they were favorite ambuscades of outlaws.

Night seemed blacker. Stars receded, bare pin points in the narrow strip of sky between the tall canes on either side of their road. The pulpy mud-sound of horses' hoofs combined with the sigh of stalks swaying slightly in the faint chill breeze.

Nez Coupé's throat filled with apprehension. He heard something: or thought he did. No sound, so much as an instinctive conviction of some near presence . . .

"Jim—Jim——" Whisper of terror.

"What?"

"Best turn back—something here—I don't like—plenty——"

Terror in Nez Coupé's voice brought Bowie to alertness. Instinctively he loosed the knife in its scabbard.

A scream from Nez Coupé. *"Mon Dieu*—Jim—they *got* us——"

The Cajun was trying to turn his pony. A shot thudded right beside them in the cane tangle. Nez Coupé pitched out of his saddle, and Bowie's horse reared high in the air, with a rough brute of a fellow clinging to his bridle.

Bowie leaned across the sorrel's neck and drove his knife hilt deep into the man's chest. He loosed his hold on the bridle and dropped with a sob.

The sorrel leaped forward as Bowie dug in his spurs.

Two lurid flashes in the canes and a double report. The horse stumbled in mid-leap and came to earth in a crashing fall, throwing his rider twenty feet forward over his head.

Half stunned, Bowie rolled over. Two leaping black shapes were on him. He heard a great blasphemous oath.

No time to think: action was reflex, purely. He twisted aside. Searing pain in his leg. Half on one knee, he swung the knife and felt it go in to the guard.

With a wet groan a man fell and did not move.

Bowie was on his feet. There was still a third assailant. But this one had seen enough. He was fleeing down the trail, dodging like a rabbit.

No hope of overtaking him. Ten feet more and he would be lost in the canebrake.

Bowie's arm whipped, the knife whistled through the air. At the very moment when the fellow was sure of escape, at the instant he changed plunging direction to duck into the covert, the point of the heavy blade caught him full in the back of the head. He went down, slobbering and kicking, dead in an instant, his skull split as by a butcher's cleaver.

3

Bowie recovered the knife, then looked around.

There were no others.

He heard a faint sound and limped toward it. Beside the canes he found Nez Coupé.

"Jim . . . Jim . . ."

The voice was barely audible. Bowie lifted his head.

"Hold me, Jim . . . so dark . . . I can't see . . ."

"I'll hold you, Nez Coupé."

With his hand Bowie felt the hot blood where the bullet had torn a hole in his friend's side.

" 'By, Jim . . . my friend . . . best hunter . . . best fighter . . . in the world."

His voice sank, died away.

In all his life Bowie had never known a helplessness of this kind. "God —God——" he moaned. A prayer.

Nez Coupé stirred.

"Jim . . . always . . . we make plenty fun . . . us . . ."

He was dead.

Bowie felt the tears sliding down his face. Alone, more alone than ever before, he wept over this friend of his life in the night canebrake.

He had controlled his grief, and laid his friend down, and was sitting on the dead horse, making some shift to bind up the stab wound in his leg, from which the blood had soaked his breeches to the knee, when he heard a halloo. Through the canes a distant light sparkled. He answered the call.

Around a bend came a horn lantern and two men carrying long rifles.

"Who's thar?" a voice inquired.

Bowie said, "Five of us. Only one alive. James Bowie."

"Four daid?"

The lantern came cautiously forward. The man carrying it lifted it high. "What we got hyar?"

He was short and lean, with a leathery face, long, ropy black hair, and a beady black eye that caught the light like a cat's.

"Ain't it so!" he said. "Four daid." He cast the light around. "You kill 'em all?"

"No. This one's my friend. They killed him."

"Then you killed *them?*"

"Yes."

"Whut with?"

"A knife."

"That knife? Glory be." He gave Bowie a sudden sharp look. "Say, I heerd about you. Jim Bowie? Shore."

Bowie said nothing. The man looked at Nez Coupé's dead face closely, then shone his light in the faces of the waylayers, one after another.

"Glory be," he said again.

He came back. "I don't know 'em," he said, "but it'd be danged funny if the authorities didn't."

Bowie was still too sick with grief to answer.

"Jethro," the man said to his companion, a boy as lean and lantern-jawed as himself, but taller, "go fotch ol' Topsy an' the cyart. We'll take these yere to the cabin, an' notify the sheriff."

To Bowie, he said, "We heerd the shootin' an' concluded to see whut was up. Kind of lucky we done so. My name's Roger Hatteras. If ye kin walk, better come back to the cabin. If not, ye kin ride with them corpses ye created."

Bowie found he could walk.

Hatteras was a small cropper and hunter, whose cabin they had passed just before entering the canebrake. He was a squatter, he told Bowie, but it made no never mind, because he could leave what he had any time without a how-de-do. Already he had plans to quit here and go to, maybe, Texas, where he heard folks got free land for just settling.

The cabin was of felled logs, with a bare earth floor, loft above, and a roof of bark slabs. Bowie's wounded leg was bathed and bound with clean cloths by Mrs. Hatteras, a quick, withered woman, and her daughter Selina, sixteen perhaps, with a ripening body curving under her linsey dress. There were three younger children, a boy and two girls, ranging from six to three, all wearing the "toga" of the frontier: a long shirt like a nightgown, the boy's having two slits in the tail, those of the girls only one.

Jethro, the eldest son, perhaps two years older than Selina, presently arrived with the cart and the dead.

Nez Coupé they laid on a clean blanket beside the porch and covered his face. The others Bowie examined by lantern. Fat, red-faced, and bald, for one: harmless-looking and bloody-acting, for two: cadaverous, with bird-of-prey features, for the third. Jo Burke, Buck Sorrels, and Steve Heacock, Sturdevant's creatures.

With unalloyed respect Roger Hatteras and his son looked at Bowie. They had observed the wounds: Burke and Sorrels stabbed to their hearts, and Heacock's cloven skull. How one man could accomplish this was more than the squatters could imagine. In the darkness, too.

Jethro Hatteras took a club and sat up that night to keep the hogs away from the bodies. Bowie slept uneasily on a corn-shuck mattress laid on the floor. In the same room his host snored with his wife in a homemade bedstead. Selina and the children occupied the loft.

Dawn found them up, Bowie's leg very stiff. The elder Hatteras took Nez Coupé's pony, which was found grazing near the cabin, and rode to Natchez. By noon he was back with the coroner and sheriff. Processes of law were quick here. The sheriff blandly identified the three criminals, the bodies of which the coroner equally blandly took into custody.

"Wanted, every one of 'em," the sheriff said. "Rewards somewhere for all three, I reckon. Ye might look into it an' collect."

Bowie said, "If there's a reward, you take it, Sheriff."

This pleased the official, who, as it turned out, collected nine hundred dollars on the three men, offered by authorities at Memphis and Lexington. When he took the dead ruffians to Natchez, he carried with him also the story of the fight, three to one in the dark, and the knife the victor.

Men dug into their memories for other Bowie episodes. The duel at Galvez-town and the dark-room meeting in New Orleans were refurbished. All details of the Vidalia sand bar were savored over. Eyewitnesses elaborated on the fight with Bloody Sturdevant. Bowie, it was freely stated, had killed a dozen, perhaps a score of men. All with the knife. The knife itself was dwelt upon. Dozens had seen it, and these agreed that a knife like that had never before been made.

Who made it? That was the next question.

James Black of Washington, Arkansas.

In those days, while he nursed his wound at the Hatteras cabin, Bowie was becoming, without knowing it, a legend all up and down the Mississippi.

As for James Black, his benefits were practical. Sundry gentlemen began to wait on him, asking for knives exactly like the one he made for Jim Bowie. He obliged, at one hundred dollars apiece. Bowie knives came in dozens, then scores, from his forges. Other steelworkers imitated his weapons. Fame spread. Far across the Atlantic, in England, great cutlery makers of Sheffield and Bristol produced bowie knives modeled on James Black's pattern. On the frontier, until the day when the nimble six-shooter made its advent—and that was long after Bowie—the knife named after him, devised and demonstrated by him, was the most universal and deadliest weapon of the West.

In his great sudden tide of prosperity, James Black kept only one secret. The steel in his blades was the best, but none of his later knives ever could equal the archetype which Bowie himself carried: for alone of them all, it carried in it the brilliant fragment of a star.

Chapter Twenty-seven

I

One morning early, Bowie looked at his shadow, and saw that it pointed west. All at once this seemed a portent. A clean wet air was abroad. Thin blue was the sky. Dew lay like jewels on the bushes. A fresh day was like a fresh life.

His life demanded new turnings. When he buried Nez Coupé, it seemed that every vital link between him and the old life was severed. He had brooded much, and his thoughts had not been palatable. The shame of a man who has supposed himself strong and wise and discovered himself weak and foolish was his, and the bitterness.

Sometimes, to escape from their thoughts, and more particularly their memories, men take to the sea. On this morning Bowie thought longingly of a sea: not a sea of water waves, but a sea of grass.

233

The impression made on him by the land called Texas had never departed. It was far. It was vast. It was haunted by emptiness and unknown peoples. It lay beyond everything, as mysterious as the wild mountains, or the ocean, of which it was neither.

Bowie knew men who had gone thither: young men, riding away, light of heart, confident, and bold. None had ever seen them come back. Whither had they gone, and what had become of them? Did they yet roam in that vast melancholy, gaunt with a never-ending struggle for life? Or had they entered into a strange new kind of existence among a people who spoke not their tongue and knew not their beginnings? Or might their bones be whitening among the stark thorn and cactus thickets?

Texas had swallowed them up, and there was no guessing to what wild uses she had put them. Bowie thought of the limitless blue horizons and felt suddenly that he would know no rest now until Texas had been finally probed by him, appeased by his death, or subjugated to him.

Two notes of briefest form he wrote, one to his brother John, and one to his mother, telling of his plenary plans: and he was gone.

2

A journey alone, and now it was good-by. Good-by to Natchez, to New Orleans, to Arcadia: good-by to everything they stood for.

New horse, a fast claybank, with a dark stripe along his spine and zebra markings on his legs; new buckskin suit; new wide-brimmed, low-crowned hat. New garments on the pack horse he led. It was as if he cast off everything relating to the past, as a snake sloughs its old skin in the springtime.

Everything but the knife. The knife had taken possession of him. He remembered how it had served him, in a manner miraculous almost. Perhaps it was, somehow, unworldly. The knife became bound up with him in a manner nothing less than talismanic. This feeling continued in him as he rode westward: continued through his life thereafter.

His journey was long and leisurely, cutting straight across by way of Natchitoches and Nacogdoches: outlandish but strangely similar names for towns, the one in Louisiana, the other in Texas, pegs on a route into the unknown.

One record of his passage was contained in a letter written home to Boston by a young minister. His name was Bacon: the Reverend Sumner Bacon, only recently ordained, and on his first journey to the awesome new land. Since some paragraphs of his report to his home conference were pertinent, they are worth recording:

On the first day after leaving the river I was overtaken by a large man, well-mounted and armed with rifle, pistol and knife. When we learned that we had a mutual destination we rode together, and I was obliged for the company.

Soon after crossing the border into Texas, that area known as the Neutral Strip, which is filled with every kind of outcast, gallows-bird, and depraved criminal, we came to a small village. Being filled with zeal for the work of God, I proposed to preach here, and lacking suitable meeting place, attempted to conduct services in the public house or saloon, where the chief part of the population, rough and dirty, all armed to the teeth, already had gathered, drinking and carousing.

I therefore mounted on a bench, and announced my purpose to gain their attention, then started a hymn, which I sang pretty much as a solo. Next I offered prayer to Almighty God, and though there were hawkings and coughs, and stirring of feet, concluded it. But when I launched into my sermon, taking as my text, Jeremiah 7:3, "Amend your ways and your doings," and hoping by proving to them the transience of earthly pleasures to deliver to these people the blessed truths which would save their souls, I was most rudely interrupted by shouts, hoots, and catcalls. So loud did this become that I could hardly hear my own voice, and had not even completed Firstly, when I ceased speaking in embarrassment and dismay.

Then I saw my companion, who had been in the audience, advancing toward me. He mounted on the bench beside me and raised a voice like unto the trumpets of Jericho, saying:

"I want every man here to listen to me!"

The very force of his utterance won him attention.

He then said, "This minister has come from the States to preach to you people. And I never saw men that needed preaching to worse than you do. You're free to leave if you want to, but by God, he's going to have a chance to preach, and if you stay you're going to stop this racket so he can be heard!"

After this there was a momentary silence, and then a large and ferocious bully right in front of us, who had been very loud and seemed to be the leader of the rowdies, took a swaggering step forward, all bedecked with knives and pistols. I confess I uttered a little silent prayer for my soul, for it seemed sure to me that bullets would be flying soon, and I might very well be stricken down on this, the very dawn of my mission.

"And who is going to make us stop, my fine cock?" the ruffian said. "What's your name, and where did you drop from?"

"That's immaterial," replied my companion, "but if you want my name, it's Bowie. James Bowie."

The result of this announcement was to me astonishing. In the ruffian crowd was a little subdued murmuring, as if the name was repeated among them, then utter silence. The bully stepped back without a word, and with something akin to awe on his dirty visage. It appeared that my friend was well known, at least by reputation, by what acts or deeds I do not know. But his mere name cowed this barroom full of drunken desperadoes, so that I can most truthfully say that from that moment on, I never had a more respectful or attentive audience. I did not, however, make any converts that night.

The report of the Reverend Mr. Bacon was interesting, for it demonstrated something the seedling minister hardly appreciated. Bowie's reputation had preceded him. Every word and movement of his was now significant on the frontier. He had been cut free from any questionable mediocrity now and forever: had become a law unto himself which few men would question.

3

In April he reached San Antonio de Bexar—usually known as Bexar—and found lodgings in a *fonda* called the León de Oro, which was on one of the city's two main squares, the Plaza de la Constitución. On the opposite side of the square from the inn was the cemetery of the Church of San Fernando, and beyond that the church itself, fronting on the second chief square, known as the Plaza Militar, where the soldiers' barracks were situated.

In Bexar all people were Mexican, and there was a Mexican proverb to the effect that time was made by God, but hurrying was only the futility of man. Everyone was leisurely: men lounged in the streets or *cantinas,* women languidly did their household tasks between cat naps and shrill chattering conversation. Dogs napped in the shade, swine slept in mudholes in the center of the thoroughfares. Only the fleas of Bexar seemed to have energy, and Bowie, scratching himself, sometimes wished they shared the otherwise universal somnolence.

Leisure took possession of him. He slept easily and woke to the sound of church bells. The bells sounded their mellow music almost every hour of the day. The city lay in a perfect nest of ancient missions which clustered about it—Concepción, San José, San Juan, Espada, and the Alamo, the roof of which had fallen in, its walls ruinous. Religion was much in the minds of the people.

Well pleased, Bowie wandered through the streets. The sun wooed him like a lover; forgotten sweetness came back to the mere act of living. He felt his strength returning to his body with every pulse of his blood.

He observed that the *presidio* in the Military Plaza was practically abandoned, and the Mexican soldiers in garrison hardly knew how to stand formation, spending their time swaggering aimlessly among the shops or sometimes on guard at the *palacio* of the vice-governor, whose name was Don Juan Martin de Veramendi.

Very much he liked the adobe houses with their soft pastel tints, the quaint old bridges spanning the San Antonio River which meandered through the town, the gardens and orchards, the carved front doors, the barred windows of the greater *casas,* behind which one sometimes caught a glimpse of a cloud of dark hair and bright eyes flashing, and the market with its awnings of skin or canvas, beneath which vendors squatted sleepily beside their wares. He became accustomed to the groaning of the ungreased wooden wheels of the *carretas,* and the sight of tiny burros almost concealed beneath huge loads of mesquite or live-oak firewood, with the master, almost larger than the beast, perched like as not on top of the heap.

Though he made no especial effort, he found friends among the Mexican populace. The Mexican is by nature shy and a close observer, with an inborn distrust of foreigners. To an infinite degree is the Mexican woman, in particular, expert in reading character. To this natural reserve, the extreme isolation of Bexar had added, so that a stranger's slightest syllable was weighed.

It was, therefore, something of a tribute to Bowie that women with complexions varying from palest olive to deepest brown, and without exception having magnificent eyes, gazed at him, on the street, with shy admiration. His type drew them, he had a courtly manner, and it was notable that once he knew your name he did not forget it. The women, baking *tortillas* or washing their garments on the banks of the river, giggled and gossiped, and sometimes teased one another about him.

But to the men also Bowie was acceptable. Faces broke into smiles when he entered a *cantina:* for it was obvious that though their women might admire this *Americano,* he paid to their women only the attention of courtesy. A race notorious for jealousy found nothing exceptionable in him. Meantime, he had plenty of silver, displayed fondness for the *aguardiente,* of which he proved able to drink more than any three men in Bexar, and liked company: any man in the *cantina* was a companion to him, and became his guest.

So Bowie dreamed away his days, and took a refresher course in Spanish, and made a pleasurable study of the niceties. In all truth nowhere was more attention devoted to the kindly gesture and word than in Bexar. You met a friend perhaps twenty times a day, and each of those twenty times you stopped and shook his hand as if you had not seen him before in months. You passed a woman of your acquaintance: it was not sufficient merely to touch or tip the hat, you lifted it from your head entirely, and perhaps held it over your heart.

On Sundays, at the time of Mass, the square before the Church of San Fernando became a spectacle. Black-shawled women, sombreroed men, children in bright dresses, a few Indian *reducidos,* and soldiers in blue uniforms came to worship. All of these halted to gape when a closed carriage drove up and discharged one of the notable families, such as the Bustillos, the Rodriguezes, the Seguins, the Navarros, or their equals in wealth and standing.

Sometimes Bowie loitered across the street in the shade of the *presidio* buildings to watch this sight, and he noticed that always the greatest expectation was aroused by the arrival of a coach bearing on its doors the eagle-and-serpent seal of the Mexican Government, in red and gold. This was the equipage of the vice-governor. First would step out that official himself, a slender, graying man, in a blue and gold uniform. With a flourish he would hand out the female members of his family. From his place across the street Bowie saw that the vice-governor's señora had a fine figure, and that there was a señorita who seemed a pretty girl, though both she and her mother were somewhat veiled by their mantillas: also a son, and a younger daughter, still unformed.

4

In the third week of his stay in Bexar, one evening just before the Angelus bell, a *mozo* came bearing a note to Bowie:

Esteemed Señor: At your convenience it is requested that you appear at the residence of His Excellency, Don Juan Martin de Veramendi, vice-governor of Coahuila and Texas, from whom these greetings.

It was in Spanish. Bowie considered the signature, ornate with the inevitable rubrica or peculiar flourish, without which neither the nature of that which was written nor the name itself seemed to have any significance to the Mexicans.

A courteous message, certainly: but a summons, also, to be obeyed.

Bowie wondered what occasioned it. Next morning he dressed in his best, not in the buckskin, but a woollen suit, the coattails of which concealed the knife he carried as a settled habit now. Hardly more than a square was the distance to the *palacio,* but he rode, because the horse was the mark of the *caballero,* a distinction from the peasant who traveled afoot, and it was important to create proper impressions.

Before the great carved doors of the *palacio* was a soldier. The man was barefoot but he wore a tall and faded shako, a tight-fitting blue coat, and loose trousers, once white. He carried a musket with a broad-bladed bayonet, which he brought to a horizontal position, as Bowie dismounted, to sign that he was to halt.

The American smiled and presented the note which had been brought to him. For a moment the soldier stared at the paper without offering to accept it. Then he turned his head and called, *"Chapulin!",* a derisive term, a nickname, signifying grasshopper or cricket. Bowie was not surprised when a boy, hardly out of his adolescence, appeared. He had a weak, effeminate face and an indolent manner.

The soldier did not change his position while the youth, with every evidence of boredom, took the note and read it. Without a word he slouched back into the *palacio,* his loose white trousers flapping about his large bare feet. In a few minutes he reappeared, and at his word the soldier brought the musket to the position of present arms.

Bowie followed the boy and found himself in a hallway. To one side the youth opened a door and signed to him to go in.

The room was a combination library and office. The walls on two sides were lined to the ceiling with shelves of books, and a carved wooden crucifix, the tortured figure on which, almost life size, displayed over-realistic painted blood welling from five wounds, occupied the space between two windows.

Behind an ornate desk sat a man with a lean, intelligent face, a forehead polished and hollowed at the temples, thick hair and mustache iron-gray, and a costume of rich black velvet with ornamental gold buttons. Bowie recognized Don Juan de Veramendi, the vice-governor.

"Excellency," he said in Spanish, which he now used always, "I am James Bowie, presenting myself at your invitation."

Veramendi rose. "It is good of you, señor, to come so promptly. Will you sit down?"

Stiffly Bowie took a chair, and the other seated himself once more.

"A cigar?" He opened a box, and Bowie took from it and lit a fragrant Havana. In a moment a *mozo,* noiseless on bare feet, entered with a tray bearing a decanter of wine and glasses. The vice-governor poured, and they sipped. The wine was excellent. Thus far all was pure friendliness.

"You wonder why I asked you here?" said Veramendi at last.

"Perhaps I can guess, Excellency."

"And what is your conclusion?"

"I am a stranger in your city. You know nothing about me: I may be a fugitive from justice. You wish to inquire——"

The other stopped him with an uplifted hand. "You hardly do me justice. I should not be worthy of my office if I did not know that Don Jaime

Bowie, of Louisiana, is not only no criminal or fugitive, but a very famous man, greatly honored in his own country." This with a beautiful smile of real charm.

"*Gracias,*" Bowie said. "But in such case why did you summon me?"

"Do you find the climate of Bexar pleasant?"

Bowie acknowledged that he did.

"A wonderful climate," said Veramendi. "Mild. Not too warm nor yet too cold. Wonderful for growing things, señor, such as plants and animals —and perhaps ambitions."

Bowie blew a cloud of smoke, and gazed at it. "Ambitions of what kind, Excellency?"

"Of many kinds." The vice-governor shrugged. "I do not know what kinds. It is, however, my province and duty to study ambitions and see if they are healthy ones."

"I find the climate, rather than stimulating my ambition, lulls it."

"Some of your countrymen seem not to have found it so." Veramendi paused, then very abruptly asked, "You participated in the filibustering expedition of Dr. Long?"

"I did, in a minor capacity. How did you know it?"

"My dossier on you is lengthy, señor."

Bowie studied the ash on his cigar. "I entered Texas with Long in 1819, his first expedition. If you will pardon my saying it, I don't like to refer to it as filibustering. The people of Mexico were then fighting Spain for their liberty. I considered that we fought Spain also—for the Mexicans."

He paused for a moment. "I did not accompany Long on his second expedition of 1821. That was after the Treaty of Cordova, which happily established the independence of this nation, and to that expedition the term filibustering may perhaps be more truly applied. This should tell its own story to you concerning myself."

The vice-governor considered, then said, "There is an explosive quality about you Americans. Mind you, I do not say this with disparagement. On the contrary, I admire it. It resembles a force of nature. Properly harnessed, it might do very much good for Mexico or any other nation. But the difficulty is in harnessing it. You will agree that there is a certain lack of discipline among some of the Americans we see here in Texas?"

"Perhaps. But on the other hand there are Americans who have made a notable record for honesty and industry. I refer especially to Stephen Austin and his colonists."

Veramendi nodded. "You perhaps know Don Estevan?"

"No. I stopped in San Felipe to see him, but he was absent."

"He and those Americans to whom you refer have done much to de-

240

velop and civilize Texas. I value them. It is not the American of the colony about whom I sometimes wonder, but the unattached American——"

"Without visible occupation?" Bowie smiled.

The vice-governor returned the smile. "Exactly."

"I'm interested in no plots or schemes against the governor, if that will relieve your mind."

"It does relieve me in one respect, but it does not answer my speculation. As I said, your fame has preceded you. Knowing before I ever saw you that you are perhaps the most formidable fighter of duels in this hemisphere, I knew also of the—shall we say—irregular?—transactions in slaves with a certain Lafitte."

"And what conclusion did this bring to you?"

"That you are of somewhat different clay from most mortals, Don Jaime. A master of men, perhaps, but also perhaps a slave to fortune." Veramendi tasted his wine contemplatively. "In general, I will be frank, your record would not be one to predispose me in your favor."

"I am sorry."

"But wait: there is much about you which is mysterious. And I must confess that I find much about you of which I cannot help approving. Were you and I fully candid with each other, it comes to my mind that we might become very good friends."

"If not?"

"I could call the guard, arrest you, and have you transported, perhaps, to the City of Mexico, to answer to the tribunal there."

Bowie laughed. "I prefer to be candid with you. I have no desire to visit the capital, especially under such circumstances. So I will tell you truthfully that at this present I have no definite plans of any kind."

Veramendi frowned slightly.

"But I am trying to formulate some," Bowie went on. "I am not a rich man, but I own some property in the United States and have a little money besides. I have spent some of my time here studying the possibilities of investment."

Interest replaced Veramendi's frown. "And what have you seen?"

"Land, of course. There is much land in Texas. I have connections in the States whom I might interest in purchasing tracts at a good profit." The vice-governor's bright eyes became singularly watchful, but Bowie proceeded. "Another thing: in passing across Texas, I saw many fields of cotton. Cotton brought in by the American colonists. At present it is baled and exported to New Orleans."

"That is true."

"Why not weave this cotton into fabrics here? Machinery can be imported from Boston. Cloth woven here would be welcomed, for it would undersell anything from the outside on a simple basis of transportation costs. A textile mill, if a license could be obtained, would be a most attractive investment, I should think."

Veramendi's keen face lighted up. "To hear an American speak of bringing in resources, instead of merely carrying them away, is refreshing! We shall discuss this very fully." He shot a glance at Bowie. "You know, I suppose, that before you can own property here you must undergo the formality of becoming a citizen of Mexico?"

"Some thousands of American colonists have taken that step before me. Shall I tell you that I've already made up my mind to do so?"

The vice-governor rose to his feet. "Don Jaime! I find you most to my liking!"

Coming around his desk, he bestowed upon Bowie the *abrazo*, a gesture of affection given between dear friends, embracing him for several moments, patting him on the shoulders, and murmuring complimentary expressions of regard. To most Anglo-Saxons it would have seemed effusive, but Bowie found in it a warmth and vitality that pleased him. Without any self-consciousness, he returned the embrace.

Veramendi stood back, smiling warmly, and took from his pocket an English watch. *"Mira!* It is almost the *hora de comer.* You must stay. No, I insist upon it." His smile broadened. "If Doña Josefa, my wife, should discover that I have had under this roof the famous Don Jaime Bowie, without giving her an opportunity to meet him, I should be most reluctant to face her wrath."

Chapter Twenty-eight

1

The *palacio* dated from the year 1716, and had the mellowed charm of age. It was of a single story, rambling, and L-shaped, the front wing devoted to offices and a library, the rear wing used for family living quarters. A high adobe wall, extending several hundred feet from the rear of the building to the banks of the river, enclosed a flowered patio and a *huerta*—a combination of orchard and kitchen garden.

As he accompanied his host down the hall, Bowie was sensible of the honor being paid him. They entered a *sala* where the family customarily gathered before meals, and a youth rose respectfully from his chair. He had a narrow face and thick black hair cut *en brosse*.

242

"Come, Carlos," said the vice-governor. "You must meet this guest, who is a very famous man. Don Jaime Bowie, I present my only son, Carlos de Veramendi."

The youth bowed formally, but Bowie grinned and extended his hand. "The son is like the father. For both, I could say no better."

Smiles interestingly similar appeared on the faces of the boy and his parent. Before either could reply, a little apparition bounded into the room and halted, mouth open with dismay. She was perhaps fourteen, just old enough to begin trying to put on airs, and too young to carry them well. Behind her came an older girl and a woman.

Veramendi laughed at her mortification, and taking her by the hand, led her forward. "My *niña*," he said. "Her name is Teresa, and she has not yet learned that a footpace sometimes takes one farther than a gallop." He gave the child a hug. "Saints, how she is blushing!"

Bowie bowed now with the courtliness of an ambassador saluting a princess, and lifted her limp little hand to his lips. "Better a blush on the cheek than a stain on the heart," he said, quoting one of the innumerable Spanish proverbs.

Little Teresa smiled, nor did the bit of tact fail to make an impression on her father.

"Ah, here are the others," Veramendi said. "It is my great pleasure to present to you, *querida,* Señor Don Jaime Bowie. Señor Bowie, my wife whom I worship, Señora María Josefa Navarro de Veramendi."

She was dignified and dark-eyed, very gracious in her bearing, and she smiled as he bowed over her hand. "I perceive that Señor Bowie knows something of our old Spanish sayings," she said.

"Not so much as I would like of this wisdom," he replied.

"I think you may have a better wisdom, señor," she said. Then, "But you have not yet met our other daughter."

The vice-governor drew forward the girl who had entered with Señora Veramendi. "Señor Bowie, this is my daughter Ursula," he said simply, but with cordial pride and affection.

She was a gleaming girl, with heavy jet-black curls and dark eyes filled with brilliant highlights, wonderful even in this country of splendid eyes. Somewhere between sixteen and eighteen, he decided as he saluted her finger tips. Quite tall for a girl, slim-waisted but well formed, and attired in the costume of the country, the pretty *china poblina:* a very full skirt of bright crimson ornamented with white, a sheer white waist exquisitely wrought with embroidery, and high-heeled white slippers. Neck, shoulders, and arms were bare, and earrings of unusual length consisting of interwoven golden rosebuds dangled from the lobes of her ears. Her hair was caught back from her face by a blazing rhinestone fillet, rendering

243

the color and curve of her cheek more perfect. The effect was vivid, almost barbarically beautiful.

Bowie used one of the phrases of the country, "Señorita, I salute your grace with my eyes."

To his surprise, she flushed as her sister had done.

"You honor me beyond my deserts, señor," she murmured, so modestly that her gleaming appearance was momentarily subdued.

He was charmed: by her, by this whole handsome family. When they went into the *comedor grande* to dine, he had a place at Señora Veramendi's right, with Ursula opposite, and Carlos and Teresa on either side of the vice-governor, who sat at the head of the table.

"It's fortunate that for once we have no guests save yourself," said Veramendi, as the first course of the *comida,* a good mutton broth thickened with rice, *garbanzos* and cabbage, was brought on. "It gives us all an opportunity to make your acquaintance better. Usually it is otherwise: yesterday, for example, there were eighteen at table, including the commandant and Padre Garza, the priest. One could hardly give a moment's undivided attention to any one of them."

"The fortune is all mine, Excellency," Bowie said.

"Let us forget the formalities. I will call you Don Jaime, do you also call me Don Juan."

"It is a sincere pleasure, Don Juan."

Amazing, how quickly they took to him. The mother soon had him describing, as well as a bachelor might, styles of dress among women of the States. Carlos, who hoped to enter a military academy, asked some questions of a warlike nature, and Don Juan told a humorous story or two. Even Teresa interposed some laughing chatter. Only Ursula was silent. She ate, devoted herself to listening, and hardly spoke. Bowie wondered if she did not quite like him, perhaps because of the reputation which even here had preceded him.

He did not, however, permit that to spoil his appetite. The *comida* at noon was in Bexar the principal meal, plain and substantial. The soup was followed by a *puchero*—a sort of stew of beef and vegetables, with a sauce to stimulate the appetite, as hot as minced onions, parsley, garlic and dried peppers could make it. Well-fried *frijoles* came as a side dish, together with *tortillas.* Wine of excellent quality was served, and at the end a dish of dried fruit and *dulces.*

At the conclusion of the meal, the ladies departed, while Bowie remained at the table with Don Juan and Carlos. One of the *mozos* brought a dark wooden case of cigars, from which Bowie and Don Juan each took one. But Carlos looked at his father with his lustrous eyes.

"Do you grant your permission, my father?"

"Yes, my son."

No youth of good Mexican family would think of smoking in the presence of his parents without permission from them.

Veramendi spoke with concern of difficulties between the American colonists and certain Mexican officials in the vicinity of Nacogdoches which had caused a near revolt. He said also that the Indian problem was serious, and asked Bowie's opinion of the best way to handle the hostile savages on the border.

"I would establish a series of posts, each garrisoned with a small force of picked men, mounted and well armed," Bowie answered. "Such men can be obtained among the Texas Americans, many of whom are adventurous. The Indians depend on mobility to accomplish their raids. A fast-riding, hard-striking and self-sufficient detachment can cope with them best. Punishment of a few raids will discourage them."

"Such establishments would be costly," said the vice-governor.

"One Comanche raid costs more in damage and lives than the entire support for years of the posts I suggest."

"Can you convince the colonists of that?"

"Bring the matter before the *ayuntamientos* of the American settlements. It is the instinct of these people to defend themselves. Was not that the original purpose in inviting American colonists into Texas, to form a barrier against the wild Indians?"

"To a degree," admitted Don Juan.

"You observe that when the Comanches raid it is not against the American settlements."

"Some attribute that to a sinister agreement between the Americans and the Indians."

"Such a suspicion is baseless," Bowie said. "And the exemption is an illustration of my point. The Americans inflicted on the Indians such severe losses that they have since left the colonists alone."

Don Juan puffed his cigar gravely. "We must discuss this—and other matters—at greater length, Don Jaime," he said. "I perceive that you have a very statesmanlike approach to these problems."

2

In the following days, through Don Juan, Bowie was made acquainted with a number of the prominent men of Bexar. He met Erasmo Seguin, the judge of the court, Placido Benavides, Francisco Ruiz, and others. Particularly he liked Don José Antonio Navarro, a stately amiable man with surprisingly liberal political ideas, along democratic lines, who was the vice-governor's brother-in-law. Because of the auspices under which he was introduced, the warm Mexican hospitality was continuously extended to him. Hardly a day passed but a *mozo* brought to him an invitation to this *comida,* that *almuerzo,* or a *taza* yonder.

He was conversing with Navarro in the Plaza de la Constitución about a week after his visit to the *palacio,* when an odd caravan entered the square. Flat-faced dark men on little springy horses were followed by women in buckskin riding in the rear. Some of the Mexicans scowled.

"I did not know Indians were permitted in Bexar," Bowie said.

"Lipan Apaches," said Navarro. "Peaceful and friendly."

"To judge by some faces, they're not entirely welcome."

Navarro smiled. "Perhaps it's not difficult to surmise why. It's not always easy to distinguish between kinds of Indians: these Lipans, for example, and our enemies the Comanches, or the wilder Apaches of Nuevo Mexico. The vice-governor, however, has ordered that the Lipans be given free access to barter here."

"What do they barter?"

"Hides, furs and dried meat. Sometimes silver."

"Silver?" said Bowie.

"Melted silver. Not very much at any one time, but a little dribbles in continuously."

"Where do they get it?"

The Mexican shrugged. *"Quién sabe?"*

"Do they mine it?"

Navarro shook his head. "These are primitives. To labor is for them a disgrace. No, they do not mine the silver. They find it."

Bowie was interested. "There must be some special place."

Again his friend shrugged. "At one time, so they say, there were many silver mines in the upper country of Texas."

"I had not heard that."

"The early Spanish explorations had as their chief object the discovery of treasure." Navarro paused to watch the motley group of Lipans dismounting in the plaza. "It is well known that Don Bernardo de Miranda discovered and worked a mine of silver on a hill called the Cerro del Almagre."

"Near here?"

"No, many days' journey northwest. It was, according to the written record, a good mine. The principal vein of metal ore was said to be more than two *varas* in width, which is to say nearly two of your English yards, and to increase in thickness as it went downward. Miranda established near it a small *presidio* and mission. I am told that very much silver was brought by mule pack to Bexar in those days."

"What happened to the mine?"

"*Los Comanches*. In the year 1758, they destroyed the *presidio* and mission and massacred all the people and priests. Since then the country has been too dangerous to venture. The very secret of the location of the Cerro del Almagre mine has been lost for a long time."

Bowie marveled at the timidity or lack of enterprise which allowed such a thing to occur. He said nothing, but for the first time since he had been in Bexar, an exciting speculation began to grow in him. If the Lipan Apaches were bringing in silver, they must know where it came from, and the place, very likely, was this lost mine. He felt his old zest returning, the lure of adventure, and the gamble for treasure. If he could only find some way . . .

With new keen interest he studied the visitors. Already the squaws, strangely alien in appearance in this land where they were not aliens, had seated themselves in a row on the ground, wearing their best doeskin dresses well ornamented, round spots of red ocher on their cheekbones, the parting of their heavy braided hair also touched with red. Before them they arranged small handicraft articles for sale: moccasins, pottery, feather fans, and the like. Trade was slow. They sat silently, taking in everything about them. It was evident that this was their way of sightseeing, with which they were content enough.

Here and there moved the men, wrapped in their whitened buffalo robes, entering market places and stores, gravely seeking to exchange their peltries for calico, beads, steel knives, small mirrors, tiny jingling bells, gunpowder and lead. This was the real tribal business, and though they were cheated on every transaction, they seemed to expect it.

One seemed to receive a sort of deference from the others, and him Bowie noticed especially. He was perhaps sixty, with a few silver threads in his black hair. His face was very broad through the cheekbones, eyes small and glittering, mouth wide and grim. Most Lipans were spare, but this man was almost corpulent. He carried himself very proudly, like one who sets on himself a high value.

"That's old Sholic," Navarro said. "He's chief because he knows how to deal with us. So long as Sholic is chief, we do not worry about the Lipans."

It would do no harm, Bowie reflected, to make the acquaintance of old Sholic.

3

Bowie had been urged by the Veramendis to visit them frequently and he accepted the invitation. Once, finding Don Juan occupied with a delegation from the outcountry, he wandered back to the patio.

Sitting beside the fountain was Teresa, the younger daughter. At his step she quickly put behind her a book she had been reading.

"I thought you were Ursula," she said.

"Is that why you hid the book?"

"Yes." She smiled and brought it out. "It's a *romanza,* and tells of a man who lives a life of sin, and his sad end——"

"And gives a good opportunity of observing the various kinds of sin in doing it?"

"Oh, yes. But the moral is excellent."

He smiled. "Ursula, I take it, doesn't approve a study of sin, even with a moral at the end?"

"It's that she wants me instead to study my Latin grammar."

"Latin? I didn't know it was an accomplishment desirable in young ladies——"

"It's Father. He's a great scholar himself, and he thinks every educated person should know a little Latin—even girls——"

"So Ursula makes you study?"

"She is the family conscience. Even for Father: she can make him do anything she wants." Teresa sighed pensively. "It is hard to be the younger daughter."

"It doesn't seem so hard in your case, little one."

"Oh, but think how much better it will be when Ursula is married."

He was surprised. "She is going to be married soon?"

"Thinking of it. She's eighteen, you know. There are four young *caballeros* now, and I think there will be more. Her calling hour is at five in the evening. They will not allow me to go in."

"Why not?"

"They're afraid I'll giggle. It's so funny to see them, those 'playing the bear': Ramón Yburri, and José Bustillos, and Miguel Garza, and Pablo Grenados. They sit in a line of chairs, very prim. Ursula sits opposite across the room, with Mother on one side of her, and on the other side Aunt Elena de Mena—she's a *soltera,* you know, though she's five and thirty. And first Ramón seeks to impress by expanding the chest. And next Miguel attempts to look valorous. And they all sigh and consume cigarettes, and there are vast chasms of silence which Mother and Aunt Elena try to bridge over with trivialities of conversation. And at last when the hour allotted has passed, they make solemn farewells and depart until next calling hour."

"Teresa," Bowie said with mock sternness, "if you are not allowed to go in, how do you know these things?"

"I peek."

She was irresistible, and he laughed. More and more pleased was he with this demure and confiding little girl, who fancied herself so sophisticated, reading novels by stealth and "peeking" at her sister's courtship. More and more pleased, also, was he with this entire wholesome and kindly family.

A few days later, on another visit, it was the older girl he encountered. Ursula was in the *sala pequeña,* her lap filled with needlework. Her smile at him was a pretty modeling of perfect lips and teeth, and warmth and kindness.

"You mustn't spoil Teresa," she said.

"How do I spoil her?"

"Too much attention. Her little head is quite turned."

He laughed. "Should I ignore her? I can't. She's too delightful."

"You might encourage her to study her Latin grammar."

"Is she going into a convent?"

"Good heavens, no! Teresa is hardly the convent type."

"I've never seen a woman outside a convent who needed Latin."

"Latin is the basis for all good language."

"You?"

"I have read to the third book of the *Aeneid* under the teaching of the good Padre Garza."

"Teresa has something better than Latin. She's in love with life."

Ursula became serious. "It's easy to love life: hard to love responsibility."

"I had forgot. Now I remember." He twinkled genially. "What is the word—'playing the bear'? There are four now playing the bear, aren't there? And more to come?"

"Teresa!" she exclaimed, vexed.

"Observation," he said. "It's known all over Bexar that the beautiful Urusula de Veramendi has a whole retinue of worshipers."

"You make sport of me."

"Never. That would be sacrilege. Why, if I were only a hundred years or so younger, I might play the bear for you myself——"

"A hundred! You're not more than thirty——"

"Thirty-three. In actual years. But a hundred more in experiences of life."

"An old ox draws a straight furrow." She laughed impudently as she quoted the proverb.

"*Old* ox!" He laughed with her. "You pinked me there, and I deserve it."

"In any case, you would not have to play the bear."

"Why not?"

"You are my father's close friend, and this house is yours to come and go when you will."

It cut the speech clean out of him, although she laughed as she said it. He, the experienced man, was the confused one. He found himself thinking in terms of their ages: thirty-three and eighteen. Preposterous! To cover his confusion, he changed the subject.

"The merchants are complaining about the continued stay of the Lipans. Francisco Soriano, who operates the goods shop next my *fonda,* was quite wrathful this morning. 'Filthy, filching beggars,' he called them."

The girl's eyes met his with a grave clarity. "Soriano was glad enough to get a chance to cheat them out of their furs and *charque.* Now that they have nothing to trade, he would have the soldiers drive them away."

"You are *simpático* with these Indians?"

"My father, the vice-governor, is criticized because of them. But there is such a thing as fairness, and this he believes in. He desires to keep the friendship of the Lipans because they are valuable in checking the Comanches, and because even a Lipan has rights."

"*Maravilloso!*" he said softly. "I applaud such a sense of justice, Ursula. Well, in any case, they're departing tomorrow."

"How do you know?"

"Their chief, Sholic, told me. I have made quite a friend of him."

"I am astonished, Don Jaime. I thought no American could abide any person with a dark skin."

"Perhaps I have something in common with Don Juan and his beautiful daughter. I'm interested in those people."

He hesitated, toying with a thought. "I once knew a strange, but I think a wise, man named Audubon, who had a philosophy: if one is to seek for true nobility, the nearer to nature he lives, the nobler his spirit. He told me to observe the untutored savage of the wilds. I was young when he said that to me, but it made an impression that has lasted all my life." He smiled at her. "So, since old Sholic speaks Spanish not badly, I made a friend of him. And found him kind and quite intelligent."

She regarded him very seriously with her brilliant eyes. "Who in all the world has the gift for making friends that you have, Don Jaime? Never was an American so received by all classes in Bexar. My father, the vice-governor, swears by you. And our *mozo,* old Benito, who took you that message and upon whom you lavished a piece of silver and a word of kindness, almost says his prayers to you at night. Now even these Indians give to you a friendship they display toward nobody else."

She spoke with no trace of the coquette in her manner, looking at him directly. This girl was a new experience: so young, and yet somehow so rich in mind and heart.

"You give me too much credit, Ursula," he said in a low voice. "But if I have won the friendship of Don Juan de Veramendi's oldest daughter, then I have achieved beyond my deserts."

"I'm sure you must know you have that friendship."

Again he found himself almost abashed. He shook himself out of the spell, and said, "The shadows are growing long, and your father continues to be held up by his visitors. I will go. The señorita must prepare herself for her bears, and the old ox must get back to his furrow."

She half opened her lips, closed them, then dimpled with laughter.

"Bears and oxen! Please, let's call it quits! Come again, Don Jaime—very soon."

He took her white fingers and kissed them. On his face as he departed was the faintest lingering smile.

Chapter Twenty-nine

I

In the evening, silence and repose made themselves felt as soft poetry. The Lipans had departed. Bexar had gone back to its normal life. Only Bowie seemed driven by a nagging uneasiness that sent him walking out in the darkened streets.

About him he heard murmurings, laughter, distant music. A concertina far away. Nearer, the sound of a short-bodied Mexican guitar, and a tenor voice singing *appassionato:*

> *"Dulces momentos*
> *Que ya parsaron . . ."*

One of the love songs, of which these people seemed to have a supply inexhaustible.

In the shadows ahead, he heard voices and paused to listen. It was one of the typical little wrangles tinged with love-making, such as went on continually among the common people.

A man's voice: "Where are you going, *mi alma,* nice as a rose?"

A woman's reply: "Where am I going? Listen, what a question!"

"Now that you've put on a new *rebozo,* you give yourself airs!"

Evidently he caught her by the *rebozo* for her next words were, "Oh, let me alone! What a nuisance you are! What can I do with you?"

"Do you love me or no? Tell me that, or I won't let you go."

"Didn't I tell you not to bother me again? What do you want? Let me go, it's getting late."

"I must know—do you love me or not?" Wheedling voice.

She said, "I was told you are married. Go to your wife!"

"*Mira!* Who said I was married? If I had a wife, would I love you? Tell me that."

She seemed to relent. "You then love me very much?"

"More than life itself! Now, do you love me also?"

She laughed. "I love you—about as much as that wall there. Why not? It's made of dried mud—and so are you!"

She must have tossed his hand from her shoulder and released her *rebozo,* for Bowie heard her walk rapidly away. The man laughed to himself in the darkness, his feelings quite unwounded, and lit a cigarette, settling himself perhaps for the next feminine encounter.

Love-making seemed to be a principal industry in Bexar. In the daytime idle young men stood tirelessly in the streets, to watch the señoritas on their way to Mass or the shops, hoping for a glance or a sign which they almost never received. These waiting ones were called *lagartijas*—lizards—because they were always in the sun. After night they serenaded or prowled, and became *gallitos*—cockerels.

Nearing his *fonda,* Bowie passed the house of Anastasio Grenados, and saw a youth, resplendent in *charro* costume, stalking back and forth in front of it. This recalled to him that Grenados had a pretty daughter, and also that the young man was practicing the first stage of courtship as conducted by the upper classes.

When he was smitten, a youth could at first show his devotion only by pacing slowly back and forth before the house of his admired one, for hours at a time. Perhaps his companions teased him, but all Bexar knew presently he was courting. Whether because of this lugubrious walking back and forth as on a chain, or for some other reason, a lover in this period assumed the unromantic title, "playing the bear." Later he might obtain her father's consent to call. The catch in this was that a popular girl, or one of a wealthy family, often had several suitors who came simultaneously: such as the four dreary "bears" whom Teresa had so merrily described. It was not a method of courtship that appealed to Bowie, nor was it, he felt, proof against intelligent competition.

Lying sleepless in his bed that night, he found himself reviewing his own situation, stimulated by the atmosphere of love-making which seemed to exist all about him. He was thirty-three. A climactic age in man. Youth has passed: he is in his prime, but middle age is not far away. By thirty-three most men are settled, have households, responsibilities, and the standing these things give them in their communities.

He had a feeling that the Mexicans were watching him, saying to each other, "He is not married, what is the matter with the *Americano?*"

He reflected that his brothers were married and seemed happy. It was a fine thing for a man to have the right wife. But the wrong one—that was the terror.

Bowie knew his own weakness. He was a fool in the hands of a clever woman. Judalon had shown him that: and had almost succeeded in embittering him against all her kind.

Inwardly he writhed at the recollection of his actions before that woman. John James Audubon's words came back to him. *This one, I think she would require very much experience to cope with—and perhaps ruthlessness . . .*

Now, in retrospect, Judalon's ruthlessness was apparent. Seven men were dead because of her: Sturdevant's three ruffians, Norris Wright, Contrecourt, Nez Coupé and her own brother Narcisse. Dead because of the heated whirlpool in which she seemed always to move.

Looking up at the dark ceiling, Bowie resolved never again to lose himself in love: it was an experience too profoundly bitter.

But how could he avoid it? Perhaps the best way, after all, was to marry. A mating dictated by the head, not the heart, would be free of the devil-drivings of emotion. His mother's Bible phrase returned to him. *It is not good for man to live alone.*

As if all this had been erected as a preliminary, he began to think about the vice-governor's daughter.

Ursula was very young. Yet she had four suitors and would be accepting someone before long.

He began cold-bloodedly to consider her, as he might have considered a fine piece of merchandise before deciding whether to purchase. She was pretty: more than pretty. From what he had seen of her, she was well trained. Her disposition was genuine and sweet. He had found her intelligent. And she was the daughter of the most powerful, and one of the richest, men in Texas.

To be sure, she had called him an old ox . . .

2

From the *palacio,* the next day, came a note. It began with the usual flowery salutation and went on to state that Sunday was in the octave of the feast of San Diego and San Felipe and would Don Jaime honor the household of Veramendi by participating with them in the service of Mass at the church, and dinner afterward, in honor of this *día de los santos?*

A delicate compliment. San Diego was another name for St. James. Mexicans had a custom of naming a child for a saint who would be its patron for life, and in whose honor the namesake was supposed to make special observances. Thus, Bowie was being asked to be with a kindly family while they prayed for him to *his* patron saint.

That Sunday morning he dressed in his fine long-tailed blue coat, with brass buttons, salmon waistcoat, frilled shirt, white cravat, yellow nankeen trousers, and high wool hat, and walked across the square. As he stood before the church he received some stares, and the stares increased when the vice-governor's coach drew up, and he opened it to hand out the women of the Veramendi family.

He gave Ursula's fingers just the slightest squeeze, and she smiled at him. On this morning she was in flowing white, with a lace mantilla draped from the high comb in the back of her hair: and her eyes seemed singularly clear and brilliant. She accepted his arm, and they entered the church together behind her father and mother.

Far from churchly had been Bowie's life. He gazed about with curiosity at this Catholic worship and was surprised by his own subdued and thoughtful pleasure. Lighted tapers on the altar and beams from the windows dimly illuminated the interior. He did not understand the solemn rolling Latin of the service, but in its way it was beautiful. A soft undertone of music came from the choir loft. How long he remained on his knees, he did not know, but it was possibly longer than he had spent in that position in all his previous life put together. Presbyterians, like his parents, were a stiff-necked lot and did not believe in kneeling, even to God.

Beside him the girl seemed a different being. He had seen her gleaming almost barbarically, laughing impudently, discussing serious matters with intelligence and spirit. Now she appeared saintly, pure, her face softly mystical. On her other side the ruler of a territory as large as half of Europe bowed his head as humbly as the humblest. In front of him an old man, gaunt and wrinkled, his thick hair white as snow, in the ragged shirt and cotton trousers of the *mozo,* lifted a face ardent with acceptance. A black-shawled woman, with hands crippled by hard labor, leaned forward, hungrily listening. The hushed voice of prayer was all about Bowie. He bowed his head and abode on his knees, until the service ended and the stirrings of the congregation prompted him to rise.

3

Among the numerous guests at dinner at the *palacio* that Sunday was the priest of San Fernando Parish, whom Bowie here met for the first time. Padre Refugio de la Garza—the names of these people had the roll of a drum—was lean and angular, with a homely but kindly and good-humored face, a neck scrawny as a turkey's, and nearsighted eyes which gave him the appearance always of listening without seeing, yet which, weak as they were, had the reputation of noticing more than most men with perfect sight observed. When he blessed the meal, Bowie was struck by his manner, as if he spoke directly to Someone he knew well.

Ursula was placed beside Bowie at the table. "How did you like the Mass?" she asked as the meal began.

"It hurt my knees," he said.

"Heretic!" She laughed.

"I think I saw someone else shift her position once or twice."

"Those flagstones *are* hard," she confessed. "And the prayers this morning were long, Padre."

Padre Garza smiled. "It was good for you both," he said. "It is said that God adds to a man's allotted time the minutes he spends upon his knees."

"It was especially good for you, Don Jaime," the girl said, "since it was your own patron saint who was being celebrated."

"How do you know? There were two St. Jameses, weren't there?"

"Yes, St. James the Greater, and St. James the Less."

"Which was this one?"

She tilted her head prettily to one side, thinking. Then she half laughed. "I don't know. I can never keep them straight."

"Shall we ask the padre?" he said in a low voice. The priest was engaged at the moment with plump Don Saucedo, the *jefe político*.

"No! Please don't!" she begged. "He would realize my ignorance——"

"I heard you, my daughter," said Father Garza, with a twinkle. "I suppose I should tell you to learn the whole calendar of saints over again and recite it to me."

"You wouldn't be so cruel, Padre!"

He laughed. "No, *querida*. I would tremble for the soul of the man who could be cruel to such as you."

Bowie took a liking to him. The old priest was merry with the rest, discussed everyday affairs, and told a droll story or two, yet his sincerity was obvious. Accustomed to see some men of the frontier churches put on faces of sanctimony when they turned to religion, Bowie found this good.

Later, he strolled alone for a moment with Ursula in the patio. Near the fountain she picked a magnificent rose from its bush.

"Just the same," she said, "I'm sure of one thing."

"What's that?" he asked.

"That St. James the Greater must be your patron saint."

"Why?"

"St. James the Less would hardly fit your stature."

"I'm too large, perhaps?"

"I wouldn't say that." She twirled the rose under her nose, and he could see that she was laughing. "It's a matter of taste, I suppose."

"And your taste—what is it?"

"I'm . . . not sure."

"I want to know."

"Why?"

"Perhaps it's important to me."

The guests were beginning to say their farewells. She looked at him sidewise, with a tantalizing little smile.

"You won't tell me?" he pleaded.

"You can have this rose," she said.

He took it with him when he departed.

4

The very next morning, Bowie sat in the vice-governor's office and came directly to his point.

"Excellency," he said formally, "I ask of you the great favor of your permission to pay my addresses to your daughter, Ursula."

Don Juan sat back, startled. Then he leaned toward Bowie with a little frown between his eyes.

Bowie lifted a hand quickly. "Before you say anything, let me lay my cards on the table. I will give you the worst and best about me. As to the first, I am much older than Ursula. I do believe she regards me with friendship, but it is quite possible that the thought of me as a husband would not be attractive to her. Second, I am not of her people, and this may handicap me in finding favor in her sight. Third, I have, as you well know, experienced some unfortunate adventures: I have blood on my hands, and this also may be prejudicial to me. Finally, I am—or have been until lately—a wanderer, making no particular place his home."

Veramendi relaxed and leaned back in this chair, regarding Bowie with fixed attention.

"That is the worst about me, I think, with relation to a girl like Ursula," Bowie went on. "Now for the other side. I am in reasonable good health. I have never dissipated to any great extent. You have done me the compliment of investigating my past thoroughly, and therefore must know that I do not break my word. I have never been married and have no encumbrances. Lastly, I am prepared to settle down here and furnish

256

my wife with the kind of home and surroundings that would be most pleasing to her and to her family."

For five minutes there was heavy silence, the vice-governor's hand on his chin, as he studied Bowie.

At last he said, "I will be as frank with you as you have been with me. As Ursula's father, none of the things you urged against yourself seems too serious. Your age is not excessively greater than hers, and remember that our women flower early. As to the violent passages in your life, in perilous times a man must defend himself, and I am informed you provoked none of these quarrels. As to your being an American, I have not observed that it makes you too unattractive to our women."

He permitted the briefest gleam of a smile, then became serious again. "But there are two obstacles you did not mention. You are not a Catholic. You are not a citizen of Mexico. I would not have a man think of my daughter who is not of her country and her church."

"I have considered these things too," Bowie said soberly, "and have made a decision which, I want you to know, is not contingent on the matter we are discussing. I intend to live my life here. I believe there is opportunity, and I like the people with whom I am acquainted. I therefore some time ago made up my mind to apply for citizenship. The first requisite of that is that I become a Catholic, is it not?"

"Yes."

"I wish to do so."

"You will have to take instruction."

"That I am prepared to do."

"Padre Garza will see to it. You'll find him intelligent, sympathetic, and able at explanation if you have any reservations or doubts."

"I would be pleased to learn from Padre Garza."

A moment's pause. Up to now the discourse had been conducted weightily, with all formality. Now, all at once, Don Juan's face was lit with his beautiful smile.

"You are my friend, Don Jaime," he said. "I hold you in the warmest affection. It is true I have looked upon you more as a younger brother than as a son, but such a viewpoint is susceptible to change. So I give my permission to try your luck with my daughter. But let me warn you, you'll find yourself in numerous company. Do you like crowds?"

Bowie laughed. "I'm a little old to play the bear with those youngsters. Perhaps I may find a shorter route."

Don Juan smilingly shook his head. "Custom is custom, and it is particularly dear to the women. I must tell you that Ursula's mother already has spoken to me about you. As my friend, you've had access to my house. Smelling a mouse in the manner of women, she feared you might take advantage of the situation to make love to the girl on the sly. The which, of course, I knew you would not do."

"I thank you for your confidence in me, and also your kind permission. I've spoken to Ursula as a friend only, but it's through that friendship that I've come to admire her in a different way."

Don Juan chuckled. "You have a thorny path ahead. Once Doña Josefa and her cousin Doña Elena get you in their clutches, they will make you go through your paces in good earnest."

"I only hope they will be merciful." Bowie grinned wryly.

Don Juan sobered. "One more thing. You must understand that, with this changed status, it is no longer proper for you to come and go at will in this house. I regret it, and I wish it could be otherwise, but you must abide by the hours for calling, as do the others."

Chapter Thirty

I

The records of the Church of San Fernando show that on June 26, 1828, James Bowie, a citizen of the United States, was baptized by Padre Refugio de la Garza into the Roman Catholic faith. His sponsors were Don Juan Martin de Veramendi, vice-governor of Coahuila and Texas, and his wife, the Señora Maria Josefa Navarro de Veramendi.

Two days later Bowie dropped out from the sight of Bexar. He was not seen again for months.

Don Juan had spoken to his wife of Bowie's intentions toward Ursula and when, after more than a week, the American failed even to make an appearance, she went to her husband almost tearfully.

"This Señor Bowie," she said, "he is conducting himself so that I hardly know what to do about him."

"Because he has not played the bear?"

"Yes."

"Does Ursula share your disappointment?"

"Well . . . I don't know——"

"Come now, you must have given the girl at least some hint."

"I must confess she has an inkling, and I think I can read—at least—a wonder in her mind——"

"Do you think she favors this American?"

"By no means! But, after all, a girl has her right to her hour."

The vice-governor made a soothing gesture with his hand. "It appears to me that Ursula has had her 'hours'—plenty of them." He smiled upon his wife. "It would not surprise me too much if we discover that already she has had so many of those 'hours' you bespeak for her that she is weary of them. Do you remember your courting days, *mi alma?*"

She lowered her fine eyes. "Could I ever forget them?"

"Tell me, then: what about that interminable sitting, looking at young men in starched trousers, listening to vapid conversation, wondering if any of them would ever get around to making any kind of a move? Is it, after all, so pleasant to sit like a bisque doll, for someone to make up his mind about your fate?"

She looked up, then laughed a little worried laugh. "Truly, no. But it is the custom——"

"Customs change, *querida*. Remember that Don Jaime comes from a people whose customs are very different from ours, and let us see how things work out. In the meantime there are, I believe, by the last count, six young men playing the bear? If Ursula must have 'hours,' surely these can keep her sufficiently occupied."

But even Don Juan was hardly prepared for the fact that Bowie remained away from Bexar until two days before the *Navidad,* which is to say, Christmas.

2

On the morning of December 23, Bowie was ushered into the *palacio* office, and the vice-governor bestowed on him the *abrazo*.

"Ai, Don Jaime!" he said. "Where have you been? We were concerned: I was afraid you might not return for the *Navidad*. My household has been inquiring for you——"

"I hurried to return for this season. I've been looking for available tracts of land, Don Juan, and found two fine acreages, one in the Trinity bottoms, and the other on the Brazos, which I've had surveyed against the time when I become a legal citizen of Mexico and can get title to them. That's what delayed me."

"Beginning already? *Bien! Muy bien!* Well, now that you're back, you'll of course attend our *posada?*"

The Christmas *posada* was one of the distinctively national customs. Of those in Bexar the vice-governor's was the chief, to which only the most notable people received invitations.

"It will be a choice honor," Bowie said with pleasure.

"Very well." Veramendi began to laugh. "But you scamp—you'll have to make peace with my wife."

"Why peace?" Bowie asked.

"You have not performed even once at playing the bear. The *dueñas,* you know, like to have their fun, and though you may find it hard to credit, women do regard that as fun."

"I would not for my life offend Doña Josefa."

"I'm sure of that."

But Bowie did not call at the *palacio* that afternoon, or the next. It was Christmas Eve, for the *posada,* that he finally came. Every window was alight, and the halls and *salas* already crowded with guests when he arrived.

"So here you are," Don Juan said. "Ah, my friend, this will open your eyes. We've planned a *posada* to end *posadas."* He lowered his voice. "There is Ursula. To prove to you what a good friend you have in her father, I've arranged that she is to be your partner in the processional. Shall we go over to her?"

The girl had been talking with the Navarros. She turned to them with her quick smile of welcome, and Bowie suddenly realized that he was very glad to see her.

"I'm the lucky one of the evening," he said to her. "I hadn't expected to be so fortunate as to be your partner."

She laughed. "I don't think you deserve it—when we haven't even heard from you since July."

"I'm a poor hand at letter writing."

"I'll forgive you, since it's the *Navidad."* She took his arm. "We must get in line. It's time for the processional."

Up ahead could be heard a solemn chanting: the choir had begun its litanies. *Servidors* handed lighted tapers to each guest.

The word *posada* signifies inn, and its first act traditionally represented the journey of the Virgin Mary and Joseph to Bethlehem and the difficulties they experienced in finding shelter. Preceded by wax figures of the two saintly personages, borne by two young men, and then by the chanting choir, Don Juan and Doña Josefa smilingly led the guests, two by two, through the *palacio.* At each door to which they came, Don Juan knocked ceremonially, and listened for an answer. When none was heard, the procession continued, the litanies unceasing, and the knocking repeated again and again. At last the large *salón* was reached, and the door was thrown open at Don Juan's knock by old Benito. For many years this *servidor* had acted as the functionary in this brief part of the ceremony, and he was dressed in his best, his pride pleasing to see.

Arm in arm, the procession filed into the *salón,* a large chamber corresponding to the ballroom of an American house. In a niche at one side was a crucifix with candles, where at last the holy figures found rest. All present bowed and crossed themselves. This solemnity impressed Bowie not a little.

In a moment, however, the mood of the assemblage changed.

Ursula said, "Let's go to the window. It's time for the *fuegos artificiales.*"

Everyone crowded to see. At the rear of the long *huerta* a series of brilliant jets of flame in countless colors shot skyward. The fireworks, always a feature of the vice-governor's *posada*, had been anticipated by the populace, and crowds gathered outside the walls and even across the river, cheering and applauding, as one after another flaming upbursts and blazing set pieces exceeded themselves.

Bowie glanced at Ursula. She seemed intent on that vivid fiery spectacle outside, but her hand still rested on his arm.

"What do you think of it?" she asked, looking up at him.

"It's wonderful—but do you know that you, yourself, are more vivid than any of those *fuegos,* Ursula?"

She seemed startled, highlights making her eyes brilliant. She took her hand from his arm. The last climactic fiery display faded into darkness. She did not acknowledge the compliment.

"We must go to the patio," she said. "They are going to break the *piñate.*"

He felt a little sense of disappointment at her lack of response, but went with her.

In the past two days he had seen *piñates* hawked in the market place. The Mexican people were expert in making the curious earthen jars, and it was worth while to stop and examine them. Some were oval-shaped and handsomely decorated with tinsel, gay flowers, and streamers of tissue paper. Others were formed like turkeys, horses, armadillos—whatever happened to stir the fancy of the manufacturer. Sometimes they represented children, almost life size, and he had even seen a bride of clay, complete with dress, veil, and orange blossoms.

In the Veramendi patio, the *piñate,* very large, and in the form of a monkey, hung by a cord from a high beam. Its hollow interior was filled with *dulces,* to be shared by the guests when it was broken.

Someone called out, "Señor Bowie!"

His name was repeated and became a chorus. They were watching him, laughing, applauding, calling upon him to break the *piñate.*

"Shall I?" he asked Ursula.

She, too, was laughing. "You must."

He permitted her to blindfold him with a silk scarf, and felt a long pole placed in his hands.

"Swing hard," she said in his ear. "They expect much from you."

He grinned beneath the blindfold. "I can't see this object," he said, "but I'm going to smash it if I hit it, so stand away from me, everyone."

A chorus of "Bravos," and a clapping of hands.

He had fixed the position of the clay monkey in his mind, but when he swung the pole it whistled through the air without a sound of breaking pottery or falling *dulces*. Applause, laughter, and outcries.

"*Otra vez!* Again!"

Once more he struck, but still he missed the target.

"*Otra vez! Otra vez!*"

He took a firmer grip, stepped a little closer, and his next effort was prodigious. But thin air was all his pole encountered.

Laughter surrounded him. He felt Ursula removing his blindfold. Then, far above his head, he beheld the clay monkey, slowly descending, its face grinning down at him.

A wild and clamorous burst of mirth as he discovered the trick. The cord of the *piñate* had been pulled up as soon as his eyes were bandaged, so it was impossible for him to strike it. Good will was in the laughter, however, and he joined it heartily.

"Another chance! Give Don Jaime another chance! This time without the blindfold!" came a cry.

He held up his hand. "I've had my chance, friends. Lamentably I failed. I must choose a successor." His eye fell on the thin child face of Teresa. "Will you strike the *piñate* for me, little one?" he asked.

An outburst of hand clapping and "Bravos." Don Juan smiled, and Doña Josefa seemed pleased also. Teresa blushed, but accepted the pole, and with one triumphant blow severed the clay monkey. *Dulces* rattled on the floor and guests raced and chased, shouted and laughed, as they scrambled for the sweets.

3

In the *salón* an orchestra began playing, and the guests amused themselves with dancing. Bowie had been separated from Ursula by the incident of the *piñate*, and three or four young men were begging her for dances. He made his way to her, but had to await his turn, receiving the fourth dance, a quadrille.

For the first number he therefore asked Doña Josefa, and found her an agile, smiling partner in the *contradanza*. Ursula's popularity was understandable, as he quickly saw. Assuredly she had the lightest foot, the most graceful figure in all that room.

When he claimed his dance, she smiled up at him.

"The quadrille," she said.

"I hope you're courageous," he said. "I fear I'll be clumsy."

She laughed. "At least we can try it."

He found himself delighted with her: her eyes were very bright, her color high, her spirits gay as they went out on the floor.

After a few measures of the dance, he saw that she also was pleased with him. Bowie had progressed in the polite accomplishments since his New Orleans days. He had hardly done himself justice when he expressed a fear of his clumsiness, for he was at home in the quadrille and possessed a surprising grace for a man of his impressive figure. The girl was not unconscious of the picture they made together, he so blond and tall, she so slender and dark: nor, perhaps, was she entirely displeased with it. Though the evolutions of the dance separated them too often for much conversation, he did manage a few words.

"May I take you in to supper?" he asked as they joined hands once.

"José Bustillos just asked me the same question." She smiled as they parted.

When next they came together, he asked, "You promised him?"

"No," she said, "I told him I already had promised."

Again the dance carried them apart. Her smile was tantalizing.

"I should have spoken sooner; I'm always too late," he said as they approached once more.

"Are you sure?" she asked provokingly and was gone, leaving him with something to speculate on.

"What did you mean?" he demanded when next they met.

She laughed. "I didn't tell José what I promised—or to whom."

This was baffling. He awaited doggedly his next chance to speak.

"What did you promise—and to whom? You must tell me."

Her laugh was delicious. "If you must know, señor, I made a promise —to *myself*—that I would go in with *you*—if you asked me. There!"

And having played puss-and-mouse with him, she was swept away once more, giving him no time to reply, but leaving him not unpleasurably filled with thought.

The major-domo announced supper in the *comedor grande*. It was a magnificent feast, where all kinds of meats were served, together with salads, wines, dainties and desserts to tax the imagination. But Bowie hardly noticed the food. He was entranced with the girl beside him.

"It was nice of you to favor Teresa with the breaking of the *piñate*," she said to him as they were finishing the meal.

"I would rather have favored you," he said.

"Why didn't you?" She gave him a little sidelong smiling glance.

"I'll tell you—if we could escape from here—for one moment."

"It would be noticed." She looked about. "The *dádivas* are about to be given."

"Please," he begged.

"It wouldn't be proper."

"For only one moment?"

A request was given to the guests to enter the *salón,* and she rose. He led her in, but when he would have taken seats on the opposite side of the room, she indicated that she preferred a place nearer the door which stood open to admit air.

All the guests filed in. When they were seated, two *servidors* with bright sashes began passing among them with silver trays, one of which was loaded with badges in green, white, and red, the national colors, and the other with finger rings ornamented with large glass settings. The badges were given to the men, the rings to the women. Though these were sham articles of little value, each guest was supposed to wear his throughout the evening. It had the effect of putting all in good humor, with an exchange of lively sallies and repartee. Then all attention fixed on a curtain which during supper had been hung across the end of the room.

A bell rang. The curtain drew back to reveal a vine-embowered stage covered with a wealth of plants and flowers, so that it appeared to be a mossy grotto. Within this stood two young men, Pablo Grenados and Ramón Yburri, sons of aristocratic families which were close friends of the Veramendis, and both suitors of Ursula. They were dressed in court costumes of the French monarchy, with coats richly overlaid with gold and silver embroidery, one blue, the other pink, white silk knee breeches, and flowing white curled wigs. Behind them, also wigged and powdered, were two young *mozos* as pages, in satin suits.

The effect was almost fairylike and was applauded. At once the tableau broke up as the two "courtiers" took from the pages trays of liqueurs and wines in tiny glasses, with small cakes, and passed through the audience with this refreshment.

Their places were taken by two girls, dressed as nuns: but no nuns ever wore such smiles or gave such play with their eyes as these two, whose names Ursula whispered were Carmelita Seguin and Ynez Grenados, both about her age, and close friends of hers. The "nuns" also bore trays, presenting each guest with a curious and grotesque doll, carved of wood, painted, and dressed fantastically, representing noble ladies, knights, *mozos,* soldiers, Indian warriors and squaws, even an *Americano* in buckskins: which, amid laughter, the impish Ynez gave very pointedly to Ursula.

264

But there was no time for her friends even to tease her, for already the laughter at the amusing toys was silenced by the appearance once more of the "courtiers," this time with trays of dainty little parcels, tied artistically in bright-colored silk handkerchiefs, each containing a choice and valuable little gift for the person whose name was on it.

So did Don Juan Martin de Veramendi, on the eve of Christmas, 1828, genially keep his guests constantly amused and entertained with rapid and ingenious transitions from the grand and gorgeous to the mirth-provoking and hilarious.

Bowie looked at Ursula. For a moment the girl's face was still. Then she gave a quick glance about the room. Everyone seemed occupied. By the faintest degree, her dark head inclined to him, as his eyebrows lifted in question.

She rose and silently receded through the door toward the patio. In a moment he followed her.

She was waiting for him in a recess between two large clumps of oleanders, and she was frightened, her breast rising stormily.

"Ursula——" he began.

"You said—you wished to escape——" she said breathlessly.

For a moment he could not say what was in his mind.

"You said for only a moment——" she began again. "A moment is all we have——"

Still he seemed tongue-tied.

"A moment—is such a tiny—little bit of time——" she faltered.

Her eyes were wide, as if fear-stricken at his silence. Her moist lips half parted, showing the white teeth between them.

"Ursula," he said, "I wish—to ask you—to become my wife."

He kissed those lips. She seemed to relax with a sigh, as if some dread had been lifted from her, and nestled to him. It was as if she waited for something more, but he did not kiss her again.

Instead he said, "The reason I ask you at this time is that I'm going away again, perhaps this very week, to the States this time. I may not return until summer. Before I left—I hoped to know whether you could regard me with any favor——"

It was a stupid, cold way to put it, and her manner lost its eagerness. After a moment she spoke in a way strangely submissive, almost wistful.

"If you want me, señor, I will marry you. With my father's permission."

So Bowie proposed to Ursula de Veramendi and was accepted by her: and he felt failure, because instead of enrapturing her, he had disappointed and wounded her.

He was violently sorry. She deserved something better than this. But from his numbed and awkward mood he was unable to shake himself. He took from a pocket a small box.

"My Christmas gift to you," he said.

Her fingers trembled as she opened it and saw within a gold ring with a sapphire jewel.

"In my country," he said, "This sort of a ring is used by men and women to bind their betrothal."

Almost listlessly she gazed down at the ring. "I cannot wear it—on my finger—until my father gives his blessing. But if you wish—I will wear it until you come back—about my neck—next my heart . . . "

They were back in the *salón* before anyone really noticed their absence.

Chapter Thirty-one

I

John Bowie was nearing his fortieth year, growing balder and older. His family was increasing and so was his belly. John wore the sober garments and the sober face of an established man of affairs, a plantation owner and a member of the legislature. He was accustomed to the not unpleasing notice of the citizens when he was in Helena on business.

In Arkansas no man, however important, could expect any particular deference from others: but to be recognized, to receive a jocular "How be ye, Senator?", and to be consulted on matters deemed important, these were things to be prized as indications of high standing.

When his younger brother arrived from Texas in May of 1829, John found it a little difficult to accept the manner in which Jim outshone him in public interest.

Jim Bowie? Is that Jim Bowie? Arkansawyers stared gap-mouthed, treated him everywhere with profound respect, approached and addressed him with ceremony.

This was a man! A half-mythical hero, whose exploits had been told countless times among them, and perhaps had grown with the telling. Now that he appeared among them in the flesh, they found nothing to disappoint them. His size, great shoulders, massive head and steel eyes fulfilled the legends concerning him. It had been the same, all the way through Louisiana, and even in Texas, among the American colonists, as Bowie made the long ride from Bexar.

He had delayed only briefly at Arcadia, where he discussed a certain matter relating to the Lipan Apaches with his brother Rezin and spent two days with his mother. Then he had gone on to Helena, where he broached a matter that aroused an incredulous exclamation from his elder brother.

"You mean that?" said John.

"Yes, I do."

"And take the money to Texas? Why, money isn't even safe there! Look here, Jim, in spite of everything—bad cotton and hide prices, lawsuits, and all—I've increased our holdings here three or four times. There's a fine piece of bottom land in your name. Needs a little clearing, and it'll make two bales to the acre. Forget about Texas, and stay here. We'll all be rich!"

Bowie shook his head. "I'm going to sell, and I'm going to go back."

"Well, if you're set on it." John shook his head, but he knew his brother. "There's Simon Abishaber. He will buy land, if the price is right. Let's talk to Abishaber."

Abishaber, a comfortable merchant with gray whiskers, a voice deep and mechanical as if the words were being blown through him by an outside blast of air, and a habit of chewing snuff which kept the corners of his mouth always a manure-brown, knew the piece of land in question. He and Bowie agreed on a price of thirty-five thousand dollars, although John was scandalized by the figure and privately told his brother that he could get forty-five thousand for it, if he had a few weeks to work on it.

Bowie, however, wanted the money, wanted it in cash, and wanted it quick. He had bigger plans. To John it sounded crazy, but while they waited for the details of the transaction to be worked out, he did what he could to make Bowie's stay enjoyable.

Bowie was grateful, but he was not happy. He did a little gunning for small game and played a little poker for low stakes and attended a few dinners and dances. It was very pleasant, but he fidgeted, and the days dragged. He felt the ache of worries and indefinable longings. Ever since he left Bexar, these had pursued him.

He found himself thinking of Ursula and the way she looked the night he asked her to marry him—as if something were lacking. He knew what it was: he had spoken of marriage, but he had said nothing of love. He remembered her eyelashes against her cheek as she bent her head, the almost humble, submissive manner in which she replied to him, without any particular joy in it. And her little wistful smile.

Strange, about a woman's smile. It is a thing of the moment, like a thought, or a cloud shadow, gone at once, compounded of the muscles of the lips and eyes, an action less important, even, than the uplifting of a finger. But in all nature nothing matches its magical meaning and power and endless variety: friendliness or scorn, kindness or cruelty, under-standing or derision, promise or denial, courage or hopelessness, truth or deceit, calculation or selfless love. The things which are woman. The things for which a man lives and dies.

Bowie could not get out of his mind the Veramendi girl's wistful smile. It nagged at him, clawed at his conscience.

He began to wonder why she had accepted him at all: if he had been just to her in asking her, or just to himself. Sometimes the feeling was desperate, as if he had committed himself to a course from which there was no recall, the end of which he could not foresee. He had inhibited his own freedom, and he hungered for freedom like any wild animal of the forest.

He might almost have rushed back to Bexar to settle the matters that were so disturbingly and vaguely confused in his life, but he could not. His business did not proceed as rapidly as he hoped. He must still see many persons, and take back with him commissions from investors for Texas lands: and you cannot hurry a man when you are trying to induce him to consider an uncertain speculation.

2

Late on the afternoon of May 16, for lack of anything better to pass his time, Bowie walked down to the Helena river landing. Some Negro dock hands were piling merchandise on the wharf for the next steamboat. The usual sprinkling of loafers was present. Little here of interest. He was turning away when he noticed a flatboat approaching from upriver.

The craft was small, not over thirty feet, with the usual low cabin amid-ships. A lank-haired boatman in linsey stood at the steering oar and a couple of rough-haired curs snarled and barked in the bow. Behind the dogs was a young Negro. On the cabin roof, their legs dangling, two men sat together, gazing with little curiosity at the town they were approach-ing.

Bowie's eye ran indifferently over the shabby assemblage until it en-countered the visage of the larger of the two strangers on the cabin. His face showed sudden interest.

The man was more than big: he was a giant. Stained leather shirt with fringes on the sleeves, half-grown beard shot with gray, wide-brimmed wool hat with a feather stuck in the band: in every aspect of costume, he was just another riverman.

But a riverman Bowie was sure he was not. His head was huge, and its broken hat did not disguise the fact that it was an exceptional head. His mighty shoulders lacked the stoop of the frontier chawbacons. His expression proclaimed that he was out of no ordinary mold.

As the flatboat neared the wharf, the curs redoubled their furious barking, leaping about as if they were frantic to get at the people on the shore. The big man's voice boomed.

"Esau! Shut down those dogs!"

Simple command. But he said *those* instead of *them* dogs.

The Negro shouted and kicked at the curs: they retreated, snarling, to the stern where they huddled at the feet of the steersman. The giant left his seat and walked forward.

"Here, you!" he said. "Grab a rope!"

Bowie realized the command was directed at him: more, that the big man was accustomed to being obeyed. He caught the rope thrown and made it fast to a stanchion. A second rope from the stern brought the flatboat alongside the wharf.

"Tie up your dogs, Natty," the giant said, "and come up to the tavern." He lifted his eyes to the buildings of the town. "I suppose there *is* a tavern?" he growled.

Bowie said, "Of a sort, sir."

The bearded face swung around, and Bowie encountered a pair of striking eyes. Under them the skin was pouched, and all lines in the massive countenance were loose and deep, as from a long debauch. But though the eyes were bloodshot, they were unforgettable. Half slitted, shaded by heavy, bristling brows, the opaline light gray of them, intensely watchful, almost threatening, reminded Bowie of some great predatory cat.

"Perhaps, sir, you'll be good enough to indicate its direction," the stranger rumbled.

"My pleasure, sir," Bowie said.

The other clambered up on the wharf. Heavens, what a man! Bowie was not used to looking up to anyone, but he had to raise his eyes now to full six feet, six inches of height, with a great bearlike body to go with it.

"You appear to be a gentleman, sir," the man said. "May I take the liberty of inquiring whom I'm addressing?"

"My name is James Bowie."

The opalescent eyes widened a fraction of an inch, then narrowed.

"Bowie, you say? James Bowie? Is it possible that this is the *celebrated——*"

One of the loafers snickered. "That's who you're lookin' at, mister."

The huge man extended his hand and gripped Bowie's palm.

"A pleasure—and I count it an honor—to meet you, sir! Your name is a household word, sir! Permit me to introduce myself—my name is Sam Houston."

Bowie's turn to stare now. This sodden wreck, unshaved and filthy, the famous Sam Houston? Yet, sizing up the immense shoulders and huge body, he could believe the stories of how, when campaigning for the governorship of Tennessee, this man made a robust practice of challenging to a wrestling match the champion bully of each town he visited, and after throwing him, making a political speech to the crowd that had gathered to see the rough-and-tumble contest. It was said that Houston never had lost a wrestling match—or a precinct in which he made his speech after the match was over.

But what had happened to him? Houston's vast visage was flushed and puffy, his beard and hair untrimmed and unkempt, his breath heavy and sour with liquor. Yet even half drunk, this was an arresting figure. Dissipation had not diminished the jut of his great rocklike nose, nor softened his hard-lipped mouth. And there were those eyes . . .

Bowie said, "It's your own fame which extends to every part of the land, Governor——"

Houston gestured, as if brushing something aside. "Forget titles, I beg of you, Mr. Bowie. By your good leave, sir, I am plain Sam Houston, adventurer."

3

The incredible story of Houston's strange fate was all over the country. A major general, then a member of Congress, finally governor of his state, by the time he reached the age of thirty-three, he had, at the height of his career, taken himself a wife: the blond beauty, Eliza Allen, daughter of Colonel John Allen of Nashville. As Bowie remembered it, there had been somewhat of a disparity in their ages: the bride was eighteen, the governor thirty-five. It occurred to him that Ursula was eighteen her last birthday . . .

Nobody could have foreseen the strange course this match would take. After a notable wedding the couple went on a honeymoon. A few days later, they had parted. Weeping, the bride returned to her parents. Governor Houston wrote an incomprehensible letter and resigned his high office. Tennessee, the entire nation, were stunned. This man had stood on the brink of history: the heir apparent to the presidency after Andrew Jackson finished his term. He disappeared from the ken of his friends, drifting down the river courses in a flatboat with a brace of bear dogs and three companions, two of them servants, the third a ne'er-do-well Irish adventurer.

Now he stood before Bowie, drunken, fumbling, wretched, but an epic person still, who, if ever he shook off his black depression, might yet make history again.

Loafers craned, nudged, and whispered. On them Houston bent a silencing glare of distaste.

"Come aboard with me, Mr. Bowie," he said.

Bowie followed the fantastic figure in skins, whose hair fell about the ears of his massive head, whose moccasined feet were as huge as those of a grizzly bear. In the darkness of the small crowded cabin, Houston felt about.

"It was here," he said. "I remember distinctly. Right here on the floor." He was struck by a thought. "Haralson, the dog! I should have known! Mr. Bowie, you have no conception how that fellow drinks—and when the liquor's in him, the truth and honesty are out!"

Suddenly he bellowed like a bull. "Haralson! *Haralson!*"

A rakish, grinning face appeared at the door.

Houston scowled. "Where did you put the French brandy?"

Haralson was long-nosed, ruddy, obviously Irish, obviously irresponsible. His grin broadened. "In the chest, General——"

"Stop calling me General! And get it for me!"

Haralson threw open the lid of a chest, thrust his head in, and emerged with a glass jug in wicker, holding about a gallon. Houston seized it, squinted appraisingly through the wicker, and said, "Haralson, you're not worth the inroads you've made on this brandy. Now get out! This gentleman and I have something to discuss."

Still grinning, Haralson withdrew.

Houston tendered the jug to Bowie. "You first, sir. You'll find the cheer not bad."

The brandy was almost violent. Bowie returned the jug.

Houston took a long gulping swig. "Bowie," he said, wiping his bearded lips, "I'm glad to run into you at last. Why, man, you're a legend —a full-blown legend—and in your own lifetime! Mighty few in the world's history have known that experience. Bowie: the bowie knife. Is that the famous blade? I should like to examine it."

Bowie tendered the weapon, hilt first.

"This is the original?"

"Yes, sir."

"Half the men in Tennessee are carrying bowie knives these days. They're on sale everywhere. But not blades like these. I'd like to get one."

"Then order it from James Black, at Washington, Arkansas. He makes the genuine, hand-forged article—this is his manufacture."

"Washington? I may see that town in my itinerary." Houston ruminated. "I go west from here to the Rocky Mountains where, I hear, gold is to be gotten."

"I know nothing about the Rockies, but I have in mind a country you'd like. You're a big man, Mr. Houston, and that land is big enough for you. Texas."

"You're going to Texas?"

"I live there."

Houston nodded his huge, shaggy head. "There's a destiny in Texas. General Jackson, a man gifted with a prescience denied all common clay, has often told me that Texas may well be a star, a guiding star, in the history of this republic."

"Texas is a province of Mexico," Bowie reminded him politely.

"True. But history makes strange changes in the destinies of men—and nations." Houston returned the knife. "You lead a wondrous life, Bowie, doing as you desire, and going where you wish. Responsibility and disappointment do not vitiate your mind or spirit. But Houston—Houston is a ruined man."

He broke off, looking despondently at the planks under his feet, and Bowie was struck by his manner of referring to himself in the third person, a habit derived from the Indians among whom he had lived in his youth, and which grew more marked as he became older.

"Houston, the vagrant and vagabond," he continued. "Scorned and pitied by the lowliest. What a fall for a major general, member of Congress, and governor of so respectable a state as Tennessee!"

Bowie felt pity and a great liking for the huge bear of a man, sitting there in the ill-smelling cabin with his head bowed.

That night Houston was his guest at supper in the tavern, where the ex-governor drank far too much. At the end, he nodded tipsily at Bowie across the table.

"And so," he said, "though we scarcely know each other, our roads must already part?"

"Yes," Bowie said. "I go to Texas, you go to the mountains."

"In the mountains I will remember Jim Bowie in Texas."

"And in Texas I will remember Sam Houston in the mountains."

Houston nodded with the solemnity of the drunken. "Perhaps our paths will yet cross. And may our friendship never be the less."

A strange meeting and a strange parting, marking a pregnant moment in history.

Chapter Thirty-two

1

"I declare," said Simon Abishaber, as the white steamboat appeared around the upriver bend, "she's the *Orleans*. I know her captain. Jo Davis. A very high-toned gentleman. I promise you'll have excellent accommodations to Natchez."

They were waiting at Reyneud's landing. It was now June, and Bowie had said good-by to John and his family and ridden south to this place, since the deed had to be recorded in the county wherein lay the land Abishaber had bought of him. He had upon him the cash in bank notes of large denominations, but even in hundred-dollar bills, thirty-five thousand dollars made his wallet uncomfortably bulky.

With clanging bells, the stately craft drew in. She was, without question, a river queen, a floating palace of the Mississippi. Bowie noticed an oddity in her design. Instead of being rounded as usual, the wheelhouses of the *Orleans* were square, their flat tops coming up to within a couple of feet of the hurricane deck.

"I'll go aboard and introduce you to Cap'n Davis," said Abishaber amiably.

Up the lowered gangplank they went and, instead of entering the gentlemen's cabin, climbed directly to the hurricane deck, where Captain Davis stood near the pilothouse, blue-coated, bushy gray as to eyebrows, and white as to mustache, watching the roustabouts scurrying to bring aboard the freight packages.

"How be ye, Simon?" he asked Abishaber pleasantly.

"Poorly, poorly," said Abishaber with complacence. "I'm aboard, sir, to do myself the honor of bringing about an introduction between you and this gentleman. Cap'n Davis, I'm proud, certainly, to present Mr. James Bowie."

The extreme blue of the captain's gaze rested on Bowie's face. "I declare, sir, having you aboard my little old steamboat is a sure-enough event in my life. I've been hearing about you, sir, for years, it seems like——"

"Perhaps too much, sir," Bowie said, smiling.

"Well, now, Mr. Bowie, not to say that. Certainly not to say that. But it's sort of like having a fable come to life, in a way, sir. Meaning no offense in any way, sir, for nobody respects you more than your humble and obedient. But if you realize, sir, the name you've got on the river—why, I declare, Mr. Bowie, Andy Jackson hisself ain't got more say-so in these parts than you've got, if you want to use it."

Flattery is pleasant. Abishaber bade them farewell. In the bustle that marked shoving off, Bowie was left alone. He was watching the activity, when he heard beside him a voice.

"Is your name Mr. Bowie, marster?"

He turned. A bright-looking young Negress in white *tignon* and apron regarded him with liquid brown eyes.

"That's my name," he said.

"Then I is to say that a ol' friend of yours is abo'd an' craves the pleas-uah of seein' you."

A friend who sent a personal serving maid could only be a woman. Bowie followed the girl down the stairs. The ladies' cabin of the *Orleans* was immediately below the hurricane deck and above the gentlemen's cabin, which was on the main deck. When he saw Judalon he was hardly surprised.

She rose as he came to her, and smiled, saying his name. He bowed. "What kind of luck was it that put me aboard the one steamboat going down-river on which Mrs. Cabanal is a passenger?"

"Good or bad luck?"

"Good, of course. I'm always pleased to see you, Judalon."

"Then sit down here by me. What are you doing here? How are you prospering? You've no idea how everybody talks about you. What strange things have happened to you in Texas? It's a year and a half since I saw you . . . it seems like a century."

She was still beautiful, her waist no larger, her skin as fresh. Perhaps there was a faint line of discontent about her mouth, but when she smiled it disappeared.

He said, "Philippe, of course, is aboard?"

Her face lost its pleasure and its softness. "Yes."

"I haven't seen him yet."

"He's in the men's cabin."

"I must make myself known to him at once."

She hesitated. "It would hardly be worth your time, I fear." Her voice seemed suddenly to have grown dull.

"Why?"

"Philippe has been—drinking very heavily for days. He might not even know you."

He sat back and regarded her intently. Remarkable how a woman can put into a tone a shade of subtle meaning, a suggestion of something unsaid and not even meant in her words, yet underlying them as if the

274

thing unrevealed were more important in every way than that which is openly stated. Philippe was drinking. Heavily, she said. This did not seem of such great moment. Drinking was a common vice, and women as a rule put up with it in their men. But in Judalon he sensed an indefinable alarm, almost a despair.

He said, "You're on your way down from St. Louis?"

"We're returning from New York."

He was surprised. The journey to New York from Natchez was long, and not easy, particularly for a woman.

"I had always wished to see the East," she continued. "Narcisse, before his death, made constant reference to it. And life in Natchez, too—there's a certain sameness in it——" The discontent in her face was more evident now.

"I reckon it might be," he agreed, "though my memories of Natchez are pleasant. With a few exceptions."

Her eyes grew still, watching his face. "Am I one of the exceptions, Jim?"

"No. You could never be an unpleasant memory—to any man."

"You're laughing at me," she said. "I would never laugh at you."

Incomprehensibly, he experienced a sensation of alarm, as if he were near the outer but already dangerous circle of a whirlpool of emotion, toward the vortex of which he would inescapably be drawn if he did not in some manner break away from it.

To change the direction of their conversation, he said, "Was your trip for pleasure?"

"Pleasure, really." She leaned back. "But Philippe combined it with business . . . to a degree."

Again he divined that there was beneath her words an underlying meaning, but he could not be sure what it was.

After a moment she said, "But you've told me nothing of yourself. I have a never-ending interest in you—you must know that, Jim."

In her voice was the old attractive quality, the undertones of languor, mingled with warmth, which suggested her essential femininity: the femininity that perhaps allows itself to be carried along in the stream of chance, but which, when chance throws into its way what it desires, can take hold upon it and grip it closely with potent allurements and distractions.

"It's hardly worth your interest," he said.

"I disagree." She gave him her smile, and her voice was light. "You're worth any woman's interest."

Then her mood changed. She ceased smiling and leaned forward slightly, her chin resting on her soft white hand, regarding him with a

275

concentrated scrutiny in which all self-consciousness was forgotten. Then she relaxed and leaned back, her hand dropping into her lap.

"You've changed," she said. "Texas has done something for you. You're sure of yourself—I see in you the fulfillment of a promise."

He sat silent, with an almost hypnotic pleasure at her near presence.

"No man," she went on, "can possibly judge another man as well as a woman can. No man can know how good or bad, how strong or weak, other men can be. It is only woman who learns the full truth of man . . . the beast—and the god."

Engines ceaselessly throbbed beneath them, and they heard the foaming dash of water under the paddle wheels. A leadsman's musical cry came from forward.

She seemed to take possession of him—her voice, the curve of her cheek, the indescribable intimacy of her manner. Once more she was in his blood, his bones—like a thirst.

As if tearing himself up, he stood on his feet. This was Judalon. Judalon the faithless. Judalon, who promised and did not give. Judalon, who could wear upon her face a look of unassailable innocence as if she comprehended not one whit of that which she did comprehend completely.

He said, "I must pay my respects to Philippe. He will think it mighty strange if I stay here talking much longer without at least greeting him."

A clouded look came into her eyes. "Very well. You will be able to judge for yourself."

She made no offer to deter him. As he walked away, she remained seated, alone at the end of the cabin.

2

The men's cabin was larger than the ladies' cabin above it, and brilliantly lighted, for night had fallen on the river. At one end was an elaborate mahogany bar, attended by two Negro stewards in white jackets. A pair of elderly gentlemen brooded over a chessboard at one table. At another, four men played whist. Quite a group was at the bar, ordering drinks.

The largest crowd, however, stood about one table, watching a game, the players of which were hidden from Bowie's sight. He strolled over. As he half expected, Philippe was one of the four players. And as he had been warned, Philippe was quite drunk—almost incapable, in fact, of focusing his eyes on the cards.

"They've got to that fellow for almost a hundred thousand," a tall man muttered in Bowie's ear.

276

Now he understood something he had not been able to interpret in Judalon's voice: something she had been too proud to tell him outright.

The game was twenty-card poker, much in vogue then. It was played by four, and only the tens, jacks, queens, kings, and aces of the pack were used, so that all cards were dealt out on each hand. Betting was wholly blind. A game admirably adapted for what was known to the gambling fraternity as "three pluck one."

In a year and a half, Philippe had changed for the worse. He was growing stoutish, and his face had coarsened. The curling mustache was augmented now by a small chin beard, which did not, however, hide the flabby folds of soft flesh about his jowls. For all their drunken effort to focus, his eyes were desperate, almost terrified.

This, evidently, had been going on for a long time. The three playing with him, Bowie decided, were river gamblers, though somewhat less flashy in garb than most of their kind. They drank sparingly, their faces were bland, their manners smooth.

It added up suddenly to a very ugly situation. One hundred thousand dollars: that was more than Philippe could possibly possess in his own right. Whose money was it, then?

Judalon had said she and her husband had been to New York. A journey of pleasure, combined with business. Knowing the ways of planters, at least part of his answer seemed suddenly supplied to Bowie.

Considerable cotton and sugar were sold annually to buyers in New York. The means of money exchange were as yet only sketchily developed, so it was quite customary to send a representative East, sometimes with orders to purchase goods, sometimes with bills for collection from the New York brokers. Quite likely this had been Philippe's business. Judalon shrank from saying he had been gambling with the money of others.

From his acquaintance with river customs it was not difficult for Bowie now to piece together the rest of the story. All packet boats were infested with organized gangs of gamblers, frequently in connivance with the barkeepers aboard, and sometimes even with the officers. They operated a network of spies and informers in all large cities, who busied themselves spotting persons who were to travel on the river, carrying large sums of money.

Without a doubt, Philippe Cabanal, starting back to Natchez with one hundred thousand dollars collected for friends who had trusted him with the business, had been preceded down the river by full information as to himself and his wife, their characters, and an almost minute report of the amount of money he carried.

Gamblers operated in interlocking relays. The first of these very likely

277

met the Cabanals at Pittsburgh, where the down-river journey began. Mentally, Bowie reconstructed the process that followed.

Philippe discovered an affable new group of friends, whose flattery and deference were doubly enjoyable because he was so little accustomed to them. He warmed to the gentlemen, drank with them, conversed with them. It was natural to engage in a small game to pass the time, and without a doubt the game suggested was twenty-card poker. To his delight, Philippe won. The sums lost by his friends were small, but their compliments were polite and admiring. By the time they arrived in Louisville, where the Cabanals changed boats, Philippe had a happy conviction, backed up by perhaps two or three hundred dollars of winnings, that twenty-card poker was a game in which he was a natural master, for which he was ordained by nature, something the more pleasurable because in all his previous life he had shown a singular lack of ability to win at any kind of gambling.

Undoubtedly there was a layover at Louisville, and undoubtedly he was loath to part from his upriver friends. But by coincidence, these gentlemen discovered some friends of theirs, who were taking the same boat as he, all the way down the Mississippi. Introductions followed, and Philippe heard his own praises spoken in terms as extravagant as even he could wish.

The new "friends" were, of course, the down-river gambling team assigned to make the killing for which the upriver team had only baited the trap. The old story of the vain fool led subtly to his doom. A glass always on the table before Philippe as soon as the last was empty. Increased stakes, and no retreat.

Bowie wondered if Judalon had tried to get her husband away from the sharpers. She knew her husband well enough to be sure of the ruinous course he was taking. Yet, there was little she could do. On the *Orleans* women did not go to the gentlemen's cabin.

3

Philippe was too drunk to know Bowie or anyone else in the crowd about the table: but he was not too drunk to know the black disaster that had overtaken him.

The thought of confronting the men whose money he had lost made him cringe. Not only ruin but disgrace faced him at Natchez. More and more desperately, with a drunk's stubbornness, he plunged as the night wore on. Down the dark river the *Orleans* pushed her way. The men's cabin still was brightly lighted, but the ladies' cabin and the stateroom

278

passageways were dimmed. Most passengers had retired. Saying nothing, Bowie still watched the game. Midnight came and one o'clock approached. His face twisted as with a sickness, Philippe shook the last bank notes from his wallet and threw them on the table.

One by one he seized his cards as they came to him, staring at each as if it alone held his fate.

It was the last hand. As had been ordained from the beginning, Philippe had lost every dollar he had.

"I'm cleaned out," he said hoarsely. "You bastards—you've cleaned me out——"

One of the gamblers silently shuffled the cards. None of them even glanced at their victim: he had served his purpose.

With fumbling hands, Philippe attempted to straighten his coat. He peered around at the faces, recognizing none of them, and lurched away, reeling not only with the fumes of the liquor, but with the stunning realization of his disaster.

Bowie followed. Philippe continued on up past the ladies' cabin, toward the hurricane deck. When Bowie reached it a moment later, he was standing alone by the rail.

River and distant shores were dark, almost indistinguishable in the night, but the bright sparkle of a navigating light showed that the *Orleans* was booming along at full speed down the center of the channel.

Just in time Bowie leaped forward and snatched Philippe back as he tried to climb the rail, with the drunken intention of throwing himself into the river. The man struggled for a moment, in the manner of would-be suicides, then collapsed, sobbing, on the deck.

Bowie lifted him to his feet. He said, "It's time for you to go to bed, Philippe."

Cabanal peered at him. "Jim Bowie?" he said, incredulously. "Where—where'd you drop from?" In the odd, inconsequential way of drunkards, he became amazed at his own lack of observation. "Didn't even see you—know that, Jim? Didn't even see——"

Bowie started him toward the companionway. "You need sleep."

"Sleep——" Philippe said. He had forgotten suicide, forgotten everything. "Take me to m'cabin, Jim, will you——?"

He almost fell as they started down the steps, and Bowie half carried him to the deck below.

"Which is your stateroom?"

"Stateroom?" Owlish craning around. "Oh——" Philippe pointed. "Miss-issippi. Ol' Missi-ssippi——"

The door with *Mississippi* lettered upon it opened. Judalon whispered, "Bring him in."

She was in some sort of chiffon peignoir, very fluffy and soft, pale pink in color, and her face was very serious. Bowie helped Philippe into a berth, and together they removed his boots. In this proximity her delicate fragrance was very apparent.

"He—lost everything?" she said.

"Yes."

She closed her eyes, as if with a shudder. Cabanal already was asleep in the berth, snoring unpleasantly.

"He'll sleep now," Bowie said. He moved toward the door.

"Where are you going?" she whispered.

"I may be back," he said.

Chapter Thirty-three

I

Above the bar in the men's cabin, where a few still lingered taking a nightcap, the clock pointed exactly at one o'clock.

"A whiskey toddy," Bowie said.

The steward placed it before him. In the full view of all present, Bowie drew out his wallet and took from it a roll of bills. A very fat wad. Thirty-five thousand dollars. He stripped from it a hundred-dollar bill, returned the wallet to his pocket, and offered the greenback to the steward.

The Negro took the note and looked at it uncertainly. "Sorry, suh," he said. "Cain't change a bill this big."

A big plausible man, with a pallid face, the bar manager, came forward. "Policy of the boat, sir. We put the bulk of our money in the vault at midnight. I could get your change, but it would necessitate awaking the captain." He smiled. "Perhaps, however, one of these gentlemen may be able to assist you."

As at a cue, one of the gamblers stepped forward. "May I be of service, sir? I happen to have change for a hundred. Meantime, allow me the honor and privilege of paying for the refreshment you ordered."

"Why, thank you indeed, sir," Bowie said politely.

The other lingered. "May I be so bold, sir, as to inquire your destination?"

"Natchez."

A smile. "By coincidence, it's mine also. We arrive in three or four hours, I believe."

Bowie sipped his toddy. "I hadn't realized we were so near. Hardly worth going to bed. Reckon I'll go up on deck and catch the night breeze."

"Might I suggest a better way of spending the time, sir?"

"How, sir?"

"My friends and I thought of taking a turn at a friendly game of twenty-card, and we need a fourth. Care to join us?"

All most transparent. It told Bowie what he wanted to know. The three men were aware he had followed Cabanal to take care of him. His open display of the bank roll was understood also, as a sort of challenge to them, perhaps with the thought of revenging what they had done to his ostensible friend. Most important, they knew that Bowie fully discerned their knowledge of his intentions.

Bowie laughed. "Small stakes, of course?"

"Set the stakes to suit yourself, sir," the gambler said.

They were sure: yet he puzzled them. Why would anyone who had seen what happened to Cabanal willingly sit alone into a game with them? He was an adversary to be closely studied. Yet there was that big bank roll . . .

Cards were brought, a new pack. But this would be an old trick. Decks already marked were sold up and down the river to gamblers, who placed them with their confederates, the bar managers, to be brought out with the appearance of innocence when a game began and a victim was to be fleeced. Bowie knew he was confronting marked cards.

"Shall we introduce ourselves?" the first gambler said, riffling the cards. "My name, sir, is John Latour. This gentleman is Mr. William Payne, and he upon your right is Mr. Manuel Duran."

Bowie nodded. Only two men aboard knew him: Captain Davis and Cabanal. Both were abed. He thought of his Arkansas friend.

"Abishaber," he said. "Simon Abishaber."

Bets at first were small. Bowie lost and won. In fifteen minutes he knew the gamblers' plan.

"We haven't long to play," he said. "Might raise the limit a little."

"Agreed," nodded Latour.

An hour passed. Bowie had been permitted to win perhaps five thousand dollars.

Latour dealt. Bowie fanned his cards. Four kings and a ten-spot: an almost certain winner.

He glanced at the clock. They were only an hour from Natchez.

The gamblers must have decided to finish him at once by giving him cards which would induce him to bet heavily. The critical moment.

Swiftly, he appraised the situation. Since there were three of them, he could not call unless they let him, and they felt certain they could force him to put up all he had before they permitted a showdown.

His face was devoid of expression. Payne, at Latour's left, bet one hundred dollars, blind. Next to him, Duran raised to two hundred. Without hesitation Bowie saw this bet. Latour doubled it.

Payne's turn. Squinting at his cards, he said, "It's getting late. Why don't we make this worth while?"

"Agree, Abishaber?" asked Latour.

Bowie nodded.

Payne raised Latour by five hundred. Duran lifted it three hundred more.

In Bowie's mind now was only one question.

He saw Duran's bet, but did not raise. Again and again, however, the gamblers raised him, until the pot contained about fourteen thousand dollars.

Payne threw in his hand but kept the cards, face down, close to the edge of the table, toying with them, as if absently.

That answered Bowie's question. He sat back almost happily.

When the bet came around to him again, he suddenly raised· by five thousand dollars. There were three of them against him and the heap of money in the center was mounting. After several raises Duran fell out.

Matching Latour's final raise, Bowie shoved in the last of his thirty-five thousand dollars.

"That's my pile, gentlemen," he said. "I'm calling for a show."

He was morally certain that his four kings were *at that moment* the best hand. The question in his mind at the beginning was whether Latour, the dealer, had dealt all hands cold, or whether the gamblers planned to slip a winning card to one of themselves. Thus far he had seen no motion of a card, although he had never taken his eyes from Payne and Duran.

Then Payne's hand, which had been resting on top of his five discards, lifted and went to his lap. It was impossible to count the pasteboards remaining, but as well as if he had seen it, Bowie knew a card had been palmed and passed to Latour. There would be four aces against him.

But Latour had not yet time to complete his transaction.

Bowie's hand shot forward and grasped the gambler's wrist. At the same moment he whipped his knife from its sheath and held it on the table in front of him.

"Lay those cards face down on the table, Latour," he ordered.

Payne and Duran leaped to their feet. A sudden, excited stir among the onlookers. White with anger, but looking at the murderous knife, Latour put down his cards in a neat symmetrical pile.

Bowie said, "If that hand is raised and contains six cards, I will kill the man who held it." He threw down his four kings. "I claim this pot, Latour. Do you want to show?"

A new figure pushed in among the spectators. From the corner of his eye, Bowie saw it was Captain Jo Davis.

Twice Latour put out his hand toward the small heap of cards before him, and twice withdrew it. No question now that Bowie had caught him before he could get rid of the sixth card. No question, either, that he debated, perhaps, some way still to get rid of it. And no question that after another look at Bowie's face he gave up the thought.

"You concede the pot?" Bowie said.

Latour nodded sulkily.

Bowie sheathed the knife and swept the heap of bills into his tall hat. "I'm retiring now, gentlemen." He gave them a little bow.

That broke the spell.

"You can't do that!" Latour shouted.

Bowie halted.

"You'll settle with me, Abishaber!"

Bowie surveyed him almost curiously. "At your pleasure. I'll be back in five minutes."

He was gone, the gamblers glowering at each other, blaming one another for the failure in their plan.

Captain Jo Davis said, "What did you call that man?"

"Abishaber."

The captain grinned thinly. "Gentlemen, *that* is Jim Bowie."

2

Again Judalon opened the stateroom door, her eye taking in the hat he carried and its contents.

"You got it back?" she whispered.

"Most of it, anyway. There should be about one hundred and thirty-five thousand in there. I've got to return below. Count out thirty-five thousand while I'm gone, will you? That belongs to me—the money I used to gamble with. The rest is Philippe's."

She nodded. Bowie glanced at her husband, sprawled in the berth. "He all right?"

"As much as he'll ever be," she said.

"It's less than an hour to Natchez now."

His own stateroom was *Alabama,* down the hall three doors and across. He paused in it for a moment to take from his portmanteau two small pistols: Allen's patent pistols, ivory-handled and polished, the very newest thing in weapons. Merely pulling the trigger lifted the hammer and let it fall on the cap, firing it, and thus saving in time of cocking before shooting: a useful quality in Texas on occasion. He had bought the small hand guns in Helena.

As he left his stateroom, not locking it, a door opened slightly down the hall. He did not see her, but Judalon was watching him.

They were waiting for him in the gentlemen's cabin.

"You're Jim Bowie," Latour said. "The captain just told me. Well, it doesn't scare me. But we're not going to fight with butcher knives, or cane cutters, or whatever you're used to lording it around with. We're going to fight like gentlemen!"

Bowie nodded. "I reckoned you'd find out about me before I got back, so I brought along some weapons I thought might please you. Take your choice, load your pistol yourself, and I'll take the other and load it. Meantime, suppose we go up to the hurricane deck?"

"See those wheelhouses?" Bowie said, when they had gained the deck. "Square on top. They make standing platforms two feet wide, and this deck's about twelve paces across. I'll take one wheelhouse. Let Latour take the other. Captain Davis can give the word." He felt eager to get it over with.

Latour walked over toward the starboard wheelhouse.

"One of us won't need to worry about a funeral," Bowie said, as he stepped on the wheelhouse at the port side. Latour nodded.

Strange scene. The antagonists stood with the full width of the deck between them. Onlookers stared, their faces oddly lit from the pilothouse above.

Captain Davis began his count. "One——"

Both pistols came up.

"Two——"

At arm's length the two weapons still were silently aimed.

"Three——"

From Latour's pistol an orange tongue of flame and a sharp report. Bowie stood unmoved as the smoke blew away.

"Four——"

Latour was deathly white.

"Fire!"

Bowie's pistol spat. Latour staggered, turned, fell on his knees on the wheelhouse, clutched emptily at the air, and plunged off into the river.

Bowie had no compunctions about his death. He stepped on the deck and blew the smoke out of his pistol. The two remaining gamblers backed away, but Bowie paid no attention to them.

"I'm sorry," he said, "to lose the mate to this gun."

Nobody tried to stop him when he went down the companionway.

3

He opened his stateroom door. It was pitch-dark inside but from it emanated the faint fragrance of perfume. He fumbled for a sulphur match to light the lamp.

The cabin sprang out of blackness.

He saw Judalon seated on one of the two berths. Beside her was his hat, bottom up, the green paper money in it. She had been waiting for him in the darkness.

She rose, her silks whispering. "I brought it to you." Her voice was barely audible. "There it is. Thirty-five thousand dollars."

He closed the door behind him and moved toward her slowly. "I would have come for it," he said.

"I brought it . . . myself. Because there is very little time. We'll be at Natchez soon, you said."

He stopped, like a black thundercloud looming over her. Her face lifted, eyes wide, lips parted. Swirl of fragrance. Fluffy loose pink cloud of a garment. She seemed to tremble, cupped in the narrow space between the berths, and he need only reach out his two hands to capture her.

"You brought . . . *yourself* . . ." he said.

She gave a tiny nod and in her face was a desperate assent.

Here was the answer to a great question of his life, a chance for slaking old resentments, achieving old desires. The vortex of an emotional whirlpool was opening for him, to pull him down into it, steal from him all reason, all perception, save the blood-pounding intoxication of his senses.

Distantly a bell rang, a drop of clear silver sound.

He moistened his lips, and his face changed.

From the berth he took up the hat filled with money and held it before him in both hands. "Thank you for bringing this," he said. The breath slid out of him in a long exhalation. "You'd better go back to your cabin now."

She gazed at him incredulously. "I thought—you——"

"I thought so—too. But something happened."

He stepped back to open a way for her, but she followed him, standing close.

"What happened, Jim?"

He shook his head. "A sound—a bell. A signal to the engine room from the pilothouse. The pilothouse is on the hurricane deck."

"But what has that to do with . . . us?"

"I killed a man on the hurricane deck just now, Judalon."

"Killed . . . ?" Horrified, breathless question.

"One of the gamblers. Because of you."

"What did I have to do with it?"

"You always have something to do with it. This is the eighth man who has died on your account."

"How can you say that? I was not even aware . . ."

"I'm sure you were not."

Bewilderment and growing resentment on her face, and in him a strange feeling of emancipation.

"Judalon," he said, "I don't know whether I can make you understand this." He seemed to be trying to adjust things in their right perspectives. "I've been on fire for you. In love with you for years. Or thought I was. And now all at once—I'm not."

"Are you very sure?" she said. She placed her hands on his arms, and her body went against his. "Completely sure . . . dear?"

He swallowed, but his arms did not go around her yet.

"It's a mood," she whispered. "It will pass. The man deserved to be killed, didn't he? And now—for the first time—it's just you and I—alone together——"

He said, "The duel doesn't oppress me. It's just—that I don't want——"

"Don't want me?" He saw the sudden terrified hurt in her eyes.

"No woman—nobody—is worth the lives of eight men."

She bent her head and walked out past him, shutting the stateroom door behind her, leaving with him only the whisper of her going and a last faint hint of fragrance in the air.

He did not turn to look after her. When a woman, having exhausted her other resources, plays the final trump with her own body, it is decisive, in one way or the other.

The San Saba, 1831

*T*he western plains of Texas, in 1831, seemed to defy not only settlement but even exploration. Vast, much broken with canyons and gullies, in some places not well watered, they terminated in the Llano Estacado, or Staked Plain, a strange upthrust of flat tableland, which rose from the eastward levels in a steep escarpment, hundreds of miles in extent, and so dry it was called "the Sahara of America."

Yet this inhospitable immensity was the habitat and stronghold of many wild Indian tribes. Its expanses of grass were a boon to the buffalo herds. Its canyons offered protection from element or enemy. There dwelt the bloody-handed Comanches, Kiowas and Cheyennes. Not far below the escarpment of the Llano Estacado were the populous villages of the Wacos, Caddos and Wichitas. The Lipans and Tawakonis wandered in this region.

To the white man it was the great lonely land of mystery, repellent and menacing, from which the scourge of raiding red warriors came—a land of death. Texas would never settle her destiny until she found a way to cope with her wild plains.

Chapter Thirty-four

1

The heat of the day had grown steadily more oppressive. Sholic's broad greasy face ran with sweat, and Bowie felt the drops of perspiration trickling like crawling flies down his own back under his hunting shirt. Neither spoke. Men in the wilderness find less need for talk, since all have the same eyes to see and the same ears to hear.

Sholic was old and heavy for the saddle, but he pressed ahead steadily. On his arm he continued to nurse the silver-mounted rifle, although it would have been easier to slip it into the deerskin scabbard which hung limp at the side of his saddle. It was a wonderful rifle: no other Lipan had one to compare with it. The portly chief's pride in it was almost childish.

Their course led them across a stony, infertile plateau with dry exposed limestone visible frequently among the brush, and finally down into a broad valley, covered with oak and pecan, like an oasis after the desert. This was the Llano River.

Now the heat began to diminish, for an enormous cloud had grown before the westering sun. The distant horizon became gloomy with shadows, and thunder muttered. More than once Sholic glanced at that mounting cloud, and as they reached the banks of the stream, he whipped his pony hurriedly across. The little river was clear and shallow now, but if that oncoming cloud brought the rain it promised, it could very quickly become a dangerous flood. On the plains it was wise to cross a stream first and camp afterward.

Now swirling and ragged vapor masses began to sweep across the sky above them. A few drops of rain, big as hailstones, spattered down. Sholic hurried his horse to higher ground, threw himself from his saddle, and began hurriedly to gather sticks of dry wood for a fire. Bowie hastened to assist. By the time a small heap was made, it became abundantly evident that it would be of little use to kindle a blaze before the storm broke. They unsaddled and hobbled the horses. Bowie drew on his poncho; Sholic threw a horse blanket over the wood, and then wrapped his buffalo robe about him.

Almost as soon as it began, the first brief shower of large drops ceased. A low wind sighed among the oaks. To the west a cloud line approached with the speed of a running elk, its front almost perfectly straight, and beneath it a slate-gray rain that made a steady drumming roar. With a zigzag, blinding flash of lightning, the storm broke upon them.

Level lancets of water were dashed over them by a howling hurricane which blew the smaller trees almost flat and tore huge limbs from the larger ones. Startled, the hobbled horses gave a plunge or two, then turned their tails to the deluge, and drooped their wet heads in resignation. In this solid wall of rain, Bowie could feel the cold wetness beat even through his poncho of thick-woven wool. Grimly he turned his back to the storm like the horses, cursing the merciless elements.

They were lost in the immensity of the tempest, crouching with blankets thrown over their heads, hearing the earsplitting crackle of lightning followed by the thunder's deafening detonations, the scream of the wind, the pounding of the rain on the prairie. They could only endure.

Bowie hoped the storm was no ill omen. This journey had begun with a disappointment, and resulted from plans suddenly readjusted.

So long had his business delayed him in Louisiana that it was late in June of 1830 before he could return to Bexar. It had been a year and a half since he had seen his friends there, a year and a half since he had seen Ursula.

In his return journey, he had experienced a mounting eagerness to see her. Even at San Felipe, where at last he had an interview—very unsatisfactory—with Stephen Austin, the *empresario,* Ursula had been in the back of his mind at the very moment he discussed matters of importance with that strange leader of the Texas colonists.

Myriad speculations filled him. How had she changed? How did she feel toward him? Women of this clime were notoriously fickle, and in a year and a half she might well have found someone of far more interest than he was. There had been no formal betrothal . . . she might even be married now.

A thousand times he berated himself for his conduct toward her, and a thousand times he hoped for a chance to make amends. He had brought gifts for the whole Veramendi family, and for her a wonderful brocaded coat, slippers and gloves to match, and a speech all rehearsed with which to present them. These now lay in storage—speech and all—at the León de Oro. For when he finally reached Bexar, the first thing he learned was that the *palacio* was vacant, except for the *servidors:* the family had gone to Monclova, where Don Juan had a summer estate in the mountains, to escape the heat.

In his first disappointment he contemplated riding after them, but already he feared he had violated too many of the polite usages of these people. Such an act of impetuosity might be frowned upon.

At this time the Lipans arrived at Bexar for their summer trading.

Bowie had discussed with his brother Rezin a certain plan concerning these Indians, and Rezin, listening, considered the plan wilder than any to which he had ever listened, but ended by giving his support to it. In furtherance of this plan, Bowie began to cultivate Sholic, the Lipan chief.

One evening he visited the Lipan camp outside the city. In the crook of his arm he brought part of the plan: an utterly handsome silver-mounted rifle, which had come all the way from Natchez. The eyes of Sholic fixed themselves on this bright engine, fashioned as it seemed by the very gods of covetousness. He invited Bowie to sit by his fire.

No man could make himself more acceptable than Bowie when he wished. What was to be accomplished required proper ceremony, and ceremony requires time. First there was polite talk in Spanish, and Sholic's eyes hardly left the object of incredible fascination in the crook of Bowie's arm. Food was brought. After eating, the chief politely inquired if Señor Bowie would care to trade the rifle for furs, many furs of the first quality.

No, said Bowie, as Sholic eyed it with drooling avidity, he did not care to trade. He had brought the rifle as a gift for his friend Sholic.

The Lipan's pleasure was without bounds. While he lovingly fondled the splendid new possession, Bowie mentioned a wish to hunt that summer with the Lipans. Sholic thereupon proclaimed that his *amigo,* Señor Bowie, was always and forever welcome in Lipan camps, and would be an honored guest in his own lodge for such time as he desired to remain.

Bowie delayed a few days, outfitting himself, and Sholic remained after the rest of the Lipans had returned to their wilds, to guide his friend to their village. They were now seeking that rendezvous.

Meantime, Bowie huddled in his poncho, wondering how long this storm would last. An hour passed. The downpour became a little less blinding, the thunder crashed a little less frequently. Lightness grew in the west, the wind died slowly down, the deluge changed to a drizzle, then ceased. Beneath the edge of the clouds the sun, just setting, sent a sheet of warming rays. Some of the wood beneath the horse blanket was moderately dry, and a fire was soon burning. The horses turned eagerly to feeding on the soft rich grass. As the men ate their evening meal, the prairie, which a little before had seemed so furious, invited them to repose.

"Tomorrow," said Sholic, "we find Lipan village."

2

Late the following afternoon, as they descended into a beautiful meadow which Sholic said was the valley of the San Saba River, Bowie noticed what appeared to be pale indentations in the distance, somewhat like irregular teeth of a saw. With a grunt of satisfaction, Sholic pointed. The distant lodges of the Lipans created the illusion.

Filled with the doubts and anticipations with which a man always encounters something completely strange, Bowie rode toward the Indian encampment. A group of mounted braves whipped their horses out of a copse of trees, and Sholic and Bowie halted as barbaric young riders whirled about them, a frieze of savage wildness, tossing hands and shouting calls as they recognized the chief. With them Sholic exchanged some words in the Lipan tongue. Every eye fixed first on Bowie, then on the silver-mounted rifle on Sholic's arm. Falling in behind, the young men escorted the two into camp. The sun was less than an hour high.

Scores of skin lodges, with projecting poles at the top, were scattered irregularly along the small river, in which a number of young boys and girls splashed and swam, indiscriminately, utterly naked and utterly unself-conscious, screaming and laughing. Downstream, the horse herd was guarded by mounted youths. In the village itself, warriors stalked sedately among the lodges, or rode into camp, sometimes with game slung across the backs of their mounts. Squaws gabbled and worked at their sketchy housekeeping. Dogs barked and yelped and scratched and fought. In all his life Bowie had never before seen in one place so many dogs of so many colors and sizes and shapes.

"My lodge is over there," said Sholic.

It was one of the largest, standing on a commanding spot not far from the rushing stream. Before its door sat a young Indian woman, plump and with features not unpleasant, playing with a black-eyed little boy about two years old, by rolling to him white river pebbles. She rose quickly at the sight of them, gathered up her child, and disappeared into the lodge.

Sholic laughed. "That is Topsanna, my young wife," he said. "She does not know you are going to live with us." He gave Bowie a merry, sidewise look. "She will have another surprise coming to her, so I think."

A second woman, old and ugly, thrust her wrinkled face out of the lodge. She could have been the grandmother of the first.

"My old wife, Kosquida," said Sholic. The squaw hurried forward to take their horses.

Bowie followed Sholic into the lodge. Its round floor space was about fifteen feet across, with ashes of a fire in the center, and pallets of buffalo robes arranged about the sloping walls. At their entrance the young woman went quickly out, presently bringing in their baggage. The child gazed at them with unblinking eyes of silent awe.

3

In the last light of dusk, a group of savage figures gathered before Sholic's lodge. Some were mounted, others stood erect or squatted on the grass, holding the lariats of their horses. Quivers of arrows and bow cases of wildcat skin peered over the shoulders of most. A few carried guns in cases of fringed and beaded buckskin. They had an odor of their own, not unpleasant, comprised of leather, tobacco, wood smoke, and oil. All wore upon their broad faces more or less red or yellow ocher paint. All had rings of copper wire on their wrists and ankles. Their hair was parted in the middle and braided, with here and there a dangling eagle feather or small mirror attached as decoration. Most of the faces were almost flat, with little, slanting Mongolian eyes, but there also were a few conspicuous hooked noses. Without exception these men were as motionless and silent as statues, their steady, unwavering gaze on the white man who sat with Sholic just outside the lodge door.

Bowie understood that this collective stare of savage curiosity was the natural habit and custom of wild Indians, and he sustained it as indifferently as he could.

Night descended. Except for a chosen half-dozen prominent men who had been invited to remain for a feast, the onlookers began to depart to their own various lodges. Already, with some qualms, Bowie had observed the preliminary preparations for this repast. A large fat dog had been dragged by the scruff, yelping, to the lodge, and the old wife, Kosquida, had killed it with a club. She had then held the round-bellied carcass over the fire to singe off the hair, had cut it into chunks, and without further ado had dropped it into the pot already boiling. These proceedings were viewed by the Lipans with low exclamations of polite pleasure, but Bowie's stomach was doleful.

Sholic filled his red sandstone pipe with tobacco rank and odorous. With a coal from the fire he lit it, puffed at it, and passed it toward his right about the circle. It came to Bowie last, since he was at the chief's left. He took a few puffs, for this was correct usage among the Lipans.

Darkness settled over the valley. The dog stew bubbled over the fire. Kosquida, prodding in the kettle, announced that this delicacy was about ready. At that moment a new figure arrived. He had just ridden into camp, and he stalked directly up to their circle.

"*Hodie, Sholic!*" he said in a harsh voice.

"*Tres Manos, bien venido!*" responded the chief.

At once Bowie understood the significance of the name. Tres Manos. Three hands. The newcomer was younger than he, and naked to the waist, his torso ruggedly molded. His face was grim, with exceptionally wide bony cheekbones, which gave it a shape uncompromisingly triangular. About his neck was a leather thong, and dangling from this on his chest was a human hand.

Grisly object. Withered and smoke-dried and mummified. The bones of it showed yellow through the tight flinty skin. Its fingers were half closed, the nails clawlike with the distortion of age and years of desiccation. Three hands this man had: his own, and that upon his chest.

Tres Manos spoke to those in the circle, received a reply from Sholic in the Lipan tongue, and seated himself cross-legged. Again the pipe passed.

Now the squaws brought to them wooden bowls filled with unappetizing broth and boiled meat. The Indians gobbled greedily. Bowie felt his gorge rise, but to refuse would be a serious breach of etiquette. He forced a morsel of the dog into his mouth. It was almost tasteless: but all Indian cookery was tasteless, since no salt was used. He detected a slight taint, but otherwise the meat was not too objectionable, and he succeeded in eating enough of it to fulfill the amenities.

In a sapphire night sky the stars burned brilliantly. About them skin lodges took on the appearance of internally illuminated lampshades as small fires were kindled in them for light and warmth against the evening's chill. Praising their host for his feast, the guests rose and departed. Sholic and Bowie entered their own lodge.

The household was preparing for bed, and the unabashed intimacy of the Indian lodge required some getting used to for the white man. These people slept naked, and the modest conventions of civilization did not enter their minds. Already the child was asleep. Topsanna tucked the covers of soft deerskin about him, on her young face the solicitude of all motherhood. Old Kosquida dropped her mantle and crept into her bed, skinny and brown, her aged breasts withered against the ribs of her chest. Sholic stripped himself to his bare brown hide and laid himself on his pallet, wrapping his robe about him. Ostentatiously, these two turned their faces to the wall of the lodge, their backs to the others.

From Topsanna, Bowie received a half-fearful look. He made no move.

After a moment she slipped over her shoulders her pretty doeskin dress. Stark nude. Plump hips, dangling round breasts. All woman. Enough to stir any man. Softly she got into bed.

From among her robes she watched Bowie. He felt abashed, but undressed, leaving on only his shirt, and stretched himself on the pallet of robes that had been provided for him.

By the flickering light of the fire the young woman continued to regard him. He wished she would turn her back like the rest.

He tried to sleep. It was difficult. After an hour, he stole a glance at her again. Her eyes were still open, still watching him.

He smiled at her to show friendliness.

She did not smile back.

Resolutely he followed the example of Sholic and turned his face to the wall. Somehow he felt that her eyes were still on him when at last he fell off to slumber.

4

In the morning, Sholic inquired, "You sleep good, señor?"

"Good," said Bowie.

"I am glad to hear it." A pause. "We thought you might be sick."

"I feel very well. Why should you think I was sick?"

"Something made us wonder."

Sholic thoughtfully chewed some meat which Kosquida brought him. Age had made the old woman the servant of the lodge, for Topsanna sat at one side, combing her hair, carefully putting on each round cheek a disk of red ocher, and touching the parting of her glossy hair with red. She looked quite pretty and youthful at this feminine self-adornment.

Having finished eating, Sholic rose and gave instructions in the harsh Lipan tongue. Kosquida left the lodge at once, and Topsanna with the child followed her. Sholic turned to Bowie, who had risen.

"*Quedo, señor,*" he said.

Bowie wondered, but obeyed and remained in the lodge. The chief departed, with a grunt as he stooped his rotund form in the opening. At first the meaning of this was not clear. Then Bowie heard a step, the flutter of a garment, and Topsanna slipped into the lodge alone.

She stood before him, looking down at the ground.

"*Estoy aquí, señor,*" she said.

So she, too, knew Spanish. Bowie could surmise why the girl had come back to the lodge, probably sneaking away and taking good care not to be seen, and he did not like it.

"You must go back to Sholic at once," he said sternly.

295

She showed surprise. "But Sholic sent me to you, señor."

He could feel his jaw drop. *"He* sent you?"

"Yes, señor. He sent me. To see if his brother desires anything . . . of me. He thought perhaps you were too modest for it. Last night. With everyone here. So he sent me . . . alone."

A light dawned. That was why she had remained awake the night before, while the others slept with their backs turned.

Indian hospitality. Sholic was offering his guest all possible bounties. The dog feast was a gesture of magnificence: and this, a subtler intended kindness.

Though he had not seen his women for some time, Sholic abstained from them and slept alone. The reason for this, his young and pretty wife needed not to be told. She would be the one, naturally, whom the guest would prefer. In the close quarters of an Indian lodge, where a number of persons live and the normal functions of life must go on, it is polite to sleep with the back to the center, thus excluding oneself from whatever transpires elsewhere within that narrow circumscribed space. Sholic and Kosquida slept. But all night the girl, Topsanna, lay waiting, as a matter of course, for the white guest to accept the hospitality of herself which her husband tacitly offered.

Bowie now understood what had prompted Sholic's inquiries concerning his health.

The girl still stood before him, her head bowed.

"I desire nothing from you, Topsanna," he said.

"Nothing, señor?" Her eyes lifted, as if she did not believe.

"You may go back where you came from."

She sat suddenly down and pulled a blanket up over her head.

"What's the matter?" he asked.

No answer. He stooped and lifted the edge of the blanket. Stricken eyes regarded him, like the eyes of a homeless dog.

"I am shamed," she said in a muffled voice.

"For what reason, Topsanna?"

"If you make me go . . . everyone will laugh, because I am not pretty enough for the white man."

"Are you telling me that all the village knows you are here?"

"Yes, señor."

Bowie swore heartily and fluently in English. But the situation was delicate. He had no wish to wound the pride of this girl.

"I want you to listen to me, Topsanna," he said, again in Spanish. "It is not because you are not pretty enough. You are very pretty. Do you understand?"

"No, señor," she said miserably.

He groped for some way of idea transition. "It's not good——"

"Not good, señor? What is bad about this?"

He looked at her, baffled. "How can I make you understand?" All at once he hit upon a native phrase. "It is because—because among my people, to take the wife of another man is an evil medicine. Very evil."

For a moment she did not reply, but the blanket was slowly pushed back from her face. "A bad medicine, señor?"

"Yes."

"A very strange medicine," she said, considering. "I have never heard before of this medicine. Some men must not eat with any iron utensil, some men take always anything offered them with the left hand, some must purify themselves with the sweat bath whenever they have shed the blood of an enemy, and it is well known that for the shadow of a man's mother-in-law to fall on him in the sunlight is very bad. But no medicine I ever heard of will keep a man from taking a woman."

"Only the wife of another man," he said.

"Is this true of all men in your country, señor?"

"Yes." His conscience cramped him, somewhat, at this.

To her the viewpoint was most unusual. "They must not be happy. Are not most women married in your country?"

"Yes, Topsanna."

"When a man is a long time away from his own lodge, what does he do if women who are married are forbidden to him? And how can one man do honor to another, his guest, if he cannot send to him his best wife?"

"He must find other ways."

She digested this.

"Do you understand now, Topsanna?"

"Yes, señor."

"Then, since you do not wish to go, I will," Bowie said.

Her face clouded again.

"What is the matter now?" he asked.

"Señor, I believe this is your medicine. But will anybody else believe so strange a thing? When they see you leave me, they will know——"

She rocked her body back and forth, the picture of woe.

Again Bowie swore to himself. Then he grinned. It was obvious he must salvage several different kinds of pride in this village.

"We shall both stay here, Topsanna, and we will talk. Each on his side of the lodge we will abide, until time sufficient has passed . . . so that there need be no explaining. Thus Sholic will be made happy that he has made me happy, and there will be no laughing at you. Does this seem good?"

297

She brightened and nodded.

He sat down across the ashes of the fire from her.

5

The time they spent in saving Topsanna's pretty face, which he judged was the better part of an hour, was of value after all. The girl supplied him with much information.

The Lipans were great wanderers, ranging from the Mexican settlements to the Llano Estacado, but they were few in number. She told him that they were no more than three hundred, all told, and wars constantly depleted them, in spite of the fact that they frequently kidnaped Mexican women to bear children for them and thus increased their numbers by this means. Topsanna's own mother was a Mexican captive, which perhaps accounted for the girl's superior good looks. She said her mother still lived in the village and was as much Indian as anyone now, but she never talked with her because of the taboo between husbands and mothers-in-law.

It developed that there were two factions in the village. Sholic was the chief, and his policy was peace with the Mexicans, but Tres Manos opposed nearly everything Sholic stood for, and since he was the son of a chief many thought he would someday be head of the tribe.

"Where did he get that dried hand he wears on his chest?" Bowie asked.

"It is his father's hand, señor."

"The hand of his own father?" Even in an Indian village this was so ghoulish as to be shocking.

"The father of Tres Manos was Lobo Amarillo, Yellow Wolf," she said. "He was chief of the Lipans before Sholic. Somebody killed him in camp one night. After that, Sholic was chief."

"Who killed Yellow Wolf?"

"Nobody knows. Perhaps some Comanche horse thief who crept into the village, or some enemy in the tribe. Tres Manos was only a boy then. But before they buried his father, he cut off the right hand at the wrist, dried it in the sun, smoked it in the campfire, and proclaimed that he would wear it until he found his father's murderer and killed him."

That stark warrior, Tres Manos, was worthy of respect, if not liking, Bowie thought.

"Sufficient time has passed, so I think," the girl said presently. "Is the señor willing that I should depart now?"

He was willing.

l

It was September, and the last heat of summer smothered the land. The broken country, covered with scrub oak and scrub cedar, was cut across by a deep valley, at the bottom of which a stream of clear water twisted through groves of taller trees. Down the precipitous slope toward the river streamed a noisy and disorderly procession, the Lipan village on the march.

A group of young hunters, almost naked, daredevil riders who courted destruction in their rivalry to be first at the bottom, whooped as they whipped their horses in a bunch down the rocky declivity, leaping boulders, crashing through scrub. Behind them, riding more sedately and selecting the best contours for the descent, went some of the older warriors, the path makers for the baggage train. Now the first squaw, on horseback, with a half-nude child clinging to her back and the rope of a travois pony in her hand, went over the lip. The pony she led dragged a heavy burden of lodge coverings and camp equipment on the travois poles. Underfoot was hard-baked earth, with irregular patches of shale that tinkled when stepped on. The sweating little horse snorted as he slipped on one of these, but the squaw jerked the lead rope. They were committed, and they plunged downward.

The squaw was Topsanna, Sholic's wife, and her going was a signal. Behind her poured the whole rag-tag procession, travois poles rattling, horses slipping and snorting, squaws screaming warnings or directions, children squalling, dogs barking, dust rising in a swirling dun cloud.

Two riders drew up at the top of the bluff to watch the descent: Sholic, plump, good-natured, oily; and Bowie.

At least that savage figure would have answered to the name of Bowie: but had any of his former friends seen him they would have found it difficult to recognize the man they knew. He rode like an Indian, naked to the waist, his skin burned a mahogany brown, the sun-bleached hair of his bare head in two short braids, his beard whipping his chest in the wind. Long squinting in the sun had narrowed his eyes. At their corners were little twisted wire wrinkles, and from between the lids they gleamed fiercely, blue-gray in color, roving from right to left restlessly, never stopping save when they paused for a flickering instant at a movement of a distant herd of antelope, or the sight of a solitary deer standing in an open flat up the valley. A bow case and quiver of arrows jutted up between his shoulder blades. Across his saddle pommel he carried a rifle. And at his hip was the hilt of his knife.

The knife gave significance to the whole man. From the first it had been an object of especial interest to the Lipans. A born knife people, they at once recognized its peerlessness.

It would cut better than a hatchet: he had demonstrated.

It would throw: he had sent it whirling, and like a javelin it had struck its point deep in the trunk of a tree. All had marked its strange singing as it had vibrated there.

He had permitted others to try it. Its weight and balance and miraculous keenness had been studied. Even with very little practice one could make the thing work. Unlike ordinary knives, it seemed to throw itself. An incredibly fine weapon, assuredly.

From it he took his name among these people. Cuchillo Grande—Big Knife. The name was given him after the battle with the Wacos.

Bowie had not bargained for what he had been through that summer. He had come, it is true, to hunt with the Lipans. But the Lipans were nomads in the extremest meanings of the word, and no man who had not experienced it could know what a life like theirs would be. In that summer they had made, as a mere matter of course, a journey out of which the ancient Greeks would have erected an epic poem.

A thousand miles they had ridden: from the San Saba to the Colorado; thence across the height of land, traveling for days in the Cross Timbers; up the Red River to its confluence with the Washita, where they fought the bloody little engagement with the Wacos; by the Washita to the Wichita Mountains to cut new lodgepoles; westward to the escarpment of the Llano Estacado, where they traversed a deep and narrow canyon, and perhaps here Bowie was the first white man to see the Palo Duro gorge; south along the escarpment to the Concho River; thence again across a height of land—a long dry march—to the cedar breaks at the head of the Colorado; and now once more they were at the San Saba.

This, however, was far upstream from their first camp. Bowie had not seen this country before. He raised his head, which was maned like a lion's, and gazed across the valley to a steep conical hill overlooking it. The hill was peculiar in one respect: it was red—not the ordinary red of red earth, but a color more vivid, the hue of red hematite.

"They have all reached the bottom," said Sholic. "Let us go."

He kicked his horse in the ribs and the animal plunged down the sliding slope. Bowie followed.

In a pretty grass-covered opening among the trees near the river, the tall lodges already were springing up almost magically, with horse gear and family possessions about them, fires kindled before them, mounted boys taking the pony herd downstream to avoid pollution of the water, savage lords smoking comfortably in the shade, while their women prepared the evening meal.

Withered old Kosquida took Sholic's horse, and the chief entered the lodge. But Bowie did not dismount. Topsanna, who already had the meat pot boiling, gave him a white-toothed smile. They were friends. Never had Topsanna revealed what took place when Sholic sent her to the white man in the lodge that first morning. Since he paid no attention even to the prettiest of the Lipan maidens, a certain prestige attached to her, in the belief that she alone had known Cuchillo Grande. She did not dislike this, and it saved Bowie embarrassments.

From the first, he had lived like a Lipan, become a very Lipan himself in every regard save his skin and eyes and hair, which he could not change. He had adopted the bow as the best of all weapons to hunt the buffalo. One could launch arrow after arrow into the shaggy brown sides, while galloping in the stampeding herd. It did not take long to learn. An arrow well shot sank to its feathers just behind the shoulders, a mark not difficult to hit even from a running horse, since one loosed the string only six to ten feet away. Pierced through the heart or lungs, the huge beasts went down before long. Arrows, furthermore, could be identified, to prove the ownership of carcasses when the squaws went to butcher.

Infinitely better, however, the rifle was for deer. Almost any Lipan was a better bowman than Bowie: but none could compare with him as a rifleshot, and none could outride him.

His reputation as a warrior was awesome. It was based on the episode that occurred early in the summer when the Lipans were journeying up the Washita valley. Purposely, they had gone far out of their way to avoid the populous earth-lodge villages of the corn-cultivating Wacos, but by misfortune a band of hostile warriors of that tribe cut off a single lodge of Lipans.

Always there were stragglers in the Lipan march, but these, because of old Skiomah, the blind man, had fallen farther back than usual. On his first day in camp, Bowie had noticed this ancient: almost toothless, with long white hair, dressed scantily in old hides, and cowering near a fire beside one of the lodges, holding over the flames withered hands trembling from age or cold. His sunken face was filled with the immemorial hopelessness of the sightless.

Later Bowie saw the pitiable old savage dragged from place to place, never seeing where he was going or knowing who was with him, too weak to ride a horse but borne on a travois like a helpless child, living a sad, cheerless existence, dependent on chance kindnesses for his very life. Always Skiomah sat alone, patient, silent, and uncomplaining. Always he got the last dregs from the pot: and if there were no dregs, he went without supper. It was the common fate of age among savages, but even when he became accustomed to Lipan callousness, Bowie could never down his feeling of pity for poor old Skiomah.

On that particular day, along the Washita, Skiomah, because of his weakness, had caused a delay of the little group he was with. The Lipans found what was left of the old man, a squaw, and her two children. It was as if they had been worried by wolves: a causeless ferocity against these helpless ones that left Bowie sick and angry.

When the yell up the valley told of the discovery of the Wacos, he rode there at once. Tres Manos, ever alert and warlike, had cornered the enemy, a score of them, in a cul-de-sac at the base of a vertical rock cliff twenty feet high. His braves now surrounded them: but how to get at them was a problem, since the Wacos lay in a breastwork of stones and logs they had erected, and were concealed by thick undergrowth. They were canny, all armed with rifles, good shots. They refused to show themselves, driving back one or two abortive Lipan rushes with loss. Time was on their side; sooner or later they could count on reinforcements from the big villages down the river.

The Lipans were aware of this danger. At the same time it would be a tribal dishonor to retreat. They faced an impasse of the most ominous type.

The solution, unexpected and spectacular, was seen by every besieging Lipan. Without warning, Bowie appeared at the top of the cliff above the Waco defenses. All eyes saw his great knife flash from its scabbard. All saw his leap, twenty feet downward. The Wacos did not know of their danger until he landed among them, and by that time he was too close for rifles. The knife flickered in and out like sheet lightning, clearing an immediate space around the bearded white warrior.

Tres Manos himself led his braves to the barrier. It was over in five minutes: all Wacos hunted down and slaughtered without mercy. Afterward, looking over the bodies, men remarked upon the number showing evidence of the white man's knife. Some said six: some eight. Clearly the white man was a devil at fighting. From that day he bore the sobriquet of Cuchillo Grande. And later, when warriors sang their deeds at the

302

scalp dance, Cuchillo Grande sang not his deeds, whereupon it was seen that his own deed was so great that all other men, singing their deeds, sang also his deed, because it was a part of every action.

Only Tres Manos, because of Bowie's friendship with Sholic, and because he had lost face, in that Bowie saved him from an impossible situation, hated him more.

Such things as these were remembered by Topsanna. If Cuchillo Grande did not want her, she could at least smile at him, and she was happy because he smiled back.

"There are three hours of sun, Topsanna," he said. "Tell Sholic I am gone for a deer."

She nodded. The camp needed meat.

3

An hour's ride up the valley, and Bowie leaped from his horse's back. The animal stood fast, "tied to the ground" by its dangling reins. Bowie's eyes glowed fiercely as he stared with almost hypnotic intensity at a spot where he had seen a flicker in the underbrush.

Again he saw movement. Easing his rifle forward, he covered the gray patch no larger than his palm among the leaves with his sights and pulled the trigger.

The spat of the bullet followed the crack of the gun. In frantic bounds, a big white-tailed buck leaped out of the chaparral. Bowie stood still, watching the animal's tail. A deer running unharmed carries its white flag high. But this one had its tail tucked in close to the rump: a sure sign it was wounded. It disappeared among the trees.

Bowie reloaded, mounted, and rode toward the spot from which the deer had first bounded. The hoofprints were closely grouped at first. On the next jump they spread apart. They followed no straight line, but landed now on one side, then on another. He was sure he would find his game in half a mile.

Above him stood the red cone of the hill he had noticed on coming into the valley. Its upper slopes were treeless, the red rock exposed, but about its base grew a choking mass of thorny scrub. A wounded deer seeks heavy, concealing brush to bed down. He found a bright splash of blood, flecked with foam. Shot through the lungs. The deer would be dead when he reached it. He began to work his way through the brush at the base of the hill. Luck was with him. In the bushes ahead lay the gray shape. He dismounted and bled the deer.

As he prepared to hoist the carcass upon his horse, he stopped. Just beyond, in an open space, were curious heaps of stones. He led his horse over and looked at them. The stones lay in rows. There could be little doubt but that they were vestiges of buildings, the stones having fallen when the adobe which had supplemented them was melted away by decades of rains. Although much of the area was overgrown, he could trace the unmistakable lines of a quadrangle, and there were two gateposts of stone which no Indian had ever built.

A blaze of interest lit the bearded face as he glanced up to the red cone. Then he looked quickly back in the direction from which he had come and cocked his rifle. Bushes moved. A moment later he relaxed. It was Sholic.

"Topsanna said you hunted," said the chief. "I came."

This was strange.

"Cuchillo Grande has killed," continued Sholic. "I will help him load the game so he can return at once."

Such haste seemed unnecessary.

Bowie said, "Sholic, what is this hill?"

For a moment the Indian hesitated. Then he said, "It is called the Cerro del Almagre."

Bowie again stared at the red cone. At the foot of a red hill called Cerro del Almagre, he had been told, was a fabulous silver mine, discovered by the Spaniard, Miranda, and lost eighty years before.

Cerro del Almagre . . . It was a name, of course, that might be applied to many red hills. Still . . . these ruins. A *presidio,* perhaps, such as had been captured and destroyed by the Comanches?

He looked Sholic in the eye. "This is where the Lipans get the *plata?*"

After a moment the chief nodded.

Bowie said, "Let me see this place of the *plata.*"

He was very close to the fulfillment of a hope he had almost given up. This was why he had hunted with the Lipans: on the tenuous chance that they might lead him to the lost mine.

He spoke again, "Sholic has the rifle his brother gave him."

To this there was assent.

"Sholic knows this knife."

He drew it. The Lipan's eyes glittered.

"As surely as Sholic is Cuchillo Grande's brother, Sholic will have the brother to this knife, when I return to Bexar."

Sholic understood the implied conditions. "It is very dangerous," he demurred. "If others should find us at the mine of silver, which is the secret of the Lipans, we would surely die."

"The full brother, perfect in every way, of this knife, Sholic."

Such a promise could not be resisted.

"Let us hurry then," the Indian said. "The *full* brother, you say?"

"You will not be able to tell the one from the other."

"When?"

"When Sholic comes to Bexar in the spring."

"You will forget what you see here?"

"So long as both of us are alive."

Sholic turned his horse abruptly and led the way through the undergrowth.

4

As if anxious to make the errand speedy, Sholic drummed his heels against the sides of his mount. Only when the Cerro del Almagre was between them and the distant camp did he slacken his pony's pace.

Presently he began looking around carefully. Then, as if he knew exactly where he was going, he rode down into the bottom of a rocky ravine. "We will leave the horses in this arroyo," he said.

On foot, up a crooked, rocky course, Bowie followed the Indian's broad back. He did not see the opening in the side of the hill until he was almost on it, so concealed was it by the shrubbery. To have found it alone would have been an impossibility. Yet, it was evident that this was no natural orifice. Below it were the tailings of a considerable excavation, so old that among and over them climbed much thorny vegetation.

Sholic paused at the hole. "Take care. It is deep." He disappeared into the darkness.

Bowie had to stoop to enter. As his eyes adjusted to the dim light, he saw a live-oak log, sloping downward, very ancient in appearance, with steps hacked into it. He hesitated to trust his weight to it, but Sholic went down without hesitation. Steadying himself with a hand against the rocky wall, Bowie followed to the stone floor below.

He was in a lofty chamber fifteen feet wide, apparently extending deep, at one time, into the mountainside. Twenty feet above, the open entrance let in enough day so that as the eye became accustomed to the dimness objects could be identified. At some time in the past the gallery had caved in. Broken stones filled the entire passage. Undoubtedly the silver vein was walled off, and it would take a considerable engineering operation to reach it.

Then he saw something else. Against the wall, at one side of the chamber in which he stood, was the littered skeleton of a man. It lay on a heap of blackened bars of some metal.

With his knife, Bowie scraped the blackened tarnish until he saw a gleaming brightness beneath. Solid silver—every one of those bars!

Incredible. Exceeding the wildest speculations. He tried to estimate what he saw before him. Not even counting what might lie unmined behind the rubble-choked gallery, under his hand was enough smelted silver to make up loads for one hundred mules. A staggering fortune . . . if it could be gotten out. Here it was, just as it had been left when the Indians overwhelmed the *presidio*. Perhaps that partly dismembered skeleton was the last survivor, who dragged himself here to die.

The naïveté of the Lipans amazed him. By carting only a small part of this precious metal to the settlements, they could have made themselves rich, according to their ideas of wealth. But they never took away at one time more than enough to fill two hands at most. Their wants were small. Rapacious they were, but not avaricious.

"A very great supply of *plata,* indeed," Bowie said.

Sholic acknowledged this. Together they climbed out of the mine by the live-oak steps. Sholic, when they were outside, pointed to what appeared to be the vestiges of an adobe building.

"Over there they worked on the *plata,*" he said.

Bowie knew little about smelting, but he made out what remained of a very primitive furnace. There was no question but that this was Miranda's mine and that it contained enough silver to make him the richest man in Texas, perhaps in the continent.

But two things stood in the way: the difficulty of getting the silver out, and the word he had given to Sholic.

In the last days of September Bowie left the Lipans at their first San Saba camp, where he had joined them, promising to meet them in Bexar the following spring.

Chapter Thirty-six

1

Uproar and confusion at the León de Oro, that sleepy inn. Bowie arrived late in the evening, his appearance enough to make a good Christian cross himself. The *posadero,* Gregorio, was summoned.

"But—to get the effects you stored—at this time of night, señor—would require summoning *porteros* who already have returned to their families——" he squeaked.

"Get them at once. And find a barber."

"A *barbero* would be most difficult to find——"

Gold and Bowie both spoke loudly.

The *posadero* scurried. Overturned, utterly, was the somnolent schedule of the inn. From storage rooms where they had gathered dust, packages were dug and brought to Bowie's quarters. In an hour, even before his *cena* was served to him, a spry little man with eyes as black as flies had been routed from his *casa* and appeared with razors, scissors, lather cup and other instruments of his craft.

"This is Samoyedo, a very excellent *barbero*," Gregorio said.

Samoyedo gazed with alarm at the ferocious tangle he was supposed to attack. He pleaded to be allowed to come again by daylight, but Bowie demanded immediate action. Samoyedo therefore seated the American in a chair and swathed towels around his neck and shoulders. Soon the keen snip of the scissors had strewed the floor with long fair hair.

The beard was the greatest difficulty, for a man's face becomes tender when the razor has not visited it in months. This was a matter of repeated latherings, much steaming with hot cloths, and then a slow working downward from each temple, first on one side, then the other, toward the point of the chin, clearing one foothold in the jungle, as it were, before going on to the next.

The time came when Bowie could survey himself in the cracked mirror, the fierce beard a thing of the past. He grinned self-consciously as he fingered his naked jaw.

"It feels as if a part of me is gone," he said.

"The señor is magnificently improved!" exclaimed the *barbero*.

True, perhaps. Bowie's face appeared smaller, the chin shrunken with its covering gone. Peering in the mirror, he noticed with surprise how white was the lower portion of his visage, where the beard had protected it, in comparison with the excessive tan of his upper cheeks and forehead.

So much was accomplished. Now came a call for a tub and hot water and more soap. Not once but many times he scrubbed his head and his long, limber body, before he was satisfied that the last trace of Indian smoke and grease was gone from it.

After that he ate his *cena* and questioned Gregorio.

Yes, said the *posadero,* the Veramendi family had returned to Bexar a fortnight ago. The son, Carlos, remained at Monclova to attend the *academia,* so it was reported. The daughters? Yes, both were here.

Bowie found the problem of sleep difficult that night.

2

The barber and good clothes combined. El Cuchillo Grande was transformed by them into Don Jaime Bowie. Taking pleasure in the greetings from old friends along the street who were surprised to see him, but excited and worried at the prospect ahead, he rode in the morning to the *palacio*, his saddlebags well filled with bundles.

Benito, the old *servidor*, admitted him, grinning cavernously. *El gobernador?* At this moment he was occupied with the *jefe politico*. But Benito was sure that Doña Josefa would receive Don Jaime.

Bowie awaited Ursula's mother in the *sala pequeña*. Presently Señora de Veramendi entered. He kissed her fingers and remained standing, for she did not take a seat. She gazed at him coldly.

"I just returned to town last night," he began.

"You have been away a very long time, señor."

Señor. Her formality chilled him. "When I returned to Bexar in the early summer, you were gone."

"So we understand. We had thought ourselves your friends."

He was aghast. "I don't understand you, Doña Josefa. No friends mean as much to me as you and yours."

After a moment of silence, she said, "What kind of friendship is it, señor, which does not once in almost two years of time let us hear from you even so much as a greeting, or where you are?"

"I know I deserve that from you," he said slowly. "I have been through much since I left you. It would take hours in the telling. And I have thought of writing many times. But to write a letter, of the kind I would have written, is a task that appeared gigantic to me, who am little accustomed to quill and paper. And I told myself that the mail was so uncertain, my message might not even be delivered——"

"I can understand, and forgive to a degree, such a conclusion when you were in the United States. But you were here in Bexar also. Surely you knew that the post is reliable between this place and Monclova?"

"This is embarrassing to me. I cannot make excuses for it. I will only say that I would rather ride a thousand miles than write one letter, and beg you to forgive my negligence."

"It is hard to forgive, señor. Because it was cruel."

"Doña Josefa—cruel?"

"It is clear that you think little of the feelings of others, señor. I must speak openly. It is Ursula of whom I am thinking."

His expression changed. "What of Ursula?"

"I will tell you that she confessed to me the secret promise she made to you, before you went back to your country. I confronted her, when month passed after month, and she would show no interest in any of the young men who came to pay courtship to her. Her promise was given, she told me then. Señor, to a girl like my daughter, a promise is a promise, however it may be regretted, until it is given back."

"She . . . regrets it?" Bowie's heart sank.

Doña Josefa's eyes looked directly into his. "I am going to ask you, Señor Bowie, to release my daughter. Wait—don't interrupt me. In the first place, there is much to criticize in the way you got the promise from her. You didn't approach her as she should have been approached, but took her aside in secret and wrung the promise from her. You realize how guilty you are in this respect?"

He hung his head. "Yes, doña."

"In the second place, you shamefully neglected her. I cannot tell you how her pride has been hurt, how many tears she has shed, because not one little evidence has come to her in all these months that you so much as thought of her."

He nodded abjectly.

"I may as well tell you," she went on with dignity, "that I have urged her to forget such a one-sided promise. Ursula de Veramendi does not deserve such treatment from any man. She has prospects too great. Sons from half the important families in Texas and Coahuila would consider themselves thrice fortunate to have her for a wife. But in spite of this, Ursula feels herself bound by her word until you yourself free her."

In his life Bowie had never been so stunned. "I must free her?"

"It is only just, señor."

Very gravely, he said, "Just, it probably is. But let me say to you this, Doña Josefa. I love your daughter. I am a man to whom it does not come easy to say what is deepest in his heart. That is one of the reasons why I did not write. When I tried to put words on paper, they seemed not to belong to me, too weak and silly to send. I tore them up. This is no excuse, of course. If Ursula wishes me to free her, I will do so. It will be the worst thing that ever happened to me. But I will do as you say. May I see her?"

Doña Josefa thought a moment, and then said, "I cannot refuse to let you see her."

"When?"

"When you came, we were both sewing in the patio. It is possible you may find her there now."

He looked at her very seriously and turned to go. She stopped him. "I would say this much, señor. When you came here I had many resentments against you. I now believe you have been only awkward and thoughtless, not entirely insincere."

"Thank you, doña." Again he kissed her fingers.

Ursula was sitting beside the fountain. As he approached, she rose, her sewing, thread and needle, fluttering to the flagstones.

The sight of her gave him a jolting sensation of the heart. He had thought her beautiful. She was something far more. A year and three quarters can perform magic in a girl, and she had become a woman since he had last seen her.

Her glossy dark hair was piled high on her head. This in itself gave her a different, somehow more daring personality. Her shoulders and full bosom rose, snow white, out of her low-cut gown of black net. At the sight of him, she raised slender fingers to her throat, as if to quiet a throbbing there.

"Ursula——" Bowie stopped. He could not make the words come. In her was a new challenge—this brilliant luster in her eyes, the white ripeness of her bosom and shoulders—they were more than he had been prepared to face. In her attitude, her look, he recognized the woman in her full majestic power.

She did not move toward him. "You have been away a long time." It was an echo of her mother's first statement.

Like the last half day to water were those five, three steps he took toward her. She gave him her hand and he crushed it to his lips.

"I couldn't come back sooner. When I did, you were gone," he said.

"Are there no paper and ink in the United States?"

The same question her mother had asked. The same lack of any excuse on his part. With this girl, he had not been honest. It was the old grasping Bowie, who had sought in the vice-governor's daughter the best opportunity to advance his fortunes. Time and bitter experience had since taught him what Ursula really meant to him. But now he was sure it was too late. He was ashamed and afraid. She had given him her hand, but she remained cool.

He said, "Ursula——" and stopped, to control his voice and collect his thoughts. She let him go on.

"I'm not trying to pretend humbleness," he said, "or to make pretty speeches when I say this, for I never meant anything as deeply in my life: I am a man who has seen a great deal of women, and in my whole life I have never seen a woman who compares to you. I have seen a great deal of men also, and of all the men I have seen, I do not think one would have been worthy of you. And I myself . . . perhaps I am the least worthy of them all."

Her eyes searched him. "What is it you are trying to say?"

"That I love you. And—Ursula—I have not been honest in the one thing I wish most to be honest about——"

She drew herself up. "You do not need to tell me, Jaime. From the first I was sure . . . that there was someone else in your life."

"How—what made you——" he gasped.

"A woman would know it."

"In spite of this you accepted my offer of marriage?"

"Yes."

"Why, Ursula?"

"I thought—perhaps—you might get over . . . the other."

Bowie said, slowly, "It required only that I see her once—to know that in comparison with you she is worthless."

"She is married."

He was stunned. "How—how could you know that?"

"Because only a woman who is beyond reach can capture and hold a man's imagination for so long."

He bowed his head before her. "You are wise, Ursula. But—she was not beyond—my reach. Knowing this, I then knew that I was in love only with you."

He waited for her to speak, but he heard only her deep breathing.

"That was not what I wished to confess to you," he said after a minute. "Something else—the hardest thing I have ever done in my life, but it must be done. When I tell you this, you may do as you wish with me."

She said, "I am waiting."

"This is it: on the day I asked your father for permission to pay my suit, it was for a selfish reason. I thought I had reached an age when a man should take a wife, and it appeared to me . . . that you would be an advantageous match. I was fond of you. But when I spoke of marriage to you, it still was that despicable motive that impelled me. Ursula—believe this. You've done something to me I could never have thought would happen. You've taken possession of my heart. I love you, and I did not know what love was until I knew this aching you have put into me. I love you—and I'll never love anyone else. Knowing that, Ursula, can you understand? And forgive?"

He paused, very despondently, his eyes on the flagstones. "Only that, Ursula. For I cannot expect you now to return my love. And your promise to me I freely at this minute give you back."

She looked at him as if she would weep, or flee.

"Oh, Jaime . . . I do not want . . . my promise back!"

Whirling to him, she pressed her mouth against his.

For a long time they stood very close together, and he held her hungrily. After a while she freed herself.

"You—you are trembling." She gave a little, shaky laugh. "You are not, then, made of steel or wood or something. You are alive and your blood beats strong——"

"You love me as I love you?"

"Yes—oh, yes!"

"When will we be married?"

"Whenever you wish—and my father gives his permission."

The lover sought her with his arms again, but she did not this time come to him.

"Wait—there is something else to be said." She smiled and held herself away from him. "Dear Jaime—what you have told me made no difference —except that it made all the difference in the world, since it has made me supremely happy. You love me—I could not have expected so much—not from a man like you——"

"From any man——"

"Let me finish. You say you despise yourself because you began your courtship of me selfishly. Believe me, it did not occur in my heart that you sought me for any other reason."

He could not interrupt her. Almost musingly she continued, "I was a girl, young but not wise, living in this out-of-the-way place. I compared myself to the women you must have known . . . that other one, particularly, whose name I never want to know. It sometimes seemed to me impossible that you could see anything in me. Far from blaming you for wanting me because I was of a family with some wealth and importance, in my mind I plumed myself on it. I treasured it as my one point of strength. For I loved you, Jaime. From the first moment when you spoke to me, I knew no other man would ever fill my heart as you did——"

Again she drew aside from his urgent arms, her smile trembling, to finish what she had to say, as if it were a confession to be made before the final seal was placed. "When you proposed to me . . . you said nothing of love. And when in all those months you did not even send me a message, I was in terror that you might have decided I was not worth your while after all. During all that time I clung only to the promise— and the hope. And now—oh, Jaime—*querido*—nobody, *nobody* can be as happy as I—because you *do* truly love me after all——"

Such a woman did not exist. Yet here she was. Her tears did come now. She let him draw her to him, and in a soft fury she raised her face to his, her cheeks wet.

In his memory forever after lived the manner in which Ursula's mouth melted to his in a blur of ecstasy.

Chapter Thirty-seven

I

"There are," said Don Juan de Veramendi, "several little matters to be considered. It will be April, at least, before the wedding can take place——"

"Why so long?" Bowie asked.

"My friend, you do not know women. Six months is too little time for them to get ready as it is. Being a bachelor, you have not the slightest conception of the monumental importance a wedding assumes in the minds of such as my wife and your betrothed. There must be special sewing, many articles must be brought clear from New Orleans or the City of Mexico, the entire *palacio* decorated, invitations sent to distant friends, the banns read five times—it is almost as difficult and laborious to get a whole army mustered, uniformed, equipped, and ready to fight a campaign, as it is to get one small girl ready to be married."

Six months it had to be. The "little matters" of which Don Juan spoke were attended to. The records of the provincial government of Texas and Coahuila show that on October 5, 1830, James Bowie, a citizen of Louisiana, became a citizen of Mexico.

On April 22, of the following year, when the day of the wedding was near, a contract was drawn up by James Bowie before Don José María Salinas, the *alcalde* of San Antonio de Bexar, and witnessed by José Manuel de la Garza, José Cárdenas, Juan María Flores, and Ignacio Frechey, substantial citizens all. The terms of the contract, arrived at without dispute and with good will on both sides, showed the care with which the father and the prospective husband sought to safeguard the future of the bride-to-be. In part the contract read:

James Bowie, being about to undertake marriage with Ursula de Veramendi, and with due consideration for the virtue and other praiseworthy qualities of said wife, he offers her in addition to her dowry by way of marriage, to make whatever use she may of it, and in case the marriage shall be consummated, the sum of 15,000 pesos, which may be selected from his possessions, which he lists as following:

In the Territory of Arkansas, in the United States, 70,000 arpents of land at four reales each at lowest price.

In legal obligations and sufficient notes made by C. C. Walker and Wilkins Bros., residents of the Neches and of the United States.

Certain individual notes in judgment or suit.

Certain cotton and wool machinery in possession of C. Angus McNeil in the state [*sic*] of Boston.

Besides certain furniture and articles in use in his house.

Land under contract and to be acquired in this country . . . good title to 15,000 arpents of land on the banks of the Colorado River and in the Teche country, valued at 75,000 pesos.

So he binds himself to pay in money to his future wife or her representative in case the marriage be terminated for any legal cause through fault of his.

In the six months since he became the acknowledged betrothed of the vice-governor's daughter, Bowie had been far from inactive in terms of land and property. Moreover, he had built a house near the Mission San José, and furnished it for Ursula with "certain furniture and articles," which they had spent many an hour, heads close together, in planning and selecting for their new home.

2

Not in years had Bexar seen anything to equal the wedding of Ursula de Veramendi and James Bowie. On that bright morning of April, the Church of San Fernando was crowded to its doors and hundreds stood without. In the solemn hush, the lean priest, Padre Garza, uttered the words of the ceremony and blessed the couple. Bowie kissed his bride in the presence of the congregation. The bridal party moved out of the church, and Padre Garza prepared to write in the parish record this notation:

In the City of San Antonio de Bexar on the 25th of April, 1831—I—the priest—Refugio de la Garza—married and veiled in the face of the church—Señor James Bowie, a native of Louisiana, North America, and Senorita Maria Ursula de Veramendi, a native of this said city, legal daughter of Juan Martin de Veramendi and Maria Josefa Navarro, his wife—in witness whereof I affix my signature.

So much for the forms. Now it was time for the jubilation. Smiles and cheers and a shower of flower petals greeted Bowie and his bride as they issued from the church. Their carriage was brought. Bowie drove, Ursula's white-gloved hand on his arm. Riders surrounded them, sometimes a man and woman on the same horse, and many equipages followed them to the *palacio* where the festivities were to be held.

Before the *palacio* a platoon of soldiers was drawn up, and at the arrival of the carriage, they fired a salvo of muskets. The horses reared at this *feu de joie,* and for a moment Bowie was busy keeping them from bolting before some men seized their heads.

Doffing his hat, the bridegroom leaped to the ground to assist his bride. Before he could do so, however, a cry was raised. *"Espuelas! Espuelas!"*

He smiled and submitted to the custom, suffering the spurs to be taken from his heels. One was the prize of Benito. The other was captured with a triumphant flourish by Almazon, a celebrated *bastonero* and improviser of music on almost any instrument, who had been appointed to act as master of ceremonies. Later each of the spurs would be redeemed with a bottle of *aguardiente.*

He was permitted to lift the bride, light as a feather in his arms, and place her on the ground, where she clung to him for a moment, her heart beating against his, her face upturned as if for a kiss.

The great carved doors swung open. Together they passed up an avenue of grinning faces, in a barrage of good wishes and congratulations.

In the *salón,* flanked by relatives and close friends, sat Don Juan and Doña Josefa together, in high-backed chairs. Before these the new-wedded couple knelt and asked their blessing.

After it was bestowed the couple rose. Veramendi nodded toward Almazon, who stood near a window. Instantly music sounded from the direction of the patio. The vice-governor offered his arm to his daughter and Bowie took the hand of Ursula's mother. They were followed by Teresa and the other guests.

Under the apricot trees in the *huerta,* at the rear of the house, a *ramada* had been erected for the wedding dances: a wide trellis, covered with leafy branches and supplemented by a pavilion of yellow canvas open toward the earthen dance floor, in which sat the wedded couple, the vice-governor and his wife, their guests of quality, and behind these the household on rows of benches, for the family *servidors* enjoyed a special place at this celebration.

On two sides of the *ramada* were rows of seats for the girls and women who were to dance. The end opposite the pavilion was open, and guarded by a strong fence of posts. Here ranged the mounted men, spurring their horses up to the barrier, the animals dancing, rearing, circling out and coming back in, the riders laughing and calling out mock threats and jokes, skylarking, disputing for places, each striving to force his horse to the front. At times they raised a cloud of dust and created a diversion almost too great, but they added much color and excitement to the spectacle.

The orchestra struck up a lively tune. Into the center of the *ramada* advanced the small and active figure of Almazon, his face one continuous smile of joy. This was his moment of high importance and delight, and he was dressed resplendently for it. His wide yellow hat glittered with an abundance of glass seed beads, the under part of the brim nearly covered with heavy silver lace. A green satin jacket with buttons of Mexican *pesetas* with the eagle stamp on the exterior fitted his body snugly. His waistcoat was yellow satin, the pocket flaps buttoned with gold dollars. He wore tight breeches of red velvet which flared below the knees with silver buckles at the top of the side openings, which were filled with gilt lace. His boots were of buckskin, decorated with green silk ribbons and tassels.

A notable feature of his ensemble was the buttons of the breeches fly, which were plainly visible, and of *pesetas,* except the top one, which was large and of gold. This button was known as the *atrancador*—the bar to the door. On it a motto was engraved: *"No me saques sin razón; no me metas sin honor*—Do not loose me without reason; do not confine me without honor." A gay and somewhat ribald impertinence: but the women of Bexar only laughed at it, for it was a device not infrequently employed by bold young sparks.

Twice or thrice Almazon pirouetted alone in the middle of the hard-beaten floor, with graceful movements of his hands and stampings of his feet to the music, his teeth gleaming beneath his mustache as he viewed the women in their pretty dresses. It was the office of the *bastonero* to organize everything, and Almazon glanced over the assemblage as a field marshal surveys his army. All at once, clapping his hands, he took steps to a girl at the end of the *ramada.*

She rose, a smiling graceful creature. With her two hands she extended her skirts and began to dance with him. The crowd applauded as the couple twirled, their feet flying. Amid "Bravos," the smiling girl returned to her place.

Now Almazon was launched. In turn he called out every woman in the *ramada,* except those sitting in the party of the vice-governor. Most of these danced gracefully, some amazingly nimbly. A few who were too old or did not wish to dance, he led out in compliment, gave them his hand, turned them, and seated them, for none must be slighted.

All this time the *charros* at the barricade were in constant motion, jockeying their horses, calling gallantries to the women, sometime backing away and letting their mounts out for short bursts of speed across the *huerta* before returning to the spectacle.

The dances began, all of the kind known to the common people. First a *jota,* a favorite with the Mexicans. A dozen horsemen dismounted, hung their spurs on their saddles, tethered their horses, and selected partners in the *ramada*. The *músicos* launched into a very rapid tune, meantime breaking into song. The *jota* was something like a reel. During the short verses of the song, the dancers made graceful motions with their arms, advancing and retreating, smiling, bowing and coquetting. When the longer choruses began—the words were improvised and personal— the men went one way, the women another, and then began a series of balances and figures, brilliant in movement and gaiety, accompanied by soft hand clapping and cries of applause from the onlookers.

The *jota* was succeeded by a *zorita,* and that by a *fandango.* A laughing circle of men and girls formed, with an extra man in the middle, in a dance known as the burro. Music began, the circle skipped about. At a shout from Almazon, each man leaped forward and embraced one of the girls. A howl of laughter. One of the men, naturally, was left without a lady to embrace. The target of gibes and merriment, he became the burro as the dance continued with constant changes.

The dancers cleared from the floor as Almazon led out Estrella, the pretty girl he had first introduced, who was known as a fine dancer, to do a special number, the *jarabe,* with himself as partner.

Estrella blushed at the applause but accepted. Even more rapid became the music. The couple began by a quick drumming of the ground with their feet, the girl, her head tilted to one side, holding up her dress with her hands. Almazon, his sombrero undoffed, rattled his boots, his face in that continual smile of delight, his arms behind his back securing the points of his *serape.* Faster and faster they danced. All at once Almazon removed his hat and placed it on his charming partner's head. She laughed and danced even more rapidly and gracefully.

A salvo of applause. Another man approached the couple with dancing steps and placed his sombrero on top of Almazon's. One after another, others came, until Estrella danced beneath a towering pinnacle of sombreros, each fitting over the crown of the next below, until they threatened to fall with every movement she made. But still she balanced them dexterously, until the long-awaited threat came true, the spire of hats fell, and sombreros rolled everywhere on the floor.

Estrella, flushed and laughing, retreated to her seat. The radiant Almazon gathered up the hats, brought them to her and placed them in her lap, where they were redeemed by their owners for money—sometimes a few reales, sometimes as much as five pesos—with which she could buy a new dress or perhaps a necklace.

Cries of *"Bomba! Bomba!"* sounded, and someone shouted, "Señora Bowie!" It was taken up with a roar of applause and laughter. "Señora Ursula! *La Bomba!* Señora Bowie!"

The *bomba* was the most difficult and brilliant of all the dances of the

317

country, and Ursula was famous for it. She looked at her husband for permission. He smiled. She rose.

The crowd cheered. Into the center of the floor she advanced, a slender figure in white, smiling at them with dark eyes and beautiful lips. All crowded back to the walls: even the horsemen ceased their restless activity to watch.

All around the *ramada* Bowie heard the exclamations of admiration and wonder as his bride stood alone, waiting. In a moment Almazon came, bringing a tumbler of water, which he placed carefully on her head.

A gasp of expectancy through the crowd. The music struck up. Ursula began to dance.

Her skirts were held daintily, so that her little feet in their twinkling intricacy of steps could be seen by all. Around and around she twirled, always smiling, changing her movements, increasing in rapidity, but keeping always that superb carriage of her head, so that from the tumbler not one drop was splashed.

The onlookers yelled. Almazon took a large handkerchief, tied its corners together so that they formed a loop, then dropped it on the floor. About this Ursula danced brilliantly in a circle. Bowie knew what she was to attempt, and his face was anxious, as he wondered if she could meet the difficult challenge of the *bastonero*.

She seemed undismayed. Her smile still wonderful, she made three short turns of intricate steps about the handkerchief, balancing the tumbler on her head. All at once, without missing a movement of the dance, she thrust out a slippered toe. Like an arrow it caught the loop. A quick kick sent the handkerchief in mid-air, where she caught it with her hand. Still not a drop of water was lost.

Applause deafened. Other kerchiefs were thrown before her by other gallants, each retrieved without breaking her beautiful dancing rhythm, with a skill which, to her husband at least, seemed incredible. He heard the constant mounting scream of approbation, nothing less than adoration of his bride, and his heart grew great with pride in her.

Two elaborately dressed *charros* ran into the arbor with bottles of *aguardiente,* which they began sprinkling on the ground before her, shouting, *"Echelas todas, mi alma! Sabe que soy yo la amparo*—Throw everything into it, my soul! Know I am thine and will guard thee!"

To the end of the music she danced. Then, having charmed and captivated every onlooker, the girl laughed, dropped her gathered handkerchiefs on the ground, removed the tumbler from her head and handed it—still brimful—to Almazon, and returned to her seat amidst an ovation, but with a look at Bowie which said that only his applause was worth anything to her.

318

Now would come the feasting and the games. The wedding celebration must continue yet for hours, before the couple would be alone.

Chapter Thirty-eight

I

Señor Bowie was the subject of limitless speculation, especially among the women of Bexar. A man, marrying, is expected to be' changed: it is one of the pet female theories, a part of the secret war between the sexes, and considered a victory for womankind. The Mexicans had a proverb: A woman marries a man because of his character, and then spends the rest of her life trying to change it.

But already, in the first days of November, within three months of the ending of his honeymoon journey, Bowie was riding out of Bexar on another of his wild journeys. This time it was with companions, including his American brother, Señor Rezin Bowie. The loose tongues of many women were busy, and the fox laugh heard. This was considered an aspersion on Ursula, who was left alone with her servants in the new house while her husband went wandering. The inaudible whisper ran from *casa* to *casa* all through Bexar.

It was perceived now that Señor Bowie had not been changed by his pretty new wife. Also, that however much he observed Mexican custom and spoke and even thought in the Mexican tongue, he was American in every link of his spine, too restless and reckless for peace of mind. Some women who secretly had envied Ursula her marriage now secretly compensated themselves by pitying her for her inability to hold in herself all the thoughts of her husband.

Ursula herself said nothing, nor was the matter discussed by any in the household of Veramendi. Bowie, riding north out of Bexar with his brother and nine others, all heavily armed as for a war expedition, had discussed the matter thoroughly with his father-in-law and also his wife. These knew that though his unremitting fever for activity was upon him, it was by no means a reflection against Ursula.

This journey was the end result of a happening in August, within a week after the return of Bowie and Ursula from their journey to the States, where he had exhibited his bride to his friends and family.

On that day Bowie saw the Lipans come into the plaza at Bexar. They were unusually late this year. He remembered that he had now the knife—one of James Black's best—which he had promised to Sholic. A woman's head shone black in the sun: Topsanna, Sholic's wife.

Beside her he dismounted. She looked up, but without a smile. No gladness at seeing him.

"Why are the Lipans late?" he said. "Where is Sholic?"

She said, "Sholic is not here, señor."

"Then where?"

"Sholic is dead."

He was much surprised. "When did this happen, Topsanna?"

"After you left us. Very soon." She spoke in a strangely subdued, timid voice.

"How?"

She was reluctant, but in brief sentences she told him. A quarrel in the village. Sholic rushed out of his lodge to quiet it. Two or three guns were fired: the chief lay dying on the ground. The quarrel had been planned for this very purpose, she said. Afterward Tres Manos stepped forward and assumed the authority of chief.

"Tres Manos killed Sholic?" Bowie asked.

She sat with lowered head. "Tres Manos learned it was Sholic who long ago killed his father, Lobo Amarillo."

A mystery closed. A savage retribution. Bowie stared.

"Señor," she said hurriedly, "you must go now. Tres Manos would be angered if he saw me talking with you."

"Of what concern is it of his? Can he order the whole tribe?"

"Me, he can order, señor. I am his squaw."

Simple finality. Yet he knew this woman had no liking for Tres Manos. "So he took you," he said. "There was nobody to say him nay."

"Go, señor." She seemed really frightened.

But already a voice called his name.

Savage, triangular face of bony bosses. Flinty, desiccated hand on the chest. The black eyes of Tres Manos glittered from Bowie to the woman.

"Cuchillo Grande," he said, "I am chief now. There is no more fat Sholic. Cuchillo Grande is not welcome to talk to Lipan woman, not welcome to come to Lipan country."

"What quarrel have the Lipans against me?"

Tres Manos placed a hard brown hand against Bowie's chest. "It is in Tres Manos' mind that Sholic showed you a certain hill. Sholic is dead now. Take warning. If you seek that hill, you will be dead also!"

Ugly, personal challenge. Bowie threw the hand off his chest.

"It is a truth that Sholic did show me the Cerro del Almagre. It is also a truth that I promised him I would forget it, for as long as we both lived. But you, Tres Manos, have killed Sholic, and so gave my promise back

320

to me. You know me. All Lipans know me. If ever I wish to come to the Cerro del Almagre, I will come!"

Hard gray eye bored into hard black eye. Topsanna gathered her things and stole away.

2

When Bowie sat a little later in the office of the vice-governor, he already was in the grip of an idea. "Tell me again," he said, "the particulars of the new land code you have just received."

"The chief of them is that *empresario* grants may be obtained again," said Don Juan.

Bowie grunted. "After many efforts, I met the *empresario,* Stephen Austin, in San Felipe, last time I was there."

"How did you think of him?"

"Too much of some things and not enough of others. Forehead too high, eyes too large, voice too soft: not enough strength, or patience, or power as a man."

"You seem not to care for Don Estevan."

"He doesn't care for me. Said my reputation didn't recommend me. Said he was too busy with colonists who had industry and integrity to give time and assistance to a dubious adventurer——"

Veramendi laughed. "I know the man: a great lecturer."

Bowie grinned. "Dubious adventurer. It hurt my pride."

"Do not mind it, Jaime. We all know Señor Austin: a good man, I believe, but rattling around in the position he occupies. There will be no more *empresarios* like him. One must be already a citizen of Mexico. Foreigners are no longer welcomed in Texas."

Bowie began to unfold his plan. As a citizen, he could apply for a grant. Suppose Don Juan had friends in Saltillo, who as a favor would also apply for grants, and then, being uninterested in promoting colonies, would sell their rights to these tracts for a nominal sum to someone designated by Don Juan . . . ?

The vice-governor saw possibilities. As a public official he could not himself receive such a grant, but there was nothing to prevent his son-in-law from doing so. He considered, and to Bowie he gave the names of thirteen men, close *compadres,* who would be glad to oblige.

"By this means," Bowie said, "we could get hold of half a million acres of good land."

"There is the little matter of finances," said Don Juan. "Neither yours nor mine are fluid at present. We have both put a great deal into our textile mill at Saltillo. And there are the land purchases——"

"Perhaps we are more fluid than would appear," Bowie said. "Don Juan—I know where is the lost silver mine of the Cerro del Almagre!"

The vice-governor was astounded. "You know *that?*"

"With these eyes I have seen enough bar silver to fill this room!"

"Where?" Veramendi's polished forehead was rapt.

"Near the headwaters of the San Saba."

"But—but that is hostile Indian country. A risk too great——"

"The reward is great."

"What would Ursula say to this?"

"Without her consent, I would not go one step."

3

When Bowie told Ursula that evening, she sat beside him and touched her cheek against his shoulder. A horror of loneliness seemed to be upon her.

"I am afraid," she said, like a little child.

"I will be back in a month," he assured her.

"It's not that. It's something else. I believe you are able to go to the San Saba and come back to me—safe. But—it is—only that sometimes I begin to see—how little you need me. How able you are to go and do, whether I am with you or not. Then I—I grow afraid that someday you will see it, too. I could not bear for that to happen——"

He soothed her in his arms. "Without you, *querida,* I could not do anything. When I am away from you, you are in my thoughts always."

This was unvarnished truth. In a way it would have been impossible for him to believe, this girl had fulfilled him. Partly, perhaps, it was her training, the upbringing of a Mexican girl of high quality. Partly, also, it was the inborn wisdom of her sex. And partly it was her imagination, which worked continually to surprise and entrance him.

Among strange scenes and peoples in the States on their wedding trip, Ursula had won all who met her, including his brothers and his mother. In public she knew how to make him proud of her, with charm and grace and new brilliant sides of mood and character. And when they were alone she was to him all things that a woman should be. If he desired rest, she could be cool of manner and of person, as refreshing as a mountain spring. But at other times she met him with fire for fire. Above all, she was a companion to him, giving him the closest and most grateful intimacy he had ever known.

In his lifetime, Bowie had undergone every kind of adventure, seen life in all forms, and had always stood ready to gamble anything, his life the quickest of all. But now, in a woman's love, he had discovered something too precious to gamble.

He was stricken with remorse at his selfishness. "I will never do what you do not wish, *querida*. I had written already a letter to my brother. But another letter goes after it tomorrow, telling him to forget the whole matter. Ten thousand mines of silver are not worth one little Ursula——"

He kissed her. But she said, surprisingly, "You must not send that second letter."

"Why?"

"Because you must go on this expedition."

"One moment ago—you said——"

Her eyes were solemn. "You are saying something yourself, Jaime, and it is as if you spoke it aloud. You are saying you will make any change in your life and nature to make me content. You will hang about this town, like one offered for hire to a master he has never seen; come home to me in the evening, making small talk on topics of no importance; and all the time you will be eating out your heart for something else——"

"This is foolishness——"

"Jaime, I will not let you do that. What man did I fall in love with? This man you would make yourself into, to please me? No, the man you are. Will you remember that, beloved?"

So when Bowie and his companions rode out of Bexar, the second day of November, his mind was at rest concerning his wife, and he had no very great apprehension concerning his mission. The first days were pleasant, warm in the sunlight, cool at night so that a man slept well. Their party was compact and well chosen: he and Rezin; Cephas Ham, a gaunt frontiersman with a greasy beard and a humorous eye; six Texas Americans, Dave Buchanan, Bob Armstrong, Jesse Wallace, Matt Doyle, Tom McCaslin, and Jim Coryell; and two servants, Rezin's Negro boy Charles, and a Mexican youth named Gonzales, to do the camp chores. It was a good-humored, competent crowd. By the night of November 19, though traveling at a leisurely pace and hunting as they went, they were encamped about seven miles north of the Llano River, well toward its sources.

4

The instant movement of the men away from the campfire was not necessary. Bowie could hear a voice calling, *"Compañero! Amigo!"*

They waited until a Mexican in breechclout and moccasins, but otherwise naked like an Indian, rode into the circle of light. A thin beard straggled over the man's lower face, and he was unarmed. A slave, evidently, of the Indians.

"Anyone with you?" Bowie asked in Spanish.

"Yes, señor. Two Comanches."

"Comanches?"

"Friendly Comanches, señor, of Ysayune's band."

"Bring them up to the fire."

The Mexican waved an arm. Into the flickering circle of light rode two young Indians, without war paint, carrying only bows and arrows, and pointing eagerly to lead peace medals they wore on their naked chests.

"What do you want?" Bowie asked.

Food, it developed, was wanted first. Bowie jerked a hand toward the pot bubbling on the fire.

While they gorged, the Comanches talked in their rasping tongue, the Mexican slave interpreting. "Ysayune camped on the Llano. He is going to Bexar, taking back some stolen horses he recovered. Before going, he wants to know if the people there are still friendly to him."

This was understandable; relations between the Indians and Mexicans were always chancy.

"Tell Ysayune that to him, and his band, alone of all Comanches, the Bexar people are always friends," Bowie said.

He looked at the Mexican interpreter with curiosity: a prisoner, a slave, probably of years' standing. He followed the Comanches, did their menial work, probably at times was mistreated by them. Yet though opportunities for escape were many, he seemed to prefer their life to that which he had known before. Strange, the power exerted by the wilderness. Bowie had heard of white women, captured by the Indians and taken by them as squaws, who refused to return to the settlements when they had a chance.

That night the Comanches and their Mexican slept at the white men's camp. At dawn they were off for Ysayune's village, while Bowie's party resumed its march toward the San Saba.

This was rough country, hard to travel, but they reached the San Saba valley by nightfall. As they prepared to camp by a small creek in a canyon, which ran into the river a mile or two below, a shout was heard distantly, and the sound of galloping hoofs.

"It's that Mex!" said Rezin.

The man rode up, dust-covered, eyes bloodshot, weary to the bone.

"Many Indians come—to kill you!" he said.

"A war party?" Bowie asked.

"Yes, señor."

324

"How do you know?"

"They stop near Ysayune's camp last night. Tell Ysayune they trail you. Ysayune say you good white men. They say no—white men bad—kill. Ysayune send me to tell."

"What tribe?"

"Tawakoni—Waco."

"Any Lipans?"

The Mexican had not seen any.

Bowie thought. "How many?"

"*Demasiado*—too many!" With rapid motions of hands, fingers opening and closing, he signified counts of ten. Bowie tried to keep track.

"About a hundred and forty, near as I can tell," he said to Rezin.

This was grave news. Taking only time to gulp a little water, the Mexican circled his horse away, as if fearful of remaining in their company.

Bowie turned to the others. "What do you men say?"

"A hundred an' forty's a lot to handle," said McCaslin.

"I'd ruther it was Tawakonis than Comanches," Cephas Ham said.

"Why would Tawakonis an' Wacos be follerin' us?" asked Armstrong.

Bowie said, "We may be in for real trouble. There's a Lipan weasel in this bush, or I'm mistaken bad. And his name's Tres Manos."

"What do you suggest?" asked Rezin.

No panic here, among any of them. Simply sober consideration of the situation and how to cope with it. Good men, these.

"This is what I think," Bowie said. "The Cerro del Almagre has an old Spanish *presidio* at its foot. Just piles of stones, but a good place to fight. If we could reach that, we might give those Indians considerable of an argument."

"How fur is it?" asked Cephas.

"Forty miles at least, up this valley."

"Easy going?"

"Rough as hell."

"Then we'd better bed down an' start with daylight," Cephas said. "In the dark we'd only blunder out of one bad arroyo into another."

5

When darkness came the next evening, the Cerro del Almagre was still miles away. Unwillingly Bowie gave orders to unsaddle. All day they had struggled in and out of steep rocky canyons. Many of the horses were limping because of the sharp flints underfoot.

"Make things as secure as you can," he said. "It's just possible those Indians might jump us here."

For the camp he selected a small hillock, at the foot of which a clear stream, tributary to the San Saba, ran. The valley here widened into a broad almost treeless level, the river two or three miles away. At this point the creek and its steep little canyon made a sharp horseshoe bend, which accounted for the fact that on the hummock a fine grove of live oaks stood, saved by their peninsula from the prairie fires which periodically swept the country. Bowie counted them. Thirty. Each with a trunk almost as big as the body of an ordinary man.

The neck of the peninsula was choked by a thick clump of thorny brush—chaparral, prickly pear, and mesquite. On the other side of the canyon was a second small hill, also with a growth of timber. Bowie did not like that hill. If they had to fight at this place, it might shelter hostile sharpshooters.

Still, this was the best camp place available. The men unsaddled and hobbled the horses. Some cooked the evening meal. Five of them, led by Rezin, took axes and went into the thicket to chop a path into the heart of the thornbush. An old story to Texans, cutting thorn. By the last of the twilight they had hewn out a space in the center, and a pathway all around the edge of the thicket, a few feet in from its border.

In the mood of men undergoing a siege, they rolled in their blankets, with Cephas Ham and Matt Doyle taking first watch.

Chapter Thirty-nine

I

Dawn, in a flare of flame-lit cloudlets. Morning sounds: the coughing and clearing of throats always heard in a waking camp.

Rezin stood up, his blanket still about his shoulders, sleep not yet fully gone from his eyes. "Looks like those Indians gave us up."

Bowie shook his head. "Not if Tres Manos is with them. Lucky the Spanish fort's not far now."

They began breaking camp early, but some of the horses were in such bad condition from stone bruises that a rearrangement of burdens was required. By the time the loads were redistributed and lashed, it was eight o'clock. A late start but nothing alarming had thus far occurred. Bowie was cheerful as he gave the order to mount.

In that moment, Cephas Ham gave a yell. *"Injuns! By God, Injuns after all!"*

Over a rise, half a mile away, came a long file of mounted warriors. Ahead of them was the tracker, a human bloodhound on foot, stooping low, his nose near the ground, almost as if he followed their trail by scent.

Very quietly, Bowie said, "Dismount. Get the horses under cover."

Men hurried, threw off saddles and packs, led animals down in the creek bed or among the trees to tether. The approaching Indians halted. All at once, with shrill high yelps, a dozen of them whipped their ponies forward. Bowie heard rifle hammers click behind him.

"Don't shoot!" he said quickly. "They're just looking us over."

On came the scurrying Indians, bright with paint and flashing steel and fluttering feathers, dust rising like smoke behind them. At a hundred yards from the grove, they swung aside and galloped back.

Cephas Ham had studied them keenly. "Wacos, all right," he said. "Tawakonis, too. Ugly. Reckon, gents, we're in for it."

Silently, Bowie was counting. "The Mex said a hundred and forty. I make out a hundred and sixty-four. See anything besides Wacos and Tawakonis, Cephas?"

The frontiersman shook his head. "Too fur away."

One of the others, Bob Armstrong, said, "A hundred and sixty-four. Eleven of us—an' two's camp boys. Why—that's fifteen to one——"

Bowie grinned. "Nobody can say that when we pick 'em, we pick 'em easy."

"Maybe they don't want a fight," Rezin said. "Sometimes Indians just want gifts of some kind, don't they?"

"Not these," Bowie said.

"I'd like to see what we can do by parleying, anyway. If we use the right talk they might go on without giving trouble——"

"Be mighty careful, Rezin."

Rezin turned to the men. "Any of you talk their lingo?"

A short dark man, with squinting black eyes, Dave Buchanan, said hesitantly, "I talk a leetle Caddo. Caddos an' Wacos is sort of related—mebbe I could make out some——"

"Walk out with me while I give them the sign," Rezin said.

"Not too far," said Bowie. "We'll cover you."

"I've got two shots myself," Rezin said. He held up his rifle, a fine double-barreled gun of English make. "And Dave's got one."

Together, carrying their rifles, but with right hands uplifted, he and Buchanan walked toward the motionless Indian array.

It takes a special kind of courage to march toward a silent overwhelming enemy, but the two went forward for two hundred yards, until they were near enough to carry on a shouting conversation, before halting.

In the oaks the Texans heard Buchanan calling out in the Caddo tongue.

A moment's silence.

"How do! How do!"

Some warrior had shouted back. It was probably his entire stock of English, but it sounded encouraging. The men relaxed slightly.

Then a musket boomed.

Rezin and Buchanan began running backward, keeping their faces to the enemy. A solid fusillade of shots came from the Indians.

Buchanan spun over on the ground, rolling and clutching at his legs. Bowie saw Rezin lift his rifle and deliberately fire both barrels. Then he stooped, hoisted the wounded man on his back and started for the oak grove at a stumbling, overburdened run.

Yell from the Indians. Another spattering volley. Buchanan cried out again and winced.

Keen-tipped lances couched, eight Tawakonis galloped forward at a dead run to spear the retreating white men.

"Cover them!" Bowie cried.

"They'll never make it," said Cephas Ham.

"We've got to meet 'em. Who'll come with me?"

Bowie waited for no answer. Already he was running in great strides toward his brother. Behind him feet pounded. Cephas Ham, Jim Coryell, and Tom McCaslin.

Rezin was doing his best, but a man bearing one hundred and sixty pounds on his shoulders cannot make much speed.

Down upon him bore the Tawakoni rush. Fifty yards. Twenty-five. In a few seconds the lances would be dipped in blood.

Bowie said, "Start shooting!"

They stopped. Almost as if at command, the four rifles cracked together. The two Tawakonis leading pitched out of their saddles. Behind them another clutched at his horse's mane and slid into a heap on the ground. A fourth leaned forward, suddenly sick. His horse whirled in a circle and he also crashed down, his body kicking up a small cloud of dust.

Four shots. Four saddles empty. Not bad shooting.

In a series of jolting jumps the four remaining Indians pulled up their ponies. Forgetting their quarry, seeing only the four terrible riflemen running toward them, ramming home new charges, they whirled their horses and fled, bending low, yelping with fear.

For a few minutes after they brought Rezin and Buchanan back to the oaks, there was stillness: stillness so profound that the stamping of horses fighting gnats in the thicket, and the jingling of their bits as they tossed their heads, were clearly heard.

Buchanan was wounded in both legs and in the body, bleeding profusely, but perfectly conscious and cool. Rezin showed a bullet hole through his hunting jacket. He began attending to Buchanan's hurts.

From the war party on the hill just out of rifle range came a series of fierce defiant yells. The usual prelude to an Indian assault. Crouching behind the oak trunks, the men made ready, looking to Bowie for orders.

Slowly the swirling mass of fluttering plumes, gaudy paint and tossing weapons on the distant hill rolled forward into motion. Halfway to the grove it came to a halt. A single figure, devilish in a weird horned headgear, rode back and forth before the van, haranguing: evidently an important chief or medicine man, inflaming his warriors before the final charge.

"Who's loaded?" Bowie asked.

Cephas Ham said, "Me."

"Can you fetch that chief?"

The frontiersman's eye gleamed down his rifle barrel. Flat, whiplike report. Down went the distant Indian, man and horse.

"Too low!" growled Cephas bitterly.

They saw the horned chief come to his feet, hopping, one leg evidently injured, trying to reach his friends.

"Git him!" Cephas yelled.

Four of them fired, and Bowie was one. The Indian went down, his body jerked once on the ground, and was still.

"Choicely good," Bowie said with approval.

In the Indian horde uncertainty was visible. It had been about to sweep forward in a charge which might have gone right through the oaks, but the chief's death seemed to have deprived the warriors of leadership. They milled around, yipping, but coming no closer.

"Must have got the boss Indian," Rezin said.

But as Rezin spoke, Bowie almost started. His head thrust forward, his attitude was that of close attention. A smaller body of Indians had just circled out from the flank, their leader apparently giving new directions.

"It's him!" Bowie said. "Cephas, see that chief on the paint horse, with the red blanket around his hips?"

"Yep. I see him."

"You've got uncommon eyes. Can you make out anything about him?"

Ham's pale eyes narrowed as he shaded his gaze with his palm. "By jings, some kind of a dingus hangin' on his chest——"

"I'll tell you what it is. A human hand. That's Tres Manos."

"The Lipan?"

Bowie nodded. "He's stirred up the Wacos and Tawakonis to follow us. He's that smart. And he's got a sure-enough hate on me."

"They're going to be about our ears pretty quick," Rezin said.

Rifle hammers clicked as a score of Tawakonis came in a rush.

"No charge," Bowie said. "They want to carry off their dead."

He knew Indian habits better than any of them. The riders swept about the recumbent figures on the prairie. Without even dismounting, seizing two by two the prostrate forms, they carried them off between galloping ponies. As an exhibition of sheer horsemanship it excited the admiration even of the Texans. But that did not prevent their volley. Two or three more Indians were hit.

From directly behind the Texans and surprisingly close, came a rolling roar of shots, and the spiteful whine of bullets. A voice said, solemnly and hollowly, "By God! By God! I'm hit, Tom!"

Matt Doyle was clutching at his tree. His hands slipped. He went to the ground and suddenly vomited.

"Matt—God—oh, Matt!" McCaslin, rifle in hand, crawled over to where the other lay. Between them, both Irish, was a great friendship. He turned Doyle over. Blood stained his chest, his eyes were closed, his face soiled and sour with vomit in which bits of grass and dirt were stuck.

Bowie looked beyond them. The shots came from that little hill skirted by timber on the other side of the creek. While the Tawakonis had attracted the attention of the defenders, a party of warriors had ridden around, left their horses, and crept into this ambush to open fire. No telling how many there were of them.

"They got Matt! The sons-a-bitches!" McCaslin was crying with rage. He looked around wildly, picked up his rifle, and began running through the grove toward the hidden Indians.

"Come back, Mac!" shouted Bowie.

Too late. A volley from the timbered hillock. McCaslin came down thrashing on the ground, blood spilling from his mouth. He died.

A bullet carried away part of the stock of Armstrong's rifle, almost knocking it out of his hands, but he raised it again and fired.

"I got him!" he yelled. "I got the bastard that killed Mac!"

Bowie gave a sudden order. "Run for the thicket!"

Too hot to stay in the grove. Carrying Doyle and Buchanan, they plunged into the ugly mass of chaparral and prickly pear where Rezin and his party had labored the previous night.

For a moment they crouched still. There was no protection from bullets here, but all the advantage of concealment. With a brief, tight grin Bowie said to Rezin, "The two hours you and the boys put in here might be the best two hours you ever spent."

Rezin was silent, working over the wounded men.

Doyle was shot through the chest. An improvised bandage stanched his bleeding somewhat, and he lay feebly moaning. Buchanan's leg was broken. Rezin was no doctor, but with the help of Jim Coryell he set the bone by guess. Buchanan gritted his teeth and went pale with pain as they bound his leg in an improvised splint of mesquite withes.

Leaving this hospital work, Bowie took Cephas Ham, Wallace, and Armstrong to the outside passage Rezin had cut. Through the screen they peered at the trees across the stream in which the Indians lay.

"Got to drive 'em out," he said. "Don't waste bullets. Shoot when you see 'em."

He fired. Deliberately, they followed his example.

Positions were reversed, now. It was the white men who were concealed, the red men who were vulnerable. No denying the whining Texas lead. Here and there a brown body flopped and kicked under the trees. It meant death to stay there and in fifteen minutes all the Indians were gone from the skirting timber, dragging their dead with them.

3

In the distance the Indians rode about aimlessly, apparently baffled by the position of the defenders. Bowie could see Tres Manos, on his pinto horse, fiercely studying the thicket. No stop in the battle would be permitted by that implacable fighter. He gesticulated, giving instructions to two sub-chiefs who sat their horses near him.

With shrill yipping, fifty warriors thundered at a run for the thicket as Tres Manos launched a charge. The Texans were ready. A volley emptied five saddles, and as the Indians pulled up, a second volley dropped five more. They retreated in panic.

"Ten." Cephas wagged his beard. "Ought to settle 'em for a while."

"You don't know Tres Manos," Bowie said.

Gonzales, the Mexican boy, looked at him with eyes like a hunting dog. "McCaslin," he said. "I go get his gun."

Bowie hardly heard him. Tactics out there were changing. About the thicket Tres Manos was posting riflemen, who crept forward, taking advantage of every gully and little rise. Whenever a white man fired, a dozen bullets probed the thicket at the point where his rifle smoke rose. Bowie gave Tres Manos credit for that dangerous plan, too.

"I got it in the arm," Jim Coryell said calmly.

"How bad?" Bowie asked.

"Dunno."

"Have Rezin look at it." Bowie glanced around. "Boys, we've got to keep moving. Every time you fire, get away from there a few feet. If you don't, they'll get us all——"

He counted losses. One dead, three wounded. Four of eleven.

Bullets continued to comb the thicket, clipping leaves, ricocheting and howling away. Horses were wounded or killed, but as the day wore on, Bowie's tactics paid: no more casualties among the defenders, and several Indians killed by the beautiful shooting of the Texans.

Shortly before noon, Armstrong cried, "Smoke!"

It could be seen clearly, the white cloud turning black, rising and spreading upon the prairie. Beyond it moved distant Indian figures.

"They figure on burning us out," Bowie said.

The grass was tall and dry, the wind directly toward the thicket. Blinding, choking clouds of smoke filled the brush, driven before the wide front of leaping flames. Men lay on their faces, coughing, almost blinded, seeking to breathe the clearer air near the ground.

"What'll we do?" a voice strangled.

"We're goners!" gasped another.

"Hold steady," Bowie said.

Smoke blinded him, but in his mind the topography of the place was etched. Prairie fires in the past had threatened the peninsula, but the trees were uncharred. Flames never had reached them. Perhaps . . .

Down the opposite side of the ravine the fire roared. But it did not roar up. A wall of rock, intervening like the prow of a ship, had baffled the flames. They snarled on down the canyon and out across the plains beyond, driving beasts and birds before them.

"Missed us, by God!"

"Got through that all right!"

"Come so clost I could almost hear my whiskers a-singein'!"

Choked, eyes still smarting, the men were congratulating themselves.

They heard Bowie, "Get ready! Everybody load!"

Now, peering through the smoke, they saw a new charge of Indians bearing down upon them, whooping and careering across the blackened and still smoking turf. Carry this rush home, and it was over.

Rifles spat among the thornbushes. Bowie fired. And at once wished he

332

had held his shot. In the smoke he saw a triangular, vicious face nearing. It was as if one man only rode in that murderous attack.

Frantically he groped for powder horn and bullet pouch.

"Señor—here!"

A rifle butt was thrust into his hand. Little Gonzales . . . the unfired rifle of McCaslin brought back from the oak grove.

He brought it to his shoulder. Very near now was the charge, and Tres Manos was at its head. Bowie's sights caught an odd target on the naked chest and he pulled the trigger.

No longer would the mummied hand be worn as an amulet. The bullet shattered the dried bones and flinty skin like crockery. Behind the dead hand was a blue hole in the naked chest. Tres Manos was dead before he hit the ground.

Once more the Indians had seen a leader stricken before their eyes. It was daunting. They turned and rode back the way they came, though some of them remained, kicking on the charred prairie.

In the thicket men took time to quench burning thirsts from skin water bottles and roll loose rocks together to form some protection.

"You got that Lipan," said Cephas Ham. "Might cool 'em."

"Can't tell yet," said Bowie.

The wind shifted, blowing the smoke in a different direction.

"That's better." Men grinned wearily, happy at the fresh, clean air. But Bowie did not grin.

"The southeast!" he said.

They saw his meaning. The wind had swung in the one direction from which a fire might approach by the neck of their peninsula. It was seen by the Indians, too. Already, in the distance, they were setting flames to the unburned part of the prairie. The peril was now greater than before.

Bowie watched the leaping flames coming in a ten-foot wall. "Blankets!" he said. "Everybody get ready to fight fire!"

In the new blinding smoke cloud, sparks flew, searing faces, charring holes in clothes and blankets.

"Coming sure, this time," said Cephas Ham. "Better load——"

"Keep your powder horns closed!" shouted Bowie. "Want to be blown up?"

They could only pray—and hope for luck. Indian whooping could be heard over the roar of the flames. Useless rifles were set down. Bowie loosened his knife in its sheath. This was the finish. Death a certainty, now.

They began beating at the flames, which were in the very edge of the thicket. As from a gigantic oven, heat seared their faces. The outer growth of the thicket frizzled in the flames. Fighting with blankets,

333

wasting the little that was left of their precious water, the men were driven back. But somehow they stopped the fire.

So little of the thicket was left that it hardly furnished concealment. In every direction the land lay black and smoking.

The Indians had not charged. The last fire stratagem had been to cover them while they carried off their comrades, slain around the deadly thicket.

The sun was setting, lurid red in the smoke over the prairie.

4

On December 6, a haggard, scarecrow band stumbled into Bexar. They were near starving, they carried with them three men badly wounded, and had buried one who was dead. They had not reached the Cerro del Almagre, because their horses were almost all destroyed, and their wounded needed care.

In that respect, their expedition had been a defeat.

But though they had remained on their hillock three days, no Indian was seen by them after the fight. Later Ysayune's friendly Comanches told them they had come upon the Tawakonis while they mourned. Fifty-two of the allied tribes were dead, a havoc almost incredible. Rarely in the history of the West had so small a band as Bowie's so severely mauled a much greater force of Indians.

Bowie laughed, but tenderly, when Ursula sobbed in his arms.

"Your tears are making clean spots on my face, *querida,*" he said.

Now that she had got her husband back, she revealed to him a secret: a matter of transcendent importance, which she had planned to tell him the night he spoke to her of his expedition, but which she had withheld until such time as he finished this one more adventure on which she had let him go.

Chapter Forty

1

In Bexar, Bowie was the man most gazed upon, most discussed. Now that the full story of the San Saba fight was known, not only by word, but also through a written report he made to the *jefe político* and the vice-governor, men acceded to him the highest place, and to have a glass with him in a *cantina* became a matter to be boasted of afterward.

Among the women, the discussion of the American's full meaning and the probability of his future actions became a sitting game well approved. One school held that Señor Bowie, having been allowed to take a last fling, would henceforth become a settled husband like other men, in view particularly of the established fact that Doña Ursula was soon to have a baby. Fatherhood is a well-known tamer of men.

Another school, however, prophesied that Don Jaime was too restless ever to be contained for long, and heads were shaken over needlework, as unhappiness was foreseen in this tumultuous passion for wandering and discovering danger to encounter. This extended even to the *palacio*, where Ursula's mother was concerned over it.

But Don Juan found amusement in it. "Is not Jaime good to our child?" he asked.

"No man could be more devoted. But——"

Don Juan quoted a Spanish proverb in couplet:

> *"El lobo pierde los dientes,*
> *Pero no las mientes."*

The free translation of this is, "The wolf loses his teeth, but not his inclination." It did not comfort Doña Josefa, and the vice-governor had to admit he had used a bad proverb, his only intention being to say that you cannot easily change a man's nature.

"One thing I know well," he said, to bring the discussion to an end, "I would not relish trying to tell Jaime what his business is."

Bowie and Ursula behaved as if unconscious of all this speculation, and in the early months of 1832 there was, certainly, no other example of such perfect conjugality in Bexar. They attended Mass together regularly. They entertained friends at their table and were entertained. He handed her about, the women said laughing, as if she were a piece of glass which he feared might break: a symptom well known and amusing in a man during his wife's first pregnancy.

A day in April, the house was filled with women and a bustle of purposeful activity in which Bowie had no place. Ursula turned eyes to him impersonal and numb, occupied solely by her own intimate, acute crisis, and he was in terror for her when they put him out of the room. He sat with Don Juan and Navarro, drinking wine, for what seemed aeons of time. At last came a stir, female voices in sudden jubilant laughter, and thin grating cries of a new soul born into a troubled world.

Doña Josefa herself, shining with the joy of women at the miracle of reproduction, brought the small bundle pillowed against her breast. "A daughter, Jaime. A beautiful, beautiful little daughter."

She thrust the bundle into his arms. So slight. Hardly anything at all.

335

Tiny head covered with straggling black hair. Red, wrinkled, old-looking little monkey face with tight-shut eyes.

Not yet had his fatherhood taken possession of him: his concern was for the girl in the room beyond.

"She is safe, but weary," said Doña Josefa.

He carried in the child to Ursula, kneeling by her bed. So drained of all color was her face that he was sick with fear, until she smiled at him, weak but filled with happiness, at rest now, the ordeal over.

2

Not very long after this, the female wiseacres who prophesied that not even Ursula and a new baby together could long hold Bowie at home were nodding their heads. For he began disappearing from Bexar, sometimes for quite protracted absences. He had affairs in partnership with his father-in-law, and since the latter must of necessity be at the *palacio* for his duties, Bowie was the traveling member of the firm.

Once he visited Monclova and made the acquaintance and friendship of thirteen Mexican gentlemen there, who were close friends of Don Juan, and would be of use to him if the project of collecting land grants into one huge block became feasible. He visited and watched in operation the new textile mill he and Veramendi had built on a water-power site near Saltillo. There were lands in the Brazos and Trinity valleys, in which they had invested heavily. Bowie was surveying these lands into parcels which he would sell in the States.

Out of one of these journeyings, a new story concerning him trickled back into Bexar. A bitter ferment was stirring in the land. Anastasio Bustamante, that ambitious man, had engineered a *coup d'état,* declared himself dictator of Mexico, overturned the Constitution of 1824, proclaimed new oppressive colonization and customs laws, and sent troops to affirm his authority.

Texas, particularly the American part, was stirred, for it was against the colonists that most of Bustamante's measures seemed directed. Don Juan himself was deeply concerned. A liberal, he now placed his chief reliance in a certain General Antonio López de Santa Anna, who had declared for the Constitution and was reported leading a revolt in the south of Mexico. He told Bowie he knew Santa Anna well: in fact the general was one of Ursula's godfathers. The name of Santa Anna was much spoken that summer by men of sober thought like Don José Navarro, Judge Seguin, and their circle.

What happened at Nacogdoches in July was an outright revolt of the

336

citizens against the Bustamante garrison, and particularly its arrogant, bullet-headed commandant, Colonel José de las Piedras.

Bowie, who rode into town from his Brazos land surveying, was at first an onlooker. He witnessed the opening skirmish in the streets, in which the *alcalde,* a distinguished old Mexican named Don Encarnación Chirino, was killed. Later, he wielded a rifle a few times in the all-day fight, when the Texans, more a posse than an army, took possession of the houses surrounding the church in the plaza, into which Piedras had withdrawn his troops. Adobe walls hung out curtains of smoke and spasms of sound quivered the eardrums. Piedras discovered that fighting American hunters and ranchers, whose rifles were as obedient to them as their eyes and hands, was a different matter from fighting Mexicans, or even Spaniards. In the night he retreated, leaving forty dead.

At this point Bowie became the leader. With twenty men and horses, the best of both, he circled, riding hard, by a lower road, to cut off Piedras at the Angelina River crossing. The plan agreed upon was for the main body from Nacogdoches to come up and fall on the rear of the Mexicans, while Bowie's small force held the ford. After nineteen miles of galloping, he reached the river crossing, which widened like the mouth of a bag, edged with oak, cottonwood, and willow, admirably suited to ambuscade.

In a few minutes the approaching dust cloud was seen. Bowie adjusted his flexible force in concealment, and when the advance squad of lancers came down to the river, he himself fired the signal shot. From hidden rifles a volley rippled. The squad lost some men, including a sergeant, and fled back in the direction it had come from.

Bowie's men did not exhibit themselves, nor did Piedras appear. With one companion, Bowie circled away from the road and saw the Mexican camp in evident confusion, a mile from the river.

By sunup there was still no sign of the Nacogdoches reinforcements. Through the thickets Bowie's twenty stole. Piedras had made no move.

The boldness of Bowie's next act lived afterward. He chose two men, provided them with a white shirt flapping from a chinquapin pole as a flag of truce, and sent them to demand Piedras' immediate surrender. Before they went, he gave them brief instruction in the manner in which they were to bear themselves before the commandant.

"When you bluff, boys," he concluded, "bet your cards as if you had them."

A metaphor in poker was understood by Texans. Bowie's messengers talked to Piedras with such arrogant assurance that in half an hour the Mexican colonel surrendered his entire force of three hundred men, never dreaming that he did not face overwhelming numbers. With their prisoners, Bowie's twenty trotted laughing back to Nacogdoches to find the "army" in that city still locked in joint debate as to whether it should follow him or no.

Liberals among the Mexicans mightily approved this blow against the dictator Bustamante.

Out of this battle, and out of his fatherhood, Bowie achieved high standing. Men poured out gallons of wine and *aguardiente* in his honor, as if he had accomplished great things in both. Yet to him they were similar in one respect: he had done little in either, yet had received plentiful credit for both. The Nacogdoches affair was accomplished with little difficulty, the praise given him not fully justified. As to the matter of his child, looking back on it, his part in it was the easiest thing he had ever done. Certainly he deserved for it no commendation.

3

A truly important event of the year 1832 was a chance encounter Bowie made at about Christmas time. He had ridden to San Felipe to attend a meeting of the assembly. Always San Felipe was busied with assemblies, or meetings of boards, committees, and councils. A continuous atmosphere of debate was in the air. This, Bowie believed, was chiefly because Stephen Austin was enamored of forensics. A forceful administrator would have dispensed with nine tenths of the talk: but to preside at meetings, to wield a gavel, was meat and drink to Austin. Bowie yawned at speech making and damned rules of order, but since Don Juan wished to know the doings of the assembly, he rode to San Felipe under a sky which was a dripping grayness, splashed with mire, his breath visible as a mist.

Taking off his chill with a glass of toddy at Peyton's taproom, he at first hardly noticed the stranger who entered and stood shaking raindrops from his hat. He heard the man rumble a question, and the bartender reply that Mr. Austin lived in the other end of the town. The voice stirred a recollection. Bowie looked up: the stranger was a giant, his shoulders immense, his booted feet huge.

Bowie rose. "If I'm not mistaken, sir, you'll be Sam Houston, of Tennessee."

The big man turned and for an instant his opalescent eyes searched Bowie's face. Then his lips parted and his teeth gleamed in a vast purple-and-yellow grin.

"James Bowie—or I'm a liar!"

With his beard shaved away Houston appeared younger and somehow more powerful, since he possessed a craglike chin to which concealment did a disservice. They dined together: venison and wild turkey and whiskey and mutual disclosures and discussions of matters of moment.

Houston was direct from Nacogdoches, where he had heard the story of Bowie and the throwing out of Bustamante's garrison.

"Things seem shaken up like a besom in a fit in Texas," he observed.

"Nobody knows what's happening in Mexico City," said Bowie. "We hear Santa Anna's in control now. The country was sick of Bustamante."

"What manner of man is Santa Anna?"

"I've never seen him. The vice-governor admires him, but Santa Anna's record is a little tricky for my taste. He's changed coats twice, and I wouldn't be surprised that he operates the puppet strings of both the Federal and Centrist parties to serve his own purpose."

Thus from Bowie, Sam Houston received his first insight into the man who was to be his great adversary.

"How is Texas toward the United States?" Houston asked.

"Friendly. The Americans especially, and also many of the native Mexicans, such as those of my own family by marriage."

Houston's cat eyes regarded Bowie intently. "The President of the United States is profoundly interested in the welfare of the people of Texas."

"He has expressed this to you?"

It was well known that between Houston and Andrew Jackson was a regard such as the hard, canny old President held for almost nobody else, and which had not been diminished by Houston's spectacular fall.

"Not in so many words," Houston said. "But I believe I know his mind."

Bowie turned the subject. "Did you go to the Rockies?"

"No, I've been domiciled among the Cherokees in the Indian Territory. Went to Washington for them—as their official ambassador." Houston chuckled. "Would that you could have seen Houston then—presenting himself at the White House, with his credentials, in a scarlet blanket, moccasins, and eagle plume, the garb of the people he represented—and on a night when a formal ball was being held. The major-domo looked as if he expected a war whoop and a scalping knife; women tittered, and men stared. But the President—God bless him—showed no reservation, no hesitation. Seldom does he smile, but his smile warmed all who saw it. Ignoring the others, he advanced, his arms extended, and Houston, the despised outcast, was in the strong and fervent embrace of the world's greatest and noblest man!"

As he concluded his voice deepened with emotion, and his eyes grew moist. He lifted his glass and said with hushed reverence, "To my chief: for him no risk is too severe, no sacrifice too great."

Bowie drank the toast. He admired a man who could greatly love a friend. Their hands moved out across the table, each taken by the other: allegiance made significant by strong clasped pressure.

Their business in San Felipe concluded, Houston went back to Bexar with Bowie. On the way, Bowie mentioned that he expected to return to the States on business the next summer.

"I trust the pestilence will be abated by then," Houston said.

"What pestilence?"

"You've not heard of the Asiatic cholera which since late summer has been ravaging the whole Mississippi Valley?"

"No. We're much cut off in Bexar."

"Nobody knows how it came. Some say a sailor was brought ashore from a ship out of the Black Sea, suffering from the ailment. Those attending him were taken soon by violent vomiting and flux, agonized cramping in legs, feet and abdomen, the surface of the body becoming cold and blue, the pulse imperceptible, the voice a hoarse whisper, death coming suddenly and terribly in most cases."

"Good God!" exclaimed Bowie. "And it's prevalent, you say?"

"What happened in New Orleans alone is a tale of horror: physicians worked day and night, yet in less than two weeks there were five thousand deaths. It was impossible to bury all the corpses. They awaited their turn, heaped in horizontal layers like cordwood. Great trenches were dug as on battlefields, and into these bodies were indiscriminately thrown. Hundreds, with bricks and stones tied to their feet, were flung into the river. In countless cases no record was even made of their passing——"

"We knew nothing of it here," Bowie said. It was as if an icy hand had been laid on his spine.

"You don't realize how fortunate you are. From New Orleans it spread upriver. Natchez, Vicksburg, Memphis, St. Louis—all the river towns were stricken. Fur traders carried it up the Missouri and wild Indians perished on the plains by thousands. In many towns hardly a house but had its sick, its dying, and its dead—sometimes all three in the same room. A peculiarity of the dreadful disease is that the bodies of its victims remain warm a long time, and the temperature may even rise after death. Horrible muscular contractions, too, are sometimes observed after life is gone, so that the position of the limbs becomes altered, as if even in death the body is tormented. Terror takes possession of the living. Wild, panic-stricken flights from the cities occurred, thousands rushing out into the country, always carrying with them the plague. Nobody will ever know how many have perished."

340

Bowie was silent and serious.

"Happily," Houston said after a time, "the epidemic seems to have run its course, and Texas has escaped it."

"Thank God for that," Bowie said. Then, "Do me a favor and say nothing about this to my wife. If she knows she will very strongly oppose my journey to the States, which I must make."

They spoke nothing more about it.

4

Nobody ever made a deeper impression on Bexar than Sam Houston. His Spanish was perhaps halting, but his bow was not, and neither was his kiss upon a lady's hand. Men and women liked equally this great Don Samuel, whose stature loomed among men of ordinary height, and who addressed everyone with respect, and listened to everyone with close attention.

Only the vice-governor had reservations.

"What does he want in Bexar?" he asked Bowie privately.

"He came as my guest, for a visit only. And he hopes to give the Indians certain peace medals from the United States."

"American peace medals? Why should he come thus far into Mexico to give peace medals?"

"He seeks the Comanches, who in summer are north on the American border. Now, however, they are far south."

Veramendi shrugged. "He may locate Ysayune's band, but that's all. And Ysayune needs no peace medals. Other Comanches are far out on the winter plains. Has he shown a disposition to make such a journey?"

Bowie shook his head.

"I confess that I don't like it," Don Juan said. "Houston is an American, and an American with close connections in Washington."

"As to that, he informs me he's to become a citizen of Mexico and set up law offices at Nacogdoches. Don't forget, Don Juan, that I also was once an American."

"I do not forget it. But you and this Don Samuel are different men, with different motives and ambitions. You have loyalties and loves which he does not."

"We have one in common: he is my very good friend."

"That I understand. And also that he is the very good friend of Andrew Jackson: Jackson, the imperialist; Jackson of the Florida seizure; Jackson who speaks of the 'manifest destiny' of his young American nation. Is it accident, entirely, that brings Jackson's trusted friend to Texas? This is a very deep and subtle man, Jaime."

Bowie could not bring himself to believe that Sam Houston had any but an honest interest in the country of which he was going to become a part. He took his guest out to Ysayune's camp on the San Gabriel River, watched him present medals with Jackson's likeness on them, and was sorry to see him depart for Nacogdoches, which he did soon, leaving a kiss on Ursula's hand, and a laugh that seemed to echo still in the house a long time after he was gone.

Bowie did not know of a certain letter written very soon thereafter. The letter was addressed to Andrew Jackson, President of the United States, and was dated February 13, 1833. To Bowie, some paragraphs would have been interesting, even illuminating:

Dear Sir: Having been as far as Bexar, in the province of Texas, where I had an interview with the Comanche Indians, I am in possession of some information that will doubtless be interesting to you, and may be calculated to forward your views, if you should entertain any, touching the acquisition of Texas by the United States. That such a measure is desirable by nineteen-twentieths of the population, I cannot doubt. Mexico is involved in civil war, the government is despotic, the rulers have not honesty, and the people have not intelligence.

Texas has already beaten and expelled all troops of Mexico from her soil, nor will she permit them to return. She can defend herself against the whole power of Mexico. Her want of money, taken in connection with the course which Texas must and will adopt, will render a transfer inevitable to some power: and if the United States does not press for it, England most assuredly will obtain it by some means.

If Texas is desirable to the United States, it is now in the most favorable attitude to obtain it on fair terms.

The letter, with an elaborate concluding paragraph of solicitude for the health, future glory, and happiness of the eminent addressee, was signed by Sam Houston.

A deep and subtle man indeed, Don Samuel.

5

Winter passed. The April convention at San Felipe drew up a memorial to the Mexican Government, asking separation of Texas from Coahuila, and tendering a proposed constitution for the new state. Bowie's friend, Sam Houston, distinguished himself as a delegate, being chairman of the constitutional committee. Stephen Austin was on his way to the national capital of Mexico to lay these documents before President Santa Anna, who had been declared elected on the last day of March.

In May, Bowie prepared to take the long road to Louisiana. Events forced this. The liberalized colonization laws had been repealed, and natives of the United States were excluded from owning land, although property rights already established were recognized. In this was one saving clause: existing contracts were valid, and the time for fulfillment extended.

This was of prime importance to Bowie and Veramendi. On the strength of Bowie's commissions to purchase land, they had sunk almost all their capital in eastern Texas acreage. Unless these lands could be delivered to their purchasers, financial disaster, even ruin, threatened. Bowie must go at once to the States with the deeds and other legal papers, and collect the money for them, because there was no telling when the time limit might be abrogated.

But here occurred a small complication. For the first time, Ursula was rebellious. It had been impossible to keep from her word of the cholera plague which had wreaked such havoc in the United States, and she feared for him. She was, furthermore, now pregnant again, her second child to be born in July. Very much she wished her husband to be with her then. Sometimes it was difficult to sit at home alone with other women, who had husbands near at hand, and were not above a subtle vivisection of one of their number who had not. Once she turned on them with a beautiful blaze of contempt.

"What do *you* know of a man?" she said. "Your husbands are *flacitos* —magpies—pieces of tallow. Not once in an eternity does one of them do anything exciting, or worthy of pride! *My* man is no more to be compared to them than is the blooded stallion to the gelded burro. Have you heard of the San Saba? Of Nacogdoches? Have you seen how all men honor him, even the great American general, Don Samuel Houston, who prefers his company to that of all men in Texas? If my Jaime desires to travel, at least he is accomplishing something. Always he returns to me, more of a man than all your weaklings combined. Me, he holds in arms of a strength you *pobrecitas* can never know. In my ears he whispers words of love—*his* words, not the outworn words that come so glibly to the lips of your *perezores*. He kisses me—as you know not how it is to be kissed. Silly ones, you have never known a *man!*"

But for all this bravery, she knew the malicious whispers still ran, and so she pleaded with Bowie not to go. "You cannot leave me—at a time like this!" she cried. "The cholera—I hear it is everywhere. You will be in danger . . . I want you with me when my baby is born."

He found it hard to explain the urgency of this journey, in the face of the necessity to her of his presence. "You will be in Monclova," he told her. "I want you to go with your parents in June. The air is purer there, the atmosphere cooler, the climate more healthful. I would have to remain here, at least most of the time, so we would be separated anyway. And this trip is as gravely important for Don Juan as for you and me."

After a time she ceased protesting, and lowered her head. "I only know I want you," she said pathetically.

He kissed her tears, and promised to make haste: even that, if all went well, he might be back at Monclova by the time the little one was born, in July.

"And hear me, *querida*," he said. "This will be the last, the very last long journey I will ever make away from you. Now, let me see no more tears."

She helped him pack his things for the journey. Only once did he hear the wistful note in her voice again. It was the morning he rode away. While pulling on his buckskin shirt, he laid his belt, with the knife in its sheath, upon the bed. She drew the blade and looked down on it for a moment.

"Jaime," she said, "can one envy something that does not live? If so, I envy this knife of yours."

"That is foolishness," he chided.

"Is it? Sometimes I think this knife is my rival. She is with you always, while I am with you only when you find time to be at home. In far places she lies by your side, like a mistress—an iron mistress—intimate with you, while I lie here by myself hoping for your return. She is never lonely, as I am often lonely. Sometimes I think I hate this knife, because she is so much a part of you . . . more a part, perhaps, than I can ever be . . ."

When she was in this mood, his heart went out to her. He comforted her with caresses and endearments. Afterward, however, he remembered those words of hers . . . the Iron Mistress . . .

At the last, Ursula clung to him, her mouth to his for a long time. Then she winked her eyes to dry her gleaming jet lashes and smiled at him.

She sent her husband away with the beautiful Mexican farewell, which is also a prayer, *"Vaya con Dios*—go with God."

Chapter Forty-one

1

Not in July did Bowie return. His business in the States was like walking in molasses. In July, when he hoped to be at Monclova, he was still at Rezin's house in Arcadia, held by maddening delays of the law, for the brothers had sold the plantation Sedalia, and two months were required to clear the title. During this time he had word of his old friend Audubon, now celebrated in both America and Europe, his great elephant folio book of bird engravings prized everywhere, his standing as a naturalist recognized, his fortune assured. Bowie heard that Audubon had made a triumphal journey down the Mississippi and would have liked to see him, to discuss an old subject: the natural man as the noblest product of humanity.

Bowie had lived with the natural man, and had some notions of his own on the subject. The Lipans had formed an interesting study. They represented the negation of civilization, but among them all manner of men were in evidence—wise counselors, knaves and clowns, fastidious dandies and hopeless failures. Human beings seemed to be human beings under whatever conditions they lived, and Bowie found that his Indian acquaintances differed little, fundamentally, from those in any other communities.

He did not, however, get to visit Audubon, because business intervened and made it impossible. Still, it was a happiness to know of the artist's success.

In August he was still fretting and traveling wearily from Louisiana, to Mississippi, to Arkansas, and back. He had in his pocket commissions for land purchase from gentlemen whom he had supposed to be perfectly honorable, and the Texas titles ready to deliver to them: yet he had to pursue, confront, and argue with each of them, to induce them to live up not only to their spoken, but to their written, words.

Some of his prospective purchasers were dead: he came to understand the horror of the Asiatic cholera in the number of his former acquaintances who had perished in the great epidemic. Of his immediate family in the States, fortunately, all had been spared, and though he heard from them hair-raising stories of the visitation, and the dread of pestilence still brooded over the country, with a few outbreaks of it yet reported here and there, his own health remained superb as usual.

Not until the end of September did he at last have the bank drafts in his possession which guaranteed solvency for Don Juan de Veramendi and himself. Then he could begin the many-league journey home.

Miles and time both dragged. He spent two days in Nacogdoches with Sam Houston, where, he found, the cholera had appeared, although not so severely as in the States. Small epidemics also had been reported in Galveston, Brazoria, and San Felipe, all quickly ended. More than ever he thanked Providence that he had sent Ursula to Monclova, which was entirely out of Texas, for he did not wish her even to experience the slight risk of the epidemic, however weak it had been.

On the last evening in Nacogdoches he dined with Houston's close circle of friends: Adolphus Sterne, the brothers John and William Wharton, Henry Raguet, Thomas McKinney—all of whom he had previously known—and one other whom he had never before met. Houston brought them together. "You two should know each other," he said. "James Bowie, shake hands with William Barrett Travis, better known as Buck."

A glance and a handshake, and the two were friends. Bowie was the taller, the more powerful, and the older: but all who witnessed their meeting remarked in them similarities that might have been those of close kinship: fair complexions, blue-gray eyes, high broad foreheads, strong jaws, crisp tawny hair, all alike.

The talk was of war. Never had Bowie heard so much war talk as in Nacogdoches. He listened with surprise and misgivings: things had changed during his absence in the States. It appeared that Santa Anna at last had thrown off the mask of liberality and assumed the dictatorship of Mexico. No more stability of principle was observable in him than in Bustamante. Both had used the Constitution of 1824 as a claptrap to introduce themselves into power, and then both had cast it aside. Discrimination against the American colonists was beginning all over again, and in a worse form than before.

One of the Whartons said savagely that the time was coming soon when Texas must fight. All nodded agreement when Houston rumbled that he was convinced the vast majority in the province favored independence at once, if not outright annexation to the United States.

"What do you think, Jim?" he said to Bowie, giving the visitor opportunity to echo the general feeling of those present.

"You ask me what I think," Bowie said slowly. "I have to say to you that I do not agree."

They were surprised and not pleased.

Bowie felt it due himself to elaborate. "It may be as you say that this feeling exists in Nacogdoches. But not in the Austin colony, and certainly

346

not among citizens of Mexican ancestry. What's Stephen Austin doing now?"

"He's still in Mexico City."

"I would say that the least we who sent him can do is wait until he gets back, to hear his firsthand impression and counsel."

"Austin!" Houston snorted. "A vain talker, a political manipulator. I hardly think we can expect much from Austin."

"I'll confess, gentlemen," said Bowie, conscious of Houston's penetrating cat eyes, "that Mr. Austin has at times not been to my liking. Nor has he shown any particular fondness for me. But he is acting as our representative within the framework of the laws of Mexico, which all of us have sworn to uphold. I'd never lend myself to any action that doesn't take into consideration the results of Austin's journey to the capital."

All this did not increase his popularity in Nacogdoches, although to Houston, who was well accustomed to have men disagree with him, and trusted to his ability to bring them around later on to his viewpoint, it seemed to make no especial difference in his friendliness.

Before Bowie left, Travis privately shook his hand.

"I didn't agree with what you had to say, Bowie," Travis said. "But I admire your guts in saying it. I think you and I are likely to see a good deal of each other, before things are settled in Texas."

2

The first chill of the great shadow fell when Bowie rode into San Felipe. He now was on the last stage of his journey, looking forward eagerly to seeing Ursula and the children. There must be two now, and he wondered if the new one was a boy or girl, as he put up his horse and went into Peyton's tavern for the night.

Strange was the manner in which he was greeted. He nodded to men he knew. They spoke to him, but his smile was answered by no other smile. On all faces was a look withdrawn, secretive, even pitying.

"What's the matter with you fellows?" he said genially. "Solemn as a bunch of hoot owls. Come up and wet a throttle with me!"

A Mexican boy stood at his elbow. "Señor, the *alcalde* sends to ask you to come at once to his office. The matter is urgent."

Like a wave of sickness, dread swept over Bowie. He did not taste the drink he had just ordered. He never tasted it. He left it on the bar and followed the youth out.

S. M. Williams, the *alcalde* of San Felipe since the death from cholera of John Austin, was at his desk, a meaty body, a sweeping mustache, and a face shot with blood capillaries under the skin. A bluff and hearty man, ordinarily, but now no humor was in him.

"Good day, Mr. Bowie." His voice was like a stone.

"The boy said you sent for me," said Bowie.

"I saw you ride into town. Took the liberty . . . have a drink?" Williams poured a dribble of whiskey into a small glass.

"No, thanks."

"Better have one."

"No."

"Then I will." Williams tossed off the liquor, and then sat for several minutes silently regarding Bowie.

"What do you want?" Bowie said at last.

"I—believe me, Mr. Bowie—I am your well-wisher and friend——"

Bowie felt irritation compounded of impatience and strange cold terror. "Very well. We'll agree you're my well-wisher. Now—if it's bad news—for God's sake tell me!"

The *alcalde's* face was a blob of dough with tiny purple veins on the surface. His hand shook as from his desk he took a folded letter.

"This came—a few days ago. From Don José Antonio Navarro of Bexar. It—it—adverts to you—my poor friend——"

As Bowie read the letter, the words twisted and blurred and crawled, yet every syllable of their meaning was burned in his brain.

San Antonio de Bexar, Sept. 26, 1833.

Esteemed Señor Williams: When I told you my fears of the cholera it looks as if I had a sad premonition, because my brother-in-law Veramendi, my sister Josefa, his wife, and Ursula Bowie and her children died unexpectedly in Monclova. I have lost a very loyal brother-in-law in Veramendi, and Texas a good son, a faithful and interested friend. Texas is now a political orphan, in the government of the state. Three days' illness were enough—from the 5th to the 8th of this month—to end all these precious lives. In fact during the first 18 days of this month 571 persons died in Monclova. Poor Bowie is a widower. I wish you would in some way advise him of this sad news.

Your friend, José Antonio Navarro.

Bowie laid the letter on Williams' desk and walked out. On the street he passed friends of years' standing without seeing or knowing them. Night already was beginning to fall, but he called for his horse and rode westward.

At dusk, three days later, he rode into Bexar and directly to the home of Don José Navarro, across from the military plaza. All the way from San Felipe a torment had crouched like a beast at the back of his mind, yet he refused to accept what he knew was true, until he had it from the lips of his friend and Ursula's uncle, Navarro himself. The incredible thing about it was that Bowie had been the one who had gone into the supposed danger, and Ursula had been sent to safety. Yet . . . Ursula, *Ursula* . . .

Don José came to the door. The sight of Bowie's face filled his warm brown eyes with concern and sorrow.

"Come in, my son."

Bowie stood before him staring like a man bereft, saying nothing.

"My heart bleeds with your heart," Navarro said. "My house is your house——"

Bowie shook his head.

"Then I will come out with you, Jaime. Let us go into the garden."

In that darkening place they talked briefly.

"When—did you hear?" was Bowie's first halting question.

"The day I wrote Señor Williams."

"The new child?"

"It was born in July. A son. She named it for you."

"None—not *one*—escaped?"

"Not . . . one." Solemn and final as a tolling bell.

Now at last Bowie believed.

In that hour he leaned his head on his arm against the wall and gave voice to his anguish.

He did not sob, or weep, like ordinary men. He cried with a despairing stridency, like an animal, bound and helpless, which is being flayed alive with knives and cannot bear its agony.

It was too terrible. Navarro drew away and left him.

For two hours Bowie remained alone in the garden.

He became quiet. All tears were shed. Remaining in him was a sea of pain which had no horizons or limits.

Why had he left Ursula, why had he not stayed with her? If he had remained, the cholera might have taken him also. To die with her would have been a thing infinitely to be desired.

He remembered her as he had seen her the last night before his departure from her. He had awakened long after midnight. The skies had cleared after a series of spring rains, and the moon had reached its full-ness, flooding the earth with beauty. The bed was placed near a window, and the clear soft light from without fell in a long slant through the open shutters, lingering on Ursula, sleeping beside him, touching her hair, caressing her features so childlike in slumber, stealing downward along her figure.

That was his memory of her, his most precious memory of beauty. It did not soothe his grief. It only served to make more maddening his sense of loss.

Without going into Navarro's house he passed down the street, his face haggard as from months of sickness, on his lips a seal of pain that never again left them.

The Mission Alamo, 1836

*I*n *terms of numbers, the Texas Revolution of 1836 would hardly
qualify as a good skirmish in modern mass wars. At San Jacinto, the revo-
lutionists mustered less than one thousand men. At the Alamo, which
preceded it, the defending Texans numbered just one hundred and
eighty-three.*

*Yet, the mastery of a continent was in contention between the cham-
pions of democracy and absolutism. Compared to this issue, the racial
rivalry was hardly important, especially inasmuch as many Mexicans
fought bravely in the Texas ranks. San Jacinto, in which Houston crushed
the invading Mexican army, captured General Santa Anna, its commander, and wrung from him terms which brought independence to
Texas, has been listed as one of the great decisive battles of the world,
along with such classic struggles as Marathon, Waterloo, Gettysburg, and
the Marne.*

*But if San Jacinto was decisive, the Alamo prepared the stage for it,
made its final stroke against aggression possible.*

*The Mission San Antonio de Valero, known to history as the Alamo,
was one of the least of the religious centers planted by the Spaniards in
Texas. The word "álamo" signified the cottonwood tree, in a grove of
which the small church and its surrounding walled plaza were erected in
1718. Before many years it was deserted, its priests and Indian converts
transferred to a more prosperous neighboring rival, its records gone, its
roof partly fallen in, bats and owls finding nesting places in its ruinous
yellow stone walls.*

Yet this despised and neglected child of the Spanish mission system, in its neglect and decay, became the most notable of them all, a place of pilgrimage for all who cherish liberty and feel the inspiration of men who were willing to die for it. Today the Alamo is visited by more people than any other historic place of Texas. It is the finest shrine of that great state, the sacred heart of its history.

During the thirteen days that Santa Anna dashed his army of six thousand men against the walls from which American sharpshooters kept up their unremitting withering fire, his battalions were so shattered, his losses so heavy, that when finally the defenses were overwhelmed, the defenders all killed, Colonel Juan N. Almonte, his chief aid, said that "Another such victory will ruin us."

Ruin Santa Anna's ambitions the Alamo did. In the weeks El Presidente spent regrouping and reanimating his forces after the fearful mauling they received from the heroic handful, Houston had the time he so desperately needed, to organize, maneuver, and prepare his little army for the final, climactic blow at San Jacinto.

The men of the Alamo knew what they were doing, when they elected to die within it. One among them was gifted with the imagination and perception to see the major strategy of this delaying action, and to make the decision for them, which they loyally accepted.

That man was James Bowie.

Chapter Forty-two

1

The big man should have seen the horse cantering down the street in San Felipe, but he almost blundered into it, saving himself only by a lurching retrogression that brought him down hard on his buttocks in the dirt. The rider shouted his contempt over his shoulder.

"Borrachón! Bufón!"

The big man put his hands awkwardly on the ground and levered himself up, rump first in the manner of bovines, achieving an upright position only by exaggerated balancing. His hands made loose flapping motions, trying to brush the dust from the seat of his pants.

"Borrachón! Hi—yi—Borrachón!"

Diabolic chant from a half-dozen Mexican urchins. The big man swung his head stupidly, and the urchins, with a derisive shriek of laughter, scampered around a corner in a flutter of ragged shirttails.

Borrachón. Drunkard.

A stubble of beard disfiguring his chin, eyes bloodshot, face marred by loose lines of a long debauch, James Bowie, sometime gentleman, dust-covered and ridiculous, lurched toward Peyton's tavern.

An incredulous voice on the tavern gallery said, *"That's Bowie?"*

"That's him. Biggest drunk in Texas."

"Funny," said the first, "how liquor gets them spectacular fellers."

"Yeah," the second agreed. "That Bowie—considerable of a man in his day. But when he got to hittin' the bottle, the weaknesses showed up on him. Now he's just a human hog—wallowin' in his own mire——"

A low, menacing rumble interrupted the two. "I'd be careful in my remarks about a man like Bowie. In times past he'd have cut your livers out for what you just said. And don't count on his not doing it now, if he hears you. Even drunk, Jim Bowie's a better man than most anyone in Texas."

353

The two critics mumbled excuses to the owner of the rumbling voice, and hastened to take themselves away.

2

Bowie slumped into a chair at a table.

"*Mozo—una bebida——*"

The waiter knew what he wanted.

Bowie ignored the glass and lifted the bottle to his lips. A throaty gulping. He put the bottle down and gripped the edge of the table as revulsion shook him. It had not been this way when he started his heavy drinking. He could put away a lot of liquor in those days, without changing his face. But now whiskey twisted his body, made him grimace wretchedly.

Drink. A year and a half of drink. Stumbling from one *cantina* to the next. Sprawling flat on the sidewalk or in the street. Sleeping off debauches in tavern rooms. Eighteen months of chaotic wandering, groping, not to find something, but to escape from something.

This was June of 1835. A terrible thing to lose a year and a half out of a man's life.

Bowie had vague recollections of various places: Gonzales, San Felipe, Arcadia, Monclova. Anywhere but Bexar. He could not bear Bexar.

He tried to remember the things he had done . . . no, that was bad. Memory was the enemy. The anesthetic of alcohol alone could drive from his mind memory . . .

Again he sucked at the bottle. Then he took it by the neck and stumbled up the stairs. Some place . . . any place . . . he was in a room. Liquor ran down his stubbled chin. He could smell the sour sickening odor of it and his stomach rose, but he downed it again.

He staggered back. Something pressed against the backs of his knees. He was falling . . . falling uncounted miles through black space. His falling ceased. Bed. Only his bed after all.

He closed his eyes to shut out the room which was whirling about him in dizzy circles, faster, smaller, narrower.

After a moment he lost consciousness of the room, of everything. His mouth was half open, his lungs pulled in the air, vibrating his soft palate with unpleasant tearing sounds. Sleep. Swinish, snoring sleep.

A faint gurgling. The last of the whiskey escaped on the floor from the open bottle his numbed hand had dropped.

With a mighty effort he fought upward out of the abyss. He was Sisera, with an iron spike driven through his skull at the temples, a blinding torque of pain.

His lungs labored and seemed unable to get air. The arch of his ribs rose and fell like a bellows, and from his throat escaped a guttural animal sound of terror: terror a man feels in the nightmare, when there is no mind or will to control the wild instinctive panic.

It was as if a hand clasped his in the darkness to pull him out of the pit. He clung to the hand. It possessed strength and calmness, and from it assurance seemed to pass into his fingers, infusing his being with the beginnings of confidence.

In the lightless vacuum of horror the hand supported him. It alone, by its solitary strength, held him from plummeting headlong into the bottomless void of eternal oblivion. Devils of night clung to his legs, his waist, his throat, every part of his body, uniting their vampire strength in hauling him downward, jerking and twisting at him, clawing at his windpipe and eyeballs. They hung upon him like a foul festoon of bats, obscene, evilly squamous.

He could resist them no longer. Strength was spent. He must loose his grip, slide down, down, down . . .

But he could not loose his grip. When he no longer clung to the hand, the hand clung to him. Against the power of the fiends of the pit, it drew him upward. Light appeared above, and toward this he strained.

At last he seemed to rest safe, for the time being at least.

Through the lids of his eyes, he felt the beams of blessed light, but he did not dare open them, and still he clung, childlike, to the hand. Pain ran through his temples in great throbs. Sweat stood on his forehead and trickled down in little rivulets along his cheeks.

A wet cloth, wondrous relief, was laid across his forehead and pressed down over his eyes.

Later, hours later, between times when cold wet cloths were put upon him, he struggled to open his eyelids. He could not bear the light at first. But again he tried. This time he had a reeling vision of the ceiling, and a double face, bending over him. The face became twins, separated, slid together, joined into one, widened, became two again, and gradually focused into a single set of features.

Like some huge carved granite boulder. Deep shadows under the jutting brows. Nose vast. Mouth rocky. Chin a thrusting monolith. The mouth opened and became a cavern, and from it issued a rumble.

"You feel better, Jim?"

Sam Houston's voice. Sam Houston's rocklike head. Sam Houston's hand which had dragged him back from the pitch-black void.

4

Still haggard and shaken, Bowie could eat with more appetite next day. They were alone together in Houston's room, where the meal had been brought. Houston said, "Looks as if you hadn't taken solid nourishment for quite a while."

Bowie chewed on a piece of fried beefsteak.

"I've been hunting you for weeks," Houston said. "Looked for you in Nacogdoches, Goliad, Gonzales, Bexar——"

"Never go to Bexar!"

Houston nodded. "By accident I happened to see you yesterday."

"And sobered me up?"

"For old friendship's sake."

"For old friendship's sake—I want a drink."

"I want to talk to you first——"

"I want it now!"

The great stone face did not change. "There's a bottle in my portmanteau."

Bowie groped for it, pulled the cork with his teeth, and drank. He put the bottle on the table, wiping his mouth with the back of his hand.

Houston took the bottle and put it back in the portmanteau.

"He needs a bath," he said sneeringly, as if he spoke to someone other than Bowie in the room. "He stinks."

"What do you mean?" Bowie growled.

"The rotgut's coming out of his pores. He smells like sour hog swill."

A wild-beast look came into Bowie's face.

"And I've seen him," Houston went on contemptuously, "in the crown of manhood, when his name would silence a barroom full of ruffians, and his figure caused women to turn their heads to look when he went by. Now the very children in the streets hoot at him!"

Bowie groped savagely at his side.

"Never mind the knife," Houston said. "I put it away."

"Let me out of here——"

"You sit there. I gave you your drink. Now you listen to me."

"What do you want?"

"I want to make a man of you again."

Bowie's turn to sneer. "Impossible. I'm satisfied the way things are."

356

"But I'm not. First-class fighting men are too scarce."

"I'm done fighting."

"No you're not."

"Let me go——"

Bowie tried to rise, but Houston pushed him back with an almost negligent gesture. Overwhelmingly Bowie realized how his strength had gone from him.

"Hear this, Jim Bowie. No man in Texas understands you like Houston. Houston was in his time also a driveling drunkard."

Driveling drunkard. There was nothing Bowie could say.

"I hear them call you *borrachón*. The word for me was *Ootsetee Arditaskee*. In Spanish and Cherokee the meanings are identical."

Houston smiled grimly. "They do not understand us, the men of lesser breeds. That a giant should plunge lower than other men is incomprehensible. But we know, you and I, the pain beyond pain, the bitterness beyond bitterness . . ."

5

No man living but Sam Houston could have done it. And he only because of equal experience, having once been lost in a great drunkenness also, which gave him intimate understanding.

For him, Bowie ceased drinking. Days passed and he grew more alert. He took long horseback rides to regain his muscle tone. Gradually, in separate conversations, he learned from Houston what had taken place in his lost months.

"Santa Anna has become a peril which concerns every man and woman in Texas," Houston said. "Consider his devious actions. After he took the oath of office, there was a revolt—carefully planned—which he marched south to 'crush.' His own troops 'mutinied,' in connivance with the very 'insurgents' they had started to fight, and made a great demonstration, declaring Santa Anna dictator of Mexico. All very ably stage-managed. The ruse signaled an uprising in the capital to establish his power, but it lacked thoroughness. Santa Anna 'escaped' from his army, and made a public apostasy, published in the so-called 'Plan of Cuernavaca,' disavowing the reforms he had 'contemplated.' Now he is in fact dictator, but he is supported by the reactionary Centrist elements and opposed to the forces that put him in power. With a ferocity which must have its basis in his own betrayed conscience, he turns against any who oppose him, prison and firing squads his weapons."

To this Bowie listened as if it had just happened, so completely had he lost all account of events.

"I'm deeply worried about Santa Anna's present movements," Houston said. "His troops already garrison Coahuila. Gossip brought by Mexican traders from south of the Rio Grande says he also is organizing an army to overrun Texas, which has been without any real Mexican forces since the uprising against Bustamante in 1832."

"Will Texas resist?"

"Would you?"

Bowie thought. "Yes. I would fight."

"Do you know what they're saying about you?"

"No."

"Houston," said the big man, "did some things in his months of inebriation which he does not yet remember. Perhaps you also——"

"Give it to me straight," Bowie said.

"What do you know of the John Mason grant?"

The Mason grant? Recollection would not quite pin it down. Bowie shook his head.

"There were," said Houston, "certain irregularities in the conduct of the last Monclova legislature—before Santa Anna took over." He hesitated, then said, "One James Bowie is reported to have wielded the influence that got for one John Mason a hundred *sitios* of land—nearly half a million acres—a grant that is a stench in the nostrils of certain Texans today."

Bowie held his head and tried hard to think. He remembered faces. At Monclova he had been half sober for weeks, while business of some kind was transacted. Friends were there, or so they told him: S. M. Williams, the *alcalde* of San Felipe; Dr. James Grant, who had estates in Coahuila; Robert Peebles and John Cameron, whom he had known before; John Mason, smooth-handed and smooth-acting; old Ben Milam.

Bowie liked Milam best: a humorous plainsman, and a good drinking companion. But all were on the same errand—something about land. Just what was it?

Houston said, "Texas land has been given away wholesale to political string-pullers in the past year. The memorial to the central government asking that Texas be created as a state separate from Coahuila seems to have prompted the politicians at Monclova to act quick, in hope of getting what profit they could out of us before we separated from them. Result: huge tracts of unoccupied Texas land sold to speculators for little or nothing. The biggest went to the man Mason I was speaking about. Naturally Texans regard such squandering of their public lands as highway robbery and are a little heated up about it, since those lands constitute their future capital as a state."

Now Bowie began to remember a little. That group—Mason, Milam and the rest—had been most generous and hospitable, particularly with the liquor. He never lacked a companion, or a glass. And their prime interest in him, he seemed to recollect, was his acquaintanceship. Those thirteen friends of Don Juan de Veramendi . . . for the sake of the vice-governor's memory, they were willing to do certain things which Bowie asked of them. After that everyone seemed happy, and there was more drinking, until one day the whole crowd hurriedly rode out of Monclova, taking him with them, on some kind of an alarm.

"It isn't clear to you?" Houston asked.

"No, hazy—all hazy."

"I believe you. As I say, a man can do the strangest things when he's liquored up. You didn't even know what you were doing, I'll take bail on it. But to show you how some feel, a letter has come into my possession, written by James Kerr, a sober gentleman of Gonzales, to T. J. Chambers of Anáhuac. Read it."

Bowie did so. One paragraph almost struck him in the face.

Williams, Johnson, Carbajal, Bowie, and others cry, "Wolf, wolf, condemnation, destruction, war, to arms!" In regard to these delinquents against the laws of the country and against honor and morality, who were concerned in the illicit buying and selling of 650 *sitios* of land in Monclova, there is not one single person, who would wittingly seek his own ruin to save Williams and the others. It is my opinion a war would inevitably be disastrous for Texas, and what would the nation not lose by it! Imagine it for yourself, some 20,000 or 30,000 men. What, all that for Bowie and some ten other rascals? God forbid!

Bowie's recollection went back to soft jowls, high white forehead, fixed smile, and unctuous voice. Mason . . . John Mason. The man who had befriended him in days when friends were not many. A favor for John Mason . . . and now it was "Bowie and some ten other rascals."

He closed his eyes tightly for a moment, then opened them.

"Have I been 'crying war'?" he asked.

Houston shook his head. "Kerr only uses you as an example, because at this present you are in none too good repute."

"I don't even know Kerr. To have my name used this way—what can I do?"

"Bear it, for the present. It's a penalty you've incurred." Houston paused. "You've heard that Stephen Austin is imprisoned in Mexico City?"

"For what, in God's name?"

"He wrote a letter home, urging united action for Texas. It was intercepted."

"I owe Stephen Austin an apology. I didn't think he'd ever do anything decisive," Bowie said.

"A great many people have misjudged Austin. I among them."

"But this war party and peace party question?" Bowie asked.

"The old story, since time immemorial. Some men will fight to defend their rights and liberties. Others will submit to any kind of tyranny and abuse for the sake of peace. Athens had a war and peace party. Rome had a war and peace party. England had a war and peace party. America always has had a war and peace party, whenever an emergency arose. Now Texas has a war and peace party. Man has to wring liberty not only from tyrants, but also from his fellow men who not only are unwilling to fight for it, but to let anyone else fight for it."

Bowie said, "I reckon nobody in Texas has more to lose than I have. I have property and friends which I'd have to give up if Texas became independent from Mexico or if I fought for Texas in a war that failed. I stand to lose in either case, if I take any part."

Very gravely, Houston said, "That has an element of truth, Jim."

For a moment they both thought profoundly. At last Bowie said, "I was born an American, Sam. Blood's thicker than water. I'm with you, for better or for worse, till we see the end of this."

6

It was heard that from the south a Mexican army was marching: such an army as never had been sent to Texas before. No mere column of lancers, this, with weary foot soldiers kicking up the dust behind, to occupy some frontier post. It was a true army: cavalry, infantry, artillery, a supply train, and commanded by General Martín Perfecto de Cos. This last indicated Santa Anna's grim purpose: General Cos was El Presidente's most trusted subordinate and brother-in-law.

So far a distant rumbling only. There was a little grim joking. If Cos occupied Texas, who would find himself looking into the musket barrels of the firing squads? Bowie discovered that he was considered a candidate for this honor, since Colonel Piedras, returning to the capital after the Nacogdoches affair, had spoken of him as a great barbarian, the most turbulent, the most dangerous, of all Americans.

To hear rumors is one thing: to see for oneself is another. Without consulting anyone, Bowie rode south toward Matamoros, which was a port on the south bank of the Rio Grande, closest to the Gulf. It was therefore, to his mind, strategic for the massing of any invasion since water-borne supplies could be embarked there. His garments, even his saddle, with broad tilted horn and large square skirts, were Mexican. He spoke Spanish with native ease and fluency, and there were Mexicans of fair hair and blue eyes. Even so, this was a dangerous mission.

He entered Matamoros by night and left before morning. His report to Dr. J. B. Miller, the *jefe político* of Brazoria, the colony most intimately concerned, was made in writing from a ranch just north of the border.

Sir: I have just arrived here from Matamoros and as all communication is cut off between Texas and other parts of the Republic, I take this opportunity of giving you some information that may be useful. I left Matamoros the 12th of this month. All vessels in the port were embargoed for the purpose of transporting troops to the coast of Texas. The commandant, General Cos, forbid all foreigners from leaving the city under any circumstances. I run away and succeeded in getting this far safely. Three thousand troops have reached Saltillo on their way to Texas. All this may or may not be news to you. I will be with you in a few days by way of Brazoria. James Bowie.

The substance of this letter, from one so well qualified to know, crossed Texas with a celerity which only fear could impart. Here and there committees of safety were formed, and men began gathering at night to drill as informal companies of volunteer soldiers. Bowie remained at Nacogdoches, hoping for the return of Houston, who had gone to seek aid for Texas in the States. One day he received a letter from Buck Travis, then in San Felipe, which better than anything expressed the disorganized confusion of the frightened province.

Dear Bowie: The truth is the people are much divided here. The peace party, I believe are the strongest and make the most noise. Unless we could be united, had we better not be quiet and settle down for awhile? There is now no doubt but that a Centrist government will be established. What will Texas do in that case? Dr. J. H. C. Miller, and Chambers, from Gonzales are, I believe, for unqualified submission. I don't know the minds of the people upon the subject, but if they had a bold and determined leader, I am inclined to think they would kick against it. General Cos writes that he wants to be at peace with us; and he appears to be disposed to cajole and soothe us. Urgartechea does the same. God knows what we are to do! I am determined, for one, to go with my countrymen: "right or wrong, sink or swim, live or die, survive or perish," I am with them. Buck Travis.

A fighting man's protest against indecision and weakness.

Then, on September 1, Stephen Austin, who after months in prison had been released at last, arrived in Texas. He called upon the people to maintain themselves and their constitutional liberties. Coming from him, that forthright declaration removed all disunion.

361

Three weeks later ominous news came from the south. General Cos was marching with an army for Bexar. The fuse of war was lighted.

7

In Nacogdoches, Bowie made up his mind. No use waiting any longer for Houston. A Texas army was forming, and as he looked at it, that meant fight. He said to himself that if there was one thing he was good for, it was fighting. Some folks in Texas still held it against him that he had been mixed up in the Monclova land dealings, but he reckoned that a lot would be forgiven in a man who showed that he wasn't afraid to eat powder smoke and listen to lead bullets whine, to defend Texas from her enemies.

Most especially, however, his nature craved action, and to palliate this secret wish suddenly became enormously important to him.

He laid aside broadcloth once more for buckskin, and early in October began a cross-country ride to join the Texas provisional army, which was reported to be advancing on Bexar with Stephen Austin at its head. Slapping his hip was the knife he always carried, in its old leather sheath.

Chapter Forty-three

1

Stephen Austin was not happy as a general. On the twelfth day of October, 1835, he was camped with his army—if it could be called an army—on the Guadalupe River, not far from Gonzales. The *empresario* found himself in command almost without his volition: a sort of impulse had generated into a military movement, and Austin was swept along with it, until he found himself actual leader of the force in the field, a responsibility which he had not sought.

Nothing went right in this army. Austin had, it is true, managed to get the tents—such as there were of them—pitched in a sort of line, but otherwise there was nothing in the camp to satisfy his orderly mind. He had with him about four hundred men, and they were without any pretense at uniforms, except that they were all unwashed, ragged and dirty, and homespun was the common material of their garments. They possessed no standard arms: each man carried his own Kentucky rifle, jaeger, smoothbore, horse pistol, or shotgun, which he had picked up when he left home. Austin remembered pleasant pictures of military encampments, and the pyramids of gleaming, bayoneted guns, stacked in a fine show before the clean white tents. But how can you stack arms when lengths of barrel vary by as much as two feet, and there is not one bayonet in the entire command?

With loathing and sickly anger, the general looked about him. Flies were thick from the offal of cattle slaughtered not far away, which had not even been removed. The men lounged about, chewing and spitting tobacco, playing cards or telling stories, swearing and laughing, completely out of hand, the officers no better than the men.

With this force, he thought scornfully yet with self-pity, he was expected to confront a well-uniformed, armed, and disciplined Mexican army, led by trained officers, with fortifications as an added advantage. Impossible! He could have wrung his hands and wept, if it would have done any good.

To have, at this hour, the man he least liked in all Texas ride in and present himself was to put a capsheaf on his difficulties. But Stephen Austin was of a nature that would be polite to the devil, if that dark personage presented himself. He rose at the table where he had been writing one of the endless lengthy dispatches, which now served as a substitute for the debates he loved.

"Mr. Bowie," he said, "your presence is unexpected but welcome, sir."

"General Austin, I have ridden from Nacogdoches to offer my services."

"We accept them, gladly." Austin stopped to think. He knew that Bowie was popular with the Texans. It would not do to put him in the ranks: that might be resented by the men. On the other hand, Austin had no wish to put him in active command of troops. After all, the *empresario* had always looked on Bowie as a land speculator, with none too clean a reputation.

"I shall attach you to my personal staff, as a volunteer aide, with the rank of colonel, Mr. Bowie," he said after a moment.

Bowie stared at him. "Staff, sir? I want to fight."

"A staff assignment is all I can give you at present," Austin said coldly. "We hold a council of war in an hour."

Bowie walked away, not pleased.

An hour later he attended the war council. Austin looked about at his officers: Colonel Edward Burleson, portly and aging, the typical politician-soldier and Austin's personal friend; picturesque Deaf Smith, in moccasins and buckskin, his hand behind his ear, a tireless scout and courier; Captain William Barrett Travis, quite neat and soldierly, the kind of man who appealed to Austin's mind; Colonel Joseph Neill, square-faced, with a viny, dark mustache and a thick throat; Colonel

Francis Johnson, whose ability at voluminous correspondence was almost equal to the general's own; and Captain J. W. Fannin, hardheaded and horse-faced, but a real fighting man. At the rear of the group, almost as if he wished to efface himself, stood Bowie, with his new rank of colonel and his debatable position, taller, broader-shouldered, and more silent than any of them, and in buckskin like Deaf Smith.

"You've heard the news from Goliad, gentlemen?" Austin's eyes turned from one to another. "Captain George Collingsworth attacked a Mexican marauding force, beat and captured it, together with two pieces of artillery and three hundred stand of arms. He brought in also Colonel Ben Milam, who had lately escaped from prison in Coahuila where he had been held by the Mexicans. In view of these developments, what is your opinion of our next move?"

"I say press on at once to Bexar," said Travis.

"A courier should be sent to Collingsworth to join us," said Burleson. "We can use those brass fieldpieces and small arms."

"I should tell you," Austin said, "that I do not consider that we are ready to attempt an operation of the magnitude we may face at Bexar, with the men and organization we possess."

"Why?" Bowie's voice from the rear, speaking for the first time.

Austin gestured wearily. "You can see for yourself the lack of discipline——"

"I can see for myself born fighting men," Bowie said. "They may not be much for spit-and-polish, close-order drill, and policing camp grounds. But put an enemy before them and I can tell you—from experience, sir —what Texas rifles can do."

About the council circle ran a series of nods. Austin felt that his officers were listening to the newcomer more closely, accepting his judgment more readily, than they did his own. This was unpalatable. But it was not in his nature to give direct opposition.

"Very well," he said drearily, "if it is the agreement of this war council, we will get under way in the morning."

2

The morning of October 27 was chill and foggy. Bowie had slept in his saddle blanket and was taking a cup of coffee when a messenger brought him a written order from Austin. Bowie was to proceed with Captain Fannin and ninety-two men, to select a camp ground for the army on the river as near Bexar as possible. There was a good deal of wordage to the order, but two paragraphs of it were of especial importance:

You will also reconnoitre, so far as time and circumstances will permit, the situation of the outskirts of the town and the approaches to it.

You will make your report with as little delay as possible, so as to give time to the army to march and take up its position before night. Should you be attacked by a large force, send expresses immediately with particulars.

Bowie rose and saddled his horse at once. This was better: only a reconnoitering command, to be sure, but action, nevertheless. He mounted and counted his horsemen ranged before him. All at once it seemed to him that he was stepping into a role for which he had been preparing all his life. He felt unconcerned, fully confident of his powers. Raising an arm, he shouted his command and led the ninety-two toward Bexar.

Nobody knew this country better than Bowie. Outside Bexar lay the whole series of old Spanish missions, planted like outposts: San Juan, Espada, San José, Concepción, San Francisco, the Alamo. All were deserted now, and in ruins, but each was capable of being defended: potential forts if the Mexicans chose to use them as such.

He led the way straight to the Mission San Juan. A few *mozos* dwelt in nearby huts, but otherwise there was no occupation. As if moving from strong point to strong point, he took his detachment a mile farther to Espada, thence three and a half miles northeast to San José.

Down the road from this mission was the stone-and-adobe home he had built for Ursula. He did not permit his eyes to turn that way as he rode on.

Ahead were the twin towers of Concepción, the nearest of all missions to Bexar, save only the Alamo. At this point the San Antonio River made a wide sweeping bend and provided what seemed a suitable camping ground for Austin's army. Extending toward the town was a nearly level plain, adjoined by timbered land chiefly of pecan trees which formed two sides of a triangle, the apex of which was on the river, the base on the plain. Five hundred feet away stood the mission.

"We'll camp here," Bowie told Fannin. "Send Lieutenant MacComb back to report this position in accordance with orders."

To right and left men began picketing horses, lighting campfires. He looked about, the recollection of the San Saba on him: a little preliminary work by Rezin had saved them then. Now he called a party of men and set them cutting a long step in the clay bluff which fell to the river, just far enough down so that riflemen could stand on it and fire over it with protection for all but their heads. Then he walked through the woods at either side, noting the cover and protection they afforded.

Sundown came and still there was no sign of Austin. Bowie ate a light supper, left Fannin in charge at the camp, and rode alone down the road toward the distant lights of Bexar. In the darkness ahead were small

365

thatched *jacales*. He left the road and guided his horse through the fields to avoid them. Then he came across an arroyo which he knew led toward the center of the town.

He left his horse tethered in a small live-oak grove and scrambled down to the bottom in the darkness, where he began a stealthy progress. After a time the arroyo widened, offering less concealment, so that he felt it expedient to creep on hands and knees. Houses on either side of him now. He saw not only the lights in windows and doorways, but figures of people moving in the streets. A guitar strummed, and a voice wailed a mournful love song concerning a dove. From a *cantina,* a few blocks below, came a growl of laughter. In the light of an open doorway, a soldier, vivid in blue, stood with his arm about a laughing woman's waist.

Bowie placed his hands on the rough slope of the arroyo and drew himself up to the level of the ground. From here he could see the distant plaza. It seemed crowded. Hardly sullen or resentful was the native population of Bexar at the presence of General Cos's army.

He thought of his friends: The Navarros, Padre Garza, Judge Seguin, other men and women with whom he had feasted and attended Mass and danced and gossiped during his brief period of great happiness when Ursula was his wife. What did they think of this military instrument of the dictator, Santa Anna? Reluctantly, he decided that even these were smiling at the invading troops, inviting officers into their homes, protesting loyalty to El Presidente.

In good faith Bowie had sought to be a Mexican, had married into a Mexican family, and considered himself one of its sons. Yet in this hour he was an alien, an American: and to these people the tyranny of Santa Anna, because he was a Mexican, probably seemed preferable to association, even on a democratic basis, with men of another race.

Another thought came to him: among Americans in the Texas army, a line also was drawn against him. They were chiefly colonists, who never had compromised with the Mexican way of life, and to many of them he was an object of suspicion, even dislike.

Bowie licked his dry, dusty lips and crept closer. Breast down, his ear to the ground, he heard the tread of feet on the earth, the stamping of horses and mules in the corrals, the rumbling of wheels. Smells of the city passed faintly into his nostrils: smells of *carne,* of *pulque,* of *ron blanco,* of tobacco, of stable manure, of wood fire, of outhouses—all blending into one hanging taint on the cold October air.

Slowly he drew back, returning to his horse. He had assured himself there would be no attack during the night hours.

But when he returned to the Mission Concepción, Austin still had not come. Had something gone wrong? He consulted his orders again. *Make your report with as little delay as possible, so as to give time to the army to march and take up its position before night . . .*

No directions for falling back. Clearly he was expected to stay at this camping place until Austin arrived.

That night, however, he did not sleep. He had placed his own head, the head of his entire command, in the mouth of the lion, and it remained to be seen if he could extricate it should the army's march be too long delayed. Ninety-two men, huddled sleeping in their blankets, seemed pathetically few compared to the military forces in the town so near.

Well . . . if MacComb made a speedy ride, Austin might be on the march already. Meantime, he would sit up, wrapped in a blanket by a fire, to make sure that his sentries kept alert.

Chapter Forty-four

I

Dawn of October 28. First only a gray glimmering through heavy fog which obscured the landscape. Bowie still sat by the small fire with his horse blanket wrapped about his shoulders, and Austin still had not come.

The whiplash crack of a rifle brought him to his feet.

"Where was that shot?"

"From the mission tower," someone said. Bowie had placed lookouts in that vantage point.

There were shadowy movements, ghostly figures in the ragged mist, a sharp rat-tat of gunfire, followed by a sudden, half-incredulous shout, "They're here, boys! They're here!"

Through the fog toward Bowie careened a short, wide shape: Henry Karnes, one of the outpost. In a high-pitched, wrathful voice, he yelled, "The damned rascals have shot out the bottom of my powder horn!"

Bowie tossed the blanket aside and ran in the direction from which Karnes had come. He should have been jaded from a sleepless night, but he experienced instead an inexplicable new lightness of limb.

Through a break in the fog, as if a curtain were pulled away, he saw the long rank of blue coats, white crossbelts in an X-pattern across them.

A moment before the Texans had been seated by their fires or still asleep. Now every man was on his feet. They heard Bowie's yell, "Open up on them, boys!"

Frontier habits paid dividends. Many of the Texans had that night slept cold in order that they might wrap their blankets about their loaded rifles against the foggy damp. At Bowie's left and right jets of flame sprang out instantaneously. Then a round score of rapid reports. Sudden empty places appeared in the distant blue line, like gaps left in a row of teeth.

The blue line began falling back, went to pieces, fled into the fog bank.

"Cease fire!" Bowie shouted. "It's only an advance guard!"

Earth gave off its dawn chill: fog caused the cold to hang in a heavy layer. Teeth chattered beside him. He glanced at the man: Henry Karnes again, but shivering from dampness, not fear. He had been supplied with a spare powder horn. His rifle was at the ready.

Then from the blank face of the fog came a volley of bullets that whined overhead.

"They're shooting blind," Bowie said.

His men flattened themselves on the ground, raising heads to watch. The blind volley claimed no casualties.

Bowie walked along the scattered prostrate line, giving orders.

"We may be in for a good old-fashioned Virginia reel, boys. Cos has sent out a reception committee. Let's sashay with 'em and show 'em how Texas cuts the pigeon's wing."

The men laughed.

Fog still hid the enemy. For a moment Bowie stared at the baffling gray bank, while his men, every one of them, watched him. Then he began giving his assignments to action.

"Fannin, take thirty men and find cover in those trees to the right, making sure your cross fire doesn't go into the trees on the other side of the open field."

The long-faced captain saluted, told off his thirty, and moved away.

"Coleman!" Fannin's second-in-command gazed at him eagerly. "You put those other thirty boys in the woods over to the left. Quick, now."

He turned to the remaining third of his command. "You others come with me." They ranged themselves behind the riverbank, where the foot-walk had been cut in the clay bluff the night before.

The fog thinned, lifted, and the Mexican array, infantry and cavalry, was clearly seen.

2

"Keep your heads down," Bowie said.

"God a'mighty—they's an awful sight of 'em—ain't they?" Henry Karnes quavered nervously.

"I reckon three hundred infantry," Bowie said. "And five companies

368

of lancers behind 'em—say forty to the company. That's five hundred men. Looky yonder—isn't that a piece of artillery being brought up?"

Sharp Mexican commands, clearly heard in the crisp air. Bayoneted muskets came to blue shoulders, legs tramped in cadence, the enemy began moving forward.

"Only five hundred of them, boys," Bowie said, "and ninety-two of us. Everyone knows one Texas rifle's worth ten Mexicans. Why—look at it —the odds are all in our favor!"

He had made them laugh again.

In full double line the Mexican infantry rolled forward toward the silent Texas position.

From the woods far on the right, where Fannin's detachment lay, came the deadly crack of a rifle. All saw a blue infantryman double up.

The Mexican advance halted. Drums rolled. These seemed well-drilled troops: every movement was according to order. They heard the order to fire.

"Tirán!"

A cloud of white smoke jetted toward them. With the crash of the volley came the hum of bullets overhead, but again, nobody was hurt.

The wisdom of Bowie's dispositions became apparent. Only in the open field, which was flanked by the two woods, could the troops be maneuvered. Attacking across it, the enemy would encounter a crisscross fire from men who knew just where their lead was going.

The white cloud of the first volley drifted away. The Mexican front blazed again.

Slowly and deliberately Texas rifles began to answer. The range was long, but here and there new blank spaces began to appear in the blue ranks. A musket ball buried itself in the bank six inches from Bowie's face, but he hardly knew it. A different movement caught his attention.

"Brass gun," he said. "Four-pounder, it looks like."

Men strained, pushing the fieldpiece forward by hand through an opening in the Mexican ranks, to a position toward the right and much nearer the Texas lines. Gunners busied themselves. All at once the brass gun boomed, a hoarse bellow that drowned all lesser sounds. Grapeshot whirled through the branches of the trees over the heads of Fannin's men.

"Let's help Fannin!" came a yell.

"Stay down——" Bowie said. Too late. Four men scrambled over the bank and raced for the woods at the right, across open ground.

Instantly, from the Mexican line, another volley erupted. One of the four Texans was down. His friends seized his arms and dragged him into the trees. Orders disobeyed. A casualty.

Along the step below the bank Bowie made his way until he could get

369

into the woods at the right. As he pushed through the thick growth, another bellow came from the fieldpiece. Involuntarily he ducked as the shot screamed overhead, bringing down branches and leaves.

He looked around. Nobody had seen him. He grinned, embarrassed, to himself.

A few more steps and he found three of his men. They lay stuffing their pockets with the ripe nuts which the cannon balls had brought down from the pecan trees over them. One of them was apologetic.

"Somep'n to eat, Colonel, if we git a lull."

Bowie laughed. "Get all you want, but look sharp."

His men seemed far from cowed by the Mexican fieldpiece. Still, that gun could be dangerous. He found Fannin, on one knee, shading his eyes with his hand as he peered through the bushes. Another charge of grapeshot tore through the branches above them, showering them with leaves.

"I don't like that birdshot rattling about my ears," Bowie said.

"Neither do I," agreed the captain. "If they depress that muzzle a little lower, they might do us some ugly damage."

Bowie crept forward. From one side came a whistling moan. He glanced beneath the bushes. It was the man who had been shot in the open. Bowie knew him: Dick Andrews. His face was gray, his eyes closed. The bullet had cut a hole under the ribs on his left side, and he was dying.

No time to stop here. Bowie crawled to the edge of the woods. A dozen Texans lay there, firing coolly at the Mexicans.

"Forget the main body," he said. "Pick off some of those artillerymen for me."

Rifles began looking toward the brass gun. It had just been reloaded, and the gunner with the lighted match stood ready to touch the firing hole. From the woods a tattoo of shots. The gunner spun to the ground like a rabbit.

The others of the crew stared as if they could not believe. Then one of them ran forward and picked up the match. He also fell as lead smacked into him before he touched the fuse hole.

A third crouched low, attempting to recover the match. His body pitched across those of his comrades. The survivors of the gun crew had seen enough. Doubling and dodging, they ran to join the main body.

From the Texas woods came a great roar of laughter, cockcrows, and the shrill whoops by which hounds are encouraged after rabbits.

Bowie was concerned with something else than mirth. Hardly more than halfway to the Mexican lines he saw the brass gun glinting in the sun. He stood up.

"Boys," he said, "let's get that gun!"

The knife leaped from its sheath, and flourishing it in his hand, he ran toward the cannon. Behind him men sprang to join him.

This was no steady, slow infantry advance that the Mexicans saw erupting from the woods. Buckskin Texans bounded toward them like bristling panthers, stopping now and then to fire with deadly accuracy, reload, and gallop forward at the same breathless pace. A great blond *diablo* ran at their head, his hat in one hand, a great knife in the other. Nothing like this existed in the textbooks of war. But regardless of textbooks, Mexican infantrymen were flopping on the ground and biting at nothing.

There was only one hurried, ill-directed volley from the blue lines before Bowie had reached the gun. He gave a stentorian shout, "Swing her around!"

Eager hands on the trail. The brazen thing was whirled until its muzzle pointed directly at the blue ranks a hundred yards away. The fuse stick was still burning, clutched in the hand of the last gunner to fall. Bowie seized it and touched it to the vent.

Deafening roar. Blinding billow of smoke. The gun leaped backward with its recoil.

Smoke cleared. In the Mexican ranks a gaping hole was torn. Men were breaking, beginning to fall back.

From the woods on either side and from the riverbank came the Texas yell, a wild shriek, compounded of Indian war whoops and cattle cries. They had seen Bowie's charge for the cannon, and now every man was springing toward the Mexican array.

A spontaneous attack, but it could not have been better timed. At the eruption of homespun and buckskin, the flanks of the blue line began to shred, the center seemed to push in on itself, officers beat frantically and angrily at men with the flats of their swords, trying to hold them in their ranks. Then the whole mass was flying, panic spurring speed, blind with fear; the array swirled about the mounted lancers in the rear, and carried them away in the wild rout. The Mexican force was gone, and in its place were scattered blue figures receding over the distant landscape, each man for himself, seeking safety where he might find it.

3

Austin, nervous and irritable as a fidgety old lady, slapped his tightened knuckles sharply on his saddle pommel.

"Why didn't you follow them?" he snapped. "Why didn't you pursue them all the way to Bexar?"

He did not like war, the sight of death made him squeamish, and before him were sixty-seven Mexican dead, beside one Texan. But above everything, Austin did not like criticism, real or implied, and he read criticism in his officers' faces as every one of them thought how victory might have been decisive and Bexar taken, had the commander acted with more celerity, and brought up the main army the night before, as he had promised to do.

A good man was Stephen Austin, but he should have spent his life quietly as a schoolteacher or at the ledger of some countinghouse. Responsibility had never been pleasant to him, although he accepted it as his cross to bear. It had been bad enough when he had to make decisions and adjudicate disputes among his colonists in peacetimes, after his father died and left the load on his shoulders. But now, in the field of war, where he could not shave regularly, or even wash his face, much less take a bath, so that he seemed always in acute discomfort, and where his terrible position of leadership kept him from sleeping well at nights, life was well-nigh insupportable.

Bowie and Fannin, who had ridden up to meet the general, stared at him in amazement after his peevish outburst. The former's surprise at this proof of lack of capacity in his superior was changing to anger. But he answered simply and formally.

"Because we had written orders to do the opposite, sir."

Austin frowned. It was true he had put certain restrictions on the commander of his advance column, but it was unpleasant to be reminded of it this way. He changed his ground of criticism.

"You have no idea how you worried me by your maneuver, Bowie," he said querulously, and it was to be noticed that he did not use the title of colonel, although he was very fond of employing titles to everyone whom he addressed. "I meant for you to return to the main body last night, and you should have done so. Why, by staying at Concepción, you might easily have had your command annihilated!"

Bowie felt a weariness at this *volte-face* in the general's carping. He might have quoted the exact words of Austin's order to him: *You will make your report with as little delay as possible, so as to give time to the army to march and take up its position before night.*

But he did not. He merely said, "Well, as it happens we weren't annihilated. But you'll find quite a few Mexicans lying out there in need of a funeral."

A little snicker in the staff at this. Austin's irritation grew. He was always conscious of any audience, and to have to bandy words with a subordinate, especially when his own remarks made him look a little foolish, aroused in him a brittle anger. He saw he was getting nowhere.

"We'll move forward at once," he said.

To his surprise, Bowie stiffened and said, "By your leave, sir, I'd advise against it."

"Why?" A little sneer in the single word.

"With all due respect to your position as commander-in-chief, sir, I happen to have lived in Bexar for years and believe I know something about the fortifications defending the city. They have, if I may say so, been extended and altered during the two years you were absent in Mexico. It's no good sending men on a suicide attack."

Austin's frown deepened. He had always disliked Bowie, about whom he thought there was a good deal of a brute, and who was a member of the growing Houston party in Texas. The dislike intensified as he now found himself brought up short whichever way he turned in this discussion. Almost hopefully he turned to Fannin.

"What's your opinion, Captain?"

"Sir, I agree with Colonel Bowie," Fannin said.

Austin's eyes, pin-pointed with distrust and antipathy, turned stonily on Bowie's face.

"At least we can find a more strategic camping place," he said with hostile niceness. "You will remain here with your command, Bowie. I shall take the main army to that old mill, a mile north of the Alamo."

Chapter Forty-five

I

Council of war. Council of war. Rostrums and gavels and rules of order. Debates and oratory and figures of speech.

Austin was up to his old practices, and nothing was accomplished. In his exposed position far from the main force, Bowie was ordered to do senseless things like "demonstrating" with his ninety men in front of the enemy position, in the expectation that disaffected Mexican troops would desert to the Texas army. Silly and futile, but typical of the visionary Austin. A cheap victory, as easy as that—a snap of the fingers!

Bowie obeyed that order. No Mexican troops deserted to him, nor had he expected them to do so.

Once he wrote out his resignation to his nominal command, but instead of accepting it, Austin relented and ordered him to join the main body, a step Bowie had been urging from the first.

Dreary days passed. Men drifted away from the camp and were seen no more. But others came to take their places. One of these was a raw-boned six-footer with a long, sly nose, and a mouth the corners of which were forever stained with tobacco juice. He was Colonel Ben Milam, a friend of Bowie's from the Monclova days.

"Heerd thar was a leetle shindig brewin'. Concluded to come an' look on," he told Bowie with a twinkle.

Bowie grinned. Everyone knew old Ben loved a fight. He had been fighting most of his life—against the British, the Spanish, the Emperor Iturbide, the Indians, and most recently at Goliad against Santa Anna.

Another arrival was a full-bodied, urbane man with a Scottish burr in his speech: Dr. James Grant, whose *hacienda* in Coahuila had been confiscated, and who therefore preached a descent on Matamoros instead of this profitless siege of Bexar. Both Milam and Grant were Monclova land speculators, tarred with the same brush as Bowie, but neither of them was so coldly treated by Austin as was Bowie.

Finally, one afternoon, a detachment of cavalry rode into camp, uniformed with splendor in comparison to the rags of the rest of the Texas army: gray jackets with black froggings and brass buttons, flat gray caps set at jaunty angles, tight white trousers, gleaming side arms and accouterments. These were the New Orleans Grays, who had outfitted themselves at their own expense, and come to help the Texas revolt, youthful, somewhat vainglorious, and not a little disdainful of the slovenly butternut crowd that gaped at them.

Toward the end of November, Austin called still another council of war, and once more suggested a direct assault on Bexar. The staff dissented.

"Such being the case," said Austin, sadly bowing to the majority will as he always did, "I have to inform you that I must take my departure. A provisional government has been organized for Texas. Our new governor is Mr. Henry Smith, of Brazoria, whom I consider most able. The commander-in-chief of the army is Sam Houston." He paused. "I have been named a commissioner to the United States, to seek aid from that country."

He said it simply and looked them directly in the faces, as if this were the highest of honors. But it shocked them. Henry Smith the governor? It should have been Austin himself.

As much as he disliked the man, Bowie at that moment felt real pity for him, and a sense of injustice in his behalf. While Austin was with the army, his quondam political friends had overlooked him in the important offices of the new government and given him a sort of diplomatic post as an almost insulting sop.

Austin seemed to read their minds. "I can only say that I am ready at

374

all times to serve Texas in any station where it is considered I can be useful."

His credo. Whatever his failings, Stephen Austin never deviated in his dedication to Texas. A bigger man, Bowie considered, than he had thought. Thereafter much, very much, could be forgiven him.

2

Deaf Smith's horse pounded up, soaped from neck to flanks, with little clots of foam blowing from its muzzle. The scout's brown beard was sugared with dust as he wheeled before Burleson's tent and jerked a hand southward.

"Hossmen! Ugartechea an' reinforcements for Cos, likely!"

Colonel Burleson, the heavy-faced politico-soldier, who had been appointed commander by Austin before his departure, stood in the tent door, the pulse visibly beating in his thick, loose neck.

"Where?" he asked.

"Laredo way."

Burelson's eye fell on Bowie. "Colonel, take your men and try to intercept the enemy. I'll follow with infantry and support you."

Bowie went at a run. Up and down the river the Texas camp was scattered for half a mile with no attempt to keep company lines. He found only forty of his command—the rest off somewhere gambling or skylarking—but these were on their feet as soon as he appeared among them.

"A little fun coming up, boys," he said. "Get your horses."

They trotted in a long detour north of Bexar, then headed southwest to cut the Laredo road. Five miles beyond the city they halted. A dust cloud was approaching. He indicated a dry arroyo angling toward the road.

"Dismount. Take your horses down there and secure them. Then take cover behind that cut bank."

If this was the Mexican reinforcing column, Colonel Ugartechea, who was second-in-command to General Cos, might have five hundred men or more with him. And Bowie had only forty. But the forty obeyed smartly. This part of the army, at least, had complete confidence in its leader. Horses were picketed. Like lizards they crept up the side of the arroyo, laying their rifles on the sod at the top, powder horns and bullets convenient to hand.

"How many?" Bowie asked, staring across the plain.

Henry Karnes said, "Looks like a lot. Burleson better get up before long."

When the dust cloud neared so individuals could be counted, Bowie was surprised. Cavalry, to be sure. Dragoons. One hundred—one hundred and twenty—one hundred and fifty, he counted. These could not be Ugartechea's reinforcements. They must be an escort of some kind.

Bowie strained his eyes. Pack mules, heavily burdened. Supplies? Perhaps—yes, very likely—the pay-roll train from Laredo.

"Boys," he said with conviction, "I'll bet you're looking at Mexican silver coming up that road. Cutting off this *conducta* might be as important as stopping Ugartechea himself."

A new eagerness appeared in their faces. To plunge arms elbow-deep in chests of Mexican silver pesos . . . They licked lips hungrily.

At a hundred yards, Texas rifles began to crackle. A dozen saddles emptied. There was confusion and surprise in the Mexican ranks. The dragoons tumbled from their horses and took refuge in a dry creek bed, answering with musketoons a foe they could not see.

Bowie gave the cease-fire order. No reason to waste ammunition. The Mexicans desisted also. Between the hostile lines lay a few dark twisted shapes, and a voice was calling upon Mary the Mother of God.

"Burleson's coming," said Karnes.

They saw the brown-clad Texas foot, angling across the field at a quick-step. At least Burleson was prompt.

"Where are they heading?" Bowie said suddenly in amazement.

"They don't see us—they're blundering right between us and the Mexicans——" said Karnes.

"Yell at them—warn them——"

But already the Mexican volley crashed, exploding almost under the feet of Burleson's men. Some were hit. Burleson's voice was lifted above the tumult, but the Texans recoiled and some began running, scattering like a panic-stricken herd.

"Come on, boys!" Bowie shouted. "We've got to get those Mexicans out of there——"

With a screech the forty were out of the arroyo, charging wildly behind him across the plain toward the creek bed. Some of Burleson's soldiers ceased retreating and roared after them.

The Mexican dragoons did not wait. Scrambling out of the creek bed, they threw themselves on their horses and careered away.

No catching them on foot.

"Let's look at what we've got." Bowie turned to the abandoned pack mules, drawing the knife from its sheath. He ripped open a pack.

"Grass!"

One after another they tore them open. New hay stuffed the loads. Not a single peso in the entire *conducta*. All this fight over a forage train.

376

Laughter grew. Texans slapped each other on the backs and sobbed with joy. They held their sides, tears running down their dirty faces. They collapsed on the prairie, helpless heaps of shuddering mirth.

The laughing did not cease even when a Mexican force appeared from Bexar, evidently to retrieve the *conducta*.

Texans sniggered as they drew beads, burst into new guffaws as soon as they had pulled triggers. But this did not impair their shooting. The Morales battalion, which Cos had sent, withdrew. Forty Mexicans died that day, with many wounded. Only four Texans were wounded, none killed.

Bowie rode crestfallen back to camp with his men. The anticlimax to his brilliant little maneuver had completely obscured his success, caused men to forget the blundering of Burleson, and to lose track of his prompt charge that saved everything at the moment of disaster.

These things were remembered and appreciated only long after.

3

More inaction. More discontent.

The Grass Fight men felt their position unhappily. Endless jokes were concocted, mostly of the stupid variety. There were some rough-and-tumble fights in camp over it, and innumerable wordy arguments.

Bowie brooded. His fight had caused him to lose reputation instead of gaining it. He and his men were pelted with laughter. Even after the Grass Fight joke became stale and men ceased to repeat it, he was sensitive about it.

In those days, Dr. Grant, who had big notions and a persuasive tongue, all but talked the army into abandoning its siege of Bexar, and going with him to descend upon the rich port of Matamoros. But the desertion did not occur. It was rumored that the long-awaited storming of Bexar was to come at last. The rumor was denied: confirmed again. On December 3, came a call for volunteers to attack next morning. This was followed by an announcement from Burleson's headquarters that there would be no assault at all, and the army was to relinquish its camp, retiring to winter quarters at Gonzales.

The Texans were furious, astonished. Mutiny threatened. Entire companies refused to parade. Men stood about, surly and indifferent to orders, glaring fiercely off toward Bexar, as if it were a prey of which they had been cheated.

Before them walked a whimsical figure in buckskins, with a rifle in the crook of his arm.

"Who'll go into Bexar with old Ben Milam?"

There was a sudden roar of relief and eagerness. Men crowded about Milam, tossing rifles in air, howling like a pack of wolves. Nothing could stop this spontaneous surge of the common soldiers. Burleson acquiesced and began naming officers to command the two columns of assault: Milam, York, Patton, Llewellyn for one. Johnson, Cook, Swisher, Edwards, Benavides for the other. There was no mention of Bowie.

In the gray dawn of December 5, Bowie watched them march away. He was to remain in camp on "staff duty."

They listened to the distant opening shots, building up to a steady concentrated roar. Couriers came at intervals with reports on the progress of the battle: Milam was progressing down Acequia Street, Johnson down Soledad.

Big guns from the military plaza and the Alamo began to speak. Against the heavier beating of Mexican muskets and cannon, the snarl of the Texas rifles was bitter sharp, and the smoke of burning houses obscured the distant sky.

The attackers were reported working their way from house to house, tearing holes through adobe walls with crowbars and pickaxes. By nightfall, they were said to be well fortified in the north part of the town.

On the second day the advance began again. Now there was word that they had pushed beyond the house of Antonio de la Garza, the priest's brother, and had entered the Veramendi *palacio*. Bowie drew plans of the town for Burleson to show just where the spearheads were thrusting.

The morning of December 7, old Ben Milam was killed—shot down by a Mexican sharpshooter from the riverbank, as he was crossing the patio of the *palacio*.

Bowie heard this news unmoved. In his mind was less the thought of Milam than the picture of that patio: as it had looked the day when he and Ursula together had watched the wedding dances. It was torn up now. Ripped. Bloody. Another thing to live only in his memory.

General Martín Perfecto de Cos, a small, compact man with vivid dark eyes, sent a flag of truce asking terms of surrender on December 9. The defeats his troops had suffered at the Mission Concepción and on the Laredo road had broken their morale, and by the time the Texans penetrated into Bexar, desertion and insubordination were manifest.

In this manner, Bexar was captured by four hundred Texas fighting men, when every military expert, including Sam Houston himself, had said it was impossible to take the place without heavy reinforcements and siege artillery.

Bowie was oppressed with the question: *why?*

He, himself, had given the first and best demonstrations of the formidability of Texas irregulars against Mexican troops. In a joking manner, to keep up the spirits of his men, he had coined the saying that one Texas rifle was worth ten Mexicans. Twice he had led wild charges of Texans in buskskin and homespun, to shatter superior Mexican forces and drive them from the field. It was, although he did not know it, a pattern which would be continued, until Sam Houston one day would use it to change the history of the hemisphere at San Jacinto.

Meantime, Bowie sought an answer. He knew these native Mexicans. Among them were few cowards. He had beloved friends among them, had considered himself a son in a Mexican family. In a manner of speaking the weakness they had shown was a reflection on himself, since he had freely taken the Mexican ways for his own, and identified himself with the Mexican people.

There was some reason for it, not at first apparent. Even in his own detachment were fighting men of the Mexican race, and they had been among the foremost when the rifles were speaking and the bullets kicking up the dust. Why, therefore, the panics and quick retreats of regular Mexican troops, drilled and uniformed and well armed?

He remembered a dead Mexican soldier upon whom he had looked after the Concepción battle. The poor corpse was attired in the long-tailed blue uniform coat, and the tall plumed shako of the Mexican infantry lay beside it. Across the still bosom gleamed the white crossbelts, and a stripe ran down the side of each trousers leg. So far, everything was military.

But the feet were bare. The bare brown feet of the Mexican *mozo.* They had known sandals of rawhide, but never shoes. This was not military.

How long had that man been away from the maize field he had cultivated all his life? How long from his simple village, his *jacal*, his church and padre, his wife and children? Not long. A few weeks, at most a few months.

Herein lay the answer to Bowie's question. Santa Anna's conscription ruthlessly had torn men from peaceful little villages, even had emptied prisons, to fill the ranks of his army. Hardly comprehending, these poor creatures were herded into barracks, issued uniforms and weapons, whipped into some sort of cohesive organization and an understanding of simple commands, by loud-voiced and abusive officers. But something more than a uniform and the manual of arms was required to make a soldier. These had no incentive to fight, other than a fear of their superiors. When they were confronted by a deadly shooting enemy, they ran away without shame, inasmuch as they saw no good reason for remaining where they were to get killed.

Given a reason for it, Bowie considered, Mexican soldiers might fight savagely. It required a motive.

Santa Anna knew as well as anyone the necessity for a war spirit. In the manner of dictators, he had already raised the issue that seemed most likely to inflame his people—the issue of race. Bowie had read some of the *pronunciamientos* that were being circulated even in Texas.

Foreigners. Invaders. North American Barbarians. Warmongers. Traitors. Filibusters.

So ran the epithets applied to the Texans. Hatred was a stronger motive than love of country, even. Those of Mexican blood numbered a hundred times more than those of American blood in Mexico. Invoking the race question, Santa Anna hoped to unite his nation in a crusade of hate, so that his own despotic crimes would be forgotten. Perhaps, when enough incoherent emotional fury had been fomented, he would himself lead back into Texas an army inspired by it.

When the Texans occupied Bexar, Bowie did not go into the city. He could not yet bring himself to look upon the old scenes and meet the old friends of his happiness.

Christmas, also, was almost upon them. Christmas was the worst season to abide, in his ache for Ursula which time did not seem to blunt. He therefore asked Burleson to relieve him of his duties, and rode back toward San Felipe.

Chapter Forty-six

1

The strangest thing had taken place: an army had been stolen from its commander. It was unprecedented almost in the annals of war: and a tribute to the persuasiveness of one man, Dr. James Grant.

General Sam Houston, by law commander-in-chief of the military forces of Texas, rode fuming across the country. So stripped was he of any semblance of a following that he had with him not even an orderly or any baggage, other than what he carried in his saddlebags. A lone man, frowning and biting his lips, he urged his horse down the mesquite-lined road, with the darkness of night gathering, a dubious symbol of the gloom settling over the future of Texas.

Never had Houston experienced so terrible a feeling of impotence. A winter storm had passed, leaving cold behind it, and the washed countryside seemed empty, but placid, as if it did not know the fate stored up for it. He ignored the refreshment of the bitter, lucid air. No matter how, he was determined to overtake his army before it left Texas, to try to dissuade it from the mad course on which it was bent. In real emergencies, he had always been the master, he could make himself agreeable to soldiers, and this was his only hope now.

Lights blinked ahead. That would be Goliad, where the army was reported camped.

As he rode into town, however, it was apparent that no army was here. He saw a few lounging butternut figures who might be soldiers, but hardly more of them than enough to make up a corporal's guard.

His nerves were aquiver as he dismounted before the lone *fonda*. Might as well stay here the night and make inquiries. Perhaps this was the finish, the end of all. He had written a despairing letter to Henry Smith, the governor, ending, "No language can express the anguish of my soul. Oh, save our poor country!"

It was enough to make a man throw up his hands, resign his commission, everything, and get back to the United States where at least he could call the President his firm friend.

The door of the *fonda* opened, and for a moment the light from within outlined a figure in buckskin. Houston stared.

"Bowie!" he cried.

The buckskin man peered into the darkness. "Who is it—General Houston!"

They half embraced, hands on each other's shoulders, eyes searching eyes, faces of relief and gladness.

"A drink?" said Bowie, as he drew Houston into the inn.

"I need one!"

"Muchacho—aguardiente."

"You?"

Bowie shook his head. "Not since—the day in San Felipe."

"Good man!" Houston nodded with approval.

He studied Bowie: he was thinner, seemingly older than when Houston had seen him last. A man mauled by the hands of fate. No happy warrior, but a brooding spirit questing for repose in a pathway of storms. Yet the one man in all Texas on whom Houston could depend, absolutely. The last thought alone lifted a part of the burden he carried.

Houston said, "I sent you some orders. Instructions I hoped might forestall this ridiculous Matamoros fever."

Bowie showed astonishment. "I regret. The courier never reached me."

"Too late now," Houston almost groaned. "Where's the army?"

"Marched yesterday, the bulk of it, with Grant, Johnson and Fannin, for Refugio, on the border."

"I must overtake it. There was a proclamation on a wall, calling for volunteers to attack Matamoros, and promising that troops would be paid 'out of the first spoils taken from the enemy.' Signed by Colonel J. W. Fannin, as 'acting commander-in-chief.' I gave him no such authority, and at best this represents a serious indiscretion. A looting raid will win over to us no Mexican liberals. How do you account for what's happened?"

Bowie was grave. "Dr. Grant has succeeded in his design. All through the Bexar siege, he belittled it, and kept urging instead the march on Matamoros. Wrong, wrong, he'd say, that concentration of strength at Bexar, when Matamoros, so much more important and rich, was a defenseless open gateway to the interior of Mexico, with disaffected Mexicans ready to join and help the Texas invasion."

"Perfidy! His expedition is plain piratical war!"

Bowie nodded. "I've had dealings with the doctor before, and they didn't improve my belief in his honor. I kept remembering that his confiscated estates are at Parras, which can be reached from Monterrey, which can in turn be reached from Matamoros."

"Using the army to recover his personal lands! But others, I take it, found him more convincing than you?"

"Yes: especially the gilded young gentlemen of the New Orleans Grays."

Houston brooded, unsmiling. "I can see it. They found Grant's urbane and highly literate discourse more to their taste than the talk of blunt and sometimes uncouth Texans."

"Enough 'uncouth Texans' went along so there's hardly a company left at the Alamo in Bexar."

"What a disaster!" Houston's massive face was furrowed. "You know as well as I that Mexican pride will try to revenge Bexar. Somehow, Texas must build an army to oppose Santa Anna when he comes. And now our one force of any size, and all the supplies we have, are committed to this insane visitation, which can only further incite Mexico to anger. How many men are here?"

"Thirty. Members of my old command of the Concepción fight whom I talked into staying, although I had no authority for doing it."

Bowie said this with a tinge of bitterness. Houston understood it, and did not blame him. Action was the only thing this sad man wanted. In the hot minutes when death flew on the air at Concepción and on the Laredo road, he had been nearer to happiness than at any time since Ursula's death nearly deprived him of reason. He could forget when the lead was whistling. It was the old fever of gambling, with huge stakes,

382

greater than his own life, which in this game was no more than a single chip. He wanted a command in the army, to fight and gain such credit as was in it, as some reason for continuing his existence.

Other men had been promoted and given responsibilities. Buck Travis, one of Austin's pets, was a colonel now, as a result of capturing a herd of Mexican horses. So was Fannin, in recognition of his services as Bowie's subordinate at Concepción. But nothing for Bowie himself, who had done much more than either of them.

To Houston, the injustice was as great as the reason was evident. The men in power at San Felipe were colonists. Bowie was not. A distinction was drawn by them, between themselves and the man who had married a woman of the Mexican people, lived the Mexican life, and honestly adopted Mexico as his country. A renegade, some called Bowie. Yet he was the best fighting leader Houston had in all Texas.

While they still sat talking, a dusty courier on a weary horse rode into Goliad. He asked a direction from a soldier and stumbled with whizzing spurs into the *fonda.*

"General," he made a weary half effort at a salute, "dispatches for you, sir."

Houston scanned the written sheets. He said to the courier, "Get some rest and something to eat. I'll have a message to send back in the morning."

The man nodded and disappeared.

Houston turned to Bowie. "This is heavy, very heavy news."

"Where from?" said Bowie.

"From Colonel Neill at Bexar. A desperate plea for reinforcements. He has only about eighty men, he says, besides the sick and wounded. But the portentous information is this: Santa Anna is at Laredo, with not less than four thousand men."

Stunned silence. "Laredo?" Bowie said. "That's on Texas soil. It means . . . it means Santa Anna's major move!"

"What can I do?" Houston sounded imploring. "There are limits to what one man can accomplish. I should be going on to Refugio to save my army, and at the same time be back in San Felipe, trying to pull together some sort of defense force. Now Bexar calls for me! Time! Time is what I need. If I only had a little time, a few weeks to prepare—but Santa Anna is upon us——"

Bowie said, "I could go to Bexar for you."

Houston looked at him. "You're the one man who can. It seems providential that I found you here. Take every soldier you can find and head for Bexar first thing in the morning, will you?"

"Why not tonight?"

"Even better. Let's see—I hardly know what to tell you to do. Look the situation over. If it's as bad as Neill says, demolish all fortifications, remove the cannon and other munitions, blow up the Alamo, and abandon Bexar."

For a moment they sat in silence together. Then Bowie departed to gather up his men and go to his new war.

2

Colonel Joseph C. Neill wore an untrimmed dark mustache which drooped heavily, hiding his mouth, and had a habit of standing with his feet apart, hands clasped behind his back. He was a Regular Army man, one of Houston's own choosing, unimaginative but conscientious.

"You brought only thirty men?" he asked peevishly.

"All there were at Goliad," said Bowie.

"What can we do with thirty? I tell you Santa Anna has thousands!" Neill looked desperately weary. "And he won't wait forever."

"Give me time to think. I want to look around."

A matter of inspecting the Alamo first. It was in exactly the same condition General Cos had left it. Two enclosures, one large, one small, surrounded by walls of masonry from two feet to a yard thick and eight feet high. The smaller was the convent yard, and the old convent, no more than a long row of two-story dormitories, had been used by the Mexican troops, and Texas soldiers who followed them, as barracks. At the southeast corner of all this, the chapel, a squat, square ruin of hewn stone. Half the roof had fallen in, the rear wall having crumbled from the top, and the overhead masonry given away. Two enclosed rooms flanked the door, the baptistry and the sacristy. The latter now did service as a powder magazine, the former as a dispensary. All told, the church and its walls enclosed a space of two or three acres. There was a plentiful water supply, since two aqueducts ran close to the eastern and western walls.

"What do you think?" asked Neill after the inspection.

Bowie shook his head. "Not much here."

Before he made a decision, however, he rode into Bexar itself. Not since the night of his interview with Don José Navarro had he been in the city. For a brief moment, he pulled up his horse before the *palacio*. Hardly could he bear looking now at that half-ruined old abode of happiness. The great cedar doors hung open. Bullet holes pocked the walls. At one place an ugly gap, large enough to permit the passage of men, had been torn in the side of the house. The interior, after the fighting and looting, was a chaos of wreckage.

384

Sick at heart, Bowie shook his bridle. Once again he stood at the door of Ursula's uncle. Don José Navarro possessed the magnificent eyes of the family, the eyes Ursula had inherited from her mother.

"Don Jaime——" He almost stepped back in surprise. "I have not seen you in many months——"

"I found it—very hard——"

Navarro made a little hushing gesture. "Of course. I understand. Come in, my son. You are here for some special reason?"

"I want your counsel."

"Gladly."

"You know Santa Anna is on the border?"

"Yes."

"What do the people of Bexar think of that?"

Don José pulled his mustache and studied the floor. "For myself, I can only tell you this: I leave in a few days for San Felipe, as a delegate to the convention summoned for the first of March."

"It's to discuss the question of independence, isn't it?"

"More than that, Jaime. To declare independence, to elect a president, and to adopt a constitution for Texas. We're taking the big jump, for good or ill, this time."

"You favor these steps?"

"I must. And if your friend and mine, Don Juan de Veramendi, were here with us today, it would be he, not I, who would be going. He also hated despotism."

Bowie drew a deep breath. "It makes me very happy to know you are on my side in this."

"Many in Bexar are with us. Judge Erasmo Seguin, his son Captain Juan Seguin who is with Neill's command, his nephew Blaz Herrera, our *alcalde* Don Pancho Ruiz—they are all stanch. I could name others. But not everyone. There has been more of Santa Anna's propaganda believed than you might think."

"Could we get recruits in the city?"

"I doubt it. The fear of Santa Anna is too great. He is a terrible man, Jaime. Have you heard of his massacres in Zacatecas? Hundreds were stood against a wall and shot down. That, he would do here also. In knowledge of this, I'm taking my family to the interior of Texas. And I urge you to get out of here. For Santa Anna I have no admiration, but I know that he comes with too much in men and weapons for what you have in this place. To stay would be death."

With these grave words in his mind, Bowie returned to the Alamo.

There he counted fourteen pieces of artillery. It would be criminal to surrender them to the enemy, yet there were no horses to take them away.

Beyond this was an even more serious consideration. He remembered Houston's haggard visage. Houston was a giant, seeking to hold together with one man's strength the timbers of this ship of state, to keep them from riving apart. And Houston's plea was time . . . time . . .

That evening, at the Alamo, Bowie made his life's most important decision.

He wrote next morning a letter, which amounted to a disobedience of his superior's orders.

· Relief at this post in men, money and provisions is of vital importance. The salvation of Texas depends on keeping Bexar out of the hands of the enemy. Colonel Neill and myself have come to the same conclusion, that we will rather die in these ditches than give it up to the enemy . . .

This was followed by a statement of the situation: his own forces, one hundred and twenty men and officers; those known to be converging on him, seven thousand.

Not yet had the word "expendable" come into military parlance. Bowie thought rather in the terms of a gigantic duel. A duel not of single men but of nations. Once, in a duel, he had deliberately taken a flesh wound, to be able to give a death thrust. Texas could spare a little of its blood—his and that of the men with him—for the sake of making it very costly to Santa Anna to reduce the Alamo. If this gambit were not given, the country would be swept clean to the Sabine, for Houston was not yet ready. Time—weeks, days, hours even—had become more precious than diamonds and rubies.

3

Lieutenant Colonel William Barrett Travis went to the Alamo unwillingly. Twice he had written Governor Smith, begging to be relieved of the order to proceed there, once complaining that he was being "sacrificed," once threatening to resign his commission. In the end, however, he went, bringing with him thirty more men. He reached Bexar a few days after Bowie wrote his decisive letter.

Bowie was glad to see him, but there was a surprise for him, not pleasant. Travis met him in a manner stiffly cold and formal. While Bowie wondered at this attitude, there was a new development. It now appeared that though he had given Colonel Neill full credit for sharing his decision to hold the Alamo at all costs, Neill was in reality none too enthusiastic about "dying in these trenches." His relief when Travis arrived was visible, and the following day, pleading there was a sickness in his family requiring his presence, he left Bexar. Going, he suggested, as it were over his shoulder, that Travis take command of the post.

Bowie grinned and said, "Reckon we can adjust that between us, Buck."

Travis' face chilled. "You heard Colonel Neill's order. From here on, you will regard yourself as under my command, Colonel Bowie."

Bowie stared. Then displeasure answered displeasure. "If that's your position, Colonel Travis, I've got something to say on the subject myself. Neill had no authority to name a commander. If we're standing on strict military procedure, I'll call your attention to the fact that I'm senior to you in rank and that the commanding general sent me here with orders to take command. He has sent no orders relieving me. Until such orders come, I'll continue in command of the Alamo."

They bristled, steel glance clashing with steel glance.

In half an hour Bowie left the Alamo and rode into Bexar.

A military impasse. Here again was the evil of the cleavages in Texas. The rift between Austin and Houston created two factions that split the political and social structure in two, vertically. There were, in addition, other horizontal lines of cleavage, such as the difference between those of American and Mexican blood, the colonists and non-colonists, the farmers and the land speculators, which, like geological seams, ran across both segments.

Travis was an Austin man: Neill was a Houston man. But here appeared another of those horizontal cleavages. Neill was a Regular, subscribing to the conception of a professional army as against an improvised fighting force. In this category Travis also stood. Hence, Neill's farewell, almost malicious, "conferring" of the command on Travis.

It appeared also to Bowie that Travis had changed in character. He had considered Buck one of his close friends. Something had broken that friendship. Attentions he had received and reputation he had earned seemed to have endowed Travis with new arrogance. He had become an assertive man, believing in his own star, filled with ambitions.

Bowie felt weary. The taste had gone out of his meat.

He dragged himself into the *cantina* at the old León de Oro and called for *ron blanco*. The white, clear rum. The bottle stood on the table before him. For a long time he looked upon it, his face deep-set in melancholy. Then at last he reached for the bottle and poured into a glass. He lifted it and smelled it, and a craving possessed him. Not in months had he tasted spirits. So quickly that his eagerness betrayed him, he raised the glass to his mouth, moistening his lips, grown suddenly dry, with his tongue. The fiery liquor was grateful in his throat.

Caution whispered in the back of his mind, but he poured another glass. Again the fiery swallowing. Caution died. Warm waves surged through his body. Responsibilities seemed far away and not pressing . . .

4

Travis fumed and wrote letters to anyone who might read them, complaining of Bowie, who had been drunk on three successive days. He felt that he rightly should be in chief authority, and also that Bowie was leaving the whole load on his shoulders. Meantime the danger from south of the Rio Grande grew more ominous each day.

One ray of brightness was the unexpected arrival of eighty men. They were buckskin-clad Tennesseans, armed with long rifles, their leader a tall man with iron-gray hair falling to his shoulders, and a coonskin cap. This was the famous Colonel Davy Crockett, a legendary figure. Travis was most delighted.

But after the preliminary greetings, Crockett said, "I hear Jim Bowie's in this camp. Whar mought I find him?"

Travis soured. Bowie, he said, was probably in a *cantina* on the plaza, drunk as usual.

In that case, Crockett observed with a sly grin, he ought to have company.

Travis felt that courtesy demanded he conduct Crockett into Bexar in person.

It was a singular meeting. Bowie and Crockett struck hands and looked each other up and down. Pleasure was evident on each face, for these men long had heard about one another, and this meeting was an event.

Crockett took off his coonskin cap, hung it on the muzzle of his rifle, and leaned the rifle in a corner of the *cantina*.

"You an' me's got a lot to talk about, Bowie," he said.

Travis felt neglected, forgotten. He excused himself and went back to the Alamo. The others hardly knew he had left, so deep were they in the comparison of ideas, the exchange of reminiscence. Rarely had Bowie encountered a man to whom he took so immediately. The Tennessean had a sly grin, a dry way. The whole man, physical and mental, was a frontier growth. To Bowie he gave a brief vignette of his life.

"I fit in the war of 1812, though I'm no admirer of parades an' drills. Later I lived as a hunter an' planter in Tennessee. The wayfarer was ever welcome to a meal an' a glass of redeye at my house."

He grinned, and ran his gnarled fingers through his long gray hair. "My mistook was goin' into politics. I reckoned I was an honest man, an' if thar was many of the same stamp in Congress, the newspapers

388

strangely lied. I'd mastered the varmints of the woods, why shouldn't I use up the prowlers who preyed on the commonwealth? So I run, I stumped, I got elected. But Congress is enough to make a man puke. I was plumb disgusted with politics when I got home, an' findin' thar was a fracas down hyar, I took old Betsey, my rifle, off the pegs, an' come a-runnin'."

Listening, Bowie absently drew his knife to cut a loose string from his buckskin fringe.

Crockett said, "Is that the knife I've heerd about?"

Bowie offered it to him. Over and over in his hands, Crockett turned the blade. "Tarnation, if the very sight of it ain't enough to give a man a squeamish stummick, specially before breakfast!"

Bowie grinned. "You might tickle a fellow's ribs a long time with that before you'd make him laugh."

Crockett drew his own knife and compared it. "They call this of mine a bowie," he said sadly. "Made in Bristol, England. Ain't a man of my company but's got one. Good in their way, but compared to this old sockdolager of yours, they ain't hardly worth mentionin'."

5

Travis, the letter writer, dispatched an unhappy missive to Governor Smith.

Dear Sir: My situation here is truly awkward and delicate. Colonel Neill left me in command, but wishing to give satisfaction to the volunteers here and not wishing to assume command over them, I issued an order for an election of an officer to command them, with the exception of one company that had previously engaged to serve under me.

Bowie was elected, and since his election has been roaring drunk all the time, has assumed all command and is proceeding in a most disorderly and irregular manner.

If I did not feel my honor and that of my country compromised, I would leave here instantly for some other point with the troops under my immediate command, as I am unwilling to be responsible for the drunken irregularities of any man.

I hope you will order immediately some regular troops here as it is more important to occupy this post than I imagined. It is the key to Texas. Without a footing here the enemy can do nothing against us in the colonies . . .

A querulous letter, almost childish. But the last paragraph saved it. The charge that Bowie was "roaring drunk all the time" was hardly

389

justified. He had, to be sure, made a congenial round of the *cantinas,* arm in arm with Crockett, in a frontierwise celebration of a new friendship. But Travis' own disappointment spoke there.

With some confidence, since to his mind there was little question but that the men would choose the efficient, spruce, neatly uniformed officer over the buckskin roisterer, he had called for the election of officers. In this, however, he failed to understand the Texas race.

An independent people, a stiff-necked congregation, they were not easily swept by any assumption of authority. To gain authority, a man had to be such as they admired. In this the Tennesseans, including Crockett, saw eye to eye with the Texans. An overwhelming majority at the Alamo voted for Bowie as commander.

The disappointment of Travis may be understood, but the last paragraph of his letter showed the man's thoroughbred strain. He had concurred with Bowie's view of the strategic importance of the Alamo. A good fighting man, William Barrett Travis, as the days were to prove.

A conference was held between him, Bowie and Crockett, and the following day he put his name to still a further letter to the governor.

Sir: By an understanding of today, Colonel James Bowie has command of the volunteers of the garrison, and Colonel W. B. Travis of the regulars and volunteer cavalry. All general orders and correspondence will henceforth be signed by both.

An adjustment having been reached, Bowie, who was now looked to for orders by the whole Alamo, save Travis' thirty men, turned his attention to something very pressing and important.

Chapter Forty-seven

I

From the beginning Bowie saw the weakness of the Alamo. Now he turned to strengthening this wherever possible. With his own hands he labored among the men, building a palisade of cedar logs and an entrenchment to guard the opening between the church and the wall of the main enclosure. There could be no redoubts or bastions to command the lines of the fort, so the best thought must be given to placing the fourteen cannon in positions most strategic.

Four already stood on a platform above the apse of the church, placed there by the Mexicans under Cos before his surrender. At various other places he saw to the placing of others: four in the nook covered by the log palisade, the point of greatest danger; four on the walls of the chief enclosure, and two for the wall above the main gate. Here a planking of heavy cedar timbers was built, fifteen feet above the ground, and sweating men hauled the cannon up by block and tackle.

Bowie stood on the platform, directing. One cannon had been placed, a heavy piece. The other was coming up, the pulleys creaking. A swing started. A cry of warning.

Bowie did something he had rarely done in his whole life. He took a backward step without looking.

The whole thing had the curious unreality of a dream. For an incredible time he seemed to be hanging in space. Then came a stunning concussion as his body hurtled to the ground. He struck so heavily that for a moment he was unconscious.

He opened his eyes. His head was supported by a soldier.

"Are you bad hurt, Colonel?"

Sharp pain, like a knife blade, went through him as he caught his breath. Words came hard, managed with effort.

"Feels like . . . busted somewhere . . . get doctor . . ."

New face bent above. Sober, bearded. Dr. Edward Mitchasson. Pain. Hands feeling and molding where nerves were lacerated. Bowie coughed. An agony. He saw the scarlet stain on the ground.

"Bad . . . Doctor?"

"I'm afraid, Colonel . . . the hip is broken. Ribs, too—penetration of the lung."

The final stroke of misfortune. "How long . . . ?"

"Six weeks. At least."

Bowie closed his eyes. "Santa Anna won't wait six weeks."

Men lifted and bore him to a cot in the old baptistry where the surgeon labored over him.

"We'll put a box splint on this hip, colonel. You'll have to lie on your back till it heals, or you'll have a crooked leg all your life."

Bowie coughed again. A bloody foam came on his lips. The doctor's face clouded with gravity.

2

He was easier. The ribs and hip were set, and though his lung still pained each time he breathed, there was not at this present that sharp shooting anguish. In his mind, however, he was low beyond all the depths he had yet known.

They had left him alone in the baptistry. A smell of disinfectants and drugs still hung on the air, but the medicines had been taken to another place where the main hospital was set up, since here the space was insufficient. He looked at the stained old walls, and at the ceiling, and time dragged as heavily as a log through a morass.

He was concerned greatly over the situation of the Alamo and its defenders, and he did not receive half as much information as he desired about the progress of affairs. If he could only be on the walls now . . . perhaps there was still some last preparation that might be made . . .

He knew this was futile and foolish, and for a time he lay trying not to think at all. Then the thought of Ursula came to him like a faint, sad chord of distant music.

Ursula . . . He sometimes wondered at the change she had wrought in him. One girl, out of millions of girls, had in some manner bound his heart to hers with bonds invisible yet strong as welded steel. Why and how?

Ursula had not that assurance of her power over men some women seem to feel. Judalon had it, the supreme egotism of sex. Catherine Villars, even, had it in certain measure. But Ursula, who was superior immeasurably to both of them, had it not. She gave, but did not take. Her love asked only to be permitted to love.

Bowie never had admired the submissive, the self-immolating. To his forthright masculine viewpoint, humility was a confession of weakness. Strength took what it could, gave up only what it must. No ability is required to yield: the prone position is ever the easiest, whether it be physical or psychic, and the weakling is the most successful in subservience.

But through Ursula he had come to understand a strength also in sacrifice, a pride in humility, a power in thinking, not of oneself, but of others. Never in one moment of their life together had she brought him anything but joy, and now he still thought of her, as a man dying in the sun-blasted desert thinks of the bliss of thirst-quenching water.

The door of the baptistry opened. A thin, seamed face looked in, followed by a lean figure in a black cassock.

"Padre Garza——" There was gladness in Bowie's voice.

The priest came over and stood beside the cot. "I just learned, my son, of your accident. I came quickly——"

"Is it as bad as that, Padre?" Bowie said with a half-smile.

"No. Not that. But Santa Anna is reported in half a day's march of Bexar. I came because—I thought it might be a wish of yours—to——"

"It's been long, Padre. Two years and more since I went to confession."

Padre Garza regarded him patiently. "There will be a severe battle here, my son, and this may be the last time that I will see you."

392

"Sit down beside me."

The priest seated himself on a stool.

"I wish to ask a question," Bowie said. "Does Almighty God fix every man's destiny?"

"God knows what will come to pass, my son."

"I might be living at ease now, a small planter on some back bayou in Louisiana, with a wife and children, perhaps, like my brothers. But instead, I am here—perhaps near my end. Why?"

"Who can answer such a question? No man knows the mind of God or His reasons for working His wonders. Some men are pivots upon whom the history of all men turns. I think, my son, that you are such a man. What the good God above intends with you, it is past our poor ability to find out. But rest assured it is good."

"All things are good?"

"All things except sin."

"What about Ursula? Was there good in her being taken away?"

"I cannot answer this with wisdom, my son. I can only say to you what many men have said to themselves before you in great adversity—you must have faith."

Bowie's hand stirred on the cover of his bed. "I am—oppressed—with a great guilt, Padre."

"For what, my son?"

"I sent Ursula—and the others—to Monclova. I sent her to her death. A horrible death—it was as if I myself caused her to be executed by torment. It is this thought that has hit me so hard that my heart cannot recover from the soreness of it——"

"Now I am glad I came to you," Padre Garza said. "For I can bring you peace from this bitterness. You are a just man, my son. Be just to yourself, as you are to others, and do not blame yourself for this which you could not help. First, you acted with all wisdom and judgment in sending your family to Monclova. Second, even had they remained here in Bexar, they might as easily have been taken: for in Bexar the cholera raged likewise. God himself would absolve you from all guilt. And be of good cheer, for if you are at peace with God, He is merciful to grant that you will see her again, whom you love so greatly. You speak of Ursula as dead? I say to you there are no dead. There are no dead. Nearness to a loved one is not mere proximity of body, but nearness to the spirit. She is in God's care, but are we not all, my son? There are no dead. Only believe. The splendor of God, the just, the merciful, surrounds her now, and one day will surround you also as you will be happy with her, more happy than you ever were capable of being happy here . . ."

393

The kindly old face, the warm old heart, the gentle soft voice brought a peace he had not felt in months to Bowie's spirit.

"Padre," he said, "I have made one chief mistake. It is that long ago I should have come to you. Now confess me, and bless me."

3

The next afternoon a heavy explosion shook the building. Bowie was weaker this day and coughing much, but he half raised himself on an elbow. In a moment a woman came in, Mrs. Dickenson, wife of one of the officers in the Alamo.

"What was that?" he asked her.

"The Mexicans have appeared. That was a cannon on the platform. Colonel Travis himself fired it."

"Was anybody hit?"

"No. They say the Mexicans fell back."

"Why did he do that? I could myself hear, even in this room, the Mexican bugles sounding the call for a parley. Travis was too quick. He should have listened to what they had to say."

Through the open door he heard a stir and excited voices. "Find out what it is, will you?" he said.

In a moment the woman returned. "Something ominous has taken place. A blood-red flag has been run up on the flagpole of San Fernando Church."

"The no-quarter flag," Bowie said. "I thought so. Get me a paper and ink, and ask Benito Jameson to come to me."

In Spanish he wrote:

Commander of the Army of Texas: Because a shot was fired from a cannon of this fort at the time that a red flag was raised over the tower, and because a little afterward they told me that a part of your army had sounded a parley which however was not heard before the firing of said shot, I wish, sir, to ascertain if it be true that a parley was called, for which reason I send my second aide, under guarantee of a white flag which I believe will be respected by you and your forces.

James Bowie, commander of the volunteers of Bexar, to the commander of the invading forces below Bexar. February 23, 1836.

Jameson departed with the flag of truce. A moment later Travis, white and furious, came into the baptistry.

"Why did you do that, Bowie?" he stormed. "Do you realize it's tantamount to denying my authority? I want an explanation, sir!"

Bowie could not summon energy to reply to this anger with any heat of his own. "Wait till Jameson returns," was all he said.

In half an hour the aide brought back the reply.

As the aide-de-camp of His Excellency the President of the Republic, I reply to you, according to the order of His Excellency, that the Mexican army cannot come to terms under any conditions with the rebellious foreigners to whom there is no other recourse left, if they wish to save their lives, than to place themselves immediately at the disposal of the supreme government from whom alone they may expect clemency after some considerations are taken up.

> José Batres, to James Bowie, General Headquarters at San Antonio de Bexar. February 23, 1836.

Bowie handed the communication to Travis. "There, Buck. It's to the finish now. I can't help you much in the shape I'm in. But you're the commander, and I'll so notify the entire garrison. You can count on me to follow loyally every order you give from this moment."

Travis' strong hand gripped Bowie's weak hand. "Sorry, Jim—about this." He gestured at the bandages. "Sorry, too, for the differences we've had. I've always respected you as a man and a soldier, and I would to God you could be with us on the parapets."

A ripping roar came from without, a thundering report from above: the first Mexican volley, and the answer of the Alamo's cannon.

Santa Anna's first assault was defeated with loss.

Next day Travis sent out the last word the world was to hear from the Alamo.

To the People of Texas and all Americans in the World, Commandancy of the Alamo, Bexar. February 24, 1836.

Fellow Citizens and Compatriots: I am besieged by a thousand or more of Mexicans under Santa Anna. I have sustained a continual bombardment for twenty-four hours and have not lost a man. The enemy have demanded surrender at discretion; otherwise the garrison is to be put to the sword if the place is taken. I have answered the summons with cannon-shot and our flag still waves proudly from the walls. I shall never surrender or retreat. Then I call upon you, in the name of liberty, of patriotism, and of everything dear to the American character, to come to our aid with all dispatch. The enemy are receiving reinforcements daily and will no doubt increase to three or four thousand in four or five days. Though this call may be neglected, I am determined to sustain myself as long as possible and die like a soldier who never forgets what is due to his honor and that of his country. Victory or death!

> W. Barrett Travis, Lt. Col. Commanding.

For two days and nights, the firing was almost continual.

At the end of that time Bowie felt cold when he sweated. His bones ached, and his chest was filled with knife blades that slashed him every time he drew a breath. Days and nights began to slide into each other.

Dr. Mitchasson muttered and shook his head. "Pneumonia. The ribs punctured his lungs."

In all his life Bowie had never known a sickness like this. It became a battle, and everything seemed centered in his chest. When he coughed a raw-edged saw rasped his lungs. His bones, his head, all his tissues, ached. His body, the great superb body, rallied like a heroic army to fight off the assaults of this deadly enemy. Immense violences took place around and in him. Time ceased to have any meaning. His will fought to keep him alive, even in the periods when his mind knew nothing.

A moment came when there was clarity, and he heard silence.

It was actual, he *heard* silence. So accustomed had his ears become to the continual noise of bombardment, that a sort of reverse impression was made on them by the lack of any firing whatsoever.

Davy Crockett, gaunt now but still grimly humorous, came in to his cotside. "How ye doin', Jim?"

Bowie said, weakly, "I feel a little better."

Crockett grinned. "You're too ornery to pass in your chips. We'll pull ye through yet."

Bowie was listening to a sound of feet, a steady tramping.

"What's going on?"

"The Mexicans has let up on the shooting. Travis is taking the opportunity to call a meetin' of the men in the courtyard."

"To give them the bad news?"

"I reckon." Crockett's smile faded.

"I'd like to be there, Davy."

"Why, if ye want, I reckon we kin arrange it. I'll git some of the boys."

For the first time in days Bowie saw the sun. An immense change had taken place in the chapel, he saw as four men carried him through the door. To one side was a hospital, where doctors bent over sick and wounded. Most of these lay on the floor, with small piles of straw to ease their bones. Three or four women acted as nurses.

He closed his eyes and put the back of his hand over them when they carried him into the direct sunlight. In a few minutes, however, he became accustomed to it, and lay weakly back on his cot, able to watch what was happening.

"What's today?" he asked Crockett.

"March third, about two hours before sunset."

"The siege has been going on *ten days?*"

Crockett nodded. Astonishment filled Bowie. He had hardly marked the passage of time in his illness.

Save for the sentries on guard, every able-bodied man and many of the sick and wounded ranged in a line across the courtyard. Bowie marked the great change in them, their weary, haggard gauntness.

Buck Travis faced them, in the front of the center. Of them all, he showed the greatest changes. Less than thirty, his appearance was that of a man fifty years old. His eyes were sunk and bloodshot from sleeplessness. All parade and flourish were gone. The responsibilities he had carried and the sacrifices he had made had refined the man.

Bowie heard him, his voice a hoarse croak, "My brave companions, stern necessity compels me to employ the few moments of this brief cessation from conflict in making known to you the most interesting, yet the most solemn, melancholy and unwelcome fact that humanity can realize."

He paused. His voice deepened, "Our fate is sealed. Within a very few days, perhaps a very few hours, we must all be in eternity."

Again he stopped, and Bowie saw him swallow before he went on, "I have deceived you long by the promise of help. For that I crave your pardon, hoping that after you hear my explanation you will not only regard my conduct as pardonable but heartily sympathize with me in my extreme necessity. I have continually received the strongest assurances of help from home——"

At this point he digressed, to list letters and messages which had promised assistance. Then he continued, "In the honest and simple confidence of my heart, I have transmitted to you these promises and my confident hope of success, but the promised help has not come and our hopes are not to be realized."

Briefly he attempted to explain the difficulties of bringing adequate relief. In this hour Buck Travis was too great a man to feel bitterness or lay blame on anyone. He went on, "Then we must die. Our business is not to make a fruitless effort to save our lives, but to choose the manner of our death."

His eye ran down the line of his men. "As I see it, only three methods are presented to us. Let us choose that one by which we may best serve our country. Shall we surrender, and be deliberately shot, without taking the life of a single enemy? Shall we try to cut our way out through the Mexican lines and be butchered before we can kill twenty of our adversaries? I, for one, am opposed to either method. Let us resolve, instead, to withstand our adversaries to the last, *from these walls!*"

His voice lifted in exhortation. "At each advance, kill as many of them as possible! And when at last they shall storm our fortress, let us kill them as they come! Kill them as they scale our walls! Kill them as they leap within! Kill them as they raise their weapons and as they use them! Kill them as they kill our companions! And continue to kill them as long as any one of us shall remain alive!"

Every man in that haggard line straightened. Travis' voice became lower, reasonable, understanding.

"But I leave every man to his own choice. Should any man prefer to surrender or to attempt an escape, he is at liberty to do so. My own choice is to stay in the fort and die for my country, fighting as long as breath shall remain in my body. This I will do, even if you leave me alone. Do as you think best. But no man can die with me, without affording me comfort in that hour of death."

All of Bowie's heart went out to Travis. The disagreements, the bickerings, the man's previous pettiness and ambition, were erased by the simple grandeur of this moment.

Travis drew his sword and with its point drew a long line on the ground a yard in front of the rank of men. Then he assumed again his position before them.

"I now want every man who is determined to stay here and die with me—to come across this line! Who will be first? March!"

A young man sprang across.

A cheer. "That's young Tapley Holland."

Man after man the defenders of the Alamo stepped across the line to join their leader. Sick and wounded crowded over.

Bowie tried to rise in his cot, but he was too weak. He lifted his voice, and it surprised him, because it sounded like the croaking of an old man. "Boys . . . I can't come over to you. But I wish some of you . . . would be so kind as to move my cot over there."

A wild storm of cheering from the soldiers. Four of them took the cot, each by a corner, across the line.

One man only remained where he had been: Moses Rose, a trader. He had been brave enough in the fighting, but now he sank to the ground, covering his face with his hands. Taking his hands from his face, his eyes sought out, not Travis, but Bowie.

Crockett was leaning over the cot, talking. Bowie said, "Wait a minute, Davy." He spoke to Rose. "You seem not willing to die with us, Rose?"

"No," the man sobbed. "I'm not ready to die. I can't——"

"You mought as well conclude to die with us, old man," Crockett said. "Escape's impossible."

Rose looked at the top of the wall. Of a sudden he stood up, seized a bundle of his clothes, and began climbing the wall. At the top he gave one last glance back at his friends. They were watching him, but no one spoke to him.

He was gone on the other side. Not any of those he left behind knew that he was fated to make his escape good, to bring the record of that last hour to the world.

A few minutes later a new thunder broke out. The bombardment had begun once more.

Crockett said, "Four of you boys take Colonel Bowie back to his room. I'll be in to see you later, Jim."

Chapter Forty-eight

I

Sunday, March 6, the day of God's peace. Yet though it still was two hours until dawn, man had been making a hell of war almost since midnight.

Bowie lay fully conscious and awake. They were not fighting at this minute. The incessant rising roar of the rifles, punctuated by the jolting crash of Travis' cannon, and the frenzied screams and yells of men in deadly struggle, had quieted. Once again Santa Anna had retreated to regroup his forces.

He had need to do it. The Mexicans had been reinforced again and again, until eight thousand men surrounded the Alamo's walls. Assaults had been delivered, one upon another, like blows from a trip hammer, and all of them had thus far been beaten back during the night. The ground outside for hundreds of yards was strewn with wrecked bodies of men, some dead, some feebly moaning for help.

But this was the final lull. Every man knew it. It presaged the final, climactic effort of Santa Anna's army.

Alone, the heavy door shut and his only light a candle flickering, Bowie could hear the murmur of moans and groans and pleading voices in the church, with now and then the peculiar babbling wail of a man wounded to death and out of his mind.

Hardly enough defenders were left now to man even thinly the widespread walls. None had slept for two days and nights. They crouched, wherever they were, peering through the pre-dawn darkness, waiting like strange votaries for the end of the Alamo, which had been built for the worship of God, and had been diverted to a temple of warfare.

Bowie did not think they would wait long. Santa Anna would come at them again while it was yet dark. Hopeless impatience gripped him in that lonely room. He kept thinking of himself as one of the defenders, and yet for all the help he could give, he might as well be underground already. Yet he must continue to link himself with them, for his fate was bound with theirs inextricably. Above all, it was he who had made the initial decision by which all these brave men were going to lay down their lives.

Bowie lay on his cot in an overwhelming weakness of fever that burned him up, so that his constant cough, his broken hip, and his shattered chest seemed unimportant by comparison. James Bowie, he thought. Only a name now, but a name that still meant something. Santa Anna had said that above anyone in the Alamo he would rather hang Bowie. So much at least his name had done for him. It was a name some had hated, some feared, and some loved. It was a name which, perhaps, would not be entirely forgotten when all this was done . . .

The name was about all there was left of him. He gazed down at his right hand, the grasp of which had been like that of a blacksmith's vise, and it seemed impossible that it could be the hand of Bowie. The great frame of it was there, with the strong bones of the fingers and the wrist unchanged, and the knotted veins and corded muscles. Yet he scarcely had the strength to lift it from the blanket.

He looked down also at his body, stretched on the cot which creaked with his weight when he feebly stirred, and marveled at how that six feet and two inches of bone and gristle could, in a few days, become so helpless, so unfit for mere existence.

Yet this was Bowie. Colonel James Bowie, soldier and adventurer and, he hoped, gentleman. A man who had been reckoned with in his time . . .

It was very quiet just now. Bowie supposed the men on the walls were taking cat naps wherever they were stationed, except for the few sentries. The suspense was growing unbearable.

2

In these last hours he had experienced a remarkable clarity of mind. Sometimes he seemed to lack bodily sense, to be floating alone out in the world, not dreaming but more widely awake than ever in his life before, seeing things and events from distant perspectives that gave them new meanings.

He was dying. He knew he was dying, for he could tell it by the broad pallid face of Dr. Mitchasson, by the high-bred weary face of Buck Travis, by the weather-beaten face of Davy Crockett. One and all they had visited him during the night, catching minutes from their fighting, their expressions charged with forced cheerfulness. Yes, even while Crockett jested and recounted a funny episode of the battle, Bowie could read in his black eyes that he knew his fate.

For himself, Bowie did not fear death. Never had he feared it unduly. He had respected it, and more than once had looked it between the eyes. But he had not cowered before it. Now that it was very near, he feared death less than ever before.

Yet, before he encountered the great mystery, he desired to consider some of the things of his life. It was not a long life, for he was now only forty-one. But it was long in events, for in his years he had seen more and taken part in more than is given to most men, even those who live past the allotted threescore and ten.

Every man's life is an ocean, charted by jutting headlands. He thought of the headlands of his sea, and wondered which of them had most influenced its currents.

Sam Houston, that great roan bear of a man, upon whom must hang the fate of Texas now. Juan de Veramendi, his friend and father-in-law, a gentleman in the truest sense, gifted with kindness and understanding. Padre Refugio de la Garza, the wise and saintly. Sholic, the fat Lipan chief, who showed him the treasure which even now he regretted that he never had gone back to see, because it represented a failure. Tres Manos, the vengeful and murderous. Major Norris Wright, with whom he fought a feud based on jealousy over a woman to whom neither of them had a right. Philippe Cabanal, weak and despicable, living off his wife, protected by her for all of her contempt of him. Jean Lafitte, the polite and bitter buccaneer. Nez Coupé, more faithful than any dog, who died in Bowie's arms. John James Audubon, the gentle artist, now a famous man, ever urging the way of nature as the answer to life. Narcisse de Bornay, lighthearted and cynical, but loyal to the death. Rezin and John, his brothers, who in spite of their misgivings ever rallied to him.

Which had most dominated the rough wave-lashed ocean of his life? He considered them and knew it was none of them. There were others.

Judalon de Bornay. Bowie did not know, he could not judge the problems or motives or necessities of her sex. It struck him with peculiar force that Judalon, as a woman, gambled with life, even as he himself gambled with it in the way of a man. And though the memory of her was at times sharp with anger, and at times charged with mystery beyond solution, he saluted her because to the very end she carried her courage high and was unafraid.

Last of all, Ursula. The thought of her played upon the chords of his being like some unearthly music, soundless except to his own spirit. Now at last he could think of her without torment. Ursula was too good for him. Bowie thought that if he had had his deserts, he might perhaps have had someone like Judalon. But it had been his life's great fortune to have Ursula.

Bowie, who never was a woman's man, to whom always they had seemed something of the background, who at times did not even see them for months on end, was suddenly confronted by the fact that his life's great currents had flowed not around men, but around women, as any man's must. For twelve years, far and near from him, Judalon had molded his life. At the last Ursula had made him a different man and in her death had influenced him even more strangely. These women were his loftiest headlands, and he had not even known it.

3

What of his life? Would he change it if he had it to live over? He had known pain and weariness and hunger, danger and disappointment and sorrow. He had made mistakes, many, very many mistakes. Much and grievously had he sinned. Of the Ten Commandments given by God he could think now only of one of which he stood guiltless. He had never failed, so far as he knew how, in giving proper respect to his father and mother.

But the others: false gods, unholy Sabbaths, false witness, theft—if sharp dealing were theft—taking the lives of other men, coveting not only the goods of others but the wife of another, and that sin called adultery: of these he had been guilty, each and all. Yet for these Padre Garza had promised forgiveness. He hoped the promise would be fulfilled.

Lying alone now with only the guttering tallow dip to keep him company, Bowie decided that with all his imperfections he would not wish to have lived any other kind of life. Nor even to live that life over. He was not healing. The crude boxlike structure made by the doctor to hold his broken hip seemed filled with fiery coals. He called for breath, and it came slowly.

He heard outside voices, the steps of people. His people. This was among the great changes in his understanding. Before, those of his own blood were set apart, and his friends, from all the rest. But now he thought in terms of all in the Alamo, all others, countless others in Texas. Having lived without thought and for himself, in his death he was moved only by a wish for the good of his country. A refinement out of the dross of his nature, which he found strange and satisfying.

Yet in dying he was accomplishing nothing. Until now he had never stopped in all his life. Now nothing was asked of him: he was through, his part played, no words to say in the curtain's fall. An anticlimax.

The fighting death, that was the thing. If he could only have been spared helpless passing in bed, the crawling cold of his limbs.

Silence continued outside. No sharp rat-tat of rifles. Without the walls lay blue figures, almost beyond counting. When the Mexicans came again the ground would be littered with another carpeting of blue. A bloodletting such as Texas had never seen, such as Santa Anna had never dreamed. He would carry the Alamo, but in taking this forlorn outpost he was shattering his army so that it would take him long weeks to rebuild it.

Bowie thought with a grim satisfaction that Houston, after all, was to have the time he prayed for because of the Alamo. To make its cost the last ultimate payment in life and blood for the invaders, that was the dedication of every man in these walls, the thing Bowie himself had foreseen and decided . . . and he was not a part of it.

His eye rested on the stool beside his cot. Sitting on that stool, Padre Garza, Davy Crockett, Buck Travis, and others had visited with him. Now upon it were arranged five objects which he had requested. Four pistols, primed and loaded. And his knife, unsheathed.

One by one he lifted the pistols and laid them on his cot on either side of him. He still had strength enough to lift pistols.

Last of all he took the knife.

Heavy coughing seemed to tear out his lungs. He had no way of knowing how high his fever was, but now his body, which had been cold, seemed burning into a cinder. Hardly enough of a body for Santa Anna to swing from the gibbet he had promised. If Santa Anna did not come soon, there might not even be a living body for his bayonets . . .

He considered the knife. This metal thing had been a headland in his life, too, made him the kind of man he was. Bowie and his knife—the Iron Mistress, always faithful to him—to go down together at last. His fist closed on the haft lovingly.

4

A sharp rifle report was followed by another, and another. Shooting all at once became heavy, a thundering roar.

Daylight was breaking. The Mexicans were coming again.

Five thousand men charged from all directions. Artillery hurled shells into the enclosure, followed by scaling ladders, hand grenades, bayonets.

Massed bands played the assassin notes of the *Degüello*—meaning no quarter. Three thousand more troops waited in reserve to take the places of the ones in the assault if they failed.

Travis' cannon thundered on the western wall. Down before the chapel, the Tennessee rifles crackled keenly where Crockett defended the angle.

The heaviest toll would be taken now, the final payment from Santa Anna for the Alamo.

Uproar built to ear-shattering crescendo. Muskets and rifles and big guns, and the throaty roar of thousands converging on the tottering walls.

Now came other sounds: shouts, curses, groans and screams of agony. Without doubt the Mexicans had carried the outer parapet.

Mrs. Dickenson entered, weeping.

"We're gone—all gone," she sobbed to Bowie. "My husband's dead——"

Dread news, she told him. Travis was dead, a bullet through his brain, lying across the trail of a cannon. Crockett was fighting alone for his life, his rifle flailing like a club in the snarling mob about him, and must be gone by now.

Bowie said, "Go out and leave me. They will not hurt you."

The door closed.

He heard the cheer as the Mexicans burst into the chapel. Walls were shaken by the thudding of musket shots as the sick and wounded were massacred. None were to live: not even the non-combatant doctors.

It was all over. He, James Bowie, lying on his cot almost too weak to lift his head, was the last man who could resist in the Alamo.

A lightness of heart came over him. So he was to make a fine end after all.

He lay with his eyes fixed on that door.

It opened. Brown, fierce face peered in. Another and another. They crowded in, rushed across the floor.

Strange that the thin, blond man grinned so fiercely and so happily at their coming . . .

Yes, Bowie still could lift his pistols. The recoils jolted his hands. In the powder smoke a trail of stricken enemies extended from the door to his cot. The last, the boldest of them, lay with the knife buried in his heart.

Bowie was dead even before the bayonets reached him.

Dead? There are no dead . . .